THE MODERN LIBRARY
OF THE WORLD'S BEST BOOKS

SELECTED SHORT STORIES OF
IRWIN SHAW

The Publishers will be pleased to send, upon request, an illustrated folder setting forth the purpose and scope of THE MODERN LIBRARY, *and listing each volume in the series. Every reader of books will find titles he has been looking for, handsomely printed, in definitive editions, and at an unusually low price.*

SELECTED SHORT STORIES OF

IRWIN SHAW

WITH A PREFACE BY THE AUTHOR

THE MODERN LIBRARY · NEW YORK

Library of Congress Catalog Card Number: 61-10674

Acknowledgment is made to *The New Yorker, McCall's*
magazine, *Collier's, Harper's* magazine, and *Esquire* who first
published the stories in their pages.

Random House is THE PUBLISHER OF *The Modern Library*
Bennett Cerf · Donald S. Klopfer

Preface

I have been writing short stories since I was twelve. Do not be alarmed—none of the vintage of that year, or of several years thereafter, is included in the present collection. This book has been considerably limited to those stories of mine that have been published in magazines and books during the last twenty-odd years. Even so, there was a generous number—nearly eighty—from which to choose. The editor who helped me in this choice was Mr. Albert Erskine, of Random House. We had no set qualifications for our choices, except to extract from the mass of print the stories we both liked best. When the time came to arrange the stories in the sequence in which they can be read in this book, it occurred to both of us that by printing the stories in the order in which they were written, which was also, with one or two exceptions, the order in which they were first published, a kind of running account of the years from 1935 to 1960 might be achieved. The gaps in the account are, naturally, very large. For one thing, the shape of the book is a result of accretion and selection and not of a preconceived plan. For another, only a few of the stories are based on specific public events, such as the beginning of World War II or the landings in North Africa of American troops. But to me, at

least, the stories all seemed to be anchored in some remembered, isolated moment of my own time, and they
reflect, I believe, the moods which I experienced in common with many of the men and women of my generation,
and the ideas that moved us in the time which these
stories span.

In that time, in the places I have passed through, there
have been hope, despair, defiance, courage, resignation,
brutality, laughter, and love, as in all other times, but
all in the special and peculiar light of our epoch. Now, as
I re-read this sampling of nearly a quarter of a century's
work, I see that I was trying, as the politicians phrase it,
to put it on the record.

I await with lively interest the Modern Library volume
of a selection of stories from my next twenty-five years
work.

                                                      I. S.

CONTENTS

CONTENTS

The Eighty-Yard Run

The pass was high and wide and he jumped for it, feeling
it slap flatly against his hands, as he shook his hips to
throw off the halfback who was diving at him. The center
floated by, his hands desperately brushing Darling's knee
as Darling picked his feet up high and delicately ran over
a blocker and an opposing linesman in a jumble on the
ground near the scrimmage line. He had ten yards in the
clear and picked up speed, breathing easily, feeling his
thigh pads rising and falling against his legs, listening to
the sound of cleats behind him, pulling away from them,
watching the other backs heading him off toward the side-
line, the whole picture, the men closing in on him, the
blockers fighting for position, the ground he had to cross,
all suddenly clear in his head, for the first time in his life
not a meaningless confusion of men, sounds, speed. He
smiled a little to himself as he ran, holding the ball lightly
in front of him with his two hands, his knees pumping
high, his hips twisting in the almost girlish run of a back
in a broken field. The first halfback came at him and he
fed him his leg, then swung at the last moment, took the
shock of the man's shoulder without breaking stride, ran
right through him, his cleats biting securely into the turf.
There was only the safety man now, coming warily at

1

him, his arms crooked, hands spread. Darling tucked the ball in, spurted at him, driving hard, hurling himself along, his legs pounding, knees high, all two hundred pounds bunched into controlled attack. He was sure he was going to get past the safety man. Without thought, his arms and legs working beautifully together, he headed right for the safety man, stiff-armed him, feeling blood spurt instantaneously from the man's nose onto his hand, seeing his face go awry, head turned, mouth pulled to one side. He pivoted away, keeping the arm locked, dropping the safety man as he ran easily toward the goal line, with the drumming of cleats diminishing behind him.

How long ago? It was autumn then, and the ground was getting hard because the nights were cold and leaves from the maples around the stadium blew across the practice fields in gusts of wind, and the girls were beginning to put polo coats over their sweaters when they came to watch practice in the afternoons. . . . Fifteen years. Darling walked slowly over the same ground in the spring twilight, in his neat shoes, a man of thirty-five dressed in a double-breasted suit, ten pounds heavier in the fifteen years, but not fat, with the years between 1925 and 1940 showing in his face.

The coach was smiling quietly to himself and the assistant coaches were looking at each other with pleasure the way they always did when one of the second stringers suddenly did something fine, bringing credit to them, making their $2,000 a year a tiny bit more secure.

Darling trotted back, smiling, breathing deeply but easily, feeling wonderful, not tired, though this was the tail end of practice and he'd run eighty yards. The sweat poured off his face and soaked his jersey and he liked the feeling, the warm moistness lubricating his skin like oil. Off in a corner of the field some players were punting and the smack of leather against the ball came pleasantly through the afternoon air. The freshmen were running signals on the next field and the quarterback's sharp voice, the pound of the eleven pairs of cleats, the "Dig, now

dig!" of the coaches, the laughter of the players all somehow made him feel happy as he trotted back to midfield,
listening to the applause and shouts of the students along
the sidelines, knowing that after that run the coach would
have to start him Saturday against Illinois.

Fifteen years, Darling thought, remembering the
shower after the workout, the hot water steaming off his
skin and the deep soapsuds and all the young voices singing with the water streaming down and towels going and
managers running in and out and the sharp sweet smell
of oil of wintergreen and everybody clapping him on the
back as he dressed and Packard, the captain, who took
being captain very seriously, coming over to him and
shaking his hand and saying, "Darling, you're going to go
places in the next two years."

The assistant manager fussed over him, wiping a cut
on his leg with alcohol and iodine, the little sting making
him realize suddenly how fresh and whole and solid his
body felt. The manager slapped a piece of adhesive tape
over the cut, and Darling noticed the sharp clean white of
the tape against the ruddiness of the skin, fresh from the
shower.

He dressed slowly, the softness of his shirt and the soft
warmth of his wool socks and his flannel trousers a reward
against his skin after the harsh pressure of the shoulder
harness and thigh and hip pads. He drank three glasses
of cold water, the liquid reaching down coldly inside of
him, soothing the harsh dry places in his throat and belly
left by the sweat and running and shouting of practice.

Fifteen years.

The sun had gone down and the sky was green behind
the stadium and he laughed quietly to himself as he
looked at the stadium, rearing above the trees, and knew
that on Saturday when the 70,000 voices roared as the
team came running out onto the field, part of that enormous salute would be for him. He walked slowly, listening
to the gravel crunch satisfactorily under his shoes in the
still twilight, feeling his clothes swing lightly against his

skin, breathing the thin evening air, feeling the wind move softly in his damp hair, wonderfully cool behind his ears and at the nape of his neck.

Louise was waiting for him at the road, in her car. The top was down and he noticed all over again, as he always did when he saw her, how pretty she was, the rough blonde hair and the large, inquiring eyes and the bright mouth, smiling now.

She threw the door open. "Were you good today?" she asked.

"Pretty good," he said. He climbed in, sank luxuriously into the soft leather, stretched his legs far out. He smiled, thinking of the eighty yards. "Pretty damn good."

She looked at him seriously for a moment, then scrambled around, like a little girl, kneeling on the seat next to him, grabbed him, her hands along his ears, and kissed him as he sprawled, head back, on the seat cushion. She let go of him, but kept her head close to his, over his. Darling reached up slowly and rubbed the back of his hand against her cheek, lit softly by a street lamp a hundred feet away. They looked at each other, smiling.

Louise drove down to the lake and they sat there silently, watching the moon rise behind the hills on the other side. Finally he reached over, pulled her gently to him, kissed her. Her lips grew soft, her body sank into his, tears formed slowly in her eyes. He knew, for the first time, that he could do whatever he wanted with her.

"Tonight," he said. "I'll call for you at seven-thirty. Can you get out?"

She looked at him. She was smiling, but the tears were still full in her eyes. "All right," she said. "I'll get out. How about you? Won't the coach raise hell?"

Darling grinned. "I got the coach in the palm of my hand," he said. "Can you wait till seven-thirty?"

She grinned back at him. "No," she said.

They kissed and she started the car and they went back to town for dinner. He sang on the way home.

Christian Darling, thirty-five years old, sat on the frail spring grass, greener now than it ever would be again on the practice field, looked thoughtfully up at the stadium, a deserted ruin in the twilight. He had started on the first team that Saturday and every Saturday after that for the next two years, but it had never been as satisfactory as it should have been. He never had broken away, the longest run he'd ever made was thirty-five yards, and that in a game that was already won, and then that kid had come up from the third team, Diederich, a blank-faced German kid from Wisconsin, who ran like a bull, ripping lines to pieces Saturday after Saturday, plowing through, never getting hurt, never changing his expression, scoring more points, gaining more ground than all the rest of the team put together, making everybody's All-American, carrying the ball three times out of four, keeping everybody else out of the headlines. Darling was a good blocker and he spent his Saturday afternoons working on the big Swedes and Polacks who played tackle and end for Michigan, Illinois, Purdue, hurling into huge pile-ups, bobbing his head wildly to elude the great raw hands swinging like meat-cleavers at him as he went charging in to open up holes for Diederich coming through like a locomotive behind him. Still, it wasn't so bad. Everybody liked him and he did his job and he was pointed out on the campus and boys always felt important when they introduced their girls to him at their proms, and Louise loved him and watched him faithfully in the games, even in the mud, when your own mother wouldn't know you, and drove him around in her car keeping the top down because she was proud of him and wanted to show everybody that she was Christian Darling's girl. She bought him crazy presents because her father was rich, watches, pipes, humidors, an icebox for beer for his room, curtains, wallets, a fifty-dollar dictionary.

"You'll spend every cent your old man owns," Darling protested once when she showed up at his rooms with seven different packages in her arms and tossed them onto the couch.

"Kiss me," Louise said, "and shut up."

"Do you want to break your poor old man?"

"I don't mind. I want to buy you presents."

"Why?"

"It makes me feel good. Kiss me. I don't know why. Did you know that you're an important figure?"

"Yes," Darling said gravely.

"When I was waiting for you at the library yesterday two girls saw you coming and one of them said to the other, 'That's Christian Darling. He's an important figure.'"

"You're a liar."

"I'm in love with an important figure."

"Still, why the hell did you have to give me a forty-pound dictionary?"

"I wanted to make sure," Louise said, "that you had a token of my esteem. I want to smother you in tokens of my esteem."

Fifteen years ago.

They'd married when they got out of college. There'd been other women for him, but all casual and secret, more for curiosity's sake, and vanity, women who'd thrown themselves at him and flattered him, a pretty mother at a summer camp for boys, an old girl from his home town who'd suddenly blossomed into a coquette, a friend of Louise's who had dogged him grimly for six months and had taken advantage of the two weeks that Louise went home when her mother died. Perhaps Louise had known, but she'd kept quiet, loving him completely, filling his rooms with presents, religiously watching him battling with the big Swedes and Polacks on the line of scrimmage on Saturday afternoons, making plans for marrying him and living with him in New York and going with him there to the night clubs, the theaters, the good restaurants, being proud of him in advance, tall, white-teethed, smiling, large, yet moving lightly, with an athlete's grace,

dressed in evening clothes, approvingly eyed by magnificently dressed and famous women in theater lobbies,
with Louise adoringly at his side.

Her father, who manufactured inks, set up a New York
office for Darling to manage and presented him with three
hundred accounts, and they lived on Beekman Place with
a view of the river with fifteen thousand dollars a year between them, because everybody was buying everything
in those days, including ink. They saw all the shows and
went to all the speakeasies and spent their fifteen thousand dollars a year and in the afternoons Louise went to
the art galleries and the matinees of the more serious plays
that Darling didn't like to sit through and Darling slept
with a girl who danced in the chorus of *Rosalie* and with
the wife of a man who owned three copper mines. Darling
played squash three times a week and remained as solid
as a stone barn and Louise never took her eyes off him
when they were in the same room together, watching him
with a secret, miser's smile, with a trick of coming over
to him in the middle of a crowded room and saying
gravely, in a low voice, "You're the handsomest man I've
ever seen in my whole life. Want a drink?"

Nineteen twenty-nine came to Darling and to his wife
and father-in-law, the maker of inks, just as it came to
everyone else. The father-in-law waited until 1933 and
then blew his brains out and when Darling went to Chicago to see what the books of the firm looked like he
found out all that was left were debts and three or four
gallons of unbought ink.

"Please, Christian," Louise said, sitting in their neat
Beekman Place apartment, with a view of the river and
prints of paintings by Dufy and Braque and Picasso on
the wall, "please, why do you want to start drinking at
two o'clock in the afternoon?"

"I have nothing else to do," Darling said, putting down
his glass, emptied of its fourth drink. "Please pass the
whisky."

Louise filled his glass. "Come take a walk with me," she said. "We'll walk along the river."

"I don't want to walk along the river," Darling said, squinting intensely at the prints of paintings by Dufy, Braque and Picasso.

"We'll walk along Fifth Avenue."

"I don't want to walk along Fifth Avenue."

"Maybe," Louise said gently, "you'd like to come with me to some art galleries. There's an exhibition by a man named Klee. . . ."

"I don't want to go to any art galleries. I want to sit here and drink Scotch whisky," Darling said. "Who the hell hung those goddam pictures up on the wall?"

"I did," Louise said.

"I hate them."

"I'll take them down," Louise said.

"Leave them there. It gives me something to do in the afternoon. I can hate them." Darling took a long swallow. "Is that the way people paint these days?"

"Yes, Christian. Please don't drink any more."

"Do you like painting like that?"

"Yes, dear."

"Really?"

"Really."

Darling looked carefully at the prints once more. "Little Louise Tucker. The middle-western beauty. I like pictures with horses in them. Why should you like pictures like that?"

"I just happen to have gone to a lot of galleries in the last few years . . ."

"Is that what you do in the afternoon?"

"That's what I do in the afternoon," Louise said.

"I drink in the afternoon."

Louise kissed him lightly on the top of his head as he sat there squinting at the pictures on the wall, the glass of whisky held firmly in his hand. She put on her coat and went out without saying another word. When she came back in the early evening, she had a job on a woman's fashion magazine.

They moved downtown and Louise went out to work every morning and Darling sat home and drank and Louise paid the bills as they came up. She made believe she was going to quit work as soon as Darling found a job, even though she was taking over more responsibility day by day at the magazine, interviewing authors, picking painters for the illustrations and covers, getting actresses to pose for pictures, going out for drinks with the right people, making a thousand new friends whom she loyally introduced to Darling.

"I don't like your hat," Darling said, once, when she came in in the evening and kissed him, her breath rich with martinis.

"What's the matter with my hat, Baby?" she asked, running her fingers through his hair. "Everybody says it's very smart."

"It's too damned smart," he said. "It's not for you. It's for a rich, sophisticated woman of thirty-five with admirers."

Louise laughed. "I'm practicing to be a rich, sophisticated woman of thirty-five with admirers," she said. He stared soberly at her. "Now, don't look so grim, Baby. It's still the same simple little wife under the hat." She took the hat off, threw it into a corner, sat on his lap. "See? Homebody Number One."

"Your breath could run a train," Darling said, not wanting to be mean, but talking out of boredom, and sudden shock at seeing his wife curiously a stranger in a new hat, with a new expression in her eyes under the little brim, secret, confident, knowing.

Louise tucked her head under his chin so he couldn't smell her breath. "I had to take an author out for cocktails," she said. "He's a boy from the Ozark Mountains and he drinks like a fish. He's a Communist."

"What the hell is a Communist from the Ozarks doing writing for a woman's fashion magazine?"

Louise chuckled. "The magazine business is getting all mixed up these days. The publishers want to have a foot in every camp. And anyway, you can't find an author under seventy these days who isn't a Communist."

"I don't think I like you to associate with all those people, Louise," Darling said. "Drinking with them."

"He's a very nice, gentle boy," Louise said. "He reads Ernest Dowson."

"Who's Ernest Dowson?"

Louise patted his arm, stood up, fixed her hair. "He's an English poet."

Darling felt that somehow he had disappointed her. "Am I supposed to know who Ernest Dowson is?"

"No, dear. I'd better go in and take a bath."

After she had gone, Darling went over to the corner where the hat was lying and picked it up. It was nothing, a scrap of straw, a red flower, a veil, meaningless on his big hand, but on his wife's head a signal of something . . . big city, smart and knowing women drinking and dining with men other than their husbands, conversation about things a normal man wouldn't know much about, Frenchmen who painted as though they used their elbows instead of brushes, composers who wrote whole symphonies without a single melody in them, writers who knew all about politics and women who knew all about writers, the movement of the proletariat, Marx, somehow mixed up with five-dollar dinners and the best-looking women in America and fairies who made them laugh and half-sentences immediately understood and secretly hilarious and wives who called their husbands "Baby." He put the hat down, a scrap of straw and a red flower, and a little veil. He drank some whisky straight and went into the bathroom where his wife was lying deep in her bath, singing to herself and smiling from time to time like a little girl, paddling the water gently with her hands, sending up a slight spicy fragrance from the bath salts she used.

He stood over her, looking down at her. She smiled up at him, her eyes half closed, her body pink and shimmer-

ing in the warm, scented water. All over again, with all
the old suddenness, he was hit deep inside him with the
knowledge of how beautiful she was, how much he needed
her.

"I came in here," he said, "to tell you I wish you
wouldn't call me 'Baby.' "

She looked up at him from the bath, her eyes quickly
full of sorrow, half-understanding what he meant. He
knelt and put his arms around her, his sleeves plunged
heedlessly in the water, his shirt and jacket soaking wet as
he clutched her wordlessly, holding her crazily tight,
crushing her breath from her, kissing her desperately,
searchingly, regretfully.

He got jobs after that, selling real estate and automobiles, but somehow, although he had a desk with
his name on a wooden wedge on it, and he went to the
office religiously at nine each morning, he never managed
to sell anything and he never made any money.

Louise was made assistant editor, and the house was
always full of strange men and women who talked fast
and got angry on abstract subjects like mural painting,
novelists, labor unions. Negro short-story writers drank
Louise's liquor, and a lot of Jews, and big solemn men
with scarred faces and knotted hands who talked slowly
but clearly about picket lines and battles with guns and
leadpipe at mine-shaft-heads and in front of factory gates.
And Louise moved among them all, confidently, knowing what they were talking about, with opinions that they
listened to and argued about just as though she were a
man. She knew everybody, condescended to no one, devoured books that Darling had never heard of, walked
along the streets of the city, excited, at home, soaking in
all the million tides of New York without fear, with constant wonder.

Her friends liked Darling and sometimes he found a
man who wanted to get off in the corner and talk about
the new boy who played fullback for Princeton, and the
decline of the double wing-back, or even the state of the

stock market, but for the most part he sat on the edge of things, solid and quiet in the high storm of words. "The dialectics of the situation . . . The theater has been given over to expert jugglers . . . Picasso? What man has a right to paint old bones and collect ten thousand dollars for them? . . . I stand firmly behind Trotsky . . . Poe was the last American critic. When he died they put lilies on the grave of American criticism. I don't say this because they panned my last book, but . . ."

Once in a while he caught Louise looking soberly and consideringly at him through the cigarette smoke and the noise and he avoided her eyes and found an excuse to get up and go into the kitchen for more ice or to open another bottle.

"Come on," Cathal Flaherty was saying, standing at the door with a girl, "you've got to come down and see this. It's down on Fourteenth Street, in the old Civic Repertory, and you can only see it on Sunday nights and I guarantee you'll come out of the theater singing." Flaherty was a big young Irishman with a broken nose who was the lawyer for a longshoreman's union, and he had been hanging around the house for six months on and off, roaring and shutting everybody else up when he got in an argument. "It's a new play, *Waiting for Lefty;* it's about taxi-drivers."

"Odets," the girl with Flaherty said. "It's by a guy named Odets."

"I never heard of him," Darling said.

"He's a new one," the girl said.

"It's like watching a bombardment," Flaherty said. "I saw it last Sunday night. You've got to see it."

"Come on, Baby," Louise said to Darling, excitement in her eyes already. "We've been sitting in the Sunday *Times* all day, this'll be a great change."

"I see enough taxi-drivers every day," Darling said, not because he meant that, but because he didn't like to be around Flaherty, who said things that made Louise laugh a lot and whose judgment she accepted on almost every subject. "Let's go to the movies."

"You've never seen anything like this before," Flaherty said. "He wrote this play with a baseball bat."

"Come on," Louise coaxed, "I bet it's wonderful."

"He has long hair," the girl with Flaherty said. "Odets. I met him at a party. He's an actor. He didn't say a goddam thing all night."

"I don't feel like going down to Fourteenth Street," Darling said, wishing Flaherty and his girl would get out. "It's gloomy."

"Oh, hell!" Louise said loudly. She looked coolly at Darling, as though she'd just been introduced to him and was making up her mind about him, and not very favorably. He saw her looking at him, knowing there was something new and dangerous in her face and he wanted to say something, but Flaherty was there and his damned girl, and anyway, he didn't know what to say.

"I'm going," Louise said, getting her coat. "I don't think Fourteenth Street is gloomy."

"I'm telling you," Flaherty was saying, helping her on with her coat, "it's the Battle of Gettysburg, in Brooklynese."

"Nobody could get a word out of him," Flaherty's girl was saying as they went through the door. "He just sat there all night."

The door closed. Louise hadn't said good night to him. Darling walked around the room four times, then sprawled out on the sofa, on top of the Sunday *Times*. He lay there for five minutes looking at the ceiling, thinking of Flaherty walking down the street talking in that booming voice, between the girls, holding their arms.

Louise had looked wonderful. She'd washed her hair in the afternoon and it had been very soft and light and clung close to her head as she stood there angrily putting her coat on. Louise was getting prettier every year, partly because she knew by now how pretty she was, and made the most of it.

"Nuts," Darling said, standing up. "Oh, nuts."

He put on his coat and went down to the nearest bar and had five drinks off by himself in a corner before his money ran out.

The years since then had been foggy and downhill. Louise had been nice to him, and in a way, loving and kind, and they'd fought only once, when he said he was going to vote for Landon. ("Oh, Christ," she'd said, "doesn't *anything* happen inside your head? Don't you read the papers? The penniless Republican!") She'd been sorry later and apologized for hurting him, but apologized as she might to a child. He'd tried hard, had gone grimly to the art galleries, the concert halls, the bookshops, trying to gain on the trail of his wife, but it was no use. He was bored, and none of what he saw or heard or dutifully read made much sense to him and finally he gave it up. He had thought, many nights as he ate dinner alone, knowing that Louise would come home late and drop silently into bed without explanation, of getting a divorce, but he knew the loneliness, the hopelessness, of not seeing her again would be too much to take. So he was good, completely devoted, ready at all times to go anyplace with her, do anything she wanted. He even got a small job, in a broker's office, and paid his own way, bought his own liquor.

Then he'd been offered the job of going from college to college as a tailor's representative. "We want a man," Mr. Rosenberg had said, "who as soon as you look at him, you say, 'There's a university man.'" Rosenberg had looked approvingly at Darling's broad shoulders and well-kept waist, at his carefully brushed hair and his honest, wrinkle-less face. "Frankly, Mr. Darling, I am willing to make you a proposition. I have inquired about you, you are favorably known on your old campus, I understand you were in the backfield with Alfred Diederich."

Darling nodded. "Whatever happened to him?"

"He is walking around in a cast for seven years now. An

iron brace. He played professional football and they broke his neck for him."

Darling smiled. That, at least, had turned out well.

"Our suits are an easy product to sell, Mr. Darling," Rosenberg said. "We have a handsome, custom-made garment. What has Brooks Brothers got that we haven't got? A name. No more."

"I can make fifty, sixty dollars a week," Darling said to Louise that night. "And expenses. I can save some money and then come back to New York and really get started here."

"Yes, Baby," Louise said.

"As it is," Darling said carefully, "I can make it back here once a month, and holidays and the summer. We can see each other often."

"Yes, Baby." He looked at her face, lovelier now at thirty-five than it had ever been before, but fogged over now as it had been for five years with a kind of patient, kindly, remote boredom.

"What do you say?" he asked. "Should I take it?" Deep within him he hoped fiercely, longingly, for her to say, "No, Baby, you stay right here," but she said, as he knew she'd say, "I think you'd better take it."

He nodded. He had to get up and stand with his back to her, looking out the window, because there were things plain on his face that she had never seen in the fifteen years she'd known him. "Fifty dollars is a lot of money," he said. "I never thought I'd ever see fifty dollars again." He laughed. Louise laughed, too.

Christian Darling sat on the frail green grass of the practice field. The shadow of the stadium had reached out and covered him. In the distance the lights of the university shone a little mistily in the light haze of evening. Fifteen years. Flaherty even now was calling for his wife, buying her a drink, filling whatever bar they were in with that voice of his and that easy laugh. Darling half-closed his eyes, almost saw the boy fifteen years ago reach for the pass, slip the halfback, go skittering lightly down the field, his knees high and fast and graceful, smiling to himself because he knew he was going to get past the safety man. That was the high point, Darling thought, fifteen years ago, on an autumn afternoon, twenty years old and far from death, with the air coming easily into his lungs, and a deep feeling inside him that he could do anything, knock over anybody, outrun whatever had to be outrun. And the shower after and the three glasses of water and the cool night air on his damp head and Louise sitting hatless in the open car with a smile and the first kiss she ever really meant. The high point, an eighty-yard run in the practice, and a girl's kiss and everything after that a decline. Darling laughed. He had practiced the wrong thing, perhaps. He hadn't practiced for 1929 and New York City and a girl who would turn into a woman. Somewhere, he thought, there must have been a point where she moved up to me, was even with me for a moment, when I could have held her hand, if I'd known, held tight, gone with her. Well, he'd never known. Here he was on a playing field that was fifteen years away and his wife was in another city having dinner with another and better man, speaking with him a different, new language, a language nobody had ever taught him.

Darling stood up, smiled a little, because if he didn't smile he knew the tears would come. He looked around him. This was the spot. O'Connor's pass had come sliding out just to here . . . the high point. Darling put up his hands, felt all over again the flat slap of the ball. He shook his hips to throw off the halfback, cut back inside the center, picked his knees high as he ran gracefully over two men jumbled on the ground at the line of scrimmage, ran easily, gaining speed, for ten yards, holding the ball lightly in his two hands, swung away from the halfback diving at him, ran, swinging his hips in the almost girlish manner of a back in a broken field, tore into the safety man, his shoes drumming heavily on the turf, stiff-armed, elbow locked, pivoted, raced lightly and exultantly for the goal line.

It was only after he had sped over the goal line and slowed to a trot that he saw the boy and girl sitting together on the turf, looking at him wonderingly.

He stopped short, dropping his arms. "I . . ." he said, gasping a little, though his condition was fine and the run hadn't winded him. "I—once I played here."

The boy and the girl said nothing. Darling laughed embarrassedly, looked hard at them sitting there, close to each other, shrugged, turned and went toward his hotel, the sweat breaking out on his face and running down into his collar.

"Flacker: All right now, Kid, now you'd better talk," Andrew dictated. "Business: Sound of the door closing, the slow turning of the key in the lock. Buddy: You're never going to get me to talk, Flacker. Business: Sound of a slap. Flacker: Maybe that'll make you think different, Kid. Where is Jerry Carmichael? Buddy: (Laughing) Wouldn't you like to know, Flacker? Flacker: Yeah. (Slowly, with great threat in his voice) And I'm going to find out. One way or another. See? Business: Siren fades in, louder, fades out. Announcer: Will Buddy talk? Will Flacker force him to disclose the whereabouts of the rescued son of the railroad king? Will Dusty Blades reach him in time? Tune in Monday at the same time, et cetera, et cetera . . ."

Andrew dropped onto the couch and put his feet up. He stretched and sighed as he watched Lenore finish scratching his dictation down in the shorthand notebook. "Thirty bucks," he said. "There's another thirty bucks. Is it the right length?"

"Uhuh," Lenore said. "Eleven and a half pages. This is a very good one, Andy."

"Yeah," Andrew said, closing his eyes. "Put it next to *Moby Dick* on your library shelf."

18

"It's very exciting," Lenore said, standing up. "I don't know what they're complaining about."

"You're a lovely girl." Andrew put his hands over his eyes and rubbed around and around. "I have wooden hinges on my eyelids. Do you sleep at night?"

"Don't do that to your eyes." Lenore started to put on her coat. "You only aggravate them."

"You're right." Andrew dug his fists into his eyes and rotated them slowly. "You don't know how right you are."

"Tomorrow. At ten o'clock?" Lenore asked.

"At ten o'clock. Dig me out of the arms of sleep. We shall leave Dusty Blades to his fate for this week and go on with the further adventures of Ronnie Cook and His Friends, forty dollars a script. I always enjoy writing Ronnie Cook much better than Dusty Blades. See what ten dollars does to a man." He opened his eyes and watched Lenore putting her hat on in front of the mirror. When he squinted, she was not so plain-looking. He felt very sorry for Lenore, plain as sand, with her flat-colored face and her hair pulled down like rope, and never a man to her name. She was putting on a red hat with a kind of ladder arrangement going up one side. It looked very funny and sad on her. Andrew realized that it was a new hat. "That's a mighty fine hat," he said.

"I thought a long time before I bought this hat," Lenore said, flushing because he'd noticed it.

"Har-*riet!*" The governess next door screamed in the alley to the next-door neighbor's little girl. "Harriet, get away from there this minute!"

Andrew turned over on his stomach on the couch and put a pillow over his head. "Have you got any ideas for Ronnie Cook and His Friends for tomorrow?" he asked Lenore.

"No. Have you?"

"No." He pulled the pillow tight around his head.

"You'll get them by tomorrow," Lenore said. "You always do."

"Yeah," said Andrew.

"You need a vacation," Lenore said.

"Get out of here."

"Good-bye." Lenore started out. "Get a good night's sleep."

"Anything you say."

Andrew watched her with one eye as she went off the porch on which he worked and through the living room and dining room, toward the stairs. She had nice legs. You were always surprised when a girl with a face like that had nice legs. But she had hair on her legs. She was not a lucky girl. "Oh, no," Andrew said as the door closed behind her, "you are not a lucky girl."

He closed his eyes and tried to sleep. The sun came in through the open windows and the curtains blew softly over his head and the sun was warm and comforting on his closed eyes. Across the street, on the public athletic field, four boys were shagging flies. There would be the neat pleasant crack of the bat and a long time later the smack of the ball in the fielder's glove. The tall trees outside, as old as Brooklyn, rustled a little from time to time as little spurts of wind swept across the baseball field.

"Har*riet*!" the governess called. "Stop that or I will make you stand by yourself in the corner all afternoon! Harriet! I demand you to stop it!" The governess was French. She had the only unpleasant French accent Andrew had ever heard.

The little girl started to cry, "Mamma! Mamma! Mamma, she's going to hit me!" The little girl hated the governess and the governess hated the little girl, and they continually reported each other to the little girl's mother. "Mamma!"

"You are a little liar," the governess screamed. "You will grow up, and you will be a liar all your life. There will be no hope for you."

"Mamma!" wailed the little girl.

They went inside the house and it was quiet again.

"Charlie," one of the boys on the baseball field yelled, "hit it to me, Charlie!"

The telephone rang, four times, and then Andrew heard his mother talking into it. She came onto the porch.

"It's a man from the bank," she said. "He wants to talk to you."

"You should've told him I wasn't home," Andrew said.

"But you are home," his mother said. "How was I to know that . . . ?"

"You're right." Andrew swung his legs over and sat up. "You're perfectly right."

He went into the dining room, to the telephone, and talked to the man at the bank.

"You're a hundred and eleven dollars overdrawn," said the man at the bank.

Andrew squinted at his mother, sitting across the room, on a straight chair, with her arms folded in her lap, her head turned just a little, so as not to miss anything.

"I thought I had about four hundred dollars in the bank," Andrew said into the phone.

"You are a hundred and eleven dollars overdrawn," said the man at the bank.

Andrew sighed. "I'll check it." He put the phone down.

"What's the matter?" his mother asked.

"I'm a hundred and eleven dollars overdrawn," he said.

"That's shameful," his mother said. "You ought to be more methodical."

"Yes." Andrew started back to the porch.

"You're awfully careless." His mother followed him. "You really ought to keep track of your money."

"Yes." Andrew sat down on the couch.

"Give me a kiss," his mother said.

"Why?"

"No particular reason." She laughed.

"O.K." He kissed her and she held him for a moment. He dropped down on the couch. She ran her finger under his eye.

"You've got rings under your eyes," she said.

"That's right."

She kissed him again and went to the rear of the house.

He closed his eyes. From the rear of the house came the sound of the vacuum cleaner. Andrew felt his muscles getting stiff in protest against the vacuum cleaner. He got up and went to her bedroom, where she was running the machine back and forth under the bed. She was down on one knee and was bent over, looking under the bed.

"Hey!" Andrew yelled. "Hey, Mom!"

She turned off the machine and looked up at him. "What's the matter?"

"I'm trying to sleep," he said.

"Well, why don't you sleep?"

"The vacuum cleaner. It's shaking the house."

His mother stood up, her face setting into stern lines. "I've got to clean the house, don't I?"

"Why do you have to clean the house while I'm trying to sleep?"

His mother bent down again. "I can't use it while you're working. I can't use it while you're reading. I can't use it until ten o'clock in the morning because you're sleeping." She started the machine. "When am I supposed to clean the house?" she called over the noise of the cleaner. "Why don't you sleep at night like everybody else?" And she put her head down low and vigorously ran the machine back and forth.

Andrew watched her for a moment. No arguments came to him. The sound of the cleaner so close to him made his nerves jump. He went out of the room, closing the door behind him.

The telephone was ringing and he picked it up and said, "Hello."

"Ahndrew?" his agent's voice asked. His agent was from Brooklyn, too, but he had a very broad A, with which he impressed actors and sponsors.

"Yes, this is Ahndrew." Andrew always made this straight-faced joke with his agent, but the agent never seemed to catch on. "You didn't have to call. The Dusty Blades scripts are all through. You'll get them tomorrow."

"I called about something else, Ahndrew," his agent

said, his voice very smooth and influential on the phone. "The complaints're piling up on the Blades scripts. They're as slow as gum. Nothing ever happens. Ahndrew, you're not writing for the *Atlantic Monthly*."

"I know I'm not writing for the *Atlantic Monthly*."

"I think you've rather run out of material," his agent said lightly, soothingly. "I think perhaps you ought to take a little vacation from the Blades scripts."

"Go to hell, Herman," Andrew said, knowing that Herman had found somebody to do the scripts more cheaply for him.

"That's hardly the way to talk, Ahndrew," Herman said, his voice still smooth, but hurt. "After all, I have to stand in the studio and listen to the complaints."

"Sad, Herman," Andrew said. "That's a sad picture," and hung up.

He rubbed the back of his neck reflectively, feeling again the little lump behind his ear.

He went into his own room and sat at his desk looking blankly at the notes for his play that lay, neatly piled, growing older, on one side. He took out his checkbook and his last month's vouchers and arranged them in front of him.

"One hundred and eleven dollars," he murmured, as he checked back and added and subtracted, his eyes smarting from the strain, his hands shaking a little because the vacuum cleaner was still going in his mother's room. Out on the athletic field more boys had arrived and formed an infield and were throwing the ball around the bases and yelling at each other.

Dr. Chalmers, seventy-five dollars. That was for his mother and her stomach.

Eighty dollars rent. The roof over his head equaled two Ronnie Cooks and His Friends. Five thousand words for rent.

Buddy was in the hands of Flacker. Flacker could torture him for six pages. Then you could have Dusty Blades speeding to the rescue with Sam, by boat, and the boat could spring a leak because the driver was in Flacker's pay, and there could be a fight for the next six pages. The driver could have a gun. You could use it, but it wouldn't be liked, because you'd done at least four like it already.

Furniture, and a hundred and thirty-seven dollars. His mother had always wanted a good dining-room table. She didn't have a maid, she said, so he ought to get her a dining-room table. How many words for a dining-room table?

"Come on, Baby, make it two," the second baseman out on the field was yelling. "Double 'em up!"

Andrew felt like picking up his old glove and going out there and joining them. When he was still in college he used to go out on a Saturday at ten o'clock in the morning and shag flies and jump around the infield and run and run all day, playing in pickup games until it got too dark to see. He was always tired now and even when he played tennis he didn't move his feet right, because he was tired, and hit flat-footed and wild.

Spain, one hundred dollars. Oh, Lord.

A hundred and fifty to his father, to meet his father's payroll. His father had nine people on his payroll, making little tin gadgets that his father tried to sell to the dime stores, and at the end of every month Andrew had to meet the payroll. His father always gravely made out a note to him.

Flacker is about to kill Buddy out of anger and desperation. In bursts Dusty, alone. Sam is hurt. On the way to the hospital. Buddy is spirited away a moment before Dusty arrives. Flacker, very smooth and oily. Confrontation. "Where is Buddy, Flacker?" "You mean the little lad?" "I mean the little lad, Flacker!"

Fifty dollars to Dorothy's piano teacher. His sister. Another plain girl. She might as well learn how to play the piano. Then one day they'd come to him and say, "Dorothy is ready for her debut. All we're asking you to do is rent Town Hall for a Wednesday evening. Just advance the money." She'd never get married. She was too smart for the men who would want her and too plain for the men she'd want herself. She bought her dresses in Saks. He would have to support, for life, a sister who would only buy her dresses in Saks and pay her piano teacher fifty dollars a month every month. She was only twenty-four, she would have a normal life expectancy of at least forty years, twelve times forty, plus dresses at Saks and Town Hall from time to time . . .

His father's teeth—ninety dollars. The money it cost to keep a man going in his losing fight against age.

The automobile. Nine hundred dollars. A nine-hundred-dollar check looked very austere and impressive, like a penal institution. He was going to go off in the automobile, find a place in the mountains, write a play. Only he could never get himself far enough ahead on Dusty Blades and Ronnie Cook and His Friends. Twenty thousand words a week, each week, recurring like Sunday on the calendar. How many words was *Hamlet*? Thirty, thirty-five thousand?

Twenty-three dollars to Best's. That was Martha's sweater for her birthday. "Either you say yes or no," Martha said Saturday night. "I want to get married and I've waited long enough." If you married you paid rent in two places, light, gas, telephone twice, and you bought stockings, dresses, toothpaste, medical attention, for your wife.

Flacker plays with something in his pocket. Dusty's hand shoots out, grabs his wrist, pulls his hand out. Buddy's little penknife, which Dusty had given him for a birthday present, is in Flacker's hand. "Flacker, tell me where Buddy Jones is, or I'll kill you with my bare hands." A gong rings. Flacker has stepped on an alarm. Doors open and the room fills with his henchmen.

Twenty dollars to Macy's for books. Parrington, *Main Currents in American Thought*. How does Dusty Blades fit into the *Main Currents of American Thought*?

Ten dollars to Dr. Farber. "I don't sleep at night. Can you help me?"

"Do you drink coffee?"

"I drink one cup of coffee in the morning. That's all."

Pills, to be taken before retiring. Ten dollars. We ransom our lives from doctors' hands.

If you marry, you take an apartment downtown because it's silly to live in Brooklyn this way; and you buy furniture, four rooms full of furniture, beds, chairs, dishrags, relatives. Martha's family was poor and getting no younger and finally there would be three families, with rent and clothes and doctors and funerals.

Andrew got up and opened the closet door. In it, stacked in files, were the scripts he had written in the last four years. They stretched from one end of a wide closet across to another, bridge from one wall to another of a million words. Four years' work.

Next script. The henchmen close in on Dusty. He hears the sounds of Buddy screaming in the next room . . .

How many years more?

The vacuum cleaner roared.

Martha was Jewish. That meant you'd have to lie your way into some hotels, if you went at all, and you never could escape from one particular meanness of the world around you; and when the bad time came there you'd be, adrift on that dangerous sea.

He sat down at his desk. One hundred dollars again to Spain. Barcelona had fallen and the long dusty lines were beating their way to the French border with the planes over them, and out of a sense of guilt at not being on a dusty road, yourself, bloody-footed and in fear of death, you gave a hundred dollars, feeling at the same time that it was too much and nothing you ever gave could be enough. Three-and-a-third The Adventures of Dusty Blades to the dead and dying of Spain.

The world loads you day by day with new burdens that increase on your shoulders. Lift a pound and you find you're carrying a ton. "Marry me," she says, "marry me." Then what does Dusty do? What the hell can he do that he hasn't done before? For five afternoons a week now, for a year, Dusty has been in Flacker's hands, or the hands of somebody else who is Flacker but has another name, and each time he has escaped. How now?

The vacuum roared in the hallway outside his room.

"Mom!" he yelled. "Please turn that thing off!"

"What did you say?" his mother called.

"Nothing."

He added up the bank balances. His figures showed that he was four hundred and twelve dollars overdrawn instead of one hundred and eleven dollars, as the bank said. He didn't feel like adding the figures over. He put the vouchers and the bank's sheet into an envelope for his income-tax returns.

"Hit it out, Charlie!" a boy called on the field. "Make it a fast one!"

Andrew felt like going out and playing with them. He changed his clothes and put on a pair of old spikes that were lying in the back of the closet. His old pants were tight on him. Fat. If he ever let go, if anything happened and he couldn't exercise, he'd blow up like a house, if he got sick and had to lie in bed and convalesce . . . Maybe Dusty has a knife in a holster up his sleeve . . . How plant that? The rent, the food, the piano teacher, the people at Saks who sold his sister dresses, the nimble girls who painted the tin gadgets in his father's shop, the teeth in his father's mouth, the doctors, the doctors, all living on the words that would have to come out of his head. See here, Flacker, I know what you're up to. Business: Sound of a shot. A groan. Hurry, before the train gets to the crossing! Look! He's gaining on us! Hurry! will he make it? Will Dusty Blades head off the desperate gang of counterfeiters and murderers in the race for the yacht? Will I be able to keep it up? The years, the years ahead . . . You grow fat and the lines become permanent under your eyes and you drink too much and you pay more to the doctors because death is nearer and there is no stop, no vacation from life, in no year can you say, "I want to sit this one out, kindly excuse me."

His mother opened the door. "Martha's on the phone."

Andrew clattered out in his spiked shoes, holding the old, torn fielder's glove. He closed the door to the dining room to show his mother this was going to be a private conversation.

"Hello," he said. "Yes." He listened gravely. "No," he said. "I guess not. Good-bye. Good luck, Martha."

He stood looking at the phone. His mother came in and he raised his head and started down the steps.

"Andrew," she said, "I want to ask you something."

"What?"

"Could you spare fifty dollars, Andrew?"

"Oh, God!"

"It's important. You know I wouldn't ask you if it wasn't important. It's for Dorothy."

"What does she need it for?"

"She's going to a party, a very important party, a lot of very big people're going to be there and she's sure they'll ask her to play. . . ."

"Do the invitations cost fifty dollars apiece?" Andrew kicked the top step and a little piece of dried mud fell off the spiked shoes.

"No, Andrew." His mother was talking in her asking-for-money voice. "It's for a dress. She can't go without a new dress, she says. There's a man there she's after."

"She won't get him, dress or no dress," Andrew said. "Your daughter's a very plain girl."

"I know." His mother's hands waved a little, helpless and sad. "But it's better if she at least does the best she can. I feel so sorry for her, Andrew . . ."

"Everybody comes to me!" Andrew yelled, his voice suddenly high. "Nobody leaves me alone! Not for a minute!"

He was crying now and he turned to hide it from his mother. She looked at him, surprised, shaking her head. She put her arms around him. "Just do what you want to, Andrew, that's all. Don't do anything you don't want to do."

"Yeah," Andrew said. "Yeah. I'm sorry. I'll give you the money. I'm sorry I yelled at you."

"Don't give it to me if you don't want to, Andrew." His mother was saying this honestly, believing it.

He laughed a little. "I want to, Mom, I want to."

He patted her shoulder and went down toward the baseball field, leaving her standing there puzzled at the top of the steps.

The sun and the breeze felt good on the baseball field, and he forgot for an hour, but he moved slowly. His arm hurt at the shoulder when he threw, and the boy playing second base called him Mister, which he wouldn't have done even last year, when Andrew was twenty-four.

The Girls in Their Summer Dresses

Fifth Avenue was shining in the sun when they left the
Brevoort and started walking toward Washington Square.
The sun was warm, even though it was November and
everything looked like Sunday morning—the buses, and
the well-dressed people walking slowly in couples and the
quiet buildings with the windows closed.

Michael held Frances' arm tightly as they walked downtown in the sunlight. They walked lightly, almost smiling,
because they had slept late and had a good breakfast and
it was Sunday. Michael unbuttoned his coat and let it flap
around him in the mild wind. They walked, without saying anything, among the young and pleasant-looking people who somehow seem to make up most of the population of that section of New York City.

"Look out," Frances said, as they crossed Eighth Street.
"You'll break your neck."

Michael laughed and Frances laughed with him.

"She's not so pretty, anyway," Frances said. "Anyway,
not pretty enough to take a chance breaking your neck
looking at her."

Michael laughed again. He laughed louder this time,
but not as solidly. "She wasn't a bad-looking girl. She had

a nice complexion. Country-girl complexion. How did you know I was looking at her?"

Frances cocked her head to one side and smiled at her husband under the tip-tilted brim of her hat. "Mike, darling . . ." she said.

Michael laughed, just a little laugh this time. "O.K.," he said. "The evidence is in. Excuse me. It was the complexion. It's not the sort of complexion you see much in New York. Excuse me."

Frances patted his arm lightly and pulled him along a little faster toward Washington Square.

"This is a nice morning," she said. "This is a wonderful morning. When I have breakfast with you it makes me feel good all day."

"Tonic," Michael said. "Morning pick-up. Rolls and coffee with Mike and you're on the alkali side, guaranteed."

"That's the story. Also, I slept all night, wound around you like a rope."

"Saturday night," he said. "I permit such liberties only when the week's work is done."

"You're getting fat," she said.

"Isn't it the truth? The lean man from Ohio."

"I love it," she said, "an extra five pounds of husband."

"I love it, too," Michael said gravely.

"I have an idea," Frances said.

"My wife has an idea. That pretty girl."

"Let's not see anybody all day," Frances said. "Let's just hang around with each other. You and me. We're always up to our neck in people, drinking their Scotch, or drinking our Scotch, we only see each other in bed . . ."

"The Great Meeting Place," Michael said. "Stay in bed long enough and everybody you ever knew will show up there."

"Wise guy," Frances said. "I'm talking serious."

"O.K., I'm listening serious."

"I want to go out with my husband all day long. I want him to talk only to me and listen only to me."

"What's to stop us?" Michael asked. "What party intends to prevent me from seeing my wife alone on Sunday? What party?"

"The Stevensons. They want us to drop by around one o'clock and they'll drive us into the country."

"The lousy Stevensons," Mike said. "Transparent. They can whistle. They can go driving in the country by themselves. My wife and I have to stay in New York and bore each other tête-à-tête."

"Is it a date?"

"It's a date."

Frances leaned over and kissed him on the tip of the ear.

"Darling," Michael said. "This is Fifth Avenue."

"Let me arrange a program," Frances said. "A planned Sunday in New York for a young couple with money to throw away."

"Go easy."

"First let's go see a football game. A professional football game," Frances said, because she knew Michael loved to watch them. "The Giants are playing. And it'll be nice to be outside all day today and get hungry and later we'll go down to Cavanagh's and get a steak as big as a blacksmith's apron, with a bottle of wine, and after that, there's a new French picture at the Filmarte that everybody says . . . Say, are you listening to me?"

"Sure," he said. He took his eyes off the hatless girl with the dark hair, cut dancer-style, like a helmet, who was walking past him with the self-conscious strength and grace dancers have. She was walking without a coat and she looked very solid and strong and her belly was flat, like a boy's, under her skirt, and her hips swung boldly because she was a dancer and also because she knew Michael was looking at her. She smiled a little to herself as she went past and Michael noticed all these things before he looked back at his wife. "Sure," he said, "we're going to watch the Giants and we're going to eat steak and we're going to see a French picture. How do you like that?"

"That's it," Frances said flatly. "That's the program for the day. Or maybe you'd just rather walk up and down Fifth Avenue."

"No," Michael said carefully. "Not at all."

"You always look at other women," Frances said. "At every damn woman in the City of New York."

"Oh, come now," Michael said, pretending to joke. "Only pretty ones. And, after all, how many pretty women *are* there in New York? Seventeen?"

"More. At least you seem to think so. Wherever you go."

"Not the truth. Occasionally, maybe, I look at a woman as she passes. In the street. I admit, perhaps in the street I look at a woman once in a while . . ."

"Everywhere," Frances said. "Every damned place we go. Restaurants, subways, theaters, lectures, concerts."

"Now, darling," Michael said, "I look at everything. God gave me eyes and I look at women and men and subway excavations and moving pictures and the little flowers of the field. I casually inspect the universe."

"You ought to see the look in your eye," Frances said, "as you casually inspect the universe on Fifth Avenue."

"I'm a happily married man." Michael pressed her elbow tenderly, knowing what he was doing. "Example for the whole twentieth century, Mr. and Mrs. Mike Loomis."

"You mean it?"

"Frances, baby . . ."

"Are you *really* happily married?"

"Sure," Michael said, feeling the whole Sunday morning sinking like lead inside him. "Now what the hell is the sense in talking like that?"

"I would like to know." Frances walked faster now, looking straight ahead, her face showing nothing, which was the way she always managed it when she was arguing or feeling bad.

"I'm wonderfully happily married," Michael said patiently. "I am the envy of all men between the ages of fifteen and sixty in the State of New York."

"Stop kidding," Frances said.

"I have a fine home," Michael said. "I got nice books and a phonograph and nice friends. I live in a town I like the way I like and I do the work I like and I live with the woman I like. Whenever something good happens, don't I run to you? When something bad happens, don't I cry on your shoulder?"

"Yes," Frances said. "You look at every woman that passes."

"That's an exaggeration."

"Every woman." Frances took her hand off Michael's arm. "If she's not pretty you turn away fairly quickly. If she's halfway pretty you watch her for about seven steps . . ."

"My lord, Frances!"

"If she's pretty you practically break your neck . . ."

"Hey, let's have a drink," Michael said, stopping.

"We just had breakfast."

"Now, listen, darling," Mike said, choosing his words with care, "it's a nice day and we both feel good and there's no reason why we have to break it up. Let's have a nice Sunday."

"I could have a fine Sunday if you didn't look as though you were dying to run after every skirt on Fifth Avenue."

"Let's have a drink," Michael said.

"I don't want a drink."

"What do you want, a fight?"

"No," Frances said so unhappily that Michael felt terribly sorry for her. "I don't want a fight. I don't know why I started this. All right, let's drop it. Let's have a good time."

They joined hands consciously and walked without talking among the baby carriages and the old Italian men in their Sunday clothes and the young women with Scotties in Washington Square Park.

"I hope it's a good game today," Frances said after a while, her tone a good imitation of the tone she had used at breakfast and at the beginning of their walk. "I like professional football games. They hit each other as though they're made out of concrete. When they tackle each other," she said, trying to make Michael laugh, "they make divots. It's very exciting."

"I want to tell you something," Michael said very seriously. "I have not touched another woman. Not once. In all the five years."

"All right," Frances said.

"You believe that, don't you?"

"All right."

They walked between the crowded benches, under the scrubby city park trees.

"I try not to notice it," Frances said, as though she were talking to herself. "I try to make believe it doesn't mean anything. Some men're like that, I tell myself, they have to see what they're missing."

"Some women're like that, too," Michael said. "In my time I've seen a couple of ladies."

"I haven't even looked at another man," Frances said, walking straight ahead, "since the second time I went out with you."

"There's no law," Michael said.

"I feel rotten inside, in my stomach, when we pass a woman and you look at her and I see that look in your eye and that's the way you looked at me the first time, in Alice Maxwell's house. Standing there in the living room, next to the radio, with a green hat on and all those people."

"I remember the hat," Michael said.

"The same look," Frances said. "And it makes me feel bad. It makes me feel terrible."

"Sssh, please, darling, sssh . . ."

"I think I would like a drink now," Frances said.

They walked over to a bar on Eighth Street, not saying anything, Michael automatically helping her over curbstones, and guiding her past automobiles. He walked, buttoning his coat, looking thoughtfully at his neatly shined heavy brown shoes as they made the steps toward the bar. They sat near a window in the bar and the sun streamed in, and there was a small cheerful fire in the fire-place. A little Japanese waiter came over and put down some pretzels and smiled happily at them.

"What do you order after breakfast?" Michael asked.

"Brandy, I suppose," Frances said.

"Courvoisier," Michael told the waiter. "Two Cour-voisier."

The waiter came with the glasses and they sat drinking the brandy, in the sunlight. Michael finished half his and drank a little water.

"I look at women," he said. "Correct. I don't say it's wrong or right, I look at them. If I pass them on the street and I don't look at them, I'm fooling you, I'm fooling my-self."

"You look at them as though you want them," Frances said, playing with her brandy glass. "Every one of them."

"In a way," Michael said, speaking softly and not to his wife, "in a way that's true. I don't do anything about it, but it's true."

"I know it. That's why I feel bad."

"Another brandy," Michael called. "Waiter, two more brandies."

"Why do you hurt me?" Frances asked. "What're you doing?"

Michael sighed and closed his eyes and rubbed them gently with his fingertips. "I love the way women look. One of the things I like best about New York is the bat-talions of women. When I first came to New York from Ohio that was the first thing I noticed, the million wonder-ful women, all over the city. I walked around with my heart in my throat."

"A kid," Frances said. "That's a kid's feeling."

"Guess again," Michael said. "Guess again. I'm older now, I'm a man getting near middle age, putting on a little fat and I still love to walk along Fifth Avenue at three o'clock on the east side of the street between Fiftieth and Fifty-seventh Streets, they're all out then, making believe they're shopping, in their furs and their crazy hats, everything all concentrated from all over the world into eight blocks, the best furs, the best clothes, the handsomest women, out to spend money and feeling good about it, looking coldly at you, making believe they're not looking at you as you go past."

The Japanese waiter put the two drinks down, smiling with great happiness.

"Everything is all right?" he asked.

"Everything is wonderful," Michael said.

"If it's just a couple of fur coats," Frances said, "and forty-five-dollar hats . . ."

"It's not the fur coats. Or the hats. That's just the scenery for that particular kind of woman. Understand," he said, "you don't have to listen to this."

"I want to listen."

"I like the girls in the offices. Neat, with their eyeglasses, smart, chipper, knowing what everything is about, taking care of themselves all the time." He kept his eye on the people going slowly past outside the window. "I like the girls on Forty-fourth Street at lunch time, the actresses, all dressed up on nothing a week, talking to the good-looking boys, wearing themselves out being young and vivacious outside Sardi's, waiting for producers to look at them. I like the salesgirls in Macy's, paying attention to you first because you're a man, leaving lady customers waiting, flirting with you over socks and books and phonograph needles. I got all this stuff accumulated in me because I've been thinking about it for ten years and now you've asked for it and here it is."

"Go ahead," Frances said.

"When I think of New York City, I think of all the girls, the Jewish girls, the Italian girls, the Irish, Polack, Chinese, German, Negro, Spanish, Russian girls, all on parade in the city. I don't know whether it's something special with me or whether every man in the city walks around with the same feeling inside him, but I feel as though I'm at a picnic in this city. I like to sit near the women in the theaters, the famous beauties who've taken six hours to get ready and look it. And the young girls at the football games, with the red cheeks, and when the warm weather comes, the girls in their summer dresses . . ." He finished his drink. "That's the story. You asked for it, remember. I can't help but look at them. I can't help but want them."

"You want them," Frances repeated without expression. "You said that."

"Right," Michael said, being cruel now and not caring, because she had made him expose himself. "You brought this subject up for discussion, we will discuss it fully."

Frances finished her drink and swallowed two or three times extra. "You say you love me?"

"I love you, but I also want them. O.K."

"I'm pretty, too," Frances said. "As pretty as any of them."

"You're beautiful," Michael said, meaning it.

"I'm good for you," Frances said, pleading. "I've made a good wife, a good housekeeper, a good friend. I'd do any damn thing for you."

"I know," Michael said. He put his hand out and grasped hers.

"You'd like to be free to . . ." Frances said.

"Sssh."

"Tell the truth." She took her hand away from under his.

Michael flicked the edge of his glass with his finger. "O.K.," he said gently. "Sometimes I feel I would like to be free."

"Well," Frances said defiantly, drumming on the table, "any time you say . . ."

"Don't be foolish." Michael swung his chair around to her side of the table and patted her thigh.

She began to cry, silently, into her handkerchief, bent over just enough so that nobody else in the bar would notice. "Some day," she said, crying, "you're going to make a move . . ."

Michael didn't say anything. He sat watching the bartender slowly peel a lemon.

"Aren't you?" Frances asked harshly. "Come on, tell me. Talk. Aren't you?"

"Maybe," Michael said. He moved his chair back again. "How the hell do I know?"

"You know," Frances persisted. "Don't you know?"

"Yes," Michael said after a while, "I know."

Frances stopped crying then. Two or three snuffles into the handkerchief and she put it away and her face didn't tell anything to anybody. "At least do me one favor," she said.

"Sure."

"Stop talking about how pretty this woman is, or that one. Nice eyes, nice breasts, a pretty figure, good voice," she mimicked his voice. "Keep it to yourself. I'm not interested."

"Excuse me." Michael waved to the waiter. "I'll keep it to myself."

Frances flicked the corner of her eyes. "Another brandy," she told the waiter.

"Two," Michael said.

"Yes, ma'am, yes, sir," said the waiter, backing away.

Frances regarded him coolly across the table. "Do you want me to call the Stevensons?" she asked. "It'll be nice in the country."

"Sure," Michael said. "Call them up."

She got up from the table and walked across the room toward the telephone. Michael watched her walk, thinking, what a pretty girl, what nice legs.

Sailor off the Bremen

They sat in the small white kitchen, Ernest and Charley and Preminger and Dr. Stryker, all bunched around the porcelain-topped table, so that the kitchen seemed to be overflowing with men. Sally stood at the stove turning griddle-cakes over thoughtfully, listening intently to what Preminger was saying.

"So," Preminger said, carefully working his knife and fork, "everything was excellent. The comrades arrived, dressed like ladies and gentlemen at the opera, in evening gowns and what do you call them?"

"Tuxedoes," Charley said. "Black ties."

"Tuxedoes," Preminger nodded, speaking with his precise educated German accent. "Very handsome people, mixing with all the other handsome people who came to say good-bye to their friends on the boat; everybody very gay, everybody with a little whisky on the breath; nobody would suspect they were Party members, they were so clean and upper class." He laughed lightly at his own joke. He looked like a young boy from a nice Middle Western college, with crew-cut hair and a straight nose and blue eyes and an easy laugh. His laugh was a little high and short, and he talked fast, as though he wanted to get a great many words out to beat a certain deadline, but otherwise, being a Communist in Germany and a deck officer on the *Bremen* hadn't made any obvious changes in him. "It is a wonderful thing," he said, "how many pretty girls there are in the Party in the United States. Wonderful!"

They all laughed, even Ernest, who put his hand up to cover the empty spaces in the front row of his teeth every time he smiled. His hand covered his mouth and the fingers cupped around the neat black patch over his eye, and he smiled secretly and swiftly behind that concealment, getting his merriment over with swiftly, so he could take his hand down and compose his face into its usual unmoved, distant expression, cultivated from the time he got out of the hospital. Sally watched him from the stove, knowing each step: the grudging smile, the hand, the consciousness and memory of deformity, the wrench to composure, the lie of peace when he took his hand down.

She shook her head, dumped three brown cakes onto a plate.

"Here," she said, putting them before Preminger. "Better than Childs restaurant."

"Wonderful," Preminger said, dousing them with syrup. "Each time I come to America I feast on these. There is nothing like it in the whole continent of Europe."

"All right," Charley said, leaning out across the kitchen table, practically covering it, because he was so big, "finish the story."

"So I gave the signal," Preminger said, waving his fork. "When everything was nice and ready, everybody having a good time, stewards running this way, that way, with champagne, a nice little signal and we had a very nice little demonstration. Nice signs, good loud yelling, the Nazi flag cut down, one, two, three, from the pole. The girls standing together singing like angels, everybody running there from all parts of the ship, everybody getting the idea very, very clear—a very nice little demonstration." He smeared butter methodically on the top cake. "So then, the rough business. Expected. Naturally. After all, we all know it is no cocktail party for Lady Astor." He pursed his lips and squinted at his plate, looking like a small boy making believe he's the head of a family. "A little pushing, expected, maybe a little crack over the head here and there, expected. Justice comes with a headache these days, we all know that. But my people, the Germans. You must always expect the worst from them. They organize like lightning. Method. How to treat a riot on a ship. Every steward, every oiler, every sailor, was there in a minute and a half. Two men would hold a comrade, the other would beat him. Nothing left to accident."

"The hell with it," Ernest said. "What's the sense in going through the whole thing again? It's all over."

"Shut up," Charley said.

"Two stewards got hold of Ernest," Preminger said softly. "And another one did the beating. Stewards are worse than sailors. All day long they take orders, they hate the world. Ernest was unlucky. All the others did their jobs, but they were human beings. The steward is a member of the Nazi party. He is an Austrian; he is not a normal man."

"Sally," Ernest said, "give Mr. Preminger some more milk."

"He kept hitting Ernest," Preminger tapped absently on the porcelain top with his fork, "and he kept laughing and laughing."

"You know who he is?" Charley asked. "You're sure you know who he is?"

"I know who he is. He is twenty-five years old, very dark and good-looking, and he sleeps with at least two ladies a voyage." Preminger slopped his milk around in the bottom of his glass. "His name is Lueger. He spies on the crew for the Nazis. He has sent two men already to concentration camps. He is a very serious character. He knew what he was doing," Preminger said clearly, "when he kept hitting Ernest in the eye. I tried to get to him, but I was in the middle of a thousand people, screaming and running. If something happens to that Lueger that will be a very good thing."

"Have a cigar," Ernest said, pulling two out of his pocket.

"Something will happen to him," Charley said, taking a deep breath, and leaning back from the table. "Something will damn sure happen to him."

"You're a dumb kid," Ernest said, in the weary tone he used now in all serious discussions. "What do you prove if you beat up one stupid sailor?"

"I don't prove anything," Charley said. "I don't prove a goddamn thing. I am just going to have a good time with the boy that knocked my brother's eye out. That's all."

"It is not a personal thing," Ernest said, in the tired voice. "It is the movement of Fascism. You don't stop Fascism with a personal crusade against one German. If I thought it would do some good, I'd say, sure, go ahead . . ."

"My brother, the Communist," Charley said bitterly. "He goes out and he gets ruined and still he talks dialectics. The Red Saint with the long view. The long view gives me a pain in the ass. I am taking a very short view of Mr. Lueger. I am going to kick the living guts out of his belly. Preminger, what do you say?"

"Speaking as a Party member," Preminger said, "I approve of your brother's attitude, Charley."

"Nuts," Charley said.

"Speaking as a man, Charley," Preminger went on, "please put Lueger on his back for at least six months. Where is that cigar, Ernest?"

Dr. Stryker spoke up in his dry, polite, dentist's voice. "As you know," he said, "I am not the type for violence." Dr. Stryker weighed a hundred and thirty-three pounds and it was almost possible to see through his wrists, he was so frail. "But as Ernest's friends, I think there would be a definite satisfaction for all of us, including Ernest, if this Lueger was taken care of. You may count on me for anything within my powers." He was very scared, Dr. Stryker, and his voice was even drier than usual, but he spoke up after reasoning the whole thing out slowly and carefully, disregarding the fear, the worry, the possible great damage. "That is my opinion," he said.

"Sally," Ernest said, "talk to these damn fools."

"I think," Sally said slowly, looking steadily at her husband's face, always stiffly composed now, like a corpse's face, "I think they know what they're talking about."

Ernest shrugged. "Emotionalism. A large useless gesture. You're all tainted by Charley's philosophy. He's a football player. He has a football player's philosophy. Somebody knocks you down, you knock him down, everything is fine."

"I want a glass of milk, too," Charley said. "Please, Sally."

"Whom're you playing this week?" Ernest said.

"Georgetown."

"Won't that be enough violence for one week?" Ernest asked.

"Nope," Charley said. "I'll take care of Georgetown first, then Lueger."

"Anything I can do," Dr. Stryker said. "Remember, anything I can do. I am at your service."

"The coach'll be sore," Ernest said, "if you get banged up, Charley."

"The hell with the coach. Please shut up, Ernest. I have got my stomachful of Communist tactics. No more. Get this in your head, Ernest." Charley stood up and banged the table. "I am disregarding the class struggle, I am disregarding the education of the proletariat, I am disregarding the fact that you are a good Communist. I am acting strictly in the capacity of your brother. If you'd had any brains you would have stayed away from that lousy boat. You're a painter, an artist, you make water colors, what the hell is it your business if lunatics're running Germany? But all right. You've got no brains. You go and get your eye beat out. O.K. Now I step in. Purely personal. None of your business. Shut your trap. I will fix everything to my own satisfaction. Please go and lie down in the bedroom. We have arrangements to make here."

Ernest stood up, hiding his mouth, which was twitching, and walked into the bedroom and closed the door and lay down on the bed, in the dark, with his eye open.

The next day, an hour before sailing time, Charley and Dr. Stryker and Sally went down to the *Bremen,* and boarded the ship on different gangplanks. They stood separately on the A Deck, up forward, waiting for Preminger. Preminger came, very boyish and crisp in his blue uniform, looked coldly past them, touched a steward on the arm, a dark, good-looking young steward, said something to him, and went aft. Charley and Dr. Stryker examined the steward closely, so that two weeks later, on a dark street, there would be no mistake, and left, leaving Sally there, smiling at Lueger.

"Yes," Sally said two weeks later, "it is very clear. I'll have dinner with him, and I'll go to a movie with him, and I'll get him to take at least two drinks, and I'll tell him I live on West Twelfth Street, near West Street. There is a whole block of apartment houses there, and I'll get him down to West Twelfth Street between a quarter to one and one in the morning, and you'll be waiting there, you and Stryker, under the Ninth Avenue L, and you'll say, 'Pardon me, can you direct me to Sheridan Square?' and I'll start running."

"That's right," Charley said, "that's fine." He blew reflectively on his huge hands, knotted and cleat-marked from last Saturday's game. "That is the whole story for Mr. Lueger. You'll go through with it now?" he asked. "You're sure you can manage it?"

"I'll go through with it," Sally said. "I had a long talk with him today when the boat came in. He is very . . . anxious. He likes small girls like me, he says, with black hair. I told him I lived alone, downtown. He looked at me very significantly. I know why he manages to sleep with two ladies a voyage, like Preminger says. I'll manage it."

"What is Ernest going to do tonight?" Dr. Stryker asked.

In the two weeks of waiting his voice had become so dry he had to swallow desperately every five words. "Somebody ought to take care of Ernest tonight."

"He's going to Carnegie Hall tonight," Sally said. "They're playing Brahms and Debussy."

"That's a good way to spend an evening," Charley said. He opened his collar absently, and pulled down his tie. "The only place I can go with Ernest these days is the movies. It's dark, so I don't have to look at him."

"He'll pull through," Dr. Stryker said professionally. "I'm making him new teeth; he won't be so self-conscious, he'll adjust himself."

"He hardly paints any more," Sally said. "He just sits around the house and looks at his old pictures."

"Mr. Lueger," Charley said. "Our pal, Mr. Lueger."

"He carries a picture of Hitler," Sally said. "In his watch. He showed me. He says he's lonely."

"How big is he?" Stryker asked nervously.

"He's a large, strong man," Sally said.

"I think you ought to have an instrument of some kind, Charley," Stryker said dryly. "Really, I do."

Charley laughed. He extended his two hands, palms up, the broken fingers curled a little, broad and muscular. "I want to do this with my own hands," he said. "I want to take care of Mr. Lueger with my bare fists. I want it to be a very personal affair."

"There is no telling what . . ." Stryker said.

"Don't worry, Stryker," Charley said. "Don't worry one bit."

At twelve that night Sally and Lueger walked down Eighth Avenue from the Fourteenth Street subway station. Lueger held Sally's arm as they walked, his fingers moving gently up and down, occasionally grasping tightly the loose cloth of her coat and the firm flesh of her arm just above the elbow.

"Oh," Sally said. "Don't. That hurts."

Lueger laughed. "It does not hurt much," he said. He

pinched her playfully. "You don't mind if it hurt, nevertheless," he said. His English was very complicated, with a thick accent.

"I mind," Sally said. "Honest, I mind."

"I like you," he said, walking very close to her. "You are a good girl. You are made excellent. I am happy to accompany you home. You are sure you live alone?"

"I'm sure," Sally said. "Don't worry. I would like a drink."

"Aaah," Lueger said. "Waste time."

"I'll pay for it," Sally said. She had learned a lot about him in one evening. "My own money. Drinks for you and me."

"If you say so," Lueger said, steering her into a bar. "One drink, because we have something to do tonight." He pinched her hard and laughed, looking obliquely into her eyes with a kind of technical suggestiveness he used on the two ladies a voyage on the *Bremen*.

Under the Ninth Avenue L on Twelfth Street, Charley and Dr. Stryker leaned against an elevated post, in deep shadow.

"I . . . I . . ." Stryker said. Then he had to swallow to wet his throat so that the words would come out. "I wonder if they're coming," he said finally in a flat, high whisper.

"They'll come," Charley said, keeping his eyes on the little triangular park up Twelfth Street where it joins Eighth Avenue. "That Sally has guts. That Sally loves my dumb brother like he was the President of the United States. As if he was a combination of Lenin and Michelangelo. And he had to go and get his eye batted out."

"He's a very fine man," Stryker said. "Your brother Ernest. A man with true ideals. I am very sorry to see what has happened to his character since . . . Is that them?"

"No," Charley said. "It's two girls from the YWCA on the corner."

"He used to be a very merry man," Stryker said, swallowing rapidly. "Always laughing. Always sure of what he was saying. Before he was married we used to go out together all the time and all the time the girls, my girl and his girl, no matter who they were, would give all their attention to him. All the time. I didn't mind. I love your brother Ernest as if he was my young brother. I could cry when I see him sitting now, covering his eye and his teeth, not saying anything, just listening to what other people have to say."

"Yeah," Charley said. "Yeah. Why don't you keep quiet, Stryker?"

"Excuse me," Stryker said, talking fast and dry. "I don't like to bother you. But I must talk. Otherwise, if I just stand here keeping still, I will suddenly start running and I'll run right up to Forty-second Street. I can't keep quiet at the moment, excuse me."

"Go ahead and talk, Stryker," Charley said gently, patting him on the shoulder. "Shoot your mouth right off, all you want."

"I am only doing this because I think it will help Ernest," Stryker said, leaning hard against the post, in the shadow, to keep his knees straight. "I have a theory. My theory is that when Ernest finds out what happens to this Lueger, he will pick up. It will be a kind of springboard to him. It is my private notion of the psychology of the situation. We should have brought an instrument with us, though. A club, a knife, brass knuckles." Stryker put his hands in his pockets, holding them tight against the cloth to keep them from trembling. "It will be very bad if we mess this up. Won't it be very bad, Charley? Say, Charley . . ."

"Sssh," said Charley.

Stryker looked up the street. "That's them. That's Sally, that's her coat. That's the bastard. The lousy German bastard."

"Sssh, Stryker. Sssh."

"I feel very cold, Charley. Do you feel cold? It's a warm night but I . . ."

"For Christ's sake, shut up!"

"We'll fix him," Stryker whispered. "Yes, Charley, I'll shut up, sure, I'll shut up, depend on me, Charley . . ."

Sally and Lueger walked slowly down Twelfth Street. Lueger had his arm around Sally's waist and their hips rubbed as they walked.

"That was a very fine film tonight," Lueger was saying. "I enjoy Deanna Durbin. Very young, fresh, sweet. Like you." He grinned at Sally in the dark and held tighter to her waist. "A small young maid. You are just the kind I like." He tried to kiss her. Sally turned her head away.

"Listen, Mr. Lueger," she said, not because she liked him, but because he was a human being and thoughtless and unsuspecting and because her heart was softer than she had thought. "Listen, I think you'd better leave me here."

"I do not understand English," Lueger said, enjoying this last coyness.

"Thank you very much for a pleasant evening," Sally said desperately, stopping in her tracks. "Thank you for taking me home. You can't come up. I was lying to you. I don't live alone . . ."

Lueger laughed. "Little frightened girl. That's nice. I love you for it."

"My brother," Sally said. "I swear to God I live with my brother."

Lueger grabbed her and kissed her, hard, bruising her lips against her teeth, his hands pressing harshly into the flesh of her back. She sobbed into his mouth with the pain, helpless. He released her. He was laughing.

"Come," he said, holding her close. "I am anxious to meet your brother. Little liar."

"All right," she said, watching Charley and Stryker move out from the L shadow. "All right. Let's not wait. Let's walk fast. Very fast. Let's not waste time."

Lueger laughed happily. "That's it. That's the way a girl should talk."

They walked swiftly toward the elevated ramp, Lueger laughing, his hand on her hip in certainty and possession.

"Pardon me," Stryker said. "Could you direct me to Sheridan Square?"

"Well," said Sally, stopping, "it's . . ."

Charley swung and Sally started running as soon as she heard the wooden little noise a fist makes on a man's face. Charley held Lueger up with one hand and chopped the lolling head with the other. He carried Lueger back into the shadows against a high iron railing. He hung Lueger by his overcoat against one of the iron points, so he could use both hands on him. Stryker watched for a moment, then turned and looked toward Eighth Avenue.

Charley worked very methodically, getting his two hundred pounds behind short, accurate, smashing blows that made Lueger's head jump and loll and roll against the iron pikes. Charley hit him in the nose three times, squarely, using his fist the way a carpenter uses a hammer. Each time Charley heard the sound of bone breaking, cartilage tearing. When he got through with the nose, Charley went after the mouth, hooking along the side of the jaws with both hands, until teeth fell out and the jaw hung open, smashed, loose with the queer looseness of flesh that is no longer moored to solid bone. Charley started crying, the tears running down into his mouth, the sobs shaking him as he swung his fists. Even then Stryker didn't turn around. He just put his hands to his ears and looked steadfastly at Eighth Avenue.

When he started on Lueger's eye, Charley talked. "You bastard. Oh, you lousy goddamn bastard," came out with the sobs and the tears as he hit at the eye with his right hand, cutting it, smashing it, tearing it again and again, his hand coming away splattered with blood each time. "Oh, you dumb, mean, skirt-chasing sonofabitch, bastard." And he kept hitting with fury and deliberation at the shattered eye. . . .

A car came up Twelfth Street from the waterfront and slowed down at the corner. Stryker jumped on the running board. "Keep moving," he said, very tough, "if you know what's good for you."

He jumped off the running board and watched the car speed away.

Charley, still sobbing, pounded Lueger in the chest and belly. With each blow Lueger slammed against the iron fence with a noise like a carpet being beaten, until his coat ripped off the pike and he slid to the sidewalk.

Charley stood back, his fists swaying, the tears still coming, the sweat running down his face inside his collar, his clothes stained with blood.

"O.K.," he said, "O.K., you bastard."

He walked swiftly up under the L in the shadows, and Stryker hurried after him.

Much later, in the hospital, Preminger stood over the bed in which Lueger lay, unconscious, in splints and bandages.

"Yes," he said to the detective and the doctor. "That's our man. Lueger. A steward. The papers on him are correct."

"Who do you think done it?" the detective asked in a routine voice. "Did he have any enemies?"

"Not that I know of," Preminger said. "He was a very popular boy. Especially with the ladies."

The detective started out of the ward. "Well," he said, "he won't be a very popular boy when he gets out of here."

Preminger shook his head. "You must be very careful in a strange city," he said to the interne, and went back to the ship.

Welcome to the City

As he drew nearer to it, Enders looked up at his hotel through the black drizzle of the city that filled the streets with rain and soot and despair. A small red neon sign bloomed over the hotel entrance, spelling out CIRCUS HOTEL, REASONABLE, turning the drizzle falling profoundly around it into blood.

Enders sighed, shivered inside his raincoat, and walked slowly up the five steps to the entrance and went in. His nostrils curled, as they did each time he opened the door of the hotel, and his nose was hit by the ancient odor of ammonia and lysol and old linoleum and old beds and people who must depend on two bathrooms to the floor, and over the other odors the odor of age and sin, all at reasonable rates.

Wysocki was at the desk, in his gray suit with the markings of all the cafeteria soup in the city on it, and the pale face shaven down to a point where at any moment you half-expected to see the bone exposed, gleaming and green. Wysocki stood against the desk with the thirty-watt bulb shining down on his thinning hair and his navy-blue shirt and the solid orange tie, bright as hope in the dark hotel lobby, gravely reading the next morning's *Mirror,* his pale, hairy hands spread importantly, with delicate possessiveness, on the desk in front of him.

Josephine was sitting in one of the three lobby chairs, facing Wysocki. She wore a purple tailored suit with a ruffled waist, and open-toed red shoes, even though the streets outside were as damp and penetratingly cold as any marsh, and Enders could see the high red polish under her stockings, on her toenails. She sat there, not reading, not talking, her face carved out of powder and rouge under the blonde hair whose last surge of life had been strangled from it a dozen years before by peroxide and small-town hairdressers and curling irons that could have been used to primp the hair of General Sherman's granite horse.

"The English," Wysocki was saying, without looking up from his paper. "I wouldn't let them conduct a war for me for one million dollars in gilt-edged securities. Debaters and herring-fishermen," he said. "That's what they are."

"I thought Jews ate herring," Josephine said. Her voice scraped in the lobby, as though the Circus Hotel itself had suddenly broken into speech in its own voice, lysol and ammonia and rotting ancient wood finally put into sound.

"Jews eat herring," Wysocki said. "And the English eat herring."

Enders sighed again and walked up to the desk. In the chair near the stairway, he noticed, a girl was sitting, a pretty girl in a handsome green coat trimmed with lynx. He watched her obliquely as he talked to Wysocki, noticed that her legs were good and the expression cool, dignified, somehow hauntingly familiar.

"Hello, Wysocki," Enders said.

"Mr. Enders." Wysocki looked up pleasantly from the newspaper. "So you decided to come in out of the rain to your cozy little nest."

"Yes," said Enders, watching the girl.

"Did you know," Josephine asked, "that the English eat herring?"

"Yes," Enders said, digging into his mind for the face the girl reminded him of.

"That's what Wysocki said." Josephine shrugged. "I was living in happy ignorance."

Enders leaned over so that he could whisper into Wysocki's ear. "Who is she?" Enders asked.

Wysocki peered at the girl in the green coat, his eyes sly and guilty, as a thief might peer at a window at Tiffany's through which he intended to heave a brick later in the evening. "Zelinka," Wysocki whispered. "Her name's Bertha Zelinka. She checked in this afternoon. You could do worse, couldn't you?" He chuckled soundlessly, his bone-shaven face creasing without mirth, green and gleaming under the thirty-watt bulb.

"I've seen her someplace," Enders whispered, looking at the girl over his shoulder. She sat remote, cold, her legs crossed beautifully under the green coat, looking under heavy lids at the scarred and battered clock over Wysocki's head. "I know that face," Enders said. "But from where?"

"She looks like Greta Garbo," Wysocki said. "That's where you know her from."

Enders stared at the girl in the green coat. She did look like Greta Garbo, the long pale face, the long eyes, the wide, firm mouth, the whole thing a mirror of passion and pain and deep, Northern melancholy and bony, stubborn beauty. Suddenly Enders realized that he was a stranger in a strange city, a thousand miles from home, that it was raining out, that he had no girl, and that no one in this huge and wrangling seven-million town had ever said anything more tender to him than "Pass the mustard." And here, before him, solid as his hand, in a green coat with a lynx collar, sat a tall, melancholy girl who looked enough like Greta Garbo, pain and passion and beauty and understanding all mixed on the bony, pale face, to be her twin sister. His voice charged at his throat, leaping to say the first tender word in this rat-eaten, roach-claimed hotel lobby.

"Enders!" His name was spoken gaily, warmly. He

turned from looking at Bertha Zelinka, wrenching his soul. "Mr. Enders, I was waiting for your appearance." It was Bishop, the owner of the hotel, a little fat, gray-faced man with wet mustaches. He was rubbing his hands jovially now. "You were just the person I wanted to see tonight," he said.

"Thanks," said Enders.

"Wait!" Bishop's voice trilled. "Don't move an inch from the spot! I have a treat in store for you."

He darted back of the desk through the door into his office. Enders turned and looked at Bertha Zelinka, sitting there as calmly, as remotely, as Garbo herself.

"Observe!" Bishop darted out again from his office. "Look!" He held his hand high above his head. From it dangled a dead, wet chicken. "See what I've saved for you. I am willing to give you this chicken for sixty cents, Mr. Enders."

Enders looked politely at the chicken, hanging sadly in death from Bishop's proud hand.

"Thanks, Mr. Bishop," Enders said. "But I have no place to cook a chicken."

"Take it to your home." Bishop whirled the chicken lovingly, giving it a spruce and electric appearance of life, the wings spreading, the feathers ruffling. "Your mother would be delighted with this bird."

"My mother's in Davenport, Iowa," Enders said.

"You must have some relatives in the city." Bishop pushed it lovingly under his nose, spreading the limp wings for inspection. "They'll receive you with open arms with this chicken. This is a guaranteed Plymouth Rock chicken. Birds like this are exhibited in poultry shows from coast to coast. Sixty cents, Mr. Enders," Bishop said winningly. "Can you go wrong for sixty cents?"

Enders shook his head. "I have no relatives in the city," he said. "Thanks a lot, but I can't use it."

Bishop looked at him coldly. He shrugged. "I could've sold this chicken five times already," he said, "but I was saving it for you because you looked so pale. You gained my sympathy." He shrugged again, and holding the Plymouth Rock by the neck, he went into his office.

"Well," said Enders loudly, looking squarely at Bertha Zelinka. "I guess I'll turn in for the night."

"Want some company, Baby?" Josephine asked, in her voice the first note of hope she had allowed to sound there all evening.

"No, thank you," Enders said, embarrassedly, glad that Miss Zelinka wasn't looking at him at the moment.

"You certainly are a great ladies' man," Josephine said, her voice rasping through the lobby. "Don't you know you'll go crazy, you go so long without a woman? You been here two weeks, you haven't had a woman all that time. They face that problem in Sing Sing, the convicts climb on the walls."

Enders looked uneasily at Miss Zelinka. He didn't want a girl who looked like Greta Garbo to hear him mixed up in that kind of a conversation. "Good night," he said, and walked past Miss Zelinka, down the hallway to his own room, which was on the ground floor, at the bottom of an airwell, three dollars a week. He looked back regretfully. Miss Zelinka's legs were visible, jutting out, like a promise of poetry and flowers, past the grime and gloom of the hallway. Sadly he opened the door and went into his room, took off his hat and coat and fell on the bed. He could hear Josephine talking, as though the walls, the vermin, the old and wailing plumbing, the very rats hurrying on their gloomy errands between the floors, had at last found a voice.

"The papers are full of boys like him," Josephine was saying. "Turning the gas on and stuffing their heads into the oven. What a night! What a stinking whore of a night! They'll find plenty of bodies in the river tomorrow morning."

"Josephine," Wysocki's voice floated down the hallway. "You ought to learn to talk with more cheerfulness. You're ruining your business, Josephine. The wholesale

butchers from Tenth Avenue, the slaughterhouse workers, your whole regular clientele, they're all avoiding you.
Should I tell you why?"

"Tell me why," Josephine said.

"Because you're gloomy!" Wysocki said. "Because you
depress them with your talk. People like a woman to be
cheerful. You can't expect to succeed in your line if you
walk around like the last day of the world is beginning in
two and three-quarter hours, Bulova watch time."

"The butchers from Tenth Avenue!" Josephine
snarled. "Who wants them? I give them to you as a gift."

Enders lay on the bed, regretting that a proud and beautiful woman like Bertha Zelinka had to sit in one of the
three chairs of the lobby of the Circus Hotel on a rainy
night and listen to a conversation like that. He put on the
light and picked up the book he was reading.

> *I was neither at the hot gates*
> *Nor fought in the warm rain*
> *Nor knee deep in the salt marsh, heaving a cutlass,*
> *Bitten by flies, fought . . .*

"What a night!" Josephine's voice scraped down the
hallway. "The river will be stuffed with bodies in the
morning."

Enders put down T. S. Eliot. It was hard to read T. S.
Eliot in the Circus Hotel without a deep feeling of irony.
Enders got up and looked around the doorpost, down
the hall. The proud, poetic legs were still there, lean, muscular, beautifully shaped, aristocratic, stemming down
into slim ankles and narrow feet. Enders leaned dreamily
against the doorpost, regarding Miss Zelinka's legs. Music
played from a well-known orchestra in a night club lit by
orange lamps, where no dish cost less than a dollar seventy-five, even tomato juice, and he danced with Bertha
Zelinka, both of them dressed beautifully, shiningly, and
he made those deep, long eyes, charged with Northern
melancholy, crinkle with laughter, and later grow sober

and reflective as he talked swiftly of culture, of art, of poetry. " 'Nor fought in the warm rain,' in the phrase of T. S. Eliot, a favorite of mine, 'nor knee deep in the salt marsh . . .' "

He walked quickly down the hallway, looking neither to right nor left until he stopped at the desk. "Have there been any telephone calls for me today?" he asked Wysocki, carefully avoiding looking at Miss Zelinka.

"No," said Wysocki. "Not a thing."

Enders turned and stared full at Miss Zelinka, trying, with the deep intensity of his glance, to get her to look at him, smile at him . . .

"Heads like yours, my friend," Josephine said, "they find in ovens."

Miss Zelinka sat passionless, expressionless, heedless, looking at a point twenty-five feet over Wysocki's shoulder, patiently, but coolly, in the attitude of a woman who is expecting a Lincoln to drive up at any moment and a uniformed chauffeur to spring from it and lead her fastidiously to the heavy, upholstered door, rich with heavy hardware.

Enders walked slowly back to his room. He tried to read some more. "April is the cruellest month . . ." He thumbed through the book. "Here, said she, is your card, the drowned Phoenician Sailor . . ." Enders put the book down. He couldn't read tonight. He went to the door and looked out. The legs, silk and skin and firm muscle, were still there. Enders took a deep breath and walked back toward the desk.

"Look," said Josephine, "the shuttle's back."

"I forgot to ask." He looked straight at Wysocki. "Is there any mail for me?"

"No mail," said Wysocki.

"I'll tell you frankly, friend," Josephine said. "You should've stayed in Davenport, Iowa. That's my honest opinion. New York City will break you like a peanut shell."

"Nobody asked for your opinion," Wysocki said, noticing Enders peering uneasily at Miss Zelinka to see what impression Josephine's advice had made on her. "He's a nice boy, he's educated, he's going to go a long way. Leave him alone."

"I'm only giving him my honest opinion," Josephine said. "I've been in New York a dozen years. I see them begin and I see them wind up in the river."

"Will you, for Christ's sake, stop talking about the river?" Wysocki slammed his hand on the desk.

Gratefully, Enders noticed that Miss Zelinka was listening to the conversation, that her head tilted just a little, a shade went across her disdainful, beautiful eyes.

"I come from Fall River," Josephine said. "I should've stayed there. At least when you're dead in Fall River they bury you. Here they leave you walk around until your friends notice it. Why did I ever leave Fall River? I was attracted by the glamor of the Great White Way." She waved her red and white umbrella ironically, in salute to the city.

Enders noticed that a hint, a twitch of a smile, played at the corner of Miss Zelinka's mouth. He was glad that she'd heard Wysocki say he was educated, he was going to go a long way.

"If you'd like," he heard his voice boom out suddenly in the direction of Miss Zelinka, "if you'd like, if you're waiting for someone, you can wait in my room. It's not so noisy there."

"No, thank you," Miss Zelinka said, speaking curiously, her lips together, not showing her teeth. Her voice, behind the closed, beautiful lips, was deep and hoarse and moving, and Enders felt it grip at his throat like a cool, firm hand. He turned to Wysocki, determined now that he was not going back to his room.

"I was curious," he said. "Where did Bishop get that chicken he wants to sell me?"

Wysocki looked behind him carefully. "Don't buy those

chickens, Enders," he said in a low voice. "I advise you
as a good friend. Bishop picks them up on Tenth Avenue, alongside the railroad tracks."

"What're they doing there?" Enders asked.

"The trains bring them in from the farms, from the
country," Wysocki said. "The ones that died on the trip
for one reason or another, the trainmen throw them off
the cars and they're piled up alongside the tracks and
Bishop picks out the ones that look as though they died
most peaceful and he tries to sell them." Wysocki slid
back to the office door, listened guiltily for a moment
for Bishop, like a spy in the movies. "I advise you not to
buy them. They're not the most nourishing articles of
food in the world."

Enders smiled. "Bishop ought to be in Wall Street," he
said. "With talent like that."

Miss Zelinka laughed. Feeling twice as tall as he had
felt a moment before, Enders noticed that Miss Zelinka
was laughing, quietly, and without opening her mouth,
but true laughter. He laughed with her and their eyes met
in friendly, understanding amusement.

"May I buy you a cup of coffee?" hurled out of his
throat, at Miss Zelinka's head, like a hand grenade.

The light of thought, consideration, appeared in the
large gray eyes, while Enders waited. Then Miss Zelinka
smiled. "All right," she said. She stood up, five feet six
inches tall, graceful as a duchess.

"I'll be right back," Enders said, quickly. "Just have to
get my coat."

He fled lightly down the hall toward his room.

"That's what keeps me poor," Josephine said. "Girls
like that. What a night, what a dirty whore of a night!"

"I'm a dancer," Bertha Zelinka was saying two hours
later, her coat off, in Enders' room, as she drank the
whisky straight in one of the two water tumblers the room
boasted. "Specialty dancing." She put the whisky down,

suddenly sank beautifully to the floor in a split. "I'm as supple as a cat."

"I see," Enders said, his eyes furious with admiration for Miss Zelinka, full-breasted, flat-bellied, steel-thighed, supple as a cat, spread magnificently on the dirty carpet. It was more pleasant to look at her body, now that he had seen her eating, mouth opened to reveal the poor, poverty-stricken, ruined teeth jagged and sorrowful in her mouth. "That looks very hard to do."

"My name's been in lights," Miss Zelinka said, from the floor. "Please pass the whisky. From one end of the country to another. I've stopped show after show. I've got an uncanny sense of timing." She stood up, after taking another draught of her whisky, closing her eyes with a kind of harsh rapture as the Four Roses went down past the miserable teeth, down inside the powerful, long white throat. "I'm an actress, too, you know, Mr. Enders."

"I'm an actor," Enders said shyly, feeling the whisky beat in his blood, keeping his eyes fiercely and wonderingly on Miss Zelinka. "That's why I'm in New York. I'm an actor."

"You ought to be a good actor," Miss Zelinka said. "You got the face for it. It's refined." She poured herself another drink, watching the amber liquor pour into her glass with a brooding, intense expression in her face. "I had my name in lights from coast to coast. Don't you believe it?"

"I believe it," Enders said sincerely, noting that half the bottle was already gone.

"That's why I'm here now," she said. She walked beautifully around the small, flaky-walled room, her hands running sorrowfully over the warped bureau, the painted bedstead. "That's why I'm here now." Her voice was faraway and echoing, hoarse with whisky and regret. "I'm very much in demand, you know. I've stopped shows for ten minutes at a time. They wouldn't let me get off the stage. Musicals that cost one hundred and fifty thousand to ring the curtain up. That's why I'm here now," she said mysteriously, and drained her glass. She threw herself on the bed next to Enders, stared moodily through almost closed eyes, at the stained and beaten ceiling. "The Shuberts're putting on a musical. They want me for it. Rehearsals are on Fifty-second Street, so I thought I'd move close by for the time being." She sat up, silently reached for the bottle, poured with the fixed expression, brooding and infatuate, which she reserved for the distillers' product. Enders, too full for words, sitting on the same bed with a woman who looked like Greta Garbo, who had stopped musical shows with specialty dancing from coast to coast, who got drunk with the assured yet ferocious grace of a young society matron, watched her every move, with hope, admiration, growing passion.

"You might ask," Miss Zelinka said, "what is a person like myself doing in a rat-hole like this." She waited, but Enders merely gulped silently at his whisky. She chuckled and patted his hand. "You're a nice boy. Iowa, you said? You come from Iowa?"

"Iowa."

"Corn," Miss Zelinka said. "That's what they grow in Iowa." She nodded, having placed Iowa and Enders firmly in her mind. "I passed through Iowa on my way to Hollywood." Half the whisky in her glass disappeared.

"Have you acted in pictures?" Enders asked, impressed, sitting on the same bed with a woman who had been in Hollywood.

Miss Zelinka laughed moodily. "Hollywood!" She finished her drink. "Don't look for my footprints in front of Grauman's Chinese." She reached fluently for the bottle.

"It seems to me," Enders said seriously, breathing deeply because Miss Zelinka was leaning across him for the moment. "It seems to me you'd do very well. You're beautiful and you've got a wonderful voice."

Miss Zelinka laughed again. "Look at me," she said.

Enders looked at her.

"Do I remind you of anybody?" Miss Zelinka asked.

Enders nodded.

Miss Zelinka drank moodily. "I look like Greta Garbo," she said. "Nobody could deny that. I'm not being vain when I tell you when I photograph you couldn't tell me apart from the Swede." She sipped her whisky, ran it lovingly around in her mouth, swallowed slowly. "A woman who looks like Greta Garbo in Hollywood is like the fifth leg on a race horse. Do you understand what I mean?"

Enders nodded sympathetically.

"It's my private curse," Miss Zelinka said, tears looming in her eyes like mist over the ocean. She jumped up, shaking her head, walked lightly and dramatically around the room. "I have no complaints," she said. "I've done very well. I live in a two-room suite on the twentieth floor of a hotel on Seventy-fifth Street. Overlooking the park. All my trunks and bags are up there. I just took a few things with me, until the rehearsals are over. Seventy-fifth Street, on the East Side, is too far away; when you're rehearsing a musical comedy, you've got to be on tap twenty-four hours a day for the Shuberts. A very luxurious two-room suite in the Hotel Chalmers. It's very exclusive, but it's too far from Fifty-second Street." She poured some more whisky for herself, and Enders noticed that the bottle was almost empty. "Oh, yes," she said, crooning to the glass in her hand, "I've done very well. I've danced all over the country. In the most exclusive nightspots, I was the featured entertainment. I'm very greatly in demand." She sat down, close to him, her body moving gently and rhythmically as she spoke. "Seattle, Chicago, Los Angeles, Detroit." She gulped her whisky and her eyes clouded with a final, deep, vague mist and her voice suddenly got very throaty and hoarse. "Miami, Florida." She sat absolutely still and the cloud dissolved into tears and the tears coursed slowly down her face.

"What's the matter?" Enders asked anxiously. "Did I do something?"

Miss Zelinka threw the empty tumbler against the opposite wall. It broke heavily and sullenly, scattered over the carpet. She threw herself back on the bed, wept. "Miami, Florida," she sobbed. "Miami, Florida . . ."

Enders patted her shoulder consolingly.

"I danced in The Golden Horn in Miami, Florida," she cried. "It was a Turkish night club. Very exclusive."

"Why're you crying, darling?" Enders asked, feeling sorry for her, but elated, too, because he had said "darling."

"Every time I think of Miami, Florida," Miss Zelinka said, "I cry."

"Can I do anything to help?" Enders held her hand softly.

"It was January, 1936." Miss Zelinka's voice throbbed with old, hopeless, broken tragedy, forlorn as the story of a siege of a lost and ruined village. "I was dressed in Turkish garments: a brassiere, and veils around my legs and nothing around the middle. At the end of the dance I had to do a back-bend. I leaned back and touched the floor with my hands, with my hair falling down to the floor. There was a bald man. There was a convention of the Metal-Trades Union in Miami, Florida. He had on a badge. The whole night club was full of them." The tears and the anguish pulled at her face. "I'll remember that bald son of a bitch until the day I die. There was no music at that part of the dance. Drums and tambourines. He leaned over and put an olive in my navel and sprinkled it with salt." Miss Zelinka rolled suddenly over on her face and, clutching the bedspread, her shoulders heaving, burrowed into the grayish cotton. "It was a cartoon. He saw it in a cartoon in a magazine. It's funny in a magazine, but wait until it happens to you! The humiliation," she wept. "Every time I think of the humiliation I want to die. Miami, Florida."

Enders watched the bedspread stain with tears, mascara and rouge. With genuine sympathy, he put his arm around her. "I want to be treated with respect," Miss Zelinka wailed. "I was brought up in a good family, why shouldn't I be treated with respect? That fat, bald man, with the badge from the Metal-Trades Union Convention. He leaned over and put the olive in my navel like an egg in an egg cup and sprinkled salt like he was starting breakfast and everybody laughed and laughed, including the orchestra. . . ." Her voice went wailing up the air well, lost, despairing, full of an ancient and irreparable sorrow.

She sat up and threw her arms around Enders, digging her grief-torn head into his shoulder, clutching him with strong hands, both of them rocking back and forth like Jews praying, on the enameled bed that squeaked and wailed in the little room.

"Hold me tight," she wept, "hold me tight. I haven't got a two-room suite on East Seventy-fifth Street. I got no trunks in the Hotel Chalmers, hold me tight." Her hands dug into him and her tears and rouge and mascara stained his coat. "The Shuberts aren't giving me a job. Why do I lie, why do I always lie?" She lifted her head, kissed his throat fiercely. He shook at the soft, violent pressure, at the wetness of her lips and the tragic and exhilarating trickle of her tears under his chin, knowing that he was going to have this woman, this Bertha Zelinka. Lonely, far from home, on a rainy night, the city was pulling him in, making a place in its wild and ludicrous life for him. As he kissed her, this woman who looked like Greta Garbo, the century's dream of passion and tragedy and beauty, this woman whom he had met in a rat-tenanted lobby off Columbus Circle, among whores thinking of death and a Pole in an orange tie checking in each night's transients, age and sin, at reasonable rates, Enders felt suddenly at home, accounted for. The city had produced for him a great beauty, supple as a cat, full of lies and whisky and ancient, shadowy victories, a woman with magnificent, proud legs and deep, stormy eyes who wept bitterly behind the frail, warped door because once, in 1936, a bald man from a Metal-Trades Union had put an olive in her navel. Enders held Bertha Zelinka's head in his two hands, looked intently at the bony, drunken, beautiful, tear-stained face. Bertha Zelinka peered longingly and sadly at him through half-closed classic lids, her mouth hanging softly open in passion and promise, her poor jagged teeth showing behind the long, heartbreaking lips. He kissed her, feeling deep within him, that in its own way, on this rainy night, the city had put out its hand in greeting, had called, in its own voice, wry and ironic, "Welcome, Citizen."

Gratefully, near tears, hating himself, his hands shaking exultantly, Enders bent to his knees and took the scraped, year-worn shoes, swollen with the streets' rain, from the long and handsome feet of Bertha Zelinka.

Weep in Years to Come

They came out of the movie house and started slowly eastward in the direction of Fifth Avenue. "Hitler!" a newsboy called. "Hitler!"

"That Fletcher," Dora said, "the one that played her father. Remember him?"

"Uh huh," Paul said, holding her hand as they walked slowly up the dark street.

"He's got stones in his kidney."

"That's the way he acts," Paul said. "Now I know how to describe the way that man acts—he acts like a man who has stones in his kidney."

Dora laughed. "I X-rayed him last winter. He's one of Dr. Thayer's best patients. He's always got something wrong with him. He's going to try to pass the stones out of his kidney this summer."

"Good luck, Fletcher, old man," Paul said.

"I used to massage his shoulder. He had neuritis. He makes fifteen hundred dollars a week."

"No wonder he has neuritis."

"He asked me to come to his house for dinner." Dora pulled her hand out of Paul's and slipped it up to his elbow and held on, hard. "He likes me."

"I bet he does."

67

"What about you?"

"What about me what?" Paul asked.

"Do you like me?"

They stopped at Rockefeller Plaza and leaned over the marble wall and looked down at the fountain and the statue and the people sitting out at the tables, drinking, and the waiters standing around, listening to the sound of the fountain.

"I can't stand you," Paul said. He kissed her hair.

"That's what I thought," Dora said. They both laughed.

They looked down at the Plaza, at the thin trees with the light-green leaves rustling in the wind that came down between the buildings. There were pansies, yellow and tight, along the borders of the small pools with the bronze sea statues, and hydrangeas, and little full trees, all shaking in the wind and the diffuse, clear light of the flood lamps above. Couples strolled slowly down from Fifth Avenue, talking amiably in low, calm, week-end voices, appreciating the Rockefeller frivolity and extravagance which had carved a place for hydrangeas and water and saplings and spring and sea-gods riding bronze dolphins out of these austere buildings, out of the bleak side of Business.

Paul and Dora walked up the promenade, looking in the windows. They stopped at a window filled with men's sports clothes—gabardine slacks and bright-colored shirts with short sleeves and brilliant handkerchiefs to tie around the throat.

"I have visions," Paul said, "of sitting in my garden, with two Great Danes, dressed like that, like a Hollywood actor in the country."

"Have you got a garden?" Dora asked.

"No."

"Those're nice pants," Dora said.

They went on to the next window. "On the other hand," Paul said, "there are days when I want to look like that. A derby hat and a stiff blue shirt with a pleated bosom and a little starched white collar and a five-dollar neat little necktie and a Burberry overcoat. Leave the office at five o'clock every day to go to a cocktail party."

"You go to a cocktail party almost every afternoon anyway," Dora said. "Without a derby hat."

"A different kind of cocktail party," Paul said. He started her across Fifth Avenue. "The kind attended by men with starched blue pleated bosoms. Some day."

"Oh, Lord," Dora said as they ran to escape a bus, "look at those dresses."

They stood in front of Saks.

"Fifth Avenue," Paul said. "Street of dreams."

"It's nice to know things like that exist," Dora murmured, looking into the stage-lit window at the yellow dress and the sign that said "Tropical Nights in Manhattan" and the little carved-stone fish that for some reason was in the same window. "Even if you can't have them."

"Uptown?" Paul asked. "Or to my house?"

"I feel like walking." Dora looked up at Paul and grinned. "For the moment." She squeezed his arm. "Only for the moment. Uptown."

They started uptown.

"I love those models," Paul said. "Each and every one of them. They're superior, yet warm; inviting, yet polite. Their breasts are always tipped at the correct angle for the season."

"Sure," Dora said, "papier-mâché. It's easy with papier-mâché. Look. Aluminum suitcases. Travel by air."

"They look like my mother's kitchen pots."

"Wouldn't you like to own a few of them?"

"Yes." Paul peered at them. "Fly away. Buy luggage and depart. Leave for the ends of the earth."

"They got a little case just for books. A whole separate little traveling bookcase."

"That's just what I need," Paul said, "for my trips on the Fifth Avenue bus every morning."

They passed St. Patrick's, dark and huge, with the moon sailing over it.

"Do you think God walks up Fifth Avenue?" Paul asked.

"Sure," said Dora. "Why not?"

"We are princes of the earth," Paul said. "All over the world men slave to bring riches to these few blocks for us to look at and say 'Yes, very nice' or 'Take it away, it stinks.' I feel very important when I walk up Fifth Avenue."

They stopped at the window of the Hamburg-American Line. Little dolls in native costumes danced endlessly around a pole while other dolls in native costume looked on. All the dolls had wide smiles on their faces. "Harvest Festival in Buckeburg, Germany," a small sign said.

A private policeman turned the corner and stood and watched them. They moved to the next window.

"'A suggestion to passengers to promote carefree travel,'" Paul read off a booklet. "Also, Hapag-Lloyd announces a twenty-per-cent reduction for all educators on sabbatical leave. They are 'Masters in the Art of Travel,' they say."

"I used to want to go to see Germany," Dora said. "I know a lot of Germans and they're nice."

"I'll be there soon," Paul said as they passed the private policeman.

"You're going to visit it?"

"Uh huh. At the expense of the government. In a well-tailored khaki uniform. I'm going to see glamorous Europe, seat of culture, at last. From a bombing plane. To our left we have the Stork Club, seat of culture for East Fifty-third Street. Look at the pretty girls. A lot of them have breasts at the correct angle, too. See how nature mimics art. New York is a wonderful city."

Dora didn't say anything. She hung onto him tightly as they went down the street. They turned at the corner and walked down Madison Avenue. After a while they stopped at a shop that had phonographs and radios in the window. "That's what I want." Paul pointed at a machine. "A Capehart. It plays two symphonies at a time.

You just lie on your back and out come Brahms and Beethoven and Prokofieff. That's the way life should be. Lie
on your back and be surrounded by great music, automatically."

Dora looked at the phonograph, all mahogany and
doors and machinery. "Do you really think there's going
to be a war?" she said.

"Sure. They're warming up the pitchers now. They're
waiting to see if the other side has right-handed or left-
handed batters before they nominate their starting pitchers."

They continued walking downtown.

"But it's in Europe," Dora said. "Do you think we'll
get into it?"

"Sure. Read the papers." He glanced at the window
they were passing. "Look at those nice tables. Informal
luncheons on your terrace. Metal and glass for outdoor
feeding. That would be nice, eating out on a terrace off
those wonderful colored plates, rich food with green sal-
ads. With a view of mountains and a lake, and inside, the
phonograph."

"That sounds good," Dora said quietly.

"I could get an extra speaker," Paul said, "and wire it
out to the terrace, so we could listen as we ate. I like Mozart with dinner." He laughed and drew her to a book-
store window.

"I always get sad," Dora said, "when I look in a book-
shop window and see all the books I'm never going to
have time to read."

Paul kissed her. "What did you think the first time you
saw me?" he asked.

"What did *you* think?"

"I thought, 'I must get that girl!' "

Dora laughed, close to him.

"What did you think?" Paul asked.

"I thought"—she giggled—"I thought, 'I must get that
man!' "

"Isn't New York marvelous?" Paul said. "Where did you say you come from?"

"Seattle," Dora said. "Seattle, Washington."

"Here we are on Madison Avenue, holding hands, shopping for the future. . . ."

"Even if there was a war," Dora said after a while, "why would you have to get mixed up in it? Why would the United States have to get mixed up in it?"

"They got into the last one, didn't they?" Paul said. "They'll get into this one."

"They were gypped the last time," Dora said. "The guys who were killed were gypped."

"That's right," said Paul. "They were killed for six-percent interest on bonds, for oil wells, for spheres of influence. I wish I had a sphere of influence."

"Still," said Dora, "you'd enlist this time?"

"Yop. The first day. I'd walk right up to the recruiting office and say, 'Paul Triplett, twenty-six years old, hard as nails, good eyes, good teeth, good feet; give me a gun. Put me in a plane, so I can do a lot of damage."

They walked a whole block in silence.

"Don't you think you'd be gypped this time, too?" Dora said. "Don't you think they'd have you fighting for bonds and oil wells all over again?"

"Uh huh."

"And even so, you'd sign up?"

"The first day."

Dora pulled her hand away from him. "Do you *like* the idea of killing people?"

"I hate the idea," Paul said slowly. "I don't want to hurt anybody. I think the idea of war is ridiculous. I want to live in a world in which everybody sits on a terrace and eats off a metal-and-glass table off colored plates and the phonograph inside turns Mozart over automatically and the music is piped out to an extra loud-speaker on the terrace. Only Hitler isn't interested in that kind of world. He's interested in another kind of world. I couldn't stand to live in his kind of world, German or homemade."

"You wouldn't kill Hitler," Dora said. "You'd just kill young boys like yourself."

"That's right."

"Do you like that?"

"I'm really not interested in killing Hitler, either," Paul said. "I want to kill the idea he represents for so many people. In years to come I'll cry over the young boys I've killed and maybe if they kill me, they'll cry over me."

"They're probably just like you." They were walking fast now.

"Sure," Paul said. "I'm sure they'd love to go to bed with you tonight. I bet they'd love to walk along the fountains with the bronze statues in Rockefeller Plaza, holding hands with you on a spring Saturday evening and looking at the sports clothes in the windows. I bet a lot of them like Mozart, too, but still I'll kill them. Gladly."

"Gladly?"

"Yes, gladly." Paul wiped his eyes with his hands, suddenly tired. "Gladly today. I'll weep for them in years to come. Today they're guns aimed at me and the world I want. Their bodies protect an idea I have to kill to live. Hey!" He stretched out his hands and caught hers. "What's the sense talking about things like this tonight?"

"But it's all a big fraud," Dora cried. "You're being used and you know it."

"That's right," Paul said. "It's all a big fraud, the whole business. Even so, I got to fight. I'll be gypped, but by a little bit I'll do something for my side, for Mozart on a terrace at dinner. What the hell, it's not even heroism. I'll be dragged in, whatever I say."

"That's too bad," Dora said softly, walking by herself. "It's too bad."

"Sure," Paul said. "Some day maybe it'll be better. Maybe some day the world'll be run for people who like Mozart. Not today."

They stopped. They were in front of a little art store. There was a reproduction of the Renoir painting of a boating party on the river. There was the woman kissing the Pekinese, and the man in his underwear with a straw hat and his red beard, solid as earth, and the wit with his cocked derby hat whispering to the woman with her hands to her ears, and there was the great still life in the foreground, of wine and bottles and glasses and grapes and food.

"I saw it in Washington," Paul said. "They had it in Washington. You can't tell why it's a great picture from the print. There's an air of pink immortality hanging over it. They got it in New York now and I go look at it three times a week. It's settled, happy, solid. It's a picture of a summertime that vanished a long time ago." Paul kissed her hand. "It's getting late, darling, the hours're dwindling. Let's go home."

They got into a cab and went downtown to his apartment.

Search Through the Streets
of the City

When he finally saw her, he nearly failed to recognize her. He walked behind her for a half block, vaguely noticing that the woman in front of him had long legs and was wearing a loose, college-girl polo coat and a plain brown felt hat.

Suddenly something about the way she walked made him remember—the almost affected rigidity of her back and straightness of throat and head, with all the movement of walking, flowing up to the hips and stopping there, like Negro women in the South and Mexican and Spanish women carrying baskets on their heads.

For a moment, silently, he watched her walk down Twelfth Street, on the sunny side of the street, in front of the little tired gardens behind which lay the quiet, pleasantly run-down old houses. Then he walked up to her and touched her arm.

"Low heels," he said. "I never thought I'd live to see the day."

She looked around in surprise, then smiled widely, took his arm. "Hello, Paul," she said. "I've gone in for health."

"Whenever I think of you," he said, "I think of the highest heels in New York City."

"The old days," Harriet said. They walked slowly down the sunny street, arm in arm, toward Sixth Avenue. "I was a frivolous creature."

"You still walk the same way. As though you ought to have a basket of laundry on your head."

"I practiced walking like that for six months. You'd be surprised how much attention I get walking into a room that way."

"I wouldn't be surprised," Paul said, looking at her. She had black hair and pale, clear skin and a long, full body, and her eyes were deep gray and always brilliant, even after she'd been drinking for three days in a row.

Harriet closed her coat quickly and walked a little faster. "I'm going to Wanamaker's," she said. "There're a couple of things I have to buy. Where are you going?"

"Wanamaker's," Paul said. "I've been dying to go to Wanamaker's for three years."

They walked slowly, in silence, Harriet's arm in his.

"Casual," Paul said. "I bet to the naked eye we look casual as hell. How do you feel?"

Harriet took her arm away. "Casual."

"O.K. Then that's how I feel, too." Paul whistled coldly to himself. He stopped and looked critically at her and she stopped, too, and turned toward him, a slight puzzled smile on her face. "What makes you dress that way?" he asked. "You look like Monday morning in Northampton."

"I just threw on whatever was nearest," Harriet said. "I'm just going to be out about an hour."

"You used to look like a nice big box of candy in your clothes." Paul took her arm again and they started off. "Viennese bonbons. Every indentation carefully exploited in silk and satin. Even if you were just going down to the corner for a pint of gin, you'd look like something that ought to be eaten for dessert. This is no improvement."

"A girl has different periods in clothes. Like Picasso," Harriet said. "And if I'd known I was going to meet you, I'd've dressed differently."

Paul patted her arm. "That's better."

Paul eyed her obliquely as they walked: the familiar, long face, the well-known wide mouth with always a little too much lipstick on it, the little teeth that made her face, when she smiled, look suddenly like a little girl's in Sunday school.

"You're getting skinny, Paul," Harriet said.

Paul nodded. "I'm as lean as a herring. I've been leading a fevered and ascetic life. What sort of life have you been leading?"

"I got married." Harriet paused a moment. "Did you hear I got married?"

"I heard," Paul said. "The last time we crossed Sixth Avenue together the L was still up. I feel a nostalgic twinge for the Sixth Avenue L." They hurried as the light changed. "On the night of January ninth, 1940," Paul said, holding her elbow, "you were not home."

"Possible," Harriet said. "I'm a big girl now; I go out at night."

"I happened to pass your house, and I noticed that the light wasn't on." They turned down toward Ninth Street. "I remembered how hot you kept that apartment—like the dahlia greenhouse in the Botanical Gardens."

"I have thin blood," Harriet said gravely. "Long years of in-breeding in Massachusetts."

"The nicest thing about you," Paul said, "was you never went to sleep."

"Every lady to her own virtue," Harriet said. "Some women're beautiful, some're smart—me—I never went to sleep. The secret of my great popularity. . . ."

Paul grinned. "Shut up."

Harriet smiled back at him and they chuckled together. "You know what I mean," he said. "Any time I called you up, two, three in the morning, you'd come right over, lively and bright-eyed, all the rouge and mascara in the right places. . . ."

"In my youth," said Harriet, "I had great powers of resistance."

"In the morning we'd eat breakfast to Beethoven. The

Masterwork Hour. WNYC. Beethoven, by special permission of His Honor, the Mayor, from nine to ten." Paul closed his eyes for a moment. "The Little Flower, Mayor for Lovers."

Paul opened his eyes and looked at the half-strange, half-familiar woman walking lightly at his side. He remembered lying close to her, dreamily watching the few lights of the towers of the night-time city, framed by the big window of his bedroom against the black sky, and one night when she moved sleepily against him and rubbed the back of his neck where the hair was sticking up in sharp little bristles because he had had his hair cut that afternoon. Harriet had rubbed them the wrong way, smiling, dreamily, without opening her eyes. "What a delicious thing a man is . . ." she'd murmured. And she'd sighed, then chuckled a little and fallen asleep, her hand still on the shaven back of his neck.

Paul smiled, remembering.

"You still laughing at my clothes?" Harriet asked.

"I remembered something I heard someplace . . ." Paul said. " 'What a delicious thing a man is . . .' "

Harriet looked at him coldly. "Who said that?"

Paul squinted suspiciously at her. "Oswald Spengler."

"Uhuh," Harriet said soberly. "It's a famous quotation."

"It's a well-turned phrase," said Paul.

"That's what I think, too." Harriet nodded agreeably and walked a little faster.

They passed the little run-down bar where they'd sat afternoons all winter drinking martinis and talking and talking, and laughing so loud the people at the other tables would turn and smile. Paul waited for Harriet to say something about the bar, but she didn't even seem to notice it. "There's Eddie's Bar," Paul said.

"Uhuh." Harriet nodded briskly.

"He's going to start making his martinis with sherry when all the French vermouth runs out," Paul said.

"It sounds horrible." Harriet made a face.

"Is that all you have to say?" Paul said loudly, remembering all the times he'd looked in to see if she was there.

"What do you want me to say?" Harriet looked honestly puzzled, but Paul had never known when she was lying to him or telling the truth, anyway, and he hadn't improved in the two years, he discovered.

"I don't want you to say anything. I'll take you in and buy you a drink."

"No, thanks. I've really got to get to Wanamaker's and back home in a hurry. Give me a raincheck."

"Yeah," Paul said sourly.

They turned up Ninth Street toward Fifth Avenue.

"I knew I'd meet you someplace, finally," Paul said. "I was curious to see what would happen."

Harriet didn't say anything. She was looking absently at the buildings across the street.

"Don't you ever talk any more?" Paul asked.

"What *did* happen?"

"Every once in a while," he started, "I meet some girl I used to know . . ."

"I bet the country's full of them," Harriet said.

"The country's full of everybody's ex-girls."

Harriet nodded. "I never thought of it that way, but you're right."

"Most of the time I think, isn't she a nice, decent person? Isn't it wonderful I'm no longer attached to her? The first girl I ever had," Paul said, "is a policewoman now. She subdued a gangster single-handed in Coney Island last summer. Her mother won't let her go out of the house in her uniform. She's ashamed for the neighbors."

"Naturally," Harriet said.

"Another girl I used to know changed her name and dances in the Russian Ballet. I went to see her dance the other night. She has legs like a Fordham tackle. I used to think she was beautiful. I used to think you were beautiful, too."

"We were a handsome couple," Harriet said. "Except you always needed a shave. That electric razor . . ."

"I've given it up."

They were passing his old house now and he looked at the doorway and remembered all the times he and Harriet had gone in and come out, the rainy days and the early snowy mornings with the milkman's horse silent on the white street behind them. They stopped and looked at the old red house with the shabby shutters and the window on the fourth floor they had both looked out of time and time again to see what the weather was and Paul remembered the first time, on a winter's night, when he and Harriet had gone through that door together.

"I was so damn polite," Paul said softly.

Harriet smiled, knowing what he was talking about. "You kept dropping the key and saying, 'Lord, Lord,' under your breath while you were looking for it."

"I was nervous. I wanted to make sure you knew exactly how matters stood—no illusions. Good friends, everybody understanding everybody else, another girl coming in from Detroit in six weeks, no claims on me, no claims on you . . ." Paul looked at the window on the fourth floor and smiled. "What a fool!"

"It's a nice, quiet street," Harriet said, looking up at the window on the fourth floor, too. She shook her head, took Paul's arm again. "I've got to get to Wanamaker's."

They started off.

"What're you buying at Wanamaker's?" Paul asked.

Harriet hesitated for a moment. "Nothing much. I'm looking at some baby clothes. I'm going to have a baby." They crowded over to one side to let a little woman with four dachshunds pass them in a busy tangle. "Isn't it funny—me with a baby?" Harriet smiled. "I lie around all day and try to imagine what it's going to be like. In between, I sleep and drink beer to nourish us. I've never had such a good time in all my life."

"Well," said Paul, "at least it'll keep your husband out of the army."

"Maybe. He's a raging patriot."

"Good. When he's at Fort Dix I'll meet you in Washington Square Park when you take the baby out for an airing in its perambulator. I'll put on a policeman's uniform to make it proper. I'm not such a raging patriot."

"They'll get you anyway, won't they?"

"Sure. I'll send you my picture in a lieutenant's suit. From Bulgaria. I have a premonition I'm going to be called on to defend a strategic point in Bulgaria."

"How do you feel about it?" For the first time Harriet looked squarely and searchingly at him.

Paul shrugged. "It's going to happen. It's all damned silly, but it isn't as silly now as it was ten years ago."

Suddenly Harriet laughed.

"What's so funny?" Paul demanded.

"My asking you how you felt about something. I never used to have a chance . . . You'd let me know how you felt about everything. Roosevelt, James Joyce, Jesus Christ, Gypsy Rose Lee, Matisse, Yogi, liquor, sex, architecture . . ."

"I was full of opinions in those days." Paul smiled a little regretfully. "Lust and conversation. The firm foundations of civilized relations between the sexes."

He turned and looked back at the window on the fourth floor. "That was a nice apartment," he said softly. "Lust and conversation . . ."

"Come on, Paul," Harriet said. "Wanamaker's isn't going to stay open all night."

Paul turned up his collar because the wind was getting stronger as they neared Fifth Avenue. "You were the only girl I ever knew I could sleep in the same bed with."

"That's a hell of a thing to say to a girl." Harriet laughed. "Is that your notion of a compliment?"

Paul shrugged. "It's an irrelevant fact. Or a relevant fact. Is it polite to talk to a married lady this way?"

"No."

Paul walked along with her. "What do you think of when you look at me?" he asked.

"Nothing much," Harriet said carefully.

"What're you lying about?"

"Nothing much," Harriet said flatly.

"Don't you even think, 'What in the name of God did I ever see in him?' "

"No." Harriet put her hands deep in her pockets and walked quickly along the railings.

"Should I tell you what I think of when I look at you?"

"No."

"I've been looking for you for two years," Paul said.

"My name's been in the telephone book." Harriet hurried even more, wrapping her coat tightly around her.

"I didn't realize I was looking for you until I saw you."

"Please, Paul . . ."

"I would walk along the street and I'd pass a bar we'd been in together and I'd go in and sit there, even though I didn't want a drink, not knowing why I was sitting there. Now I know. I was waiting for you to come in. I didn't pass your house by accident."

"Look, Paul," Harriet pleaded. "It was a long time ago and it was fine and it ended. . . ."

"I was wrong," Paul said. "Do you like hearing that? I was wrong. You know, I never did get married, after all."

"I know," Harriet said. "Please shut up."

"I walk along Fifth Avenue and every time I pass St. Patrick's I half look up to see if you're passing, because I met you that day right after you'd had a tooth pulled, and it was cold; you were walking along with the tears streaming from your eyes and your eyes red and that was the only time I ever met you by accident anyplace. . . ."

Harriet smiled. "That certainly sounds like a beautiful memory."

"Two years . . ." Paul said. "I've gone out with a lot of girls in the last two years." He shrugged. "They've bored me and I've bored them. I keep looking at every woman who passes to see if it's you. All the girls I go out with bawl the hell out of me for it. I've been walking around, following girls with dark hair to see if it'll turn out to be you, and girls with a fur jacket like that old one you had and girls that walk in that silly, beautiful way you walk. . . . I've been searching the streets of the city for you for two years and this is the first time I've admitted it even to myself. That little Spanish joint we went the first time. Every time I pass it I remember everything—how many drinks we had and what the band played and what we said and the fat Cuban who kept winking at you from the bar and the very delicate way we landed up in my apartment. . . ."

They were both walking swiftly now, Harriet holding her hands stiffly down at her sides.

"There is a particular wonderful way you are joined together . . ."

"Paul, stop it." Harriet's voice was flat but loud.

"Two years. In two years the edge should be dulled off things like that. Instead . . ." How can you make a mistake as big as that? Paul thought, how can you deliberately be as wrong as that? And no remedy. So long as you live, no remedy. He looked harshly at Harriet. Her face was set, as though she weren't listening to him and only intent on getting across the street as quickly as possible. "How about you?" he asked. "Don't you remember . . . ?"

"I don't remember anything," she said. And then, suddenly, the tears sprang up in her eyes and streamed down the tight, distorted cheeks. "I don't remember a goddamn thing!" she wept. "I'm not going to Wanamaker's. I'm going home! Good-bye!" She ran over to a cab that was parked at the corner and opened the door and sprang in. The cab spurted past Paul and he had a glimpse of Harriet sitting stiffly upright, the tears bitter and unheeded in her eyes.

He watched the cab go down Fifth Avenue until it turned. Then he turned the other way and started walking, thinking, I must move away from this neighborhood. I've lived here long enough.

Night, Birth and Opinion

"Tents!" Lubbock was saying, gloomily swishing his beer around in his glass, his voice echoing hoarsely in the empty shadows of Cody's bar, dark and almost deserted now, deep in the heel of the winter night. "Yuh join the army, yuh sit in a tent and freeze yer tail all winter. I'm a civilized man, I'm used to living in steam-heated apartments."

He looked around him challengingly. He was a big man, with huge longshoreman's hands and a long neat scar down one side of his face. The other two men at the bar looked carefully into their beer.

"National defense," the bartender said. The bartender was a pale little man in a vest and apron, with pale, hairy arms and a long, nervous nose. "Everybody has to make certain sacrifices."

"The trouble with this country," Lubbock said loudly, "is there are too goddamn many patriots walking the streets."

"Don't say anything against patriotism," said the man nearest Lubbock. "Not in my presence."

Lubbock looked consideringly at him. "What's *your* name?" he asked.

"Dominic di Calco," the man said clearly, showing that he was not to be bullied. "I don't see anything wrong with being a patriot."

84

"He doesn't see anything wrong with being a patriot," Lubbock said. "An Italian patriot."

"They need you," said Sweeney, the man on the other side of Lubbock. "They need you bad—in Greece."

The others laughed. Sweeney looked around him proudly, his little creased red face beery and complacent.

"I'm an American citizen," Di Calco shouted. "After you boys get through laughing."

"You know what I'd like to see?" Sweeney waved his arms, laughing. "I'd like to see the Italian army try to invade Red Hook."

"I'm not in favor of Mussolini," Di Calco shouted. "But keep yer trap shut about the Italian army!"

"Three Irishmen," Sweeney said. "It would take three Irishmen about a half hour. The Italians're wonderful when they fight other Italians."

"Would you like to step outside, whatever yer name is?" Di Calco asked quietly.

"Boys!" the bartender spread his hands pacifically. "Remember, we're in America."

"Remember," Di Calco said, "I offered you satisfaction, whatever yer name is."

"My name is Sweeney!" Sweeney shouted. "I got two cousins in the Royal Air Force!"

"That's a hot one," Lubbock said. "A man by the name of Sweeney with two cousins in the English army. Yuh can just about imagine"—Lubbock spoke reasonably to the bartender—"what type of Irishman yuh could get to fight in the English army."

"What do you want?" the bartender asked. "You want to disagree with every patron of this saloon?"

"That must be some family, the Sweeneys," Lubbock went over and clapped Sweeney on the back.

"They're fightin' for you and me," Sweeney said coldly. "They're fightin' to preserve our way of life."

"I agree," said Di Calco.

"Yeah," said the bartender.

Lubbock turned on the bartender. "What's *your* name?"

"Cody," said the bartender. "William Cody."

Lubbock glared at him. "You kidding me?"

"I swear to God," said the bartender.

"They got a statue in Wyoming. Buffalo Bill. Any relation?" Lubbock asked.

"It's a pure coincidence," the bartender said.

"Beer, Buffalo Bill," Lubbock said. He watched the bartender draw the beer and place it before him. "From the very hand," Lubbock marveled. "A man with a statue in Wyoming. No wonder you're so patriotic. If I had a statue in Wyoming, I'd be patriotic too."

"Pure coincidence," protested the bartender.

Lubbock drank half his glass of beer, leaned back, spoke quietly and reflectively. "I just love to think of two Sweeneys in England protecting my way of life. I just love it. I feel safer already." He smacked the bar savagely. "Tents! We'll be sitting in tents in the middle of winter!"

"What do you want?" Di Calco said. "You want Hitler to come over here and clean up?"

"I hate him; I hate the bastard," Lubbock said. "I'm a Dutchman myself, but I hate the Germans."

"Give the Dutchman a beer," Sweeney said. "On me."

"I hate the Germans," Lubbock went on, "and I hate the English and I hate the French and I hate the Americans . . ."

"Who do you like?" the bartender asked.

"The Italians. You can't get them to fight. They're civilized human beings. A man comes up to them with a gun, they run like antelopes. I admire that."

Di Calco tapped warningly on the bar. "I'm not going to stand here and have the Italian army insulted."

Lubbock ignored him. "The whole world should be full of Italians. That's my program. My name is Lubbock, boys. I come from a long line of Dutchmen, but I hate them all. If the British're defending my way of life, they can stop right now. My way of life stinks."

"Boys," the bartender said. "Talk about something else, boys."

"The truth is," Sweeney said, "I wouldn't mind if there was a war. I make eleven dollars a week. Any change would be an improvement."

"This is the war of the Hotel Pee-yeah," Lubbock said.

"What do you mean by that?" Di Calco looked at him suspiciously, sensing a new insult to the Italian army.

"On Fifth Avenue and Sixtieth Street. They tea-dance." Lubbock scowled. "They tea-dance for the Em-piuh."

"What's objectionable about *that?*" the bartender asked.

"Yuh ever see the people that go into the Hotel Pee-yeah?" Lubbock leaned over the bar and scowled at the bartender. "The little fat rabbits in the mink coats?"

"The best people," the bartender said defiantly.

"Yeah." Lubbock smiled mirthlessly. "If they're for anything, it must be wrong."

"I'm speaking carefully," Di Calco said in measured tones. "I don't want to be misconstrued, but to a neutral ear you sound like a Communist."

Lubbock laughed, drained his beer. "I hate the Communists," he said. "They are busy slitting their own throats seven days a week. Another beer, Buffalo Bill."

"I wish you wouldn't call me Buffalo Bill." The bartender filled Lubbock's glass. "You start something like that, you can wind up making life intolerable." He flipped the head off the glass and pushed it in front of Lubbock.

"A statue in Wyoming . . ." Lubbock shook his head wonderingly. "Today they tea-dance for the Empiuh, tomorrow we get shot for the Empiuh."

"It don't necessarily follow." Sweeney moved closer, earnestly.

"Mr. Sweeney, of the flying Sweeneys." Lubbock patted him gently on the wrist. "The reader of the *New York Times.* I'll put a lily on yer grave in the Balkans."

"It may be necessary," Di Calco said. "It may be necessary to supply soldiers; it may be necessary for Sweeney to get shot."

"Don't make it so personal," Sweeney said angrily.

"Before we get through, Mr. Sweeney," Lubbock put his arm confidentially around him, "this war is going to be very personal to you and me. It will not be very personal to the rabbits from the Hotel Pee-yeah."

"Why can't you leave the Hotel Pierre out of this discussion?" the bartender complained.

"The snow will fall," Lubbock shouted, "and we'll be sitting in tents!" He turned on Di Calco. "The Italian patriot. I'd like to ask yuh a question."

"Always remember," Di Calco said coldly, "that I'm an American citizen."

"How will you feel, George Washington, sitting behind a machine gun with Wops running at you?"

"I'll do my duty," Di Calco said doggedly. "And don't use the term 'Wop.' "

"What do you mean running *at* him?" Sweeney roared. "The Italian army don't run at anything but the rear."

"Remember," Di Calco shouted at Sweeney, "I have a standing invitation to meet you outside."

"Boys," the bartender cried. "Talk about other matters. Please . . ."

"One war after another," Lubbock marveled. "One after another, and they get poor sons of bitches like you into tents in the wintertime, and yuh never catch on."

"I'm overlooking the language." Sweeney took a step back and spoke dispassionately, like a debater. "But I'd like to hear your solution. Since you're so clear on the subject."

"I don't want to overlook the language," Di Calco said hotly.

"Let him talk." Sweeney waved his hand majestically. "Let's hear everybody's point of view. Let the Dutchman talk."

"Well . . ." Lubbock started.

"Don't be insulting," the bartender said. "It's late and I'm ready to close up the bar anyway, so don't insult the patrons."

Lubbock rinsed his mouth with beer, let it slide slowly

down his throat. "Don't yuh ever clean the pipes?" he asked the bartender. "Yuh know, that's the most important thing about beer—the pipes."

"He's got a comment on everything!" Di Calco said angrily. "This country's full of them!"

"They are dividing up the world," Lubbock said. "I got eighty-five cents to my name. No matter which way they finish dividing, I'll be lucky to still have eighty-five cents when it's all over."

"That's not the way to approach the problem," said Sweeney. "Your eighty-five cents."

"Will I get Greece?" Lubbock pointed his huge finger threateningly at Sweeney. "Will Di Calco get China?"

"Who wants China?" Di Calco asked triumphantly.

"We get one thing," Lubbock said soberly. "You and me and Sweeney and Buffalo Bill . . ."

"Please," said the bartender.

"We get trouble. The workingman gets trouble." Lubbock sighed and looked sadly up at the ceiling, and the other men silently drank their beer. "Military strategists agree," Lubbock said, his tongue going proudly over the phrase, "that it takes four men to attack a position defended by one man."

"What's that got to do with it?" Sweeney demanded.

"This war is going to be fought in Europe, in Africa, in Asia," Lubbock chanted. "It is not going to be fought in William Cody's Bar."

"Sorry I can't oblige you," the bartender said sarcastically.

"I've studied the situation," Lubbock said, "and I've decided that there's going to be four times as many Americans killed as anybody else. It stands to reason. They're not going to attack us here, are they? We're going to take the offensive. Four to one!" He banged the bar with savage certainty. "Us four poor dumb yokels'll get it just to put one lousy Dutchman out of the way. Military strategy guarantees!"

"Don't yell so loud," the bartender said nervously. "The people upstairs don't like me."

"The worst thing is," Lubbock shouted, glaring wildly around him, "the worst thing is I look around and I see the world full of poor dumb stupid bastards like Sweeney and Di Calco and William Cody!"

"The language," Di Calco snarled. "Watch the language."

"Hitler has to be beaten!" Sweeney yelled. "That's a fundamental fact."

"Hitler has to be beaten!" Lubbock's voice sank to a significant, harsh whisper. "Why does Hitler have to be beaten? Because poor ignorant bastards like you put him there in the first place and left him there in the second place and went out to shoot him down in the third place and in the meantime just drank yer beer and argued in bars!"

"Don't accuse me," said Sweeney. "I didn't put Hitler anyplace."

"Sweeneys all over the world!" Lubbock shouted. "And now I got to get shot for it. I got to sit in tents in the wintertime!" Suddenly he grabbed Sweeney by the collar with one hand. "Say . . ." Sweeney gasped. Lubbock's other hand shot out, grasped Di Calco by his collar. Lubbock drew the two men close to his face and stared with terrible loathing at them. "I would like to mash yer stupid thick heads," he whispered.

"Now, lissen," Di Calco gasped.

"Boys," said the bartender, reaching for the sawed-off baseball bat he kept under the counter.

"If I get shot it's your fault!" Lubbock shook the two men fiercely. "I oughta kill yuh. I feel like killin' every dumb slob walkin' the streets . . ."

Di Calco reached back for a beer bottle and Sweeney grabbed the big hand at his throat and the bartender lifted the sawed-off baseball bat. The door swung open and a girl stepped through it and looked blankly at them.

"Go right ahead," she said, the expression on her face not surprised or worried or amused. "Don't let me interrupt."

"Boys . . ." the bartender said and put the baseball bat away. Lubbock gave Sweeney and Di Calco a last little push and released them and turned back to his beer.

"People like you," Sweeney murmured, outraged, "people like you they ought to commit to asylums."

Di Calco straightened his tie and tried to smile gallantly through his rage at the girl, who was still standing by the open door, hatless, her dirty blonde hair falling straight down to her shoulders. She was a thin girl, with the bones showing plainly in her face, and her hands skinny and rough coming out of the sleeves of the light old gray coat she was wearing. Her face was very tired, as though she had been working too long, too many nights.

"Would you like to close the door, Miss?" the bartender asked. "It's getting awfully cold."

The girl wearily closed the door and stood against it for a moment, wearily surveying the four men.

"I need some help," she said.

"Now, Miss . . ." the bartender started.

"Oh, shut up!" she snapped at him. Her voice was flat and worn. "I'm not bumming anything. My sister's just had a kid and she's laying in a stinking little hospital and she was bleeding all day and they gave her two transfusions and that's all they got and they just told me maybe she's dyin'. I been walkin' past this saloon for the last half hour watchin' you four guys talkin', gettin' up nerve to come in. She needs blood. Any you guys got some blood you don't need?" The girl smiled a little.

The men carefully avoided looking at each other.

"We're busted," the girl said, her tone as flat as ever. "The kid came out seven months and her husband's a sailor; he's on his way to Portugal and there's nobody in this whole goddamned, freezin' town I can turn to." She shrugged. "My blood's the wrong type." She took a step nearer the bar. "She's only nineteen years old, my sister. She had to go marry a sailor . . ." Lubbock turned and looked at her.

"All right," Lubbock said. "I'll go with yuh."

"Me, too," said Di Calco.

Sweeney opened his mouth, closed it, opened it again. "I hate hospitals," he said. "But I'll come along."

Lubbock turned and looked slowly at the bartender.

"It's late anyway," the bartender said, nervously drying the bar with a towel. "I might as well come along, just in case. . . . My type blood might . . . Yes." He nodded vigorously, and started taking off his apron.

Lubbock reached over the bar and brought up a bottle of rye and a glass and silently poured it and pushed it in front of the girl. The girl took it without smiling and drained it in one gulp.

They all sat in the dreary hospital clinic room with the old dead light of the hospital on them and all the weary sorrowful smells of the hospital swelling around them. They sat without talking, waiting for the interne to come and tell them which one of them had the right type of blood for the transfusion. Lubbock sat with his hands between his knees, occasionally glancing sharply at Sweeney and Di Calco and Cody, all of them nervously squirming on their benches. Only the girl walked slowly back and forth down the middle of the room, smoking a cigarette, the smoke curling slowly over her lank, blonde hair.

The door opened and the interne came in and touched Lubbock on the arm. "You're elected," he said.

Lubbock took a deep breath and stood up. He looked around him, at Di Calco, at Sweeney, at Cody, triumphantly, smiled at the girl, and followed the interne out of the room.

When he was through, when the blood had poured out of his veins, slowly and delicately, into the veins of the pale, quiet girl on the table next to him, Lubbock got up and bent over her and whispered, "You're going to be all right," and she smiled weakly at him.

Then he put on his coat and went back into the clinic room. The others were still there. They stood there, scowling at him in the blue hospital light. He smiled widely at them.

"Everything all right?" Di Calco asked solemnly.

"Everything's fine," Lubbock said cheerfully. "My blood is singing in her system like whisky."

Di Calco looked at Sweeney, Sweeney at Cody, each with doubt and hesitancy in his eye.

"Say, Dutchman," Sweeney said loudly, "we'll buy you a drink. What d'yuh say?"

They waited, tense, almost ready for attack.

Lubbock looked consideringly at them. Cody put up the collar of his coat.

"Sure," Lubbock said, putting his arm around the girl. "It'll be an honor."

They walked out through the hospital doors together.

The City Was in Total Darkness

Dutcher stood at the bar, feeling clean after his shower and still thirsty, looking at the girls, glad that he was alone, listening with one ear to the conversation around him. "The British and French," a man in a hound's-tooth-check jacket was saying, "will shuttle back and forth over Germany from Paris to Warsaw. And besides, he has no oil. Everybody knows Hitler has no oil."

" 'Darling,' she says to me," a large blonde woman said loudly to another large blonde woman, " 'darling, I haven't seen you in for*ever*. Where've you been—in the summer theater?' She knows goddamn well I just finished two pictures for Fox!"

"It's a bluff," the man in the hound's-tooth-check said. "He's going to back down, Russia or no Russia. He has no oil. Where are you today without oil?"

"Mr. Dutcher." The barman brought over a phone and plugged it in. "For you."

It was Machamer on the phone. "What're you doing tonight, Ralph?" Machamer asked, his voice, as always, grating and noisy.

"I'm drinking tonight," Dutcher said. "I'm drinking and waiting for something good to happen to me."

"We're going to Mexico," Machamer said. "Want to come along?"

"Who's we?"

"Dolly and me. Want to come along?"

"What part of Mexico?" Dutcher asked. "What distant part of that verdant land? Vera Cruz, Mexico City . . . ?"

Machamer laughed. "Tia Juana. I got to be back on Tuesday to look for a job. Just overnight. For the races. Want to go?"

"Without oil," the man in the check was saying, "a war is absolutely impractical." Dutcher looked gravely at him, considering whether or not he wanted to go to Mexico. He had avoided people after playing tennis in the afternoon, because he'd wanted to be alone, by himself, with the decks clear for something special and significant to happen to him on this special and significant week end.

"Have they got bullfights in Tia Juana?" he asked Machamer.

"Maybe," Machamer said. "They have them sometimes. Come on, this is Labor Day, there's nobody in Hollywood."

"I'm tired," Dutcher said. "I've been listening to the radio for seven nights and I played tennis and I'm thirsty."

"You can lie down in the back of the car, with a bottle," Machamer said. Machamer was a young writer and very impressed with Dutcher's two novels and constantly was after him. "I'll drive."

"I never saw a bullfight," Dutcher said. "Did you ever see one there?"

"Oh, nuts!" Machamer said. "Dolly and I'll be over in fifteen minutes to pick you up."

"Tonight," Dutcher said, "I would like to have a startling adventure."

"Oh, nuts," Machamer said. "Fifteen minutes."

Dutcher gravely put the phone back on its pedestal. "I've got to find another bar," he said to the barman. "Whenever people want to find me they call me here. It's bad for the reputation. In two years nobody'll give me a job." The barman grinned. "Another Rum Collins,"

Dutcher said, looking steadfastly at a slender girl down
the bar who had long thick black hair and tremendous full
breasts that jutted out like pennants in front of her. The
barman looked too. "Doesn't it break your heart?" the
barman said.

"California," Dutcher said. "Specialty of the country."

"That cameraman," one of the blonde ladies was saying, "he made me look like William S. Hart's mother. I
told him, too, but *loud!*"

In Poland, now, the tanks were roaring over the dusty
plains. German boys were climbing into bombers now,
Dutcher thought, fiddling with the controls, peering at
the instruments, thinking in this one minute when they
were waiting and there was nothing to do, "Is this the last
time?" and then getting the signal and sweeping off the
field toward Warsaw. Cavalry, Dutcher remembered, the
Poles had wonderful cavalry. He could just see a wonderful Polish cavalryman sitting heavily on his plodding
mount, retreating, sleepless, from the border, stinking
from the horse, listening to the bombers overhead, thinking of sleep and home and the English air force, kicking
his horse wearily, saying, "Son of a bitch." And the rich
and their women, like the rich and their women everywhere, leaving quietly out the back way, while the dawn
broke and the light came up and the boy in the bomber
could get a good clear view of the cavalryman on the long,
open road below.

Dutcher looked at the girl with breasts like pennants.
He sat at the bar, making believe he was staring blankly
ahead, making believe nothing was happening inside him,
feeling lust rise within him as definitely as water rising in
a filling glass. General, non-particular lust, he thought,
looking at the girl, pretty, with her black hair and long
throat and bright print dress and that amazing bosom. I
ought to be ashamed, Dutcher thought. The reader of
Spinoza, the admirer of John Milton, the advocate of
moral and economic reforms, a sufferer from general and

indiscriminate lust ten times daily at the sight of a face, a ruffle, at the sound of a woman's laugh.

"We live on two planes," Dutcher said to the bartender. The bartender smiled weakly.

Hollywood, Dutcher thought, Hollywood had a great deal to do with it. It was the product of the neighborhood, and everywhere you went it was pushed in your face like cheese in Wisconsin, and you tried to keep yourself from thinking about *Murder at Midnight* and sex rushed in to fill the vacuum. *Murder at Midnight* was the picture he was writing. It had a long complicated story about a night-club singer who got drunks to spend money on her but who was genuine, all the way through, as everyone always said in the conferences. She had a small son from whom she bravely tried to conceal the tawdriness of her profession, and she got mixed up in a murder and she fled town in the rain with the son and the cops picked up an innocent man. . . . Dutcher shook his head. He never could get the story straight. Anyway, this was the week end. And he'd be through in two weeks and have enough money for eight months in New York. Why'm I kidding myself? he thought. I look at them in New York, too.

Hollywood, you could always blame everything on Hollywood. That was the nicest thing about Hollywood.

"Sacred and profane," he told the bartender. "That's the whole explanation."

Machamer came in with Dolly. "On to Mexico," Machamer said.

"Sit down," Dutcher said, "and give me some good arguments. Dolly, you look beautiful." Dolly looked as thin and as plain and nervous as ever, and Dutcher was always very careful, in this city of magnificent women, to be gallant and flattering to her. "Give me Dolly," he said to Machamer, "and I'll go to Mexico."

Dolly laughed. Her laugh was high and very nervous and always made Dutcher a little uncomfortable.

"Poor Dutcher," Dolly said. "Poor lonesome Dutcher."

"Get me a girl," Dutcher said, suddenly, not thinking about it or why he was saying it, "and I'll go with you."

"Now, Dutcher," Machamer protested. "Eight o'clock Saturday night, Labor Day weekend . . ."

"On a high moral plane," Dutcher said. "I just want to have somebody to talk to."

"You have plenty of girls," Machamer said.

"I'm tired of them," Dutcher said. "Tonight I'm tired of them. War, *Murder at Midnight,* the fickleness of the male character, I'm tired of them. Tonight I'm in the mood for a new face." Dutcher waved his hands elaborately, embroidering on the theme, although already half-sorry that he'd said anything about a girl. "A face moody, passionate, with the eyes cynical and despairing, the mouth lost and contemptuous and stormy, the hair tossed and black . . ."

"He wants a character out of Thomas Wolfe," Machamer said.

"A face for the week end," Dutcher said, his tongue sliding joyfully in his mouth after the Rum Collins, "a face tragic and tortured by the guilt of a slaughtering and slaughtered world . . ."

Dolly jumped off her stool. "I'm going to call Maxine," she said.

"Who's Maxine?" Dutcher asked, warily.

"She's very pretty," Dolly said. "She's an actress at Republic."

"Oh, God," Dutcher said.

"Don't be such a snob," said Dolly. "Give me a nickel."

"What do you expect at eight o'clock Saturday night?" Machamer gave her a nickel. "Hedy Lamarr?"

"She's very pretty," Dolly repeated. "She just got in from New York and she may not be busy . . ." She started toward the phone.

"On a high moral plane!" Dutcher shouted after her. "Remember!"

Dolly strode out of sight toward the telephone booth. Dutcher watched her and then turned to Machamer.

"When you read the papers," he said, "and you read about airplanes bombing people and then being shot down, do you ever think about what it's like up there, with the bullets coming at you and the plane bucking and all of a sudden just air below . . . ?"

"All the time," Machamer said soberly.

"During the Spanish War I used to dream about being machine-gunned by airplanes. I'd run and run along alleyways between garages and the planes would always come back and get me from an open side." Dutcher finished his drink. "I wonder what garages had to do with it. The trouble with the human race is it's too brave. You can get people to do anything—fly around and get shot at twenty thousand feet up, walk into hand grenades, fight naval battles. If the human race wasn't so damn courageous, this would be a much better world to live in. That's the sum total of my thinking in two months in Hollywood."

"Einstein is resting easy," Machamer said. "He's still got a good lead."

"I know," said Dutcher. "But he doesn't have to think in this climate."

Dolly slipped in between them. "It's all settled," she said. "Maxine is dying to go. She's heard about you."

"Good or bad?" Dutcher asked.

"She's just heard about you. She says you mustn't get fresh."

Dutcher wrinkled his nose. "Did she say 'fresh'?"

"Yes," Dolly said.

"I don't like Maxine."

"Nuts," Machamer said, and pulled him away from the bar and out to his car.

The big car sped toward Mexico. Dutcher sprawled luxuriously on the back seat with his head in Maxine's lap. Occasionally he moved his head lazily because Maxine was wearing a suit trimmed all the way down the front with red fox and the fur got into his nose and tickled him.

"He was an Italian," Maxine was saying. "He had large

estates in Italy and he had a good job in New York, fifteen thousand a year, but he didn't like Mussolini."

"A character," Dutcher said softly. "A beautiful character."

"We were engaged to be married," Maxine said, speaking loudly, talking to Dolly, "but two weeks later he gave up his job. He relaxed; my little Wop relaxed." She laughed a little sadly, stroked Dutcher's head absently. "As soon as I meet a man he relaxes."

Machamer turned on the radio, and a man in London said that Hitler had not as yet answered Chamberlain's ultimatum and an orchestra played, "I May Be Wrong, But I Think You're Wonderful."

Dutcher looked thoughtfully up at Maxine's face. It was a round, full face, with a little full mouth that looked as though it had been created in God's mind with a careful brilliant smear of lipstick already on it. "You're very pretty," he said seriously.

Maxine smiled. "I'm not so bad." She patted him in appreciation. "I'm a little fat at the moment. I drank too much wine in New York. Dolly, I heard that Gladys is marrying Eddie Lane. Is that true?"

"In October," Dolly said.

Maxine sighed. "That Gladys. Eddie Lane's old man is good for five hundred thousand a year. She was in my class at high school. Oil. Old man Lane is up to his navel in oil. Eddie Lane chased me for two years like a kid after a fire truck. What a goddamn fool I was to go to New York."

Dutcher laughed, looking up at her. "You have a nice, refreshing outlook on finance."

Maxine laughed with him. "Money is money," she said. "I'll get a little fatter and even Republic won't have me, and then where'll I be?"

"I'll write a play," Machamer said, at the wheel, "and you can act in it in New York. They like them fat in New York."

"I tried that, too," Maxine said grimly. "I thought of another way out. I had my step-father insured . . ."

"Holy God!" Dutcher said. "For how much?"

"Fifty thousand."

"We're in the dough," Dutcher said. "Stop and buy me a Lincoln."

"Hah," said Maxine. "I paid his insurance three years then he went and got married on me. A little Irish biddy he saw waiting on table in San Luis Obispo."

They all laughed. "You're wonderful," Dutcher said. He pulled her down and kissed her. She kissed politely, with reserve, carefully, yet with a hint of vulgar accomplishment.

Unsatisfactory, Dutcher thought, letting his head fall back, yet . . . Reader of Spinoza, admirer of John Milton . . .

"This is Berlin," a voice said on the radio. "The city is in total darkness. The Fuehrer has not replied as yet to the English ultimatum. There is constant troop movement at the Berlin railroad stations and trains are pouring toward the Polish frontier."

A band played "Begin the Beguine," and Maxine talked to Dolly about another friend of theirs who had married a seventy-year-old man with fourteen blocks of real estate in downtown Cleveland.

"The city is in total darkness," Dutcher murmured. He lay back comfortably. This wasn't so bad, racing through the night to a new country, with a new girl, even though it was only Tia Juana and only an ordinarily pretty girl, getting a little fat, and a little hard and not exactly the girl you'd pick to take with you on a visit to your old Professor of Ethics at Amherst. Still it was better than sitting at a bar all alone, thinking, "I'll wait another ten minutes and then go out and buy another paper, see what *they* have to say."

He turned and buried his face in the red fox. There was a heavy smell of perfume, which was pleasant over the old smell of leather and gasoline in the back of the car. "Prince Matchabelli," Dutcher said. "This fox fell into a well of Prince Matchabelli and drowned. A beautiful death. Machamer, did I ever tell you about Cynthia Messmore, who was a classmate of mine at PS 99 and Miss Finch's? She married old Shamus Goonan, from the eleventh assembly district . . ."

"No!" Machamer said, in tones of wonder.

"A brilliant match," Dutcher said. "He was on the WPA three days a week and he was good for seven hundred and sixty dollars a year, as long as he stayed sober. Sewer construction, he was a sewer construction magnate, he was up to his navel in . . ."

"Are you making fun of me?" Maxine's voice was hard, and Dutcher knew he ought to stop, but he couldn't. He sat up.

"I never should've left PS 99," he said sadly. "Sex is the opium of the people. Turn on the radio, Machamer."

Dolly was shaking her head at him, but Dutcher made believe he was looking out the window. Mean, he thought, I've been mean. And I liked it. Tonight I want to be everything . . . mean, angry, noble, gracious, lordly, docile, everything. I want my emotions to be engaged. I can't love her, I can't make her love me, but I can make her angry at me and then win her over, then . . ."

"This is Paris," a voice said. "All the lights are out. The Cabinet has been in conference since seven o'clock this evening."

Machamer turned the radio off.

Dutcher felt Maxine eyeing him. He turned and looked pleasantly at her. After all, he thought, regarding her, she *is* a pretty girl, with a fine figure and we *are* going to be together until tomorrow night . . .

"Is that how you're going to the races tomorrow?" Maxine asked. "Without a tie?"

Dutcher felt at his collar. He was wearing a polo shirt, open at the throat. "I guess so," he said. "It's awfully hot."

"I won't go with you," Maxine said, "unless you wear a tie."

"I haven't got a tie."

"I won't go with you," Maxine said firmly.

"We live in a tropical climate," Dutcher said. "We mustn't ever forget that. I'm a Northern man, I sweat like . . ."

"I have an extra tie," Machamer said. "You can wear that."

Dutcher nodded. "If it'll make Maxine happy . . ." He smiled at her.

"I wouldn't be seen in front of all those people with a man who wasn't wearing a tie."

"You're right," Dutcher said, smiling pleasantly at her. "Now that I think of it, you're absolutely right."

Maxine smiled back at him. At least, he thought, I haven't thought of *Murder at Midnight* since the trip began. At least, she's done that.

They stopped in San Diego and drank at a bar among a lot of sailors from the naval base. Dolly took some of the pills she was always taking and for a moment gripped Machamer's arm and leaned over and kissed his neck. It was nearly two o'clock and the bar was closing and the sailors were drunk.

"The United States will not get into any war," a big blond farm boy jutting out of his flimsy blue uniform announced. "I have the guarantee of my congressman."

"Where you from?" Dutcher asked.

"Arkansas."

Dutcher nodded as though this convinced him. The sailor gulped down what was left of his beer.

"Let the Japs come over," he called. "We'll sweep 'em from the seas. I'd like to see the Japs just try and come over. I'd just like to see . . ."

Maxine was smiling at the sailor.

"I'm hungry," Dutcher said, herding Maxine and Dolly toward the door. "I hate discussions of relative naval strength."

"That was heartening," Machamer said, as they walked toward the bright lights of a waffle shop down the street. "An official representative of the United States armed forces says we won't get into a war."

"He was a nice-looking boy," Maxine said, as they entered the waffle shop. "If you took him out of that sailor suit."

The waffle shop was crowded, and they sat at a table that had not been cleared. Maxine and Dolly went to the ladies' room and Machamer and Dutcher were left at the table, looking at each other in the garish waffle-room light, across the dirty dishes and spilled coffee on the table.

"She's all right," Machamer said loudly, grinning at Dutcher. "Dolly did all right for you, didn't she? She's got a wonderful figure."

"Machamer," Dutcher said, "if I had a cement mixer and I wanted somebody to make a speech while it was going, I would pick you."

Machamer looked around him apologetically. "Isn't it funny, how loud I talk?"

"Everybody in the Square Deal Waffle Shop now knows you think Maxine has a wonderful figure."

The waitress, very pale and harried-looking at two in the morning, rattled the dishes between them as she cleared the table.

"You're having a good time, aren't you?" Machamer asked. "She makes you laugh, doesn't she?"

"She makes me laugh," Dutcher said.

Dolly and Maxine came back. Dutcher watched Maxine walk down the aisle between the tables, her red fox shaking down the front of her suit and all the men in the place watching her. That suit, Dutcher thought, is one-half inch too tight, in all directions. Everything she wears, always, I bet, is one-half inch too tight. Even her nightgowns.

"You know what I'm thinking of?" Dutcher said to Maxine as she sat down.

"What?" Maxine asked, all newly powdered and rouged.

"Your nightgowns."

Maxine frowned. "That's not a nice thing to say."

"Dutcher's a very vulgar man," Machamer said. "You ought to read his books."

"The English," Maxine said, "just declared war on the Germans. The woman in the ladies' room told us."

That's how I found out, Dutcher thought. In the ladies' room in a waffle shop in San Diego, a woman told an actress from Republic, who drank too much wine in New York, that the English declared war on Germany, and that's how I found out.

"This fork is dirty," Maxine said loudly to the waitress, who was putting their waffles down on the table. "You have some nerve giving us dirty forks."

The waitress sighed and put down a clean fork.

"They'll get away with murder," Maxine said, "if you let them."

All through the room, people knifed slabs of butter and poured syrup and ate waffles, Dutcher noted, as he started on his. There was no change, just the usual restaurant noise of voices and plates.

"This waffle stinks," Maxine said. "That's my honest opinion. And they make a specialty of them! San Diego!"

Dutcher put his hand gently on hers to calm her.

"You got the hand of a day-laborer," Maxine said. "What do you do, hammer in nails with them at the studio?"

"It's the disgraceful heritage of my wasted youth," Dutcher said.

Maxine turned his hand over and carefully examined the palm. "You got a heart line that's branched many times," she said.

"Tell me more," said Dutcher.

"You're fickle, jealous, selfish." Maxine leaned over his hand very seriously. "And in the long run, you're not going to be very successful."

"What a catch!" Dolly said.

"Tell me more," said Dutcher.

"You're moody." Maxine ran her finger lightly over his palm. "You're a very moody man."

"They don't come any moodier," said Dutcher.

"Your life line is short."

Dutcher took his hand back gravely. "Thank you very much," he said, his hand still aware of the soft promising feel of Maxine's fingers. "Now I'm all cleared up about myself. I certainly am glad I brought you down to San Diego."

"It's all there in the palm," Maxine said defensively. "I didn't put it there." She drew her collar around her. "Let's get out of this joint." She walked toward the door, with all the men in the room watching her.

"You're not her type," Dolly whispered to Dutcher. "She told me in the ladies' room. She likes you, but you're not her type."

Dutcher shrugged. "Palmists don't like me. It's something I've always noticed."

He caught up with Maxine and held her elbow as they walked toward the car. "Now," he said, "we come to a most delicate point. We—uh . . . We have to go to a hotel— and—I . . ."

"I want my own room," Maxine said firmly.

"I just thought I'd ask." Dutcher shrugged.

"A gentleman doesn't ask," Maxine said.

"What does a gentleman do for girls?" Dutcher asked.

"He doesn't talk about it! It just happens."

"It never occurred to me before," Dutcher said as they got into the car. "But you're absolutely right."

They could only get a two-room suite at the hotel, because it was all filled up, and there were some other people from Hollywood in the lobby and Dutcher tried to appear as though he were in no way connected with Maxine. If only she didn't have that red fox, he thought. And all day tomorrow, at the races, there would be people he knew, and he'd have to try to be eight paces in front of her or at the betting windows or at the bar . . .

Upstairs, Maxine primly put her bag down next to

Dolly's in one of the two rooms. Machamer looked at Dutcher.

"We have the west wing," Dutcher said, and walked into the next room.

"Look." Machamer followed him. "This was supposed to be a holiday for Dolly and me. She lives at home and her mother prays to God every night to save her sinful daughter's soul." Dolly came in and looked at them. Then she giggled.

"Go in and talk to Maxine," Machamer shouted to Dutcher.

Dutcher shrugged. "I see my duty," he said.

He went into the next room. Maxine was sitting neatly on the bed, her hands folded, her eyes reflectively on the ceiling. "Maxine, old girl," Dutcher said.

"Don't make fun of me."

"I'm tired," Dutcher said wearily. "There's a war on. I give up. There're two beds inside. I promise not to touch you. For Machamer and Dolly . . ."

"Let Machamer be a gentleman!" Maxine said loudly. "For one night."

Dutcher went back into the other room. "She says let Machamer be a gentleman for one night," he said. He took off one shoe. "I'm going to sleep."

Dolly kissed Machamer. She hung on, her arms wound around his neck and Dutcher made a big business of carefully arranging his shoes neatly in line under a chair. Dolly came over and kissed Dutcher lightly. "You sure make a big hit with the girls," she said, and went in.

Machamer and Dutcher put on their pajamas and turned off the light and Machamer got into bed. Dutcher went to the door of the girls' room. "Latest bulletin," he announced. "Machamer has promised not to lay a hand on me. Good night."

The girls laughed and Machamer roared and Dutcher joined them, the two rooms resounding wildly with laughter, as Dutcher climbed into bed.

Outside, the newsboys, far off along the dark streets of San Diego, cried that England had declared war.

Dutcher lay in his bed and listened to the newsboys' cries, swelling and wailing in the streets, and looked up at the dark ceiling; and the hour and the war, which had been kept off all night by drink and speed and laughter and lust, like lions warded off by a trainer's chair, now closed in on him. The cavalryman in Poland now lay across the dusty Polish road, his mouth open in surprise and death and his dead horse beside him and the boy in the German bomber flew back from Warsaw saying to himself, "One more time. I came back one more time."

"It's for Dolly's sake," Machamer's voice came across the small dark abyss between the beds, grating, but young and sorrowful. "It's nothing to me, but she's crazy to grab every hour. Do you want to go to sleep, Ralph?"

"No."

"She wants to grab everything. Everything. She hates to go to sleep. She always has her hands on me. She's going to die." Dutcher heard Machamer sigh and the bedsprings click gently and the newsboys coming nearer. "She's sick; the doctors can't cure her; she has Bright's disease. She gets numb, she feels as though an eye is falling out, an ear . . . That's why she takes those pills. She doesn't tell anybody except me. Her family doesn't know, and her boss . . ."

Dutcher lay rigid in his bed, looking up at the ceiling.

"I don't love her." Machamer's voice was harsh but small. "I tell her I do, but . . . I like other girls. . . . I tell her I do. She doesn't want to lose an hour."

"Sssh," Dutcher said gently. "Don't talk so loud."

"Even now," Machamer marveled. "Even now my voice would break down a wall. Are you sad, Dutcher?"

"Yes," said Dutcher.

"It came funny, didn't it?" Machamer asked.

"You hardly felt it." Dutcher talked with his eyes closed, his head straight back on the pillow. "You were waiting for it for six years and expecting it, and each time

a shot was fired you'd say, 'Here it is,' but it wasn't, and
you read the papers every day, and by the time it came
you didn't feel it at all. We'll feel it later, we'll feel
it later . . ."

"What're you going to do now?"

Dutcher laughed. "Go to sleep."

"Good night," Machamer said.

"Good night."

The bomber was coming down to a landing and the boy
banked and looked down to see that the landing gear was
out and he, Dutcher, was on his way with a fat citizen in
a red fox-trimmed suit to a rat-eaten Mexican racetrack,
where the youngest horse running was at least nine years
old, where the Hollywood people in their scarves and dark
glasses and buckskin shoes, with their agents and beauty-
contest winners for the week end gambled their crazy easy
money in the dusty Mexican heat, talking of sex and dollars, saying over and over, "Colossal, terrific, he's hot this
year, it lost Metro a million." The war was on, and it was
on here, too, among these idle, unbombed, frivolous people. I'd stay here, in Hollywood, Dutcher thought, if I
could bear *Murder at Midnight* and all the Murders at
Midnight to come. I don't want to write any more books.
An honest book is a criticism. Why should I torture myself
into criticizing this poor, corrupt, frantic, tortured, agony-
stricken world? Later, later, let the criticism come
later. . . .

The newsboys wailed in the streets below.

Here I am, Dutcher thought, in a hotel room far from
home, with a dying and unloved girl, cheated of an hour,
and a movie writer who wanders like a refugee from studio to studio, week in, week out, beggary plain on his face,
looking for a job, and a palm-reader who could have been
bought for the night with three compliments and ten minutes of polite charade. Fickle, jealous, selfish, moody, not
successful, short of life.

"England, England . . ." The boys' voices, wavering
in the night wind, came faintly through the window. I'm

ashamed of myself, Dutcher thought. I met the tragic hour in a mournful and ludicrous costume.

Now is the time, Dutcher thought, for some noble and formidable act. Who will supply me with a noble and formidable act?

"I would like to speak to the continent of Europe," Dutcher said aloud.

"Huh?" Machamer murmured.

"Nothing." Dutcher pulled the covers up to his chin. "You know what I'm going to do?"

"Huh?"

"I'm going to get married. I'm going to have a wife and live on a farm and grow corn and wheat and grapes and watch the snow fall and slaughter pigs and become involved with the seasons. For a little while I want to become involved in an eternal motion."

"Sure," said Machamer. "I just dreamed Mervyn LeRoy was offering me a job. Isn't it too bad, isn't it too, too bad . . ." His voice trailed off.

"Involved with the seasons," Dutcher said, rolling it on his tongue. "Involved with the seasons." He closed his eyes.

Now the bomber stopped and the boy jumped out, feeling the ground solid under his feet and cold in the early morning. The boy grinned and the sweat of relief ran down under his arms and he said, "I made it, I made it again," as he went off across the field to report to his commanding officer.

Hamlets of the World

The captain was getting more and more remote every moment. He kept stuffing papers into a heavy saddle-leather bag, whistling tunelessly under his breath. From time to time he looked out over the windy plain, swirling with dust in the late afternoon sun. He would peer thoughtfully into the eye-burning distance, then shake himself a little and resume his packing, a little more quickly each time. He never looked at Lieutenant Dumestre.

Lieutenant Dumestre sat on the edge of the desk, very neat in his expensive uniform. He was a tall, fairish man, who looked too young to be in his lieutenant's uniform, too young to be so serious, too young to be in a war.

He never took his eyes off the Captain. The Captain was a round, solid man, who had been very jovial when they had met in Algiers and had paid for the wine and had sighed gallantly over all the pretty women in the café. There was nothing jovial or gallant about the Captain now, as he prepared in a businesslike way to disappear, each moment seeming more and more remote.

"Do you expect to come back, sir?" Lieutenant Dumestre finally asked, because the silence in the orderly room broken only by the low bumble of the Captain's humming was at last too much to bear.

The Captain stopped his packing and looked thoughtfully out over the plain again, as though there, in the dust and scrub, some answer to a profound although somewhat vague question was to be found. He stood silently, even forgetting to hum.

"Do you expect to come back, sir?" the Lieutenant asked loudly.

The Captain at last turned and looked at the Lieutenant. His eyes were very cool and you would never have thought from looking at him in this moment that he had ever bought a bottle of wine for a lieutenant in his life. "Come back?" the Captain said. He turned away and sturdily buckled his bag. "Who can tell?"

"What do I do with the Americans?" The Lieutenant's voice, he noticed angrily, was much higher than it should have been. At Saint Cyr they had been after him all the time to pitch his voice lower. "An order given in the soprano register, Mister, is not calculated to drive troops to impossible glories." "What happens when the Americans arrive?"

The Captain was putting his helmet on very carefully in front of a mirror. "That is just what I hope to discover," he said.

"In the meantime?"

"In the meantime your orders are to resist. Naturally."

The Lieutenant peered out over the plain, hoping painfully that over the rim of the horizon the Americans would appear before the Captain could leave on his personal retreat. But the only movement to be seen was a corporal hurrying to the battery observation post.

"They'll arrive tomorrow morning, at the latest," the Lieutenant said.

"Quite possibly." The Captain picked up his bag decisively, marched out and into the command car. The Lieutenant followed him and saluted. The Captain saluted and the car started and the Captain drove down the road.

The Lieutenant plodded slowly up the road toward the forward gun, thinking of the Captain, in the command car, speeding over a macadam road to Algiers, where there would be other men to make the decisions, other men to say, "We will move to the left, we will move to the right . . ." and the Captain would have to make no decisions himself. No matter how things turned out, he would not be committed and would be a fine fellow with whichever side turned up on top, and would jovially buy wine for his new lieutenants at the second-best restaurant in town. . . .

The Lieutenant made his way to the aimless little mud house they used as an observation post and climbed the ladder and stood under the umbrella next to the red-eyed little corporal and peered through his glasses at the plain. He looked until his eyes ached, but aside from the blowing dust there was nothing.

The men who served the forward gun had rigged up a tarpaulin to one side and lay under it, out of the wind. Usually they slept all the afternoon, but today no one was sleeping.

Sergeant Fourier even went so far as to get up and look out across the plain.

"Anything?" Labat asked.

The Sergeant squinted anxiously. "Nothing."

"Waiting, everything is waiting," Labat said. He was a long, ugly man, with a big nose and large ears. He was from Paris and excitable and given to throwing his arms around in rage and was a great patriot of the French Republic. "In a war you wait for everything! Even the Americans! At last, I thought, things will finally move. The Americans are famous for their briskness. . . . We're still waiting. . . ."

"Only a day," said Boullard. Boullard was a big, quiet man, over forty, with a wrinkled, brown, farmer's face. "They'll be here soon enough."

"I can't wait," Labat said. He stood up and peered out. "For a year I sat in the Maginot Line. Now for two years I sit here. I am finally impatient. A day is too much."

"Shut up," Boullard said calmly. "You'll get us all nervous."

Labat lay down and put his hands behind his head and looked up at the tarpaulin angrily. Sergeant Fourier came back and sat down.

"More of the same," Sergeant Fourier said. "More nothing."

"It must be worse for Americans," Corporal Millet said He was a man who, although he was nearly thirty-five, was still plagued by pimples. His face had raging red blots on it all the time and he suffered meanly under his affliction, taking his misfortune out on the work details in his charge. "It must be unbearable for Americans."

"Why?" Labat asked angrily. "What's wrong with the Americans?"

"They are not a military people," Corporal Millet said. He had a lawyer's voice, smooth and reasonable and superior, and on bad days it made men want to kill Corporal Millet. "They are used to sitting back and pushing buttons."

"Corporal," Labat said calmly, "you are perhaps the biggest idiot in the French Army of 1942."

"The jokes," Corporal Millet said. "We can do without the jokes. It is a fact that war is harder on some races than on others. The Americans must be suffering the tortures of the damned."

"I repeat," Labat said. "The biggest."

Corporal Millet was a devotee of Vichy, and Labat enjoyed making him angry.

"Push buttons," Boullard said reflectively. "I could use a few push buttons at the moment."

"See," Corporal Millet gestured to Boullard. "Boullard agrees."

"See," Boullard said. "Boullard does not agree."

There was silence for a moment, while the men thought

of the wind and the ugliness of the men around them and the possibility of dying tomorrow.

"This war," the Sergeant said. "This disease of a war."

"Somebody talk about a woman," Private Jouvet said. "I'm tired of the war. I am in the mood for breasts and hips." Private Jouvet was twenty years old and made a desperate effort to keep on an equal footing with these sun-stricken veterans of bed and battle.

"It can't be," Labat said, "that the Americans will appear and we will be asked to shoot at them. It's impossible."

"In the French Army," Boullard said, "nothing is impossible."

"Why not?" Corporal Millet asked in his bland voice. "An invasion of French soil . . ."

"I am very tired of those two words," Boullard said. "French soil."

Labat opened his canteen and took a mouthful. He closed the canteen over the precious water and then thought that perhaps he would be shot by morning, and said, "Hell," and opened the canteen and took another mouthful.

"The problem is," Private Jouvet said, "are the Americans to be regarded as friends, enemies, or tourists?"

"What a war!" Sergeant Fourier sighed. He had just married three months before, a masseuse with a good clientele in Algiers, and he was by and large as comfortable as a sergeant could hope to be in this foul year. "What a disease of a war!"

"Lafayette," Boullard said, "we are here."

"We will be given our orders," Corporal Millet said loudly.

"That's what we're afraid of," said Labat.

"After all," said Corporal Millet, tenderly touching his current most blazing pimple, "we are soldiers. We have officers. They have their instructions."

"Please, Corporal," said Labat. "Quiet. Such official sentiments have a tendency to make me throw up."

"The Americans." Sergeant Fourier sighed again. "Things were going as well as could be expected. This wasn't good, but a man could bear it. They are crazy with anxiety to make a landing someplace. . . . They have all Europe to make a landing on. No! They must choose Africa! We will all be dead."

"Be more cheerful," Boullard said, "or kindly keep quiet."

The men sat silently for a moment, everyone heavy and gloomy because the word death had finally been mentioned.

"It will be a ridiculous thing," Labat said. "To be killed by an American." Labat had fought at Sedan and made his way bitterly down the length of France, cursing the politicians, cursing the officers, cursing the Germans and English and Italians and Americans. At last he had stowed away aboard a freighter to Algiers and without losing a day had joined up all over again and had since then sat, full of pent-up vengeance, in the gloom of Africa, waiting to fight the Germans once more.

"I refuse," Labat said. "I refuse to be killed by an American."

"You will be told what your orders are," Corporal Millet said, "and you will follow them."

Labat stared gloomily and dangerously at Corporal Millet. His face, which was ugly but usually pleasant enough, now was harsh and his eyes were squinted balefully. "Corporal," he said, "Corporal of the pimples, do you know what our orders are?"

"No."

"Does anybody know?" Labat looked around, his face still flushed and glowering, angry at Corporal Millet and the government of France and his position in the world that afternoon.

Sergeant Fourier cleared his throat professionally. "The Lieutenant. He must know. The Captain's gone . . ."

"What a wonderful thing," Boullard said, "to be a captain. . . ."

"Let us ask the Lieutenant," Labat said.

"Sergeant Fourier, we make you a committee of one."

Sergeant Fourier looked around him uneasily, pulling in his round little belly nervously, uncomfortable at the thought of any action that would make him conspicuous, endanger his pleasant anonymous future with the masseuse in Algiers. "Why me?" he asked.

"Highest non-commissioned officer present," Labat chanted. "Channels of communication with the commissioned personnel."

"I haven't said two words to him," Sergeant Fourier protested. "After all, he just got here five days ago. And he's reserved. . . . All he's said to me in five days is, 'Make sure the men do not smoke in the open at night.'"

"Enough," Labat said cheerfully. "It's obvious he likes you."

"Don't joke," Boullard said sharply. "We have no more time to joke."

"I'm only joking," Labat said soberly, "because I am willing to slit my throat."

He got up and went to the edge of the tarpaulin and stood there, his back to the men, watching across the enigmatic plain for the first fateful dust cloud.

"What sort of man is this Lieutenant Dumestre?" Boullard asked.

"It's hard to tell," Sergeant Fourier said, with the caution born of three years in an army where a hasty approval of a man, before all the facts of courage, sense and rectitude were in, might one day cause your death. "He's very quiet. Stiff . . ."

"A bad sign," said Boullard.

"Very rich in the uniform department."

"Another bad sign."

"It doesn't pay to be too hurried," Sergeant Fourier protested.

"It's the Americans," Boullard said. "They're in a hurry, not me. Well, there's only one thing to be done."

He rubbed his cheek absently with the back of his hand,

like a man determining whether or not he needs a shave. The other men watched him silently, anxious and curious about a definite plan that might have finally bloomed on this last nervous afternoon. "One thing," Boullard repeated. "We kill him."

Lieutenant Dumestre stood in the observation post and felt the headache coming on like an express train. Every afternoon the boredom and misery of the day accumulated in his brain pan and punished him for still living. He stared painfully over the darkening plain, which was silently enveloping itself in blue and purple folds, intangible and deceptive, in which the shapes of men and machines might be capriciously and dangerously lost. . . .

Lieutenant Dumestre shook his head and closed his eyes, measuring gloomily the exact extent of the pain in his skull.

How do you do it? he asked himself. How does a first lieutenant hand a battery over to an advancing army, without orders? How does a first lieutenant save his life in a situation like this? In the distance there is a puff of dust and soon the first shell dropping somewhere near you, and all around you doubtful and uncertain men whom you do not know but who, for the lack of a better word, are under your command. Why had he left his post in Algiers? In this one, crazy, fateful week, his transfer had to be granted, this transfer to dilemma, this transfer to death. . . . In the days of Napoleon it was said that every French private had a marshal's baton in his knapsack. Today every French soldier had in his knapsack a fatal and insoluble conundrum.

Lieutenant Dumestre had asked to be transferred from Algiers because he had been spending too much money there. It was as simple as that. The bills came in, the monthly reckonings were made, the deductions for the money sent home to his mother and father, who were lean and ailing in Paris, and it became clear that on a lieutenant's salary you could not save money in a gay town, especially if you had been rich all your life and your family rich before you and certain habits of eating and drinking and generosity ingrained in you, war or no war. . . .

So, it was too expensive, Algiers. So, the desert would prove to be even more expensive.

. . . Back in Algiers he knew the men of his battery had mimicked him behind his back—his slow, painful way of delivering orders, full of agonized pauses, as he tried to remember to keep his voice down, tried not to sound like a young idiot imposing callously on these veterans of a war that had passed him by. . . . They had mimicked him, but he knew them and even felt they liked him, and if he were with them now in this tragedy of a situation he would be able to go to them, talk to them, draw strength and resolution, one way or another from the men who would have to bear the burden of living and dying with him.

But here he was, on the one important day of the last two years, with a group of sullen and bearded strangers, who regarded him only with steady and cool hostility, a newcomer and an officer in an army where newcomers were automatically suspect and officers automatically hated. . . .

Lieutenant Dumestre walked slowly out toward the west across the dusty scrub. The sun had set and the wind had died and the walking, he felt, might help somehow. Perhaps, he thought, smiling a little to himself, there will be an American patrol and I am unavoidably captured and there's an end to the problem. . . . It's like a child, he thought, hoping that by morning he will have a sore throat so he does not have to go to school and take his examination in arithmetic. What an arithmetic was being imposed upon him now! What a savage and pitiless calculation! He looked toward the last blur of the horizon beyond which the Americans were marching. How simple it was to be an American! In their arithmetic there was an answer to all problems. How merry and dashing a lieutenant in the artillery in the American army must feel tonight, marching beside men whom he could trust, who trusted him, who all believed the same thing, who knew an enemy when they saw one, whose parents were well-fed and healthy, in no one's power, three thousand sweet miles from all battlefields. . . .

What a tragic thing to be a Frenchman this year! Hamlet, sword out, killing Polonius and uncle in blind unprofitable lunges. . . . Frenchmen, Hamlets of the world . . .

Lieutenant Dumestre stopped and sat down like a little boy on the dark earth and put his head in his hands and wept. He stopped suddenly and bit his lips and neglected to dry the tears from his cheeks. Nonsense, he thought, a grown man . . . There must be an answer to this, too. After all, I am not the only Frenchman afloat on this continent. The thing is, the men. If I knew what they wanted . . . If there was only some way to be present, without being seen. Armies have surrendered before. Detachments have surrendered before. Officers have appeared under a flag of truce and offered their services to their official enemies. The Captain was in Algiers, there was no one to stop him. "Dear sir, is there anyone here who speaks French? Dear sir, Lieutenant Dumestre, Battery C, wishes to state that he desires to join forces with the American Army in North Africa and put himself under the flag of the United States for the duration against the common enemy. . . ." There must be a technique to surrender, just the way there was a technique for everything else in the army. His mother and father would have to look out for themselves. Now, if only the men . . .

Lieutenant Dumestre slapped his thigh briskly as he stood up. At last he had reached a decision. He had faced the arithmetic and at least he knew what answer he wanted. There only remained going in frankly to the men and putting the situation up to them, in words of one syllable, simply. . . . He started back toward the forward gun, walking more swiftly than he had walked for a week.

"Men," he would say, remembering to keep his voice pitched low, "this is the way it is. You may or may not know it, but tomorrow an American army will appear." You never knew how much the men knew, what rumors had reached them, what facts confirmed, what punishments and discharges and prophecies and movements were peddled at the latrine or over a morning cigarette. "I am under orders to resist," he would say. "Personally, I do not believe we are bound by those orders, as I believe all Frenchmen to be on the side for which the Americans are now fighting." Perhaps that was too heroic, but it was impossible to fight a war without sounding from time to time a little heroic. "I intend to go out under a flag of truce and give over the guns of this battery." Now the question of dissenters. "Anyone who does not wish to join me in this action is free to leave toward the rear. . . ." No, they'd go back and talk and by morning a troop of cavalry would come up and Lieutenant Dumestre would be finished in thirty minutes. Keep them with him? How do that? Supposing they were all Vichy men? After all, they were being paid by Vichy and there were thousands of Frenchmen in Africa who had staked their lives on a German victory. They'd shoot him in cold blood.

Once more he cursed the trick that had landed him at this moment among two hundred strangers. In his old company he would have been able to take Sergeant Goubille aside and talk honestly and get an honest answer. Sergeant Goubille was forty-five years old and there was something fatherly and tolerant of young officers in his bearing, and a man like that would be worth a man's life on this harsh and doubtful plain tonight. Well, there was no Sergeant Goubille at hand. . . . Perhaps that Breton, that farmer, Boullard. He was an older man and he looked honest and pleasant.

He took a deep breath and walked swiftly, not knowing exactly what he would do but knowing he had to do something, toward the forward gun. . . .

Under the tarpaulin, Boullard was talking, his voice low and harsh, all the kindly, old countryman's lines somehow vanished from the set, desperate face. "There will be a token resistance," he was saying to the men, who were all sitting up, looking at the ground most of the time, looking up only occasionally at Boullard with a kind of deep embarrassment. "In a token resistance there are token deaths." He looked around him calmly from face to face, his thought plain in his eyes. "A token corpse feeds as many worms as any other. . . ."

Jouvet, the young one, was the only one who could not manage to sit still. He rubbed his heels back and forth, making marks in the sand, and studying them intensely.

"Kill the pretty lieutenant," Boullard said, "and we have our own lives in our own hands. We dispose of them as we see fit."

"Let us look at it from the political angle," Labat said. "Politically, we are fried if the Germans win. . . ."

"Perhaps," Sergeant Fourier said uneasily, his voice full of the nagging pain of having to make a decision. "Perhaps we ought to wait and see what happens."

"We will wait and see ourselves buried," Boullard said.

"At least," said Labat, "we ought to talk to the Lieutenant. Sound him out."

"I was on the Meuse," said Boullard. "I know better than to talk to a lieutenant. I'll take the responsibility. If you're all afraid . . ." He looked around him with savage, peasant contempt. "There're a lot of men still to be killed in this war. I don't mind making it one more or less, personally. . . ."

"We have to talk to him first," Labat said stubbornly.

"Why?" Boullard asked loudly.

"Maybe he's with us. Maybe he wants to fight with the Americans, too. . . ."

Boullard laughed harshly. Then he spat. "I'm surrounded by children," he said. "If he's still an officer in the French Army after two years, he is not fond of the Americans. I am. At this moment, I am crazy about Americans. If there is any hope for anybody in this stinking year, it is in the Americans. I'm forty-four years old and I've fought in two wars. The third one, I want to pick my own side. . . ."

"Still," Labat said, his voice low and persistent, "still, we ought to talk to him."

"For myself," Corporal Millet said briskly, standing up, "I am on duty at the observa—"

He let his hands fall gently to his sides as Boullard brought his rifle up and touched his chest lightly with the bayonet.

"You are on duty here, Corporal." Boullard moved the bayonet tenderly on a breast button. "There is a question before the house that must be decided by a full membership."

Corporal Millet sat down carefully.

"I don't care," Labat was saying, grinning at Corporal Millet, "what you do to the fighting corporal, but nothing happens to the Lieutenant until we talk to him." He patted Boullard's shoulder, in a small, reassuring gesture. Boullard slowly took his eyes off Millet and the Corporal sighed.

Boullard looked around him searchingly at the men caught in this hour on this desert with him. Sergeant Fourier, haunted by dreams of a pension and his masseuse and still troubled by some obscure, painful sense of patriotism and honor, refused to look at him. Jouvet, faced at the age of twenty with the ancient, tangled threads of a bloody and complex century, looked ready to weep. Labat was smiling but stubborn. Corporal Millet was sweating, and was making a great effort to look like a man who did not intend to rush to the nearest officer and announce a mutiny.

"All right," Boullard said wearily, "if that's what you want. Although I tell you, two words too many and we are all against a wall, looking at a firing squad."

Jouvet fumbled with his handkerchief quickly and Boullard looked at him curiously and impersonally.

"It is not necessary to commit ourselves," said Labat. His long, workman's arms waved in argument. "We approach the subject, we skirt it, we take soundings like a boat coming into a harbor . . ."

"Better!" Sergeant Fourier said loudly, happy at all deferment. "Excellent! Much better!"

Boullard stared at him coldly and Sergeant Fourier became quiet and nervously took out a pack of cigarettes.

"It's possible," Labat was saying, convincing Boullard, "to judge a man without a direct question. . . ."

"Possibly," Boullard said with no enthusiasm. "Possibly."

"I'll do the talking," Labat said. "I'm used to things like this. I have talked at union meetings for seven years and nothing could be more delicate . . ." He looked around him anxiously, hoping for a little laughter to take some of the deadly tension away, but only little Jouvet, who was always polite, smiled nervously because he realized Labat had meant it as a little joke.

"All right," Boullard said. He fingered his rifle gently and let it dip almost imperceptibly toward Corporal Millet. "I will judge. And you . . ." The rifle dipped very clearly toward Corporal Millet. "You will not open your mouth. Is that clear?"

Corporal Millet sat up stiffly at attention, feeling sorrowfully within him that his honor demanded some show of resistance and that his life would not be worth a great deal if he was incorporated in the army of the United States. He looked at Boullard's huge crushing hands, calm on the rifle. "It is your affair," he said faintly. "I wash my hands of it."

Boullard laughed.

Sergeant Fourier lighted his cigarette, gift of his plump wife the masseuse, eating her dinner comfortably, all unknowing, in the curtainy little apartment in Algiers with three exposures. He sighed and stood up and walked between Boullard and the limp Corporal Millet and stood at the edge of the tarpaulin in the full darkness, pulling with small comfort at his cigarette, while behind him, under the tarpaulin, there was no sound from the waiting men.

Lieutenant Dumestre made his way slowly across the rough black ground toward the gun position, turning over in his mind his possible opening sentences to the gun crew. "Men," he could say, "I am going to be absolutely honest with you. I am putting a white flag up beside this gun and I am delivering this battery over to . . ." Or he could say, "There is a possibility that tomorrow morning American troops will appear. Hold your fire until I give the word . . ." while silently swearing to himself that the word would never be given. There was much to be said for this method, as it was indefinite and seemed less dangerous and didn't tip his hand until the last moment, when it would probably be too late for anyone to do anything about it. Of course there was always the possibility that he could stand up in front of the men and pour his heart out to them, remind them in ringing words of their country's shame, call upon them with blood and passion to forget themselves, forget their families in France, remember only honor and final victory. . . . He could see himself, pale and fluent, in the dim light of the moon, roaring, whispering, his voice singing in the quiet night air, the men listening entranced, the tears starting down their cheeks. . . . He shook himself, smiled wryly at the dream, remembering his harsh, slow way of speaking, plain, indefinite, without the power to move men to the nearest café, much less throw themselves grandly and thoughtlessly upon a doubtful and possibly fatal cause. . . .

Oh, Lord, he thought, I am the wrong man for this, the wrong man, the wrong man. . . .

He turned the corner of the tarpaulin, seeing the watchful, hateful shape of the gun outlined stubbornly against the starlit sky.

Sergeant Fourier was smoking pensively in the open and the other men were sitting, strangely quiet, under cover. When Sergeant Fourier saw him he started guiltily and threw his cigarette away as unostentatiously as possible. He stood at attention and saluted and with his right heel tried to douse the glowing speck in the dirt. Somehow, the sight of the small man with the comfortable little pot belly trying to pretend, like a vaudeville comedian, that he hadn't been smoking, irritated Lieutenant Dumestre, who all morning and all afternoon had been grappling bitterly with war and fratricide and tragic, bloody policy. . . .

He returned the Sergeant's salute curtly. "What's wrong with you?" he asked sharply, his high voice making all the men in the tarpaulin turn their heads coldly and automatically to watch him. "You know there's to be no smoking."

"Please, sir," Sergeant Fourier said stupidly, "I was not smoking."

"You were smoking," Lieutenant Dumestre said, weeping inside because inside he knew how ridiculous this charge and countercharge was.

"I was not smoking, sir." Sergeant Fourier stood very straight and formal and stupid with the problem of the evening, almost happy to have a simple little idiotic argument to worry about at least for ten minutes. . . .

"You've been told, you've been told!" Lieutenant Dumestre shrieked in his highest voice, mourning deep within himself for that womanly timbre, for his military insistence upon form and truth at this unmilitary hour, but somehow unable, with the Captain's departure and the imminence, potent and desperate, of the Americans over the horizon, to stop the high noise of his tongue. "At any moment we may be bombed. A cigarette glows like a lighthouse in a black desert at ten thousand feet! Why don't you draw a map of the gun position and publish it in the morning newspapers?" He saw Labat look at Boullard and shrug coldly and turn away with an air of dangerous significance and something within him clutched at his throat, but now there was no stopping that high, silly tongue, freed for a moment from the locked agony and doubt of the day's decision making. Here at least was familiar ground. Troops disobeying orders. Troops endangering security of the post or station. Troops slightly insubordinate, lying. . . . His weary, ragged mind, terribly grateful to be relieved of its unaccustomed task of painful exploration, relapsed into the formal, years-long grooves of Saint Cyr, of countless garrisons, countless lectures. . . . "There will be double security tonight, two-hour watches for everyone," the voice still high, but with the three-thousand-year-old bite of military command. "An extra half day's ammunition will be drawn up from the battery dump by three this morning." He saw the men's faces bleakly collapse and also something else in them, although he couldn't tell in the rush of his commands what it was. Even as he spoke he hated himself for what he was doing, knowing that a better man would have ignored the cigarette or joked about it. . . . He hated Sergeant Fourier, standing there, pained and stupid and impassive, but in a way he was grateful to him, because he had given him the opportunity at this late hour once more for postponement.

He turned on his heel and strode away. Later, perhaps at midnight, he would come back, he told himself, and finally get this question of the Americans settled. He pulled his shoulders high in disgust as the sound of his own voice squalling about the cigarette sounded in his ears, but there was nothing to be done about it and he walked without looking back. Midnight, he thought, midnight is still time. . . .

Back under the tarpaulin, Boullard looked around him at the men. Their faces were grave, but except for Millet, there was consent in all of them.

Boullard walked out from under the tarpaulin with his rifle.

Midnight, Lieutenant Dumestre was thinking, when the bullet struck, midnight is still time. . . .

They buried him quickly without marking the grave and sat down in front of the gun to wait for the army of the Americans.

Walking Wounded

He wondered what had happened to the curtains. He lay stiffly on the bed, listening, with the old, irritated tightening of the nerves, to the wild and grating hubbub of the Cairo street outside his window, the insane wailing of newsboys, the everlasting iron drip of garry-horses' hooves, the pained yelps of peddlers. The sun, bright and hurtful as hot nickel, cut in through the open windows. On the floor lay the curtains, torn, with bits of cord still running from them to the top of the windows, like a ruptured spider web.

"What happened to the curtains?" he asked. His voice felt dry and sandy in his throat, and the right side of his head began to ache.

Mac was shaving at the washstand. His beard made a crinkly, Spartan sound against the razor. "Last night," Mac said, without turning. "In the excitement."

"What excitement?"

"You pulled the curtains down."

"Why?"

Mac shaved quietly and intently around the short, soldierly mustache. "Don't know," he said. "Either you wanted to throw me out, or throw yourself out, or just tear down the curtains."

129

"Oh, God!"

Mac scrubbed his face with water. "Pretty drunk, Peter," he said.

"What else did I do?"

"Two lieutenants and a major. In the lounge. Ten minutes of insults."

"A major! Christ!" Peter closed his eyes.

"I think you hit a lieutenant." Mac's voice was muffled in a towel. "Anyway, you hit something. Your hand's all cut up."

Peter opened his eyes and looked at his hand. Across the back of it there was a wide, ugly wound, just beginning to puff up around the edges. As he looked at it, he realized that it was hurting him.

"I poured iodine over it," Mac said. "You won't die."

"Thanks." Peter let his hand drop, licked his dry lips. "What did I say to the major?"

" 'Base wallah.' 'Imperial vulture.' 'Gezira bloodsucker.' 'Headquarters hangman.' "

"That's enough." The right side of Peter's head hurt very strongly for a moment.

"You were a little unfair," Mac said calmly. "He was a nice type. Been in the desert three years. Just come back from Sicily with dysentery. Wounded twice. Been attached to headquarters four days."

"Oh, Christ," Peter said. "Oh, Christ."

The room was silent as Mac put on his shirt and combed his hair.

"Get his name?" Peter asked finally.

"Major Robert Lewis. Might be a good idea to say good morning."

"How about the lieutenants?"

Mac took out his notebook. "MacIntyre and Clark," he read. "They await your pleasure."

Peter sat up and swung his legs over the side of the bed. The room faded and glittered for a moment, and he had to hold on to the bed when he stood up.

"Some day, soon," he said, "I have to stop drinking."

"A little whisky," Mac said kindly, "is good for the soul. Anything I can do for you?"

"No, thanks."

Mac stood at the door.

"Mac . . ."

"Yes, Captain . . . ?" Tiny, astringent, helpful mockery in the title.

"Mac, this is the first time anything like this ever happened to me."

"I know," Mac said softly. He went quietly out of the room.

Peter walked slowly over to the wash basin, looked at himself in the mirror. The familiar long, thin face, the uneven dotted crenelation of his wound across his forehead, the strange dark mark in the eye that had been blind for three weeks, all seeming to tremble slightly now in the bitter sunlight, as it had trembled for two months.

He shaved carefully and went to take a shower. He came back, feeling better, and put on fresh clothes. He switched his tabs with the three pips to his clean shirt, looking absently and automatically to see if there was any lipstick on them. Three and a half years ago, at Arras, there had been lipstick one morning, and he had walked around all day long, ignorant, wondering why smiles hid on sergeants' lips.

Then he went down to apologize to the major.

He sat at his desk, sweating. The heat of Egypt was like the inside of a balloon. The balloon was being constantly filled; the pressure getting greater and greater. Typewriters clicked dryly in the swelling air, and flies, the true owners of Egypt, whirled cleverly and maliciously before his eyes.

Sergeant Brown, his thick glasses clouded with sweat, clumped in and put a stack of papers on his desk, clumped out again. The back of Sergeant Brown's shirt was soaked where he had been pressing against the back of a chair, and sweat ran in trickles down his infantryman legs to the heavy wool socks and gaiters.

Peter stared at the stack of papers. Ruled forms and tiny and intricate notations that had to be gone over slowly, corrected, signed.

Outside, a donkey brayed painfully. It sounded like an immense wooden machine in agony, wood grating against wood, incredibly loud. It made the little, paper-stacked room seem hotter than ever.

Peter reread the letter he had received that morning from Italy. ". . . I am taking the liberty of answering your letter to Col. Sands, who was badly wounded last week. I am afraid there is nothing we can do about requesting your being posted to this regiment, as there is no provision in our establishment for medically graded officers."

The donkey brayed again outside. It sounded like the death of all the animals of Egypt on this hot morning.

Peter stared at the papers on his desk. Three flies danced over them, lighted, swept off. The typewriters rattled flatly in the heat. He took the top paper off the pile, looked at it. The figures leapt and wavered in the heat, and a drop of sweat fell from his forehead and mistily covered a 3, a 7, an 8. His hands glistened in little sick beads, and the paper felt slippery under his fingers. Hobnails sounded on the marble floor in the corridor, ostentatious and overmilitary among the clerks and filing cabinets. His throat burned dryly with the fifteenth cigarette of the morning.

He stood up jerkily and took his hat and went out. In the corridor he passed Mrs. Burroughs. She was a tall, full-bodied girl who wore flowered prints and always seemed to manage silk stockings. She was going home to England to divorce her husband, who was a lieutenant in India. She was going to marry an American air-force major who had been switched to London from Cairo. She was very pretty and she had a soft, hesitant voice, and her bosom was always oppressively soft and noticeable under the flowered prints.

She smiled at him, hesitant, polite, gentle. She had two rosebuds clasped in her dark hair. "Good morning," she said, stopping, her voice cool, shy, inviting in the drab corridor. She always tried to stop him, talk to him.

"Good morning," Peter said stiffly. He never could look squarely at her. He looked down. No silk stockings this morning. The pretty legs bare, the skin firm and creamy. He had a sudden, hateful vision of Mrs. Burroughs landing in London, running to be crushed in the arms of the American major in the press of Waterloo Station, her eyes bright with tears of love and gratitude, her husband, used and forgotten, in India. . . .

"I'm going to Groppi's," he heard himself say, surprisingly. "Tea. Would you like to join me?"

"Sorry," Mrs. Burroughs said, her voice sounding genuinely sorry. "So much work. Some other time. I'd be delighted. . . ."

Peter nodded awkwardly, went out. He hated Mrs. Burroughs.

The street was full of heat, beggars, dirt, children with fly-eaten eyes, roaring army lorries. He put on his hat, feeling his forehead, wet and warm, rebel under the wool. A drunken New Zealander, at eleven o'clock in the morning, wobbled sorrowfully in the full glare of the sun, hatless, senseless, reft of dignity, 7,000 miles from his green and ordered island.

Groppi's was cooler, dark and shaded. The red-fezzed waiters in the long white gaballiehs moved quietly through the pleasant gloom. Two American sergeants with gunners' wings on their shirts solemnly were drinking two ice-cream sodas apiece.

Peter had tea and read the morning paper. The birth rate had gone up in England, and an American magazine had suggested that Princess Elizabeth marry an American. The *Egyptian Mail* reprinted it with approval in a flood of Anglo-American feeling. After six years, somebody said in Parliament, men in the forces were to be sent home. The Russians were pouring across the Dnieper. Peter always saved the Russian news for last. Every step the Russians took was that much nearer home, nearer the rugged and manly weather of Scotland, near Anne. . . .

He tried to think of Anne, what she looked like, what her skin felt like. He looked up at the ceiling and half closed his eyes to shut out the tea and ice-cream shop, to close out Egypt, summer, war, army, distance, absence, close out everything but his wife. But he couldn't remember what she looked like. He remembered the dress she wore when they were married and the inn they'd stayed at after Dunkirk and what they'd played at the concert the last night in London, and he remembered that he loved her. But her face, the sound of her voice . . . lost. She refused to have photographs taken of her. Some whim or female superstition, far away in England. . . .

He paid and went out and started back to his office. But when he stood in front of the peeling, ornately balconied, sand-bagged building and thought of the small, hot office, the endless papers, the sweat and hobnails, he couldn't go in. He turned and walked slowly down the street. He looked at his watch. Still an hour before the bars opened. He walked on the shady side, erect and soldierly, slowly, like a man with a grave purpose. A horribly dirty woman with a horribly dirty child, as dirty and street-worn as only Egyptians can be, followed him, whining, for half a block. Peter didn't walk any faster, although he felt his nerves jerking at the sound of the woman's voice.

The woman left him finally, and he walked deliberately through the crowded streets, stopping from time to time to peer into shop windows. French perfume, women's dresses, mangoes, books, photographs, his mind recorded heavily. He went into the photographer's and had his picture taken, refusing to smile, looking soberly square into the camera, intimidating the photographer. He would send the picture to Anne. Three years. How long could a woman be expected to remember a man? His face would stare solemnly at her morning, noon, and night, crying, "Remember me, remember your husband. . . ."

Out in the street again he resumed his grave pacing down the shady side of the street. Fifteen minutes more and the bars would open. He grinned crookedly to himself as he thought of his pose before the camera, frozen Scotch passion grimly and puritanically peering across three years and two oceans. Anne would probably giggle at the absurdly stern, accusing face.

"Officer, wanna lady, wanna lady?"

Peter looked down. A tiny, filthy ten-year-old boy, barefooted, in a torn, bag-like single garment, was smiling up at him conspiratorially, pulling at his blouse.

"French lady," the boy whispered wickedly. "Fine French lady."

Peter stared at him disbelievingly, then broke into a roar of laughter. The boy, after a moment of doubt, also laughed.

"No, thank you, sir," Peter said.

The boy shrugged, grinned up at him. "Officer," he said, "cigarette?"

Peter gave him a cigarette and lit it for him, and the boy darted off, to try the French lady on a Polish corporal.

The bar had a nice beery smell and was dark and cool and the bartender drew eight glasses at a time, letting the foam settle whitely on the glass rims.

"The two lieutenants," Peter was saying, "were a little stuffy, but the major was fine."

"I knew he would be," Mac said. "I talked to him last night."

"I had breakfast with him"—Peter waved for two more beers—"and he said he guessed he'd be doing the same thing himself if he had to hang around this town five months."

Mac comfortably drained his beer.

"The birth rate in England," Peter said, "has gone up. I read it in the *Mail* this morning. There're three million Englishmen out of the country and the birth rate's rocketing. . . ." He heard his own voice loud and angry and humorless. "How in the name of God do they dare print things like that?" He saw Mac grinning widely, but he couldn't stop. "Who're the fathers? Where're the fathers? Bloody damned newspaper!"

"My," Mac said, "you have it bad today."

Suddenly Peter realized that Mac, placid and tolerant, was bearing a great deal of the burden of Peter's nerves.

"Mac," he said quietly, "forgive me."

"Uh?" Mac looked at him, surprised.

"Wailing Wall Chrome. Agony, Cairo division." Peter shook his head in disgust. "I keep feeding it to you seven days a week."

"Oh, shut up. I've lived with lots worse."

"Any time I get on your nerves, sing out, will you?"

"Sure thing. Drink your beer." Mac was embarrassed.

"I must be going a little crazy." Peter looked at his hands, which had taken to trembling in the last few months. The cigarette jerked minutely between his fingers, in a spasmodic rhythm. "This town. When I was with the regiment . . . Oh, hell . . ." The truth was that out in the desert, under the guns, on a pint of water a day, and the sudden air often dire with Stukas, he had been much happier. There were no women in the desert, no reminders of a civilized and normal life. There was clean, sterile sand, the noise of armor, thousands of grumbling, good-humored men intimate with an equal death, and above all there was the sense of immense and hardy effort and accomplishment, as first they had held the Afrika Corps and then driven it back. Cairo then had been a beautiful town, two days at a time, a hot bath and unlimited Scotch, and sweet, clean sheets and relief from the guns. But now, under the dry flood of paper, under the stiffness and pettiness of headquarters politics, under the cheap weight of men who had clung to soft jobs for three years, with the streets full of bare-legged girls, with the war on another continent a thousand miles away . . .

Now the regiment, what was left of it, was broken up. Most of them were in graves on the road to Tunis, others were in hospitals, the rest scattered among other units, after the four years that had started in France. Mac, who had been his platoon sergeant at Arras, calmly instructing the untrained men how to load and fire the guns they had never used before, then taking them out into the fresh May fields of France hunting for parachutists. Himself, who had crawled through the German lines to Dunkirk, who had entered Tripoli the first hour, who had blown up in the jeep outside Mareth, with his driver dead in the air beside him . . . Now, both of them clerks in small offices, chained to paper and civil servants.

"Six years," he said, "some bloody MP said we'd be sent home after six years. What do you think a woman thinks when she reads that she'll get her man back in only six years?"

"Always remember," Mac grinned, "what Monty said. 'The war can't last more than seven years. We'll run out of paper.'"

"If only I could get back to England," Peter said, "and sleep with my wife for two nights, everything would be all right. Just two nights."

Mac sighed. He was a quiet, efficient, small, matter-of-fact man, noticeably graying, and sighing was strange and incongruous to him. "Peter," he said, "can I talk plainly?"

Peter nodded.

"Peter, you ought to get yourself a girl."

They sat in silence. Peter played somberly with his beer. In France, even though he had just been married, he had been the gay young officer. Handsome and debonair, he had played joyfully and thoughtlessly with the pretty ladies of the country towns at which he'd been stationed, and in Paris, when he'd had a month there, a charming, beautifully dressed wife of a French captain stationed in Algiers.

But when he'd got back to England with the gray-faced remnants of his regiment, after the hideous, bloody days of the break-through, and had taken his wife silently into his arms, all frivolity, all smallness and lack of faith had seemed wanton and irreligious in the face of so much ruin, such agony. Leaving England for Africa, he had felt that behind him he had to leave the best part of his life orderly and decent.

"Maybe," he said to Mac. "Maybe . . ."

"A man's got to be practical," Mac said. "Three years. Oh, my God!"

Peter had to smile at the drastic expression on the practical man's face.

"You'll just explode," Mac said, "and blow away."

Peter laughed loudly, nervously. "Whisky," he said, "provides certain compensations."

"Whisky," Mac said grimly, "will send you home a doddering wreck. You'll do no one any good that way."

"Maybe. Maybe . . ." Peter shrugged. "Anyway, I hate these women out here. Having the best time of their lives. Ugly, impossible girls no one would ever look at in peacetime, just because there are a hundred men for every woman . . . Snobbish, overconfident . . . Bitches, all of them. A man has to sacrifice all decent, male pride to chase after one of these. . . ." He talked faster and faster, all the bitter observation of the past years flooding to his tongue. "They demand abasement, homage, the ugliest, most horrible and meanest of them. Women," he said, "have been among the most horrible of the war's casualties. All humility's gone, all normal value, all friendship. They're man-greedy. They're profiteering on the war, like the worst usurer and manufacturer of machine tools, except that their profits are lieutenants and generals, not cash. After the war," he said, "we should have rehabilitation hospitals for women who have been in troop areas, just like the hospitals for maimed men, to teach them how to live normal lives again. . . ."

Mac was laughing by now, helplessly, into his beer. "Enough," he said. "Enough, John Knox! All I wanted to say is that I have a date tonight, and my girl has a friend who's just come from Jerusalem, and it might do you a world of good just to have dinner with a woman for once. Do you want to go?"

Peter flushed, looked down at the beer-ringed table. "I won't even know how to talk to a woman any more."

"Do you want to go?"

Peter opened his mouth, closed it. "All right," he said. "All right."

"Jerusalem is nice enough . . ." It was on the dance floor at the Auberge des Pyramides, under the stars, with the three great tombs standing huge and a rebuke to time in the darkness just outside the lights and the music. Joyce was talking as they went slowly and painfully around the dance floor. "The city's clean, and the King David's an amusing hotel, but the people're simply dreadful." She had a brittle, drawling voice, pitched just high enough so that everyone near by could hear clearly what she was saying. "There," she said brightly, as Peter managed a full turn, "we're doing much better, aren't we?"

"Yes," Peter said, sweating in the heavy Nile heat, only slightly tempered by night, as he tried to concentrate on the beat of the music. Joyce's voice distracted him and put him off, and somehow she never seemed to stop talking. She worked in the consular service, and by nine-thirty Peter had a full store of information on the doings of the consulate in Jerusalem for the last year and a half, at which time Joyce had come out from England. He had hardly said a word all night, stammering, half finishing sentences, suffering, feeling like the clumsiest farmer. Still, she was pretty, most desirable in a full white evening gown ("We always dress in Jerusalem"), with full, sleek shoulders bare and daring under the gay lights.

"That's King Farouk. . . ." For the first time all evening her voice dropped a bit. "Isn't it?"

Peter looked. "Yes," he said.

"Isn't he attractive? What an original beard!"

Peter looked at King Farouk. "He looks like a fat, self-satisfied young man," Peter said, the first full sentence he had got out all evening. "And I understand he grew the beard because he has a terrible case of acne."

"Dance around the edge of the dance floor," Joyce whispered. "I'd like people to see me."

Dutifully and heavily Peter danced around the edge of the floor until the music stopped. He followed Joyce to the table. Joyce smiled vivaciously at seven or eight officers seated at various tables throughout the establishment.

"It's amazing," she said, brightly and loudly, "how many men I know in Cairo." They sat down. There was an awful silence while Peter wondered where in the name of God Mac was, and his girl, and Joyce smiled prettily first at one table, then another.

"Are you married?" Peter heard his voice, crooked and rasping, asking inexplicably. For the first time that evening Joyce gave him her undivided attention.

"Why," she said, looking at him queerly and coldly, "what a strange question!"

"It's just that there's a girl around my office," Peter said, almost dazedly. "Married to a lieutenant in India. Marrying an American major in London . . ." The expression on Joyce's face became more and more strained. "I don't know what made me think of her," Peter said lamely.

"No," Joyce said coldly, "I'm not married."

"I am," Peter said, despairingly.

"Really." Joyce smiled automatically at a colonel four tables away.

"My wife," said Peter, not knowing why he was talking, feeling his tongue too loose from the drinking that had been continuous since six that evening, "my wife is a woman of admirable character, although I can't remember what she looks like. Her name is Anne. She works for

the Air Ministry in Manchester. After Dunkirk, I was
stationed on the beach at Dover for five months. I used to
manage to get away week ends. We'd just stay in one room
and just look at each other. After France . . . I felt as
though my wife had healed me of a dreadful disease. She
healed me of mud and death and friends dying on all sides.
She's most beautiful, but I don't remember what she looks
like. She's very calm and simple and her voice is low, although I don't remember that, either. I sent her my photograph today. Six years is too long for a man to expect a
woman to remember him. Someone ought to tell Parliament that. . . . Don't you think?"

Joyce was staring at him, her mouth frozen to one side.
"Yes," she said.

"If I could only see her for two nights . . ." Well, finally, the thought crossed his consciousness, the lady from
Jerusalem is listening to me. "Right before I came out
here, I was moved to another beach. It was raining. Autumn and miserable and barbed wire at the high-tide marks
and mines all over the beaches. I called her long-dis-
tance and she told me she had a week and asked me
if she should come down. I told her no. It was so
miserable. Cheap little shacks waiting for the Germans in
the rain. I knew we were leaving for Africa and I didn't
want our last days together to be dreary, in that
abominable place. I told her no, but she said, 'You wait
right there. I'm coming down tonight.'" Suddenly, above
the dance music in the Valley of the Nile, Peter remembered what his wife's voice had sounded like, merry and
sensual and confidently commanding over the faulty wires
on that autumn night on a wet beach on the English Channel. "She came down and we had the week together, and
the rain and the barbed wire made no difference at all.
I've never been so gay, and it was early in the war, and
we always had a coal fire and hot rum and lovely heavy
breakfasts, with the curtains still drawn. And never a tear
when she left. And I started for Africa singing in my
heart." He was talking straight ahead to the Pyramids in

the ancient desert darkness now, not to the silly, bare-shouldered girl across the table. "I haven't heard from her in two months. Not a letter in two months." He shrugged. "After the war," he said, "I'm going to go in for politics. I'm going to stand for Parliament. There must be somebody in Parliament who knows what a war is like, who knows that one war is enough, six years is too much . . ."

"Why, Joyce, how nice!" It was the colonel, standing gallantly at the table. "Dance?"

Joyce looked doubtfully at Peter. Peter stood up, a little unsteadily. "Delighted," he said ambiguously. Without looking at Peter, Joyce went off with the colonel, smiling impartially at dozens of officers in Sam Browne belts as she danced on the edge of the floor.

Peter hazily watched the flashing plump white dress among the brave khaki and brass pips. He passed his hand over his eyes, thinking, as he remembered his outburst, God, I must be going crazy.

He saw a captain step in and dance with Joyce, then an American major. "The world," he said softly to himself, "is full of American majors." He laughed gently to himself, stood up, walked slowly out of the night club. Outside, with the music thin and distant in his ears, the Pyramids loomed, crumbling in the darkness, in memory of the unremembered dead.

He got into a cab and started for Cairo.

When the cab got to Gezira Island, he tapped the driver on the shoulder. "Sporting Club," he said.

The old, wheezing taxi laboriously turned. "I need a drink," Peter told himself seriously. "I need a drink very badly." He thought of old Mac caught there with two girls and the tremendous bill. He felt bad about it, but he'd pay his share, although it would mean considerably less drinking for the rest of the month. But he couldn't stay with that damned girl. The truth was he couldn't stay with any girl. Anne, unphotographed, in Manchester . . . Still, she should write more often than once every two months. . . .

The bar at Gezira was still open. There were some South Africans and some American fliers lounging against it. One of the American fliers was singing, in a soft Southern voice, "Oh, Susannah, don't you cry for me . . ."

"Scotch," Peter said to the bartender, feeling for the first time that evening a cessation of loneliness, his constant climate.

"Fo' Ah'm gawn' t' Alabama, with mah banjo on mah knee . . ." the American pilot sang sweetly and happily.

"Gin and lime," said one of the South Africans, a gigantic captain with huge, bare arms, whom the others called Lee. "Gin and lime all around." He turned to Peter. "What're you drinking, Captain?"

"I've ordered, thanks." Peter smiled at him.

"Man says he's ordered," the American pilot sang. "What do you know about that? British captain says he's ordered. Order again and order again, oh, Captain, order again. . . ."

The bartender put two Scotches in front of Peter, grinning. The huge South African captain poured it all into one glass. They lifted their glasses.

"To South Africa," one of the Americans said.

They drank.

"To sergeants." The American who had been singing grinned at a large South African lieutenant with a mustache. The lieutenant looked around him uneasily. "Quiet, please," he said. "I'll be in jail five years."

"This gentleman looks like a gentleman." Lee put his arm around the lieutenant with the mustache. "Doesn't he?"

"Yes," said Peter.

"Jail," said the lieutenant with the mustache.

"He's not a gentleman. He is a sergeant. He is my bloody sergeant from my bloody company."

"Ten years," said the lieutenant with the mustache.

"We're all AWOL, Sergeant Monks, lieutenant for the evening, Lieutenant Fredericks . . ." He waved to a slightly smaller red-headed South African down the bar.

"And myself. We're farmers. Independent men. When the bloody O.C. said 'no leaves,' we said farewell. Sixty miles out on the desert for three weeks. Miserable little clerk of an O.C. Sergeant, I said, here's a pip. Take off those bloody stripes. We wish to show you the glories of Shepheard's and Gezira, so that you can come back and dazzle the poor bastards in the other ranks with tales of the high life in Cairo."

"I've been talking to brigadiers all afternoon and evening," Monks complained. "Wearing on the nerves."

"If the O.C. shows up, it's all taped," Lee said. "I grab Monks by one arm, Freddy grabs him by the other. 'We've just arrested the bugger, sir,' we say. 'Impersonating an officer.' "

"Ten years," Monks said, grinning. "This round is on me."

Peter laughed. He lifted his glass. "To sergeants everywhere." They all drank.

"On my right," said Lee, "is the American Air Force."

The American Air Force raised its glasses at Peter and the pilot who sang started in on "Chattanooga Choo-choo." There were two lieutenants and a twenty-four-year-old major.

"The American Air Force is going home," said Lee. "Their tour is over. Home by way of England. The infantry's tour is never over. Oh, the poor, stinking, bloody infantry, their tour is never over . . ."

"Unskilled labor," one of the pilots said calmly. "We're delicate and highly sensitive mechanisms. We are war-weary. Our Schneiders are low as an Egyptian whore. We've bombed too many places. We've seen too much flak. We are lopsided from wearing ribbons. We are going home now to instruct the young how to shoot."

"I am going home to play with my wife," the twenty-four-year-old major said soberly.

"The infantry is not under the same Awful Strain," said the pilot who had been singing. "All they have to do is walk in and be shot. Their nerves are not stretched to the breaking point like ours. Captain," he said, leaning back and talking to Peter, "you look a little war-weary yourself."

"I'm pretty war-weary," Peter said.

"He looks sensitive," the major said. "He looks fine and sensitive enough to be at least a navigator. He looks like Hamlet on a rough night."

"I was in the tanks," Peter said.

"It's possible," said the major, "to get war-weary in a tank, too, I suppose."

"It's possible," Peter said, grinning.

". . . breakfast in Carolina . . ." sang the musical pilot.

"When're you leaving for home?" Peter asked.

"6 A.M. tomorrow. 0600 hours, as they say in the army," said the major.

"Five or six glorious days in London among our brave English Allies and cousins," said the other pilot, "and then the Stork Club, the Harvard-Yale football game, all the blonde, full-bosomed, ribbon-conscious, lascivious American girls . . ."

"London," said Peter. "I wish I were going with you."

"Come along," said the major expansively. "We have a nice empty Liberator. Pleased to have you. Closer relations with our British comrades. Merely be at the airport at 0600 hours, as they say in the army."

"Did you see," asked the singing pilot, "in the *Mail* today? Some idiot wants Princess Elizabeth to marry an American."

"Excellent idea," said the major. "Some upstanding representative citizen of the Republic. Post-war planning on all fronts. My nomination for Prince Escort is Maxie Rosenbloom."

Everyone considered the suggestion gravely.

"You could do worse," the pilot said.

"Infusion of sturdy American stock into an aging dynasty," the major said. "The issue would be strongly built, with good left hands. . . ."

"Do you mean it?" Peter asked. "You really could take me?"

"Delighted," the major said.

The singing pilot started in on "All Alone," and everyone but Peter joined him. Peter stared unseeingly at the glasses and bottles behind the bar. In three days he could be home. Three days and he could walk into Anne's room, quietly, unannounced, smiling a little tremulously as she looked up unsuspectingly. Maybe it was possible. He had had no leave since he'd come to Africa, except for two weeks' convalescence. He could go immediately to Colonel Foster's apartment, explain to him. Colonel Foster liked him, was very sympathetic. If he gave him a written order, releasing him from duty for twenty-one days, he, Peter, would undertake to get transportation back. Somehow, somehow . . . He would take all the responsibility himself. He was sure that Colonel Foster, who was a good soul, would do it.

Peter stood up straight. He spoke to the American major. "Perhaps I'll see you at six o'clock."

"Fine," the major said heartily. "It's going to be a great trip. We're loaded with Scotch." He waved as Peter turned and left the bar.

"All alone, by the telephone . . ." the wailing, mocking voices quavered in the night. Peter got into a taxicab and gave Colonel Foster's address.

He felt he was trembling. He closed his eyes and leaned back. It was all absolutely possible. England was only three days away. Two weeks there and the desert and the guns and the dying and ruled paper and heat and loneliness and insane expanding tension would disappear. He could face the rest of the war calmly, knowing that he would not explode, would not lose his reason. It was possible. Men were going home to their wives. That American major. All so cheerful and matter-of-fact about it. England in three days, after the three years . . . Colonel Foster would most certainly say yes. Peter was sure of it as the taxi drove up to the dark building where Colonel

Foster lived. Peter paid the driver and looked up. The colonel's window was alight, the only one in the entire building. Peter felt his breath coming fast. It was a symbol, an omen. The man was awake. His friend, who could give him England tonight with five strokes of a pen, by luck was wakeful in the quiet night, when all the rest of the city slept around him. It would be irregular, and Colonel Foster would be running some risk, but he had rank enough and was independent enough to take the chance. . . .

Peter rang the night-bell to the side of the locked doors of the apartment building. Far in the depths of the sleeping stone and brick, a forlorn and distant bell sang weirdly.

As he waited for the hall-boy to open the doors, Peter hastily rehearsed his story. No leave in three years. The tension getting worse and worse. Medically graded, no chance of getting to an active unit. Regiment disbanded. Work deteriorating. Given to sudden fits of temper and what could only be described as melancholia, although a doctor wouldn't believe it until it was too late. He knew the British Army couldn't provide transportation, but here were these Americans with an empty Liberator. He'd get back somehow.

As he went over it, in the darkness, with the faraway bell sounding as though it were ringing at the bottom of a troubled sea, Peter was sure the logic was irrefutable; Foster couldn't refuse.

When the hall-boy finally opened the door, Peter sprang past him, raced up the steps, too impatient to take the elevator.

He was panting when he rang Colonel Foster's bell, and the sweat was streaming down the sides of his face. He rang the bell sharply, twice. He heard his breath whistling into his lungs, and he tried to compose himself, so that Colonel Foster would think him absolutely calm, absolutely lucid. . . .

The door opened. The figure at the door was silhouetted against the yellowish light behind it.

"Colonel," Peter said, panting, "I'm so glad you're up. I must talk to you. I hate to disturb you, but . . ."

"Come in." The door was opened wider and Peter strode down the hall, into the living room. He heard the door close and turned around. "I . . ." he began. He stopped. The man who was standing there was not Colonel Foster. It was a large, red-faced man, bald, in a tattered red bathrobe. He had a mustache and tired eyes and he was holding a book in his hand. Peter looked at the book. *The Poems of Robert Browning.*

The man stood there, waiting, pulling his bathrobe a little tighter, a curious little smile on his weary face.

"I . . . I saw the light, sir," Peter said. "I thought Colonel Foster would be up and I took the liberty of . . . I had some business with . . ."

"Colonel Foster doesn't live here," the man said. His voice was clipped and military, but tired, aging. "He moved out a week ago."

"Oh," Peter said. He suddenly stopped sweating. He swallowed, made a conscious effort to speak quietly. "Do you know where he lives, sir?"

"I'm afraid not. Is there anything I can do, Captain? I'm Colonel Gaines." He smiled, false teeth above the old robe. "That's why when you said Colonel, at the door, I . . ."

"No, sir," Peter said. "Nothing, sir. I'm dreadfully sorry. This time of night . . ."

"Oh, that's all right." The man waved a little embarrassedly. "I never go to sleep. I was reading."

"Well . . . Thank you, sir. Good night."

"Uh . . ." The man looked hesitantly at him, as though he felt that somehow Peter should be helped in some dubious, obscure way. "Uh—perhaps a drink. I have some whisky I was just going to—for myself . . ."

"No, thank you, sir," Peter said. "I'd better be getting along."

Clumsily, they went down the passage together to the door. The man opened the door. He stood there, red-faced, huge, British, like a living Colonel Blimp, lonely and tired, with Robert Browning in the foreign night.

"Good night, sir."

"Good night. . . ."

The door closed and Peter walked slowly down the dark stairs.

Peter started toward his hotel, but the thought of the disordered room and Mac lying there, steadily asleep, steadily and slightly snoring in the next bed, was impossible.

He walked slowly past the dark policemen standing quietly with their rifles on the street corners. Down the street garry-lights, small and flickering and lonesome, wandered past, and the sound of the horses' hooves was deliberate and weary.

He came to the English Bridge and stood on the banks of the river, looking at the dark water swirling north toward the Mediterranean. Down the river a felucca, its immense sail spread in a soaring triangle, slowly made its way among the shadows from the trees along the shore.

Across the river a minaret, poignant with faith, shone sharp and delicate in the moonlight.

Peter felt spent and drained. A nervous and hysteric pulse pulled at his bad eye and a gigantic sob seemed wedged into his throat.

Overhead, far away, there was the sound of a plane. It came nearer, passed across the stars, died away, going somewhere.

The wedge dislodged and the sob broke out like tears and blood.

Peter closed his eyes, and when he opened them again the wild pulse had stopped, his throat was clear. He stared across the river at the minaret, faithful and lovely in the light of the moon, by the side of the old river.

Tomorrow, he thought, tomorrow there may be a letter from home. . . .

Gunners' Passage

"In Brazil," Whitejack was saying, "the problem was girls. American girls."

They were lying on the comfortable cots with the mosquito netting looped gracefully over their heads and the barracks quiet and empty except for the two of them and shaded and cool when you remembered that outside the full sun of Africa stared down.

"Three months in the jungle, on rice and monkey meat." Whitejack lit a large, long, nickel cigar and puffed deeply, squinting up at the tin roof. "When we got to Rio, we felt we deserved an American girl. So the Lieutenant and Johnny and myself, we got the telephone directory of the American Embassy, and we went down the list, calling up likely names—secretaries, typists, interpreters, filing clerks. . . ." Whitejack grinned up at the ceiling. He had a large, sunburned, rough face that was broken into good looks by the white teeth of his smile, and his speech was Southern, but not the kind of Southern that puts a Northerner's teeth on edge.

"It was the Lieutenant's idea, and by the time we got to the Q's he was ready to give up but we hit pay dirt on the S's." Slowly he blew out a long draught of cigar smoke. "Uh-uh," he said, closing his eyes reflectively. "Two

months and eleven days of honey and molasses. Three
tender and affectionate American girls as loving as the
day is long, with their own flat. Beer in the icebox from
Sunday to Sunday, steaks big enough to saddle a mule
with, and nothing to do, just lie on the beach in the afternoon and go swimmin' when the mood seized yuh. On
per diem."

"How were the girls?" Stais asked. "Pretty?"

"Well, Sergeant," Whitejack paused and pursed his
lips with thoughtful honesty. "To tell you the truth, Sergeant, the girls the Lieutenant and Johnny Moffat had
were as smart and pretty as chipmunks. Mine . . ." Once
more he paused. "Ordinarily, my girl would find herself
hard put to collect a man in the middle of a full division of
infantry soldiers. She was small and runty and she had less
curves than a rifle barrel, and she wore glasses. But from
the first time she looked at me, I could see she wasn't interested in Johnny or the Lieutenant. She looked at me
and behind her glasses her eyes were soft and hopeful and
humble and appealing." Whitejack flicked the cigar ash
off into the little tin can on his bare chest he was using as
an ash tray. "Sometimes," he said slowly, "a man feels
mighty small if he just thinks of himself and turns down
an appeal like that. Let me tell you something, Sergeant,
I was in Rio two months and eleven days and I didn't look
at another woman. All those dark-brown women walkin'
along the beach three-quarters out of their bathing suits,
just wavin' it in front of your face. . . . I didn't look at
them. This runty, skinny little thing with glasses was the
most lovin' and satisfactory and decent little person a man
could possibly conceive of, and a man'd just have to be
hog-greedy with sex to have winked an eye at another
woman." Whitejack doused his cigar, took his ash tray off
his chest, rolled over on his belly, adjusted the towel prop-
erly over his bare buttocks. "Now," he said, "I'm going to
get myself a little sleep. . . ."

In a moment Whitejack was snoring gently, his tough
mountaineer's face tucked childishly into the crook of

his arm. Outside the barracks the native boy hummed low and wild to himself as he ironed a pair of suntan trousers on the shady side of the building. From the field, two hundred yards away, again and again came the sliding roar of engines climbing or descending the afternoon sky.

Stais closed his eyes wearily. Ever since he'd got into Accra he had done nothing but sleep and lie on his cot, day-dreaming, listening to Whitejack talk.

"Hi," Whitejack had said, as Stais had come slowly into the barracks two days before, "which way you going?"

"Home," Stais had said, smiling wearily as he did every time he said it. "Going home. Which way you going?"

"Not home." Whitejack had grinned a little. "Not home at all."

Stais liked to listen to Whitejack. Whitejack talked about America, about the woods of the Blue Ridge Mountains where he had been in the forestry service, about his mother's cooking and how he had owned great dogs which had been extraordinary at finding a trail and holding it, about how they had tried hunting deer in the hills from the medium bomber, no good because of the swirling winds rising from the gorges, about pleasant indiscriminate week-end parties in the woods with his friend Johnny Moffat and the girls from the mill in the next town. . . . Stais had been away from America for nineteen months now and Whitejack's talk made his native country seem present and pleasantly real to him.

"There was a man in my town by the name of Thomas Wolfe," Whitejack had said irrelevantly that morning. "He was a great big feller and he went away to New York to be an author. Maybe you heard of him?"

"Yes," said Stais. "I read two books of his."

"Well, I read that book of his," said Whitejack, "and the people in town were yellin' to lynch him for a while, but I read that book and he got that town down fair and proper, and when they brought him back dead I came down from the hills and I went to his funeral. There were a lot of important people from New York and over to Chapel Hill down for the funeral and it was a hot day, too, and I'd never met the feller, but I felt it was only right to go to his funeral after readin' his book. And the whole town was there, very quiet, although just five years before they were yellin' to lynch him, and it was a sad and impressive sight and I'm glad I went."

And another time, the slow deep voice rolling between sleep and dreams in the shaded heat. . . . "My mother takes a quail and bones it, then she scoops out a great big sweet potato and lays some bacon on it, then she puts the quail in and cooks it slow for three hours, bastin' it with butter all the time. . . . You got to try that some time. . . ."

"Yes," said Stais, "I will."

Stais did not have a high priority number and there seemed to be a flood of colonels surging toward America, taking all the seats on the C-54's setting out westward, so he'd had to wait. It hadn't been bad. Just to lie down, stretched full-out, unbothered, these days, was holiday enough after Greece, and anyway he didn't want to arrive home, in front of his mother, until he'd stopped looking like a tired old man. And the barracks had been empty and quiet and the chow good at the transient mess and you could get Coca-Cola and chocolate milk at the PX. The rest of the enlisted men in Whitejack's crew were young and ambitious and were out swimming all day and going to the movies or playing poker in another barracks all night, and Whitejack's talk was smooth and amusing in the periods between sleep and dreams. Whitejack was an aerial photographer and gunner in a mapping-and-survey squadron and he'd been in Alaska and Brazil and back to the States and now was on his way to India, full of conversation. He was in a Mitchell squadron and the whole squadron was supposed to be on its way together, but two of the Mitchells had crashed and burned on the take-off at Natal, as Whitejack's plane had circled the field, waiting to form up. The rest of the squadron had been held at Natal and Whitejack's plane had been sent on to Accra across the ocean, by itself.

Vaguely and slowly, lying on the warm cot, with the wild song of the Negro boy outside the window, Stais thought of the two Mitchells burning between sea and jungle three thousand miles away, and other planes burning elsewhere, and what it was going to be like sitting down in the armchair in his own house and looking across the room at his mother, and the pretty Viennese girl in Jerusalem, and the DC-3 coming down slowly, like an angel in the dusk to the rough secret pasture in the Peloponnesian hills. . . .

He fell asleep. His bones knit gently into dreams on the soft cot, with the sheets, in the quiet barracks, and he was over Athens again, with the ruins pale and shining on the hills, and the fighters boring in, and Lathrop saying, over the intercom, as they persisted in to a hundred, fifty yards, twisting, swiftly and shiftily in the bright Greek sky, "They grounded all the students today. They have the instructors up this afternoon. . . ." And, suddenly, and wildly, fifty feet over Ploesti, with Liberators going down into the filth in dozens, flaming. . . . Then swimming off the white beach at Bengasi with the dead boys playing in the mild, tideless swell, then the parachute pulling at every muscle in his body, then the green and forest blue of Minnesota woods and his father, fat and small, sleeping on pine needles on his Sunday off, then Athens again, Athens . . .

"I don't know what's come over the Lieutenant," a new voice was saying as Stais came out of his dream. "He passes us on the field and he just don't seem to see us."

Stais opened his eyes. Novak, a farm boy from Oklahoma, was sitting on the edge of Whitejack's bed, talking. "It has all the guys real worried." He had a high, shy, rather girlish voice. "I used to think they never came better than the Lieutenant. . . . Now . . ." Novak shrugged. "If he does see you, he snaps at you like he was General George Patton."

"Maybe," Whitejack said, "maybe seeing Lieutenant Brogan go down in Natal . . . He and Brogan were friends since they were ten years old. Like as if I saw Johnny Moffat go down . . ."

"It's not that." Novak went over to his own cot and got out his writing pad. "It began back in Miami four weeks ago. Didn't you notice it?"

"I noticed it," Whitejack said slowly.

"You ought to ask him about it." Novak started writing a letter. "You and him are good friends. After all, going into combat now, it's bad, the Lieutenant just lookin' through us when he passes us on the field. You don't think he's drunk all the time, do you?"

"He's not drunk."

"You ought to ask him."

"Maybe I will." Whitejack sat up, tying the towel around his lean middle. "Maybe I will." He looked forlornly down at his stomach. "Since I got into the Army, I've turned pig-fat. On the day I took the oath, I was twenty-eight and one-half inches around the waist. Today I'm thirty-two and three-quarters, if I'm an inch. The Army . . . Maybe I shouldn't've joined. I was in a reserved profession, and I was the sole support of an ailing mother."

"Why did you join?" Stais asked.

"Oh," Whitejack smiled at him, "you're awake. Feeling any better, Sergeant?"

"Feeling fine, thanks. Why did you join?"

"Well . . ." Whitejack rubbed the side of his jaw. "Well . . . I waited and I waited. I sat up in my cabin in the hills and I tried to avoid listenin' to the radio, and I waited and I waited, and finally I went downtown to my mother and I said, 'Ma'am, I just can't wait any longer,' and I joined up."

"When was that?" Stais asked.

"Eight days . . ." Whitejack lay down again, plumping the pillow under his head. "Eight days after Pearl Harbor."

"Sergeant," Novak said, "Sergeant Stais, you don't mind if I tell my girl you're a Greek, do you?"

"No," Stais said gravely. "I don't mind. You know, I was born in Minnesota."

"I know," said Novak, writing industriously. "But your parents came from Greece. My girl'll be very interested, your parents coming from Greece and you bombing Greece and being shot down there."

"What do you mean, your girl?" Whitejack asked. "I thought you said she was going around with a Technical Sergeant in Flushing, Long Island."

"That's true," Novak said apologetically. "But I still like to think of her as my girl."

"It's the ones that stay at home," said Whitejack darkly, "that get all the stripes and all the girls. My motto is: Don't write to a girl once you get out of pillow-case distance from her."

"I like to write to this girl in Flushing, Long Island," Novak said, his voice shy but stubborn. Then to Stais, "How many days were you in the hills before the Greek farmers found you?"

"Fourteen," said Stais.

"And how many of you were wounded?"

"Three. Out of seven. The others were dead."

"Maybe," Whitejack said, "he doesn't like to talk about it, Charley."

"Oh, I'm sorry." Novak looked up, his young, unlined face crossed with concern.

"That's all right," Stais said. "I don't mind."

"Did you tell them you were a Greek, too?" Novak asked.

"When one finally showed up who could speak English."

"That must be funny," Novak said reflectively. "Being a Greek, bombing Greece, not speaking the language

. . . Can I tell my girl they had a radio and they radioed to Cairo . . . ?"

"It's the girl of a Technical Sergeant in Flushing, Long Island," Whitejack chanted. "Why don't you look facts in the face?"

"I prefer it this way," Novak said with dignity.

"I guess you can tell about the radio," Stais said. "It was pretty long ago. Three days later, the DC-3 came down through a break in the clouds. It'd been raining all the time and it just stopped for about thirty minutes at dusk and that plane came down throwin' water fifteen feet in the air. . . . We cheered, but we couldn't get up from where we were sitting, any of us, because we were too weak to stand."

"I got to write that to my girl," Novak said. "Too weak to stand."

"Then it started to rain again and the field was hip-deep in mud and when we all got into the DC-3, we couldn't get it started." Stais spoke calmly and thoughtfully, as though he were alone, reciting to himself. "We were just bogged down in that Greek mud. Then the pilot got out—he was a captain—and he looked around, with the rain coming down and all those farmers just standing there, sympathizing with him, and nothing anyone could do and he just cursed for ten minutes. He was from San Francisco and he really knew how to curse. Then everybody started breaking branches off the trees in the woods around that pasture, even two of us who couldn't stand one hour before, and we just covered that big DC-3 complete with branches and waited for the rain to stop. We just sat in the woods and prayed no German patrols would come out in weather like that. In those three days I learned five words of Greek."

"What are they?" Novak asked.

"*Vouno,*" Stais said. "That means mountain. *Vrohi:* Rains. *Theos:* God. *Avrion:* Tomorrow. And *Yassov:* That means farewell."

"*Yassov,*" Novak said. "Farewell."

"Then the sun came out and the field started to steam and nobody said anything. We just sat there, watching the water dry off the grass, then the puddles started to go here and there, then the mud to cake a little. Then we got into the DC-3 and the Greeks pushed and hauled for a while and we broke loose and got out. And those farmers just standing below waving at us, as though they were seeing us off at Grand Central Station. Ten miles farther on we went right over a German camp. They fired at us a couple of times, but they didn't come anywhere close. The best moment of my whole life was getting into that hospital bed in Cairo, Egypt. I just stood there and looked at it for a whole minute, looking at the sheets. Then I got in very slow."

"Did you ever find out what happened to those Greeks?" Novak asked.

"No," said Stais. "I guess they're still there, waiting for us to come back some day."

There was silence, broken only by the slow scratching of Novak's pen. Stais thought of the thin, dark mountain faces of the men he had last seen, fading away, waving, standing in the scrub and short silver grass of the hill pasture near the Aegean Sea. They had been cheerful and anxious to please, and there was a look on the faces that made you feel they expected to die.

"How many missions were you on?" Novak asked.

"Twenty-one and a half," Stais said. He smiled. "I count the last one as half."

"How old are you?" Novak was obviously keeping the Technical Sergeant's girl carefully posted on all points of interest.

"Nineteen."

"You look older," said Whitejack.

"Yes," said Stais.

"A lot older."

"Yes."

"Did you shoot down any planes?" Novak peered at

him shyly, his red face uncertain and embarrassed, like a little boy asking a doubtful question about girls. "Personally?"

"Two," Stais said. "Personally."

"What did you feel?"

"Why don't you leave him alone?" Whitejack said. "He's too tired to keep his eyes open, as it is."

"I felt—relieved," Stais said. He tried to think of what he'd really felt when the tracers went in and the Focke-Wolfe started to smoke like a crazy smudge pot and the German pilot fought wildly for half a second with the cowling and then didn't fight wildly any more. There was no way of telling these men, no way of remembering, in words, himself. "You'll find out," he said. "Soon enough. The sky's full of Germans."

"Japs," Whitejack said. "We're going to India."

"The sky's full of Japs."

There was silence once more, with the echo of the word "Japs" rustling thinly in the long, quiet room, over the empty rows of cots. Stais felt the old waving dizziness starting behind his eyes that the doctor in Cairo had said came from shock or starvation or exposure or all of these things, and lay back, still keeping his eyes open, as it became worse and waved more violently when he closed his eyes.

"One more question," Novak said. "Are—are guys afraid?"

"You'll be afraid," Stais said.

"Do you want to send that back to your girl in Flushing?" Whitejack asked sardonically.

"No," said Novak quietly. "I wanted that for myself."

"If you want to sleep," said Whitejack, "I'll shut this farmer up."

"Oh, no," said Stais, "I'm pleased to talk."

"If you're not careful," Whitejack said, "he'll talk about his girl in Flushing."

"I'd be pleased to hear it," said Stais.

"It's only natural I should want to talk about her," Novak said defensively. "She was the best girl I ever knew in my whole life. I'd've married her if I could."

"My motto," said Whitejack, "is never marry a girl who goes to bed with you the first time out. The chances are she isn't pure. The second time—that, of course, is different." He winked at Stais.

"I was in Flushing, Long Island, taking a five-weeks' course in aerial cameras," Novak said, "and I was living at the YMCA. . . ."

"This is where I leave." Whitejack got off the bed and put on his pants.

"The YMCA was very nice. There were bathrooms for every two rooms, and the food was very good," said Novak, talking earnestly to Stais, "but I must confess, I was lonely in Flushing, Long Island. . . ."

"I will be back," Whitejack was buttoning up his shirt, "for the ninth installment."

"As long as you're going out," Novak said to him, "I wish you'd talk to the Lieutenant. It really makes me feel queer passing him, and him just looking through me like I was a window pane."

"Maybe I'll talk to the Lieutenant. And leave the Sergeant alone. Remember he's a tired man who's been to the war and he needs his rest." Whitejack went out.

Novak stared after him. "There's something wrong with him, too," he said. "Just lying on his back here for ten days, reading and sleeping. He never did that before. He was the liveliest man in the United States Air Force. Seeing those two planes go down . . . It's a funny thing, you fly with fellers all over the world, over America, Brazil, Alaska; you watch them shoot porpoises and sharks in gunnery practice over the Gulf Stream, you get drunk with them, go to their weddings, talk to them over the radio with their planes maybe a hundred feet away, in the air—and after all that flying, in one minute, for no reason, two planes go down. Fourteen fellers you've been livin' with for over a year. . . ." Novak shook his head.

"There was a particular friend of Whitejack's in one of those planes. Frank Sloan. Just before we left Miami, they had a big fight. Frank went off and married a girl that Whitejack's been going with off and on for a year, every time we hit Miami. Whitejack told him he was crazy, half the squadron had slept with the lady, and that was true, too, and just to teach him a lesson he'd sleep with her himself after they'd been married. And he did, too. . . ." Novak sighed. "A lot of funny things happen in the army, when fellers've been together a long time and get to know each other real well. And then, one minute, the Mitchell goes down. I guess Whitejack must've felt sort of queer, watching Frankie burn." Novak had put his writing pad down and now he screwed the top on his fountain pen. "The truth is," he said, "I don't feel so solid myself. That's why I like to talk. Especially to you . . . You've been through it. You're young, but you've been through it. But if it's any bother to you, I'll keep quiet. . . ."

"No," said Stais, still lying back, abstractedly wondering whether the waving would get worse or better, "not at all."

"This girl in Flushing, Long Island," Novak said slowly. "It's easy for Whitejack to make fun of me. The girls fall all over themselves chasing after him; he has no real conception of what it's like to be a man like me. Not very good-looking. Not much money. Not an officer. Not humorous. Shy."

Stais couldn't help grinning. "You're going to have a tough time in India."

"I know," Novak said. "I have resigned myself to not having a girl until the armistice. How did you do with the girls in the Middle East?" he asked politely.

"There was a nice Viennese girl in Jerusalem," Stais said dreamily. "But otherwise zero. You have to be very good unless you're an officer in the Middle East."

"That's what I heard," Novak said sorrowfully. "Well, it won't be so different to me from Oklahoma. That was the nice thing about this girl in Flushing, Long Island.

She saw me come into the jewelry store where she worked and . . . I was in my fatigues and I was with a very smooth feller who made a date with her for that night. But she smiled at me, and I knew if I had the guts I could ask her for a date, too. But of course I didn't. But then later that night I was sitting in my room in the YMCA and my phone rang. It was this girl. The other feller had stood her up, she said, and would I take her out." Novak smiled dimly, thinking of that tremulous moment of glory in the small hotel room far away. "I got my fatigues off in one minute and shaved and showered and I picked her up. We went to Coney Island. It was the first time in my entire life I had ever seen Coney Island. It took three and a half weeks for me to finish my course and I went out with that girl every single night. Nothing like that ever happened to me before in my life—a girl who just wanted to see me every night of the week. Then the night before I was due to leave to join my squadron she told me she had got permission to take the afternoon off and she would like to see me off if I let her. I called at the jewelry shop at noon and her boss shook my hand and she had a package under her arm and we got into the subway and we rode to New York City. Then we went into a cafeteria and had a wonderful lunch and she saw me off and gave me the package. It was Schrafft's candy, and she was crying at the gate there, crying for me, and she said she would like me to write, no matter what . . ." Novak paused and Stais could tell that the scene at the gate, the hurrying crowds, the package of Schrafft's chocolates, the weeping young girl, were as clear as the afternoon sunlight to Novak there on the coast of Africa. "So I keep writing," Novak said. "She's written me she has a Technical Sergeant now, but I keep writing. I haven't seen her in a year and a half and what's a girl to do? Do you blame her?"

"No," said Stais, "I don't blame her."

"I hope I haven't bored you," Novak said.

"Not at all." Stais smiled at him. Suddenly the dizziness had gone and he could close his eyes. As he drifted down into that weird and ever-present pool of sleep in which he half-lived these days, he heard Novak say,

"Now I have to write my mother."

Outside, the Negro boy sang and the planes grumbled down from the Atlantic and laboriously set out across the Sahara Desert.

Dreams again. Arabs, bundled in rags, driving camels along the perimeter of the field, outlined against the parked Liberators and waiting bombs, two Mitchells still burning on the shores of Brazil and Frank Sloan burning there and circling above him, Whitejack, who had told him he'd sleep with his wife and had, the hills around Jerusalem, gnarled, rocky, dusty, with the powdered green of olive groves set on slopes here and there, clinging against the desert wind, Mitchells slamming along the gorges of the Blue Ridge Mountains, bucking in the up-draughts, their guns going, hunting deer, the Mediterranean, bluer than anything in America, below them on the way home from Italy, coming down below oxygen level, with the boys singing dirty songs over the intercom and leave in Alexandria ahead of them. The girl from Flushing, Long Island, quietly going hand in hand with Novak to Coney Island on a summer's night. . . .

It was Whitejack who awakened him. He woke slowly. It was dark outside and the electric light was shining in his eyes and Whitejack was standing over him, shaking him gently.

"I thought you'd like to know," Whitejack was saying, "your name's on the bulletin board. You're leaving to-night."

"Thanks," Stais said, dimly grateful at being shaken out of the broken and somehow sorrowful dreams.

"I took the liberty of initialing it for you, opposite your name," Whitejack said. "Save you a trip up to the field."

"Thanks," said Stais. "Very kind of you."

"Also," said Whitejack, "there's fried chicken for chow."

Stais pondered over the fried chicken. He was a little hungry, but the effort of getting up and putting on his shoes and walking the hundred yards to the mess hall had to be weighed in the balance. "Thanks. I'll just lie right here," he said. "Any news of your boys?" he asked.

"Yes," said Whitejack. "The squadron came in."

"That's good."

"All except one plane." Whitejack sat down on the end of Stais' cot. His voice was soft and expressionless, under the bright electric light. "Johnny Moffat's plane."

In all the months that Stais had been in the air force, on fields to which planes had failed to return, he had learned that there was nothing to say. He was only nineteen years old, but he had learned that. So he lay quiet.

"They got separated in clouds on the way out of Ascension, and they never picked them up again. There's still a chance," Whitejack said, "that they'll drop in any minute." He looked at his watch. "Still a chance for another hour and forty minutes . . ."

There was still nothing to say, so Stais lay silent.

"Johnny Moffat," said Whitejack, "at one time looked as though he was going to marry my sister. In a way, it's a good thing he didn't. It'd be a little hard, being brothers-in-law, on some of the parties the air force goes on in one place and another." Whitejack fell silent, looked down at his belly. Deliberately, he let his belt out a notch. He pulled it to, with a severe little click. "That fried chicken was mighty good," he said. "You sure you want to pass it up?"

"I'm saving my appetite," Stais said, "for my mother's cooking."

"My sister," said Whitejack, "was passing fond of Johnny, and I have a feeling when he gets home from the war and settles down, she's going to snag him. She came to me right before I left and she asked me if I would let her have ten acres on the north side of my property and three acres of timber to build their house. I said it was OK with me." He was silent again, thinking of the rolling ten acres of upland meadow in North Carolina and the three tall acres of standing timber, oak and pine, from which it would be possible to build a strong country house. "There's nobody in the whole world I'd rather have living on my property than Johnny Moffat. I've known him for twenty years and I've had six fist fights with him and won them all, and been alone with him in the woods for two months at a time, and I still say that. . . ." He got up and went over to his own cot, then turned and came back. "By the way," he said softly, "this is between you and me, Sergeant."

"Sure," said Stais.

"My sister said she'd murder me for my hide and taller if I ever let Johnny know what was in store for him." He grinned a little. "Women're very confident in certain fields," he said. "And I never did tell Johnny, not even when I was so drunk I was singing 'Casey Jones' naked in the middle of the city of Tampa at three o'clock in the morning." He went over to his musette bag and got out a cigar and thoughtfully lit it. "You'd be surprised," he said, "how fond you become of nickel cigars in the Army."

"I tried smoking," said Stais. "I think I'll wait until I get a little older."

Whitejack sat heavily on his own cot. "Do you think they'll send you out to fight again?" he asked.

Stais stared up at the ceiling. "I wouldn't be surprised," he said. "There's nothing really wrong with me. I'm just tired."

Whitejack nodded, smoking slowly. "By the way," he said, "you heard us talking about the Lieutenant, didn't you?"

"Yes."

"I went out to the field and had a little conversation with him. He's just been sittin' there all day and most of the night since we got here, outside the Operations room, just lookin' and starin' across at the planes comin' in. Him and me, we've been good friends for a long time and I asked him pointblank. I said, 'Freddie,' I said, 'there's a question the boys're askin' themselves these days about you.' And he said, 'What's the matter?' And I said, 'The boys're asking if you've turned bad. You pass 'em and you don't even look at them as though you recognize 'em. What is it, you turn GI after a year?' I said. He looked at me and then he looked at the ground and he didn't say anything for maybe a minute. Then he said, 'I beg your pardon, Arnold. It never occurred to me.' Then he told me what was on his mind." Whitejack looked at his watch, almost automatically, then lifted his head again. "Ever since we got the order to go overseas he's been worrying. About the waist gunner and his navigator."

"What's he worrying about?" For a moment a crazy list of all the thousand things you can worry about in the crew of one airplane flashed through Stais' head.

"They're not fighting men," Whitejack said slowly. "They're both good fellers, you wouldn't want better, but the Lieutenant's been watchin' 'em for a long time on the ground, in the air, at their guns, and he's convinced they won't measure. And he feels he's responsible for taking the Mitchell in and getting it out with as many of us alive as possible and he feels the waist gunner and the navigator're dangerous to have in the plane. And he's makin' up his mind to put in a request for two new men when we get to India, and he can't bear to think of what it'll do to the gunner and the navigator when they find out he's asked to have 'em grounded, and that's why he just sits there outside Operations, not even seein' us when we go by. . . ." Whitejack sighed. "He's twenty-two years old, the Lieutenant. It's a strain, something like that, for a man twenty-two years old. If you see Novak, you won't tell him anything, will you?"

"No," said Stais.

"I suppose things like this come up all the time in any army."

"All the time," said Stais.

Whitejack looked at his watch. Outside there was the

growing and lapsing roar of engines that had been the constant sound of both their lives for so many months.

"Ah," said Whitejack, "they should've put me in the infantry. I can hit a rabbit at three hundred yards with a rifle; they put me in the Air Force and give me a camera. . . . Well, Sergeant, I think it's about time you were movin'."

Slowly, Stais got up. He put on his shoes and put his shaving kit into his musette bag and slung it over his shoulder.

"You ready?" asked Whitejack.

"Yes," said Stais.

"That all the baggage you got—that little musette bag?"

"Yes," said Stais. "I was listed as missing, presumed dead, and they sent all my stuff into the supply room and all my personal belongings home to my mother."

Stais looked around the barracks. It shone in the harsh army light of barracks at night all over the world, by now familiar, homelike, to all the men who passed through them. He had left nothing.

They walked out into the soft, engine-filled night. A beacon flashed nervously across the sky, diming the enormous pale twinkle of Southern stars for a moment. They walked slowly, stepping cautiously over the ditches dug for the flood rains of the African West Coast.

As they passed the Operations room, Stais saw a young lieutenant slumped down in a wobbly old wicker chair, staring out across the field.

"They come yet?" Whitejack asked.

"No," said the Lieutenant, without looking up.

Stais went into the building and into the room where they had the rubber raft and the patented radio and the cloth painted blue on one side and yellow on the other. A fat middle-aged ATC captain wearily told them about ditching procedure. There were more than thirty people in the room, all passengers on Stais's plane. There were two small, yellow Chinese who were going to be airsick and five bouncing fat Red Cross women, and three sergeants with a lot of Air Force medals, trying not to seem excited about going home, and two colonels in the Engineers, looking too old for this war. Stais only half listened as the fat captain explained how to inflate the raft, what strings to pull, what levers to move, where to find the waterproofed Bible. . . .

Whitejack was standing outside when Stais started for his plane. He gave Stais a slip of paper. "It's my home address," he said. "After the war, just come down sometime in October and I'll take you hunting."

"Thank you very much," said Stais gravely. Over Whitejack's shoulder he saw the Lieutenant, still slumped in the wicker chair, still staring fixedly and unrelievedly out across the dark field.

Whitejack walked out to the great plane with Stais, along the oil-spattered concrete of the runway, among the Chinese and loud Red Cross women and the sergeants. They stopped, without a word, at the steps going up to the doorway of the plane and the other passengers filed past them.

They stood there, silently, with the two days of random conversation behind them and Brazil and Athens behind them, and five hundred flights behind them, and Jerusalem and Miami behind them, and the girls from Vienna and the American Embassy and Flushing, Long Island, behind them, and the Greek mountaineers behind them and Thomas Wolfe's funeral, and friends burning like torches, and dogs under treed raccoons in the Blue Ridge Mountains behind them, and a desperate twenty-two-year-old Lieutenant painfully staring across a dusty airfield for ten days behind them, and the Mediterranean and the hospital bed in Cairo and Johnny Moffat wandering that night over the Southern Atlantic, with ten acres of meadow and three acres of timber for his house, and Whitejack's sister waiting for him, all behind them. And, ahead of Stais, home and a mother who had presumed him dead and wept over his personal belongings, and

ahead of Whitejack the cold bitter mountains of India and
China and the tearing dead sound of the fifties and the
sky full of Japs. . . .

"All right, Sergeant," the voice of the Lieutenant checking the passengers. "Get on."

Stais waved, a little broken wave, at Whitejack standing there. "See you," he said, "in North Carolina."

"Some October." Whitejack smiled a little in the light
of the floodlamps.

The door closed and Stais sat down in the seat in front
of the two Chinese.

"I think these planes are absolutely charming," one of
the Red Cross women was saying loudly. "Don't you?"

The engines started and the big plane began to roll.
Stais looked out of the window. A plane was landing. It
came slowly into the light of the runway lamps and set
down heavily, bumping wearily. Stais stared. It was a
Mitchell. Stais sighed to himself. As the big C-54 wheeled
at the head of the runway, then started clumsily down,
Stais put the slip of paper with Arnold Whitejack written
on it, and the address, in scrawling, childlike handwriting,
into his pocket. And as he saw the Mitchell pull to a stop
near the Operations room, he felt for the moment a little
less guilty for going home.

Medal from Jerusalem

"The question that haunts me," Schneider was saying in his high, soft voice, "is, my jazz, is it real jazz or is it merely European jazz?" He was leaning against the bar of the Patio restaurant between Tel Aviv and Jaffa, which used to be the old German consulate, and speaking to Lieutenant Mitchell Gunnison in short, gaspy bursts of talk, smiling a little sadly and a little archly at Mitchell, and occasionally touching his sleeve lightly with the tips of his fingers. "I mean," he said, "I know it's good enough for Palestine, but in America what would they say about a pianist like me?"

"Well," said Gunnison gravely, "I'd say they'd think it was real jazz." He was young and he spoke slowly and he seemed to think very hard before he answered a question.

"You don't know," Schneider said, sighing, "how you've encouraged me. I listen to the records, of course, but they're old, and you never know what actually is going on in America and, after all, we all know there *is* no other jazz, no place, and with a war like this, and God knows how long it's going to last, a musician gets out of touch. And once you are out of touch, you might as well die. Just die."

"You have nothing to worry about," Mitchell said. "You'll be a sensation in America."

"If I ever get there." Schneider smiled sadly and shrugged a little. "Anyway, you must come tomorrow. I'm working on a new arrangement with the drummer. A rumba, Viennese style. It's ridiculous, but I think you'll like it."

"I'm sorry," Mitchell said. "I won't be here tomorrow."

"Then next night," said Schneider.

"I won't be here then, either," Mitchell said. "I'm going tomorrow. Leave's up."

There was a little silence and Schneider looked down at the bar and flicked his beer glass with his fingernail, making a frail musical sound in the dark oak barroom. "Some more fighting?" Schneider asked.

"A little more fighting." Mitchell nodded soberly.

"You fly, no doubt," said Schneider. "I have no wish to intrude on military information, but the wings on the chest . . ."

"I'm a navigator." Mitchell smiled at him.

"It must be an interesting profession. Measuring the distance between one star and another star." Schneider finished his beer slowly. "Well, *sholom aleichem* . . . That's good luck. Or, to be more exact, peace be with you."

"Thank you," Mitchell said.

"Hebrew," said Schneider. "I'm ashamed to talk Hebrew to anybody who knows it. The accent, they tell me, is frightful. But you don't mind, do you?"

"No," said Mitchell. He turned to the bartender. "Mr. Abrams," he said, "another beer please, for Mr. Schneider."

"No, no." Schneider waved his hands in protest. "The artist should not drink before the performance. After . . . Another matter . . . Ah," he said, bowing elaborately, "*Fräulein,* we are enchanted."

Mitchell turned around. Ruth was standing there, looking a little hurried and out of breath, but smiling, and as pretty as ever in a light cotton dress, with her skin burned dark by the sun and her eyes full of welcome and pleasure at seeing him.

"I was afraid," she said, coming over to him and taking his hand, "I was afraid you were going to be angry and leave."

"I wasn't going to leave," Mitchell said. "Not until they closed the doors on me and threw me out."

"I am delighted." Ruth laughed and squeezed his arm. "I am so absolutely delighted."

"My presence," Schneider said, bowing, "I no longer consider necessary. A hundred thanks for the beer, Lieutenant. Now I play or Mr. Abrams will start complaining he is not getting his money's worth out of me. Listen, carefully, if it is not too much of a bore, to my version of 'Stardust.' "

"We'll listen very carefully," Mitchell said.

Schneider went outside to the patio, and a moment later preliminary erratic runs and fragments of melody came floating into the bar as he warmed up for the night's work.

"So." Ruth faced him, looking at him with an expression that was half ownership, half amusement. "So. What have we been doing all day?"

"Well," Mitchell started, "we . . ."

"You are the most beautiful lieutenant in the American army," Ruth said, grinning.

"Well, we went swimming," Mitchell said, pleased and embarrassed, pretending she'd said nothing. "And we hung around on the beach. And we flew a couple of barroom missions. Gin and grapefruit juice."

"Isn't Palestinian grapefruit wonderful?" Ruth asked loyally.

"Sensational," Mitchell said. "Nothing like it in America."

"You're such a liar." Ruth leaned over and kissed him lightly.

"There was an Eighth Air Force pilot down from England," Mitchell said, "and he told us how tough it was over Wilhelmshaven and we told the lies about Ploesti and then it was time to shave and come to see you."

"What did you think while you were shaving? Were you sad because you had to leave your interesting friends and see me?"

"Broken-hearted," Mitchell said.

"You've got such a nice, skinny face," Ruth touched the line of his jaw. "You're as pretty as an English lieutenant. I'm not fond of the English, but they have the prettiest lieutenants of any army."

"We send our pretty ones to the Pacific," said Mitchell. "Guadalcanal. We preserve them for American womanhood."

Ruth signaled Mr. Abrams for a drink. "I was in Jerusalem today. I told my boss I was sick and went there. It's so bad—we never got to see Jerusalem together."

"Some other time," Mitchell said. "I'll come back and we'll see Jerusalem."

"Don't lie to me," Ruth said, seriously. "Please don't lie. You won't come back. You won't see me again. Absolutely no lies, please."

Mitchell felt very young. He felt there was something to be said, and an older man would know how to say it, but he felt dumb and bereaved and clumsy, and it must have showed on his face as he peered at his glass, because Ruth laughed and touched his lips with her fingers and said, "You have such a tragic face for an American. Where do you come from in America?"

"Vermont," Mitchell said.

"Has everybody got a face like yours in Vermont?"

"Everybody."

"I will visit there," Ruth drained her glass, "at some later date."

"I'll give you my address," Mitchell said.

"Of course," said Ruth politely. "You must write it down some time."

They went out into the patio and sat down at a table

on the old flagstones under a palm tree, with the blue blackout lights shining dimly over the uniforms and pale dresses, and the moon riding over the Mediterranean and casting flickering shadows over the dancers who now claimed the spot where the German consul had lived well in days gone by. Mitchell ordered champagne because it was his last night. It was Syrian champagne, but not bad, and to both of them it gave an air of festivity and importance to the evening, as it rocked in its silver bucket of ice. Eric, the waiter with the limp, ceremoniously took Ruth's ration tickets, and Schneider, seated with the drummer across the patio, with the drum dimly lit from inside by an orange light of which Schneider was very proud, played "Summertime" because he had decided that was the song Mitchell liked best. The old song, played trickily and well in the soft, echoing patio, somehow sounded, by some ineradicable stamp in Schneider's blood, like Carolina and Vienna and the Balkans, with here and there chords of an old Hebrew chant, quite just and indigenous here between the heavy stone walls on the edge of the Sinai desert.

"I'm jealous of him," said Ruth, speaking over the edge of her glass.

"Who?"

"Schneider."

"Why?" Mitchell asked.

"Because of the way he looks at you. He's crazy about you. Has he asked you to come to tea with him and his mother?"

"Yes," said Mitchell, trying not to smile.

"I'll tear his eyes out," Ruth said. "I'm jealous of anybody who looks at you that way. The girls back in Vermont and those Red Cross girls."

"You have nothing to worry about," Mitchell said. "Nobody looks at me that way. Not even Schneider or you."

"That's the nicest thing about you," Ruth said. "You don't know anything. I'm so used to men who know just how many steps out of bed each look a woman gives them measures. I must visit America after the war. . . ."

"Where will you really go?" Mitchell asked. "Back to Berlin?"

"No." Ruth stared reflectively down at her plate. "No, not back to Berlin. Never back to Berlin. The Germans have made clear their feeling about me. A little thing like a war will not change them. The lamb does not go back to the slaughterhouse. Anyway, I have nobody there. There was a young man . . ." She leaned over and picked up the bottle and absently poured for Mitchell and herself. "I don't know what happened to him. Stalingrad, maybe, Alamein . . . who knows?"

Four men came into the patio and walked through the brief illumination of the blue lights. Three of them were Arabs in European dress, and the fourth was a man in the uniform of the American Army with the civilian technical adviser patch on his shoulder. They stopped at the table. The three Arabs bowed a little, ceremoniously, to Ruth, and the American said, "I thought you were sick."

"This is Mr. Carver," Ruth said to Mitchell, with a wave to the American. "He's my boss."

"Hi, Lieutenant," said Carver. He was a big, fat man, with a weary, puffy, intelligent face. He turned back to Ruth. "I thought you were sick," he repeated in a pleasant, loud, slightly drunken voice.

"I was sick," Ruth said, cheerfully. "I had a miraculous recovery."

"The American Army," Carver said, "expects every civilian worker to do her duty."

"Tomorrow," said Ruth. "Now please go away with your friends. The lieutenant and I are having an intimate talk."

"Lieutenant . . ." It was one of the Arabs, the shortest of the three, a slight, dark man, with a round face and liquid, veiled eyes. "My name is Ali Khazen. Permit me to introduce myself, as no one here seems to remember his manners well enough to do so."

Mitchell stood up. "Mitchell Gunnison," he said, putting out his hand.

"Forgive me," Carver said. "I'm suffering from drink. This is Sayed Taif . . ." He indicated the tallest of the Arabs, a middle-aged man with a severe, handsome, tight-lipped face. Mitchell shook hands with him.

"He doesn't like Americans," Carver said loudly. "He's the leading journalist of the local Arab world and he writes for thirty-five papers in the United States and he doesn't like Americans."

"What was that?" Taif asked politely, inclining his head in a reserved, small gesture.

"Also, he's deaf," said Carver. "Most useful equipment for any journalist."

Nobody bothered to introduce the third Arab, who stood a little to one side, watching Taif with a fierce, admiring stare, like a boxer dog at his master's feet.

"Why don't you all go away and eat your dinner?" Ruth said.

"Lieutenant," Carver said, ignoring her, "take the advice of a veteran of the Middle East. Do not become involved with Palestine."

"He's not becoming involved with Palestine," Ruth said. "He's becoming involved with me."

"Beware Palestine." Carver weaved a little as he spoke. "The human race is doomed in Palestine. For thousands of years. They chop down the forests, burn down the cities, wipe out the inhabitants. This is no place for an American."

"You drink too much, Mr. Carver," Ruth said.

"Nevertheless," Carver shook his big head heavily, "it is no accident that they picked this place to crucify Christ. You couldn't pick a better place to crucify Christ if you scoured the maps of the world for five hundred years. I'm a Quaker myself, from the city of Philadelphia, Pennsylvania, and all I see here is the blood of bleeding humanity. When this war is over I'm going back to Philadelphia and wait until I pick up the morning newspaper

and read that everybody in Palestine has exterminated
everybody else in Palestine the night before." He walked
unsteadily over to Ruth's chair and bent over and peered
intently into her face. "Beautiful girl," he said, "beautiful, forlorn girl." He straightened up. "Gunnison, I ad-
monish you, as an officer and gentleman, do not harm
one hair on this beautiful girl's head."

"Every hair," Mitchell said, gravely, "is safe with me."

"If you must drink," Ruth said to Carver sharply, "why
don't you do it with Americans? Why do you have to go
around with bandits and murderers like these?" She
waved her hand toward the Arabs. The journalist smiled,
his handsome face frosty and amused in the wavering
light.

"Impartiality," Carver boomed. "American impartiality.
We are famous for it. We are nobody's friend and no-
body's enemy. We merely build airfields and pipelines.
Impartially. Tomorrow I lunch with the President of the
Jewish Agency."

Ruth turned to the journalist. "Taif," she said, loudly,
"I read your last piece."

"Ah, yes," he said, his voice a little dead and without
timbre. "Did you like it?"

"You'll be responsible for the death of thousands of
Jews," said Ruth.

"Ah, thank you," he said. He smiled. "It is my fondest
hope." He turned to Mitchell. "Naturally, Lieutenant,"
he said, "our charming little Ruth is biased in the matter.
It is necessary to give the Arab side of the proposition."
He began to speak more seriously, with a severe, oratorical emphasis, like an evangelical preacher. "The world is
dazzled by the Jewish accomplishment in Palestine. Fine,
clean cities, with plumbing. Industries. Where once was
desert, now the rose and the olive bloom. Et cetera."

"Taif, old boy," Carver pulled at his arm, "let's eat and
you can lecture the lieutenant some other time."

"No, if you please." The journalist pulled his arm politely away from Carver's hand. "I welcome the oppor-

tunity to talk to our American friends. You see, my good Lieutenant, you may be very pleased with the factory and the plumbing, and perhaps, even, from one point of view, they may be good things. But they have nothing to do with the Arab. Perhaps the Arab prefers the desert as it was. The Arab has his own culture. . . ."

"When I hear the word 'culture,' " Carver said, "I reach for my pistol. What famous American said that?"

"To Americans and Europeans," the journalist went on, in his singsong, dead voice, "the culture of the Arab perhaps seems backward and dreadful. But, forgive us, the Arab prefers it. The virtues which are particularly Arab are kept alive by primitive living. They die among the plumbing."

"Now," said Ruth, "we have heard a new one. Kill the Jew because he brings the shower bath."

The journalist smiled indulgently at Ruth, as at a clever child. "Personally," he said, "I have nothing against the Jews. I swear that I do not wish to harm a single Jew living in Palestine today. But I will fight to the death to keep even one more Jew from entering the country. This is an Arab state, and it must remain an Arab state."

"Gunnison," Carver said, "aren't you glad you came?"

"Six million Jews have died in Europe," Ruth said, her voice harsh and passionate, and surprising to Mitchell. "Where do you want the survivors to go?" She and the journalist had forgotten the rest of them and were locked with each other across the table.

The journalist shrugged and looked for a moment up above the palm fronds at the dark sky. "That," he said, "is a question for the world to decide. Why must the poor Arab have the whole decision? We've taken in much more than our share. If the rest of the world really wants to see the Jewish race survive let them take them in. America, Britain, Russia . . . I do not notice those large countries taking in great masses of Jews."

"There are no great masses," Ruth said. "There is only a handful."

Taif shrugged. "Even so. The truth may be, perhaps," he paused, a little doubtfully, reminding Mitchell of an old Latin teacher in a class in Cicero, shrewdly hesitating for effect, before telling the class whether the word in question was in the ablative or dative absolute, "the truth may be that the rest of the world really wants to see the Jewish race die out." He turned and smiled warmly at Mitchell. "It is an interesting supposition, Lieutenant. It might be most interesting to examine it before talking any more about Palestine." He walked over to Ruth and leaned over and kissed her fleetingly on the forehead. "Good night, little Ruth," he said, and went to a table across the patio, with the silent, adoring Arab behind him.

"If I see you with that man once more," Ruth spoke to the man who had introduced himself to Mitchell, and who had remained standing at their table, "I'll never talk to you again."

The Arab looked swiftly at Mitchell, a veiled, probing flick of the eyes, and said something to Ruth in Arabic.

"No," said Ruth, her voice clipped and sharp. "Definitely no."

The Arab bowed slightly, put out his hand to Mitchell and, as they shook hands, said, "Very pleasant meeting you, Lieutenant," and went off to join his friends at their table.

"Thé dansants in old Tel Aviv," said Carver. "Bring the kiddies. Good night." He waddled over to the other table.

"Ruth," Mitchell started to talk.

"Lieutenant Gunnison . . ." It was the soft, apologetic voice of Schneider at his elbow. "I am so anxious for your opinion. What did you think of 'Stardust'?"

Mitchell turned slowly from staring at Ruth, who was sitting tense and upright in her chair. "Great, Schneider," Mitchell said. "I thought it was sensational."

Schneider beamed with pleasure. "You are too kind," he said. "I will play you 'Summertime' once more."

"Thanks a lot," said Mitchell. He put out his hand and

covered Ruth's, lying on the table. "You all right?" he asked.

She smiled up at him. "Sure," she said. "I am an admirer of abstract political discussions." Her face grew serious. "Do you want to know what Khazen asked when he spoke to me in Arabic?"

"Not if you don't want to tell me."

"I want to tell you." Ruth absently caressed his fingers. "He asked me if I would meet him later."

"Yes," said Mitchell.

"I told him no."

"I heard you." Mitchell grinned at her. "They probably heard you in Cairo."

"I didn't want you to feel disturbed or doubtful," Ruth said, "your last night."

"I feel fine," Mitchell said.

"I've been going with him for four years." She played for a moment with the food on the plate that the waiter had put before her. "When I came here in the beginning I was frightened and lonely and he was very decent. He's a contractor for the Americans and British and he's made a fortune during the war. But when Rommel was outside Alexandria he and his friends used to celebrate in secret. I can't stand him any more. I tell him when I take up with other men. But he hangs on. Ah, finally, I suppose he'll get me to marry him. I'm not strong enough any more." She looked up at Mitchell and tried to smile. "Don't be shocked, darling," she said. "Americans can't understand how tired the human race can get." She stood up suddenly. "Let's dance."

They went onto the floor and Schneider broke into "Summertime" when he saw them and smiled fondly at them as they danced. She danced very well, lightly and passionately, and Mitchell knew as he danced that he was going to remember this for a long time, at odd moments, swinging away from targets with the flak falling off behind him, and later, if he made it, in the snowy hills of his home state, the light, soft pressure of the bright cotton dress, the dark, curved, delicate face below his, the hushed sound of their feet on the old floor under the palms, the clever, rich music of the piano under the small blue lights strung out from the stone building. There were a million things that crowded his throat that he wanted to tell her, and there was no way of saying them. He kissed her cheek as the music ended, and she glanced up at him, and smiled and said, "There, that's better," and they were laughing by the time they got back to their table.

He paid the bill and they went out, saying good night to Schneider, not looking back at the table where Carver and the three Arabs sat, but hearing Carver's deep voice rolling through the music and the darkness, calling, "Does anyone want an airfield? I'll build it for him. Does anyone want a crown of thorns? I'll build it for him."

There was an old carriage waiting outside the restaurant, its driver dozing and its lights dimmed, and they climbed in and sat close together as the driver clucked to the horse and they rattled slowly back toward town. The breeze had gone down as it did at nine o'clock every night, and there was a small, warm breath of salt off the Mediterranean and every once in a while a jeep rushed past in a whistle of American wind, with its slits of cat's-eye lights cutting a darting, frail, skidding pattern in the darkness, making the creakings and rustlings of the old carriage older and dearer and more private as they sat there holding on to each other in silence.

They got off a block from where Ruth lived because the people from whom she rented her room were intensely moral and did not approve of their boarder going out with soldiers. They walked past the corner where the Italian bombers had killed a hundred and thirty people on a Friday morning the year before, and turned into Ruth's street. From a darkened window came the sound of someone practicing the third movement of the Brahms violin concerto, and Mitchell couldn't help smiling and realizing that one of his strongest memories of Tel Aviv would be the strains of Tschaikovsky and Brahms and Beethoven coming through the opened windows on every street of the town, as the furiously cultured inhabitants practiced runs and cadenzas with never-ending zeal.

All the houses were blacked out, but there was a tiny sliver of light along one of the windows in the third-floor apartment in which Ruth lived, and they stopped in dismay when they saw it.

"She's up," Ruth said.

"Doesn't she ever sleep?" Mitchell asked angrily.

Ruth giggled and kissed him. "She can't stay up forever," Ruth said. "We'll take a little walk and by the time we get back she'll be asleep."

Mitchell took her arm and they walked slowly down toward the sea. Soldiers and whores and fat, placid couples strolled on the concrete walk along the beach, and the Mediterranean heaved gently under the moon and broke in small white rolls of foam against the beach, with a steady, foreign grumble, not like the roar of the Atlantic on the cold northern beaches of home. From a café a hundred yards away came the sound of a string quartet playing a Strauss waltz as though Vienna had never been taken, the waltz never lost to the enemy.

Mitchell and Ruth went down the steps to the beach. A weaving British lance-corporal, coming up the steps with a girl, stiffened and saluted rigidly, his hand quivering with respect for authority, and Mitchell saluted back, and Ruth giggled.

"What're you laughing at?" Mitchell asked, when they had passed the lance-corporal.

"I laugh," Ruth said, "every time I see you salute."

"Why?"

"I don't know why. I just laugh. Forgive me." She took off her shoes and walked barefoot in the sand up to the water's edge. The sea swept softly in from Gibraltar and Tunis and Cyrene and Alexandria and lapped at her toes.

"The Mediterranean," Ruth said. "I hate the Mediterranean."

"What's the matter with it?" Mitchell stared out at the flickering silver path of the moon over the water.

"I was on it," Ruth said, "for thirty-three days. In the hold of a Greek steamer that used to carry cement. Maybe I oughtn't to tell you things like that. You're a tired boy who's been sent here to have a good time so he can go back and fight well. . . ."

"You tell me anything you want to tell me," Mitchell said. "I'll fight all right."

"Should I tell you about Berlin, too? Do you want to hear about Berlin?" Ruth's voice was hard and cold, and somehow a little sardonic, not at all like her voice as he had heard it in the whole week he had known her. The meeting with the journalist at the restaurant had started something stirring within her, something that he hadn't seen before, and he felt that before he left he should see that side of her too.

"Tell me about Berlin," Mitchell said.

"I worked for a newspaper," Ruth said, her toes digging lightly in the sand, "even after the Nazis came in, and I was in love with the man who wrote the Economics column and he was in love with me. . . ."

"Economics?" Mitchell was puzzled.

"The stock exchange. The prophecies and excuses."

"Oh," said Mitchell, trying to picture what a man who wrote stock-exchange tips in Berlin in 1934 would look like.

"He was very gay," Ruth said. "Very young, but elegant, with checkered vests, and he wore a monocle and he lost all his money at the races. His name was Joachim. He used to take me to the races and to the cafés and it used to drive my mother crazy, because if they ever found out I was a Jewish girl out with a Gentile man, they would have sentenced me to death for polluting the blood stream of the German nation. They'd have sent him to a concentration camp, too, but he was always easy and laughing, and he said, 'The important thing is to be brave,' and we were never questioned, and I went to every night club in Berlin, even nights that Goering and Goebbels were in the same room.

"My father was taken to a concentration camp and we decided it was time for me to leave, and Joachim got together all the money he could lay his hands on and gave it to me and I went to Vienna. I was supposed to go to Palestine, if I could, and send for my mother, and for my father, too, if he ever got out of the concentration camp. There was an office in Vienna, and it was filled with refugees from all over Germany, and we collected money to buy transportation and bribe the nations of the world to let some of us in. I slept in the bathtub and talked to sailors and thieves and murderers and crooked shipowners, and finally we got a Greek steamer that was supposed to put in at Genoa and pick us up if we managed to get there. We gave the man 75,000 dollars in cash in advance because that's the only way he would do it, and somehow we got the Austrian government and the Italian government to look the other way, at a price, and they piled us into freight cars, eight hundred of us, and locked us in, men, women and children, lying one on top of another, and the trip took a week and a day to Genoa, and when we got there the ship never arrived. The Greek took the 75,000 dollars and disappeared. There are all kinds of Greeks, and I have nothing against them, but this was a bad one. Then the Italian government sent us back to Vienna and six people committed suicide because they couldn't bear it, and we started in all over again."

Mitchell stared out at the dark line of the sea where it blended in the western distance with the purple of the sky. He tried to think of what it would have been like for his sister and mother if they had been locked into freight cars at Rutland and forced to travel for eight days up to Quebec, say, to wait for an illegal ship to an unknown country. His mother was tall and white-haired and unruffled and pleasant, and his sister was cool and pretty and had some irritating superior mannerisms that she had picked up when she had been foolishly sent for a year to a fancy girls' finishing school in Maryland.

"Let's start home," Ruth said. "If my landlady's still up, we'll shoot her."

They turned their backs on the quiet, white churn of the waves and walked, hand in hand, across the heavy sand of the beach toward the black pile of the buildings of the city.

"Well," Mitchell said, "I want to hear the rest of it."

"No, you don't," Ruth said. "Forgive me for telling you so much. It's too dreary."

"I want to hear," Mitchell said. In the week he had known Ruth, she had been gay and light-hearted, and had helped him to forget the planes spinning out of control and the dying men lying in their frozen blood on the tangled wires and broken aluminum of the Liberator floors, and now he felt as though he owed it to himself and to Ruth to take back with him some of her agony, too, not only the laughter and the tender jokes and the self-effacing merriment. Suddenly, tonight, she had become terribly dear to him, and he felt responsible to her in a way he had never felt responsible to a girl before.

"Tell me," he said.

Ruth shrugged. "Back in Vienna," she said, "we did it all over again. It took two months and the police caught a lot of us, and it meant hiding and running most of the time, but we collected the money again, and we found ourselves another Greek, and this time he turned out to be honest. Or at least as honest as people were to Jews without passports in those days in Europe. We got down to Genoa in only five days this time, and we boarded the steamer at night and they locked the hatch doors on us after we had paid every cent of the money in advance, and we set sail before dawn. The steamer had been built in 1887." They were at the edge of the beach now, and Ruth leaned on Mitchell's shoulder as she put on her shoes. "Nobody can have any idea," Ruth said, as they went up the steps to the concrete walk above, "of what dirt is like until he has been locked into the hold of a fifty-year-old Greek ship with 700 people for over a month. People died every day, and the ship captain would let a rabbi and three other people up on deck at night to perform the burial service and dump the body overboard. The only thing we got to eat was biscuit and canned beef, and there were always worms in everything, even the water we got to drink, and everybody got sores all over their bodies, and the old people got too weak to move and the children wept all day, and the relatives of the people who died screamed a good deal of the time, and it is impossible to tell anyone who was not on that boat what it smelled like, in the middle of the summer in the Mediterranean, with a ventilating system that had been installed in Salonika in 1903."

They turned off the beach walk and climbed slowly up the hill toward the center of the town, past the clean, white, very modernistic apartment houses with gardens and fountains and balconies that faced the sea.

"We were supposed to be let off in Turkey," Ruth went on, her voice almost without inflection and emotion, as though she were reciting from a ledger the business accounts of an importing firm for the year 1850. "And we had given the Greek money to pay off every officer of the port, but something went wrong and we had to put out to sea again, and we started toward Palestine, although the British had patrols along every mile of coastline. But there was no place else to go. People started to get hallucinations about food, and the sailors would sell a sandwich or a lemon for twenty dollars or a bowl of soup for a gold candlestick. And three of the girls couldn't stand it any more and allowed themselves to be taken up every night to be used by the sailors in exchange for regular meals. It was hard to blame them, but they were cursed by the older people as they walked through the crowd each night toward the ladder, and once a Polish woman with two small daughters knocked one of the girls down with an iron pin and tried to stab her with a kitchen knife she had in her bag."

They turned into Ruth's street and looked up at the window just in time to see the thin edge of light under the blind disappear. They stopped and leaned against a stucco fence in front of a plain, shining white house with cactus plants and a fig tree in the front yard.

"We were on that ship for thirty-five days," Ruth said, "and we came to the coast of Palestine between Haifa and Rehovoth, at night, and maybe someone had been bribed, and maybe it was just lucky, but people were waiting for us in rowboats and in eight hours we were all off. There was one woman, who looked as strong as anyone, a solid, sensible-looking woman, and she seemed cheerful and healthy when she got into the little boat with me, but she suddenly died ten feet off the coast, when the water was so shallow a child could have stepped out and walked ashore. Luckily, it was a dark night, and there were no patrols, and we were taken in cars to a movie theater in a little town near Haifa and put inside. The theater had been playing Betty Grable in 'Campus Confessions,' a musical picture, and there were signs with her in tights and ostrich plumes all over it, and the management had written all over the posters, 'Closed This Week for Repairs.' "

"I saw the picture," Mitchell said. He had seen it one night in Cambridge, and he remembered how some of the boys in the audience had whistled when Miss Grable had kissed the leading man.

"We were all told to keep absolutely quiet," Ruth said, "because the British had patrols going through every town. They must have known something, because that week three men high up in the police force were suspended and investigated. It wasn't so hard to keep the older people quiet, but it was awful with the children, and one man really proposed that a little girl who kept crying all day be strangled for the good of the others. We sat there for a week, whispering, making a noise like thousands of mice in a cupboard, and each night cars would come and some people would be taken away to a collective farm somewhere in the hills. Finally, my turn came and I stayed on that farm for two years, working in the fields and teaching children how to read and write German.

"After two years, the British gave you papers, if you managed to dodge them all that time, and I got my papers and started to work for a canning factory outside Tel Aviv. My father was let out of concentration camp in 1938, but his ship was turned back at Haifa, and he was put back in concentration camp in Germany, and for all I know he's still there now, although he's probably dead.

"Joachim wrote me, and my mother, from Berlin. They became good friends once I was gone, and he brought her food, and on Friday nights would come and watch her light the candles. My mother wrote me he told her he had a girl, but he was dissatisfied, he guessed he'd gotten the taste for Jewish girls." Ruth smiled slightly, thinking of the boy with the checkered vest and the monocle many years ago, and Mitchell wondered if he had dropped a bomb near the market-analyzer somewhere in Africa, or in Sicily or Italy.

"He helped my mother get out of Germany," Ruth went on, staring up at the window of her home, which was now secure and dark. "She came out in a Portuguese boat, and I heard she was coming and I was on the shore at Haifa Harbor when it came in. But the British wouldn't let it dock, and after six days they insisted that it turn back, and there were thousands of people on the shore, relatives and friends of the people on the boat, and the worst sound I've ever heard in the world was the sound those people on the shore made when the boat turned around and started to steam toward the Haifa breakwater. But the boat never got out of the harbor." Ruth paused and licked her lips, and spoke very matter of factly. "There was an explosion. We saw the puff of dirty black smoke first, then a long time later we heard the noise, and people on shore were screaming and laughing and crying. Then there was fire and the boat started to go down, and everybody grabbed at any kind of boat they could find and started out toward the steamer, and there were people who couldn't find boats who just jumped into the water, clothes and all, and started to swim, and nobody ever found out how many people drowned that way, because bodies were washed in to shore for three weeks afterward. My mother was drowned and five hundred other people on the boat, but 700 were saved, and then the British had to let them in, and I suppose that's what the people who set the bomb figured would happen. Some people would die, but some would be saved. If the boat went back to Europe, everybody would be killed. Of course, they bungled it somewhat, and they didn't figure on the fire, and they thought the boat would sink more slowly and only a few people would be killed, but even so it was a pretty fair bargain." Ruth lit a cigarette calmly and held the light for Mitchell. "My mother was washed up a week later, and at least her grave is in Palestine. I couldn't tell my father she was dead, so when I wrote to him in concentration camp, I forged letters from my mother, because I had a lot of her letters and I learned how to make good copies. Even now, through the Red Cross, I write him notes in my mother's handwriting, and if he's alive he thinks my mother is living on a farm with a family near Rehovoth."

Ruth pulled at her cigarette and inhaled deeply and in the increased glow Mitchell looked at her and thought again, as he'd thought so many times before, that it was a wonderful and terrible thing that the human race covered its scars so completely, so that Ruth, standing there, with the torture and smuggling and burning and drowning and hiding and dying behind her, looked, with her lipstick and fluffy, cleverly combed hair, and her soft, fragile, print dress, like any one of a thousand girls at a dance in America, with nothing more behind them than a weekly allowance from father, and two proms a season at New Haven or Cambridge.

"Ah," Ruth said, throwing her cigarette away, "she must be asleep by now. Come." She smiled at him, dry-eyed and pleasant, and took his hand, and they walked quietly up through the dim hallways to the apartment in which she lived. She opened the door silently and waved him in, her finger to her lips, and when they were safely in her room, with the door locked behind them, she giggled like a child who has pulled some sly trick on the grown-up world, then kissed him hungrily in the dark room, and whispered, "Mitchell, Mitchell," making the name somehow foreign and tender by the way she said it.

He held her tight, but she pulled away. "Not yet, Lieutenant," she said, grinning, "not yet." She put on a light and went over to a chest of drawers in a corner and started to rummage under some scarves. "I have something for you. Sit down and wait, like a polite boy."

Mitchell sat on the low day bed, blinking in the light. The room was small and painted white and very clean. There was a large piece of Egyptian batik in red and dark green on the wall over the bed and there were three photographs on a dressing table. Mitchell looked at the photographs—a round, smiling woman, with a healthy, simple face, Ruth's mother, the picture taken long before the morning when the ship went down in Haifa Harbor. The other two photographs were of men. There was a man who looked like Ruth, obviously her father, a studious, humorous, rather weak face, with frail, delicate bones and shy, childish eyes. And there was the young man in the checkered vest, slender and laughing and proud of himself, with the monocle in his eye like a burlesque of a German general or a British actor.

"Here." Ruth came over to him and sat down beside him. She had a soft chamois bag, and there was a little rich clinking as she put it in his hand. "To take with you," she said.

Mitchell slowly opened the bag. A heavy silver medal

on a chain, glittering dully in the lamplight, fell into his hand. Ruth was crouched on her knees on the couch beside him, looking anxiously at his face to see if her present would meet with favor. Mitchell turned it over. It was a Saint Christopher, old and irregular, of heavy silver, with the Saint awkward and angular and archaic and very religious in the loving workmanship of a silversmith who had died a long time before.

"It's for voyages," Ruth said, hurriedly. "For a navigator, I thought, it might be quite—quite useful. . . ." She smiled uncertainly at him. "Of course," she said, "it is not in my religion, but I don't think it would do any harm to give it to you. That's why I went to Jerusalem. Something like this, something holy, might have a tendency to be more effective if it comes from Jerusalem, don't you think?"

"Of course," Mitchell said. "It's bound to be."

"Will you wear it?" Ruth glanced quickly and shyly at him, sitting there, dangling the medal on its chain.

"All the time," Mitchell said. "Day and night, every mission, every jeep-ride, year in, year out."

"May I put it on for you?"

Mitchell opened his collar and gave the medal to Ruth. She stood up and he bowed his head and she slipped it on, then leaned over and kissed the back of his neck where the chain lay against the flesh.

She stepped back. "Now," she said matter-of-factly. "There we are." She went over to the lamp. "We don't need this any more." She put the light out and went over to the window and threw back the blackout blinds, and a faint breeze carrying salt and the scent of gardens came into the room. She stood at the window, looking out, and Mitchell got up and crossed over to her, feeling the unfamiliar cool jewelry of the medal dangling against his chest. He stood behind her, silently, holding her lightly, looking out over the city. The white buildings shone in the heavy moonlight machined and modern and Biblical all at once, and from the west came the faint sound of the sea. Mitchell wanted to tell her that he would remember her, remember everything about her, her drowned mother and imprisoned father, her old, courageous lover, drinking champagne with her at the Nazi cafés; he wanted to tell her that he would remember the dealings with the Greek sailor and the hold of the ship that had been built in 1887 and the dying Jews buying a lemon with a gold candlestick; he wanted to tell her that flying over the Germans in Europe or watching the first snow fall at Stowe he would remember the small boat grating on the sand in the darkness outside Rehovoth and the week in the closed movie theater with the British patrols outside; he wanted to tell her that the terror and courage would not be forgotten, but he didn't know how to say it, and besides, being honest with himself, he knew it would be difficult to remember, and finally, back in Vermont, it would blur and cloud over and seem unreal as a story in a child's book, read many years ago and now almost forgotten. He held her more tightly, but he said nothing.

"There he is," Ruth said, her voice casual and unimpressed. "See him standing down there next to the house with the picket gate. . . ."

Mitchell looked over Ruth's shoulder. Down on the street, thirty yards from the entrance of Ruth's house, was a small dark figure, almost completely lost in shadow.

"Ali Khazen," Ruth said. "He comes and waits outside my window. Ah . . ." she sighed, "I suppose finally he'll kill me."

She turned away from the window and led him back to the couch across the strip of moonlight that divided the room. She looked up at him gravely, then suddenly pushed him gently down to the couch and fell beside him, holding onto him. She held him and kissed his cheek and chuckled a little. "Now, Lieutenant," she said, "tell me about Vermont."

Act of Faith

"Present it in a pitiful light," Olson was saying, as they
picked their way through the mud toward the orderly
room tent. "Three combat-scarred veterans, who fought
their way from Omaha Beach to—what was the name of
the town we fought our way to?"

"Konigstein," Seeger said.

"Konigstein." Olson lifted his right foot heavily out of
a puddle and stared admiringly at the three pounds of
mud clinging to his overshoe. "The backbone of the army.
The noncommissioned officer. We deserve better of our
country. Mention our decorations in passing."

"What decorations should I mention?" Seeger asked.
"The marksman's medal?"

"Never quite made it," Olson said. "I had a cross-eyed
scorer at the butts. Mention the bronze star, the silver
star, the Croix de Guerre, with palms, the unit citation, the
Congressional Medal of Honor."

"I'll mention them all." Seeger grinned. "You don't
think the CO'll notice that we haven't won most of them,
do you?"

"Gad, sir," Olson said with dignity, "do you think that
one Southern military gentleman will dare doubt the word

193

of another Southern military gentleman in the hour of victory?"

"I come from Ohio," Seeger said.

"Welch comes from Kansas," Olson said, coolly staring down a second lieutenant who was passing. The lieutenant made a nervous little jerk with his hand as though he expected a salute, then kept it rigid, as a slight superior smile of scorn twisted at the corner of Olson's mouth. The lieutenant dropped his eyes and splashed on through the mud. "You've heard of Kansas," Olson said. "Magnolia-scented Kansas."

"Of course," said Seeger. "I'm no fool."

"Do your duty by your men, Sergeant." Olson stopped to wipe the rain off his face and lectured him. "Highest ranking noncom present took the initiative and saved his comrades, at great personal risk, above and beyond the call of you-know-what, in the best traditions of the American army."

"I will throw myself in the breach," Seeger said.

"Welch and I can't ask more," said Olson, approvingly.

They walked heavily through the mud on the streets between the rows of tents. The camp stretched drearily over the Rheims plain, with the rain beating on the sagging tents. The division had been there over three weeks by now, waiting to be shipped home, and all the meager diversions of the neighborhood had been sampled and exhausted, and there was an air of watchful suspicion and impatience with the military life hanging over the camp now, and there was even reputed to be a staff sergeant in C Company who was laying odds they would not get back to America before July Fourth.

"I'm redeployable," Olson sang. "It's so enjoyable . . ." It was a jingle he had composed to no recognizable melody in the early days after the victory in Europe, when he had added up his points and found they only came to 63. "Tokyo, wait for me . . ."

They were going to be discharged as soon as they got back to the States, but Olson persisted in singing the song, occasionally adding a mournful stanza about dengue fever and brown girls with venereal disease. He was a short, round boy who had been flunked out of air cadets' school and transferred to the infantry, but whose spirits had not been damaged in the process. He had a high, childish voice and a pretty baby face. He was very good-natured, and had a girl waiting for him at the University of California, where he intended to finish his course at government expense when he got out of the army, and he was just the type who is killed off early and predictably and sadly in motion pictures about the war, but he had gone through four campaigns and six major battles without a scratch.

Seeger was a large, lanky boy, with a big nose, who had been wounded at Saint Lô, but had come back to his outfit in the Siegfried Line, quite unchanged. He was cheerful and dependable, and he knew his business and had broken in five or six second lieutenants who had been killed or wounded and the CO had tried to get him commissioned in the field, but the war had ended while the paperwork was being fumbled over at headquarters.

They reached the door of the orderly tent and stopped. "Be brave, Sergeant," Olson said. "Welch and I are depending on you."

"O.K.," Seeger said, and went in.

The tent had the dank, army-canvas smell that had been so much a part of Seeger's life in the past three years. The company clerk was reading a July, 1945, issue of the *Buffalo Courier-Express,* which had just reached him, and Captain Taney, the company CO, was seated at a sawbuck table he used as a desk, writing a letter to his wife, his lips pursed with effort. He was a small, fussy man, with sandy hair that was falling out. While the fighting had been going on, he had been lean and tense and his small voice had been cold and full of authority. But now he had relaxed, and a little pot belly was creeping up under his belt and he kept the top button of his trousers open when he could do it without too public loss of dignity. During the war Seeger had thought of him as a natural soldier, tireless, fanatic about detail, aggressive, severely anxious to kill Germans. But in the past few months Seeger had seen him relapsing gradually and pleasantly into a small-town wholesale hardware merchant, which he had been before the war, sedentary and a little shy, and, as he had once told Seeger, worried, here in the bleak champagne fields of France, about his daughter, who had just turned twelve and had a tendency to go after the boys and had been caught by her mother kissing a fifteen-year-old neighbor in the hammock after school.

"Hello, Seeger," he said, returning the salute in a mild, off-hand gesture. "What's on your mind?"

"Am I disturbing you, sir?"

"Oh, no. Just writing a letter to my wife. You married, Seeger?" He peered at the tall boy standing before him.

"No, sir."

"It's very difficult," Taney sighed, pushing dissatisfiedly at the letter before him. "My wife complains I don't tell her I love her often enough. Been married fifteen years. You'd think she'd know by now." He smiled at Seeger. "I thought you were going to Paris," he said. "I signed the passes yesterday."

"That's what I came to see you about, sir."

"I suppose something's wrong with the passes." Taney spoke resignedly, like a man who has never quite got the hang of army regulations and has had requisitions, furloughs, requests for court-martial returned for correction in a baffling flood.

"No, sir," Seeger said. "The passes're fine. They start tomorrow. Well, it's just . . ." He looked around at the company clerk, who was on the sports page.

"This confidential?" Taney asked.

"If you don't mind, sir."

"Johnny," Taney said to the clerk, "go stand in the rain someplace."

"Yes, sir," the clerk said, and slowly got up and walked out.

Taney looked shrewdly at Seeger, spoke in a secret whisper. "You pick up anything?" he asked.

Seeger grinned. "No, sir, haven't had my hands on a girl since Strasbourg."

"Ah, that's good." Taney leaned back, relieved, happy he didn't have to cope with the disapproval of the Medical Corps.

"It's—well," said Seeger, embarrassed, "it's hard to say —but it's money."

Taney shook his head sadly. "I know."

"We haven't been paid for three months, sir, and . . ."

"Damn it!" Taney stood up and shouted furiously. "I would like to take every bloody chair-warming old lady in the Finance Department and wring their necks."

The clerk stuck his head into the tent. "Anything wrong? You call for me, sir?"

"No," Taney shouted. "Get out of here."

The clerk ducked out.

Taney sat down again. "I suppose," he said, in a more normal voice, "they have their problems. Outfits being broken up, being moved all over the place. But it is rugged."

"It wouldn't be so bad," Seeger said. "But we're going to Paris tomorrow. Olson, Welch and myself. And you need money in Paris."

"Don't I know it." Taney wagged his head. "Do you know what I paid for a bottle of champagne on the Place Pigalle in September . . . ?" He paused significantly. "I won't tell you. You won't have any respect for me the rest of your life."

Seeger laughed. "Hanging," he said, "is too good for the guy who thought up the rate of exchange."

"I don't care if I never see another franc as long as I live." Taney waved his letter in the air, although it had been dry for a long time.

There was silence in the tent and Seeger swallowed a little embarrassedly, watching the CO wave the flimsy sheet of paper in regular sweeping movements. "Sir," he said, "the truth is, I've come to borrow some money for Welch, Olson and myself. We'll pay it back out of the first pay we get, and that can't be too long from now. If you don't want to give it to us, just tell me and I'll understand and get the hell out of here. We don't like to ask, but you might just as well be dead as be in Paris broke."

Taney stopped waving his letter and put it down thoughtfully. He peered at it, wrinkling his brow, looking like an aged bookkeeper in the single gloomy light that hung in the middle of the tent.

"Just say the word, Captain," Seeger said, "and I'll blow . . ."

"Stay where you are, son," said Taney. He dug in his shirt pocket and took out a worn, sweat-stained wallet. He looked at it for a moment. "Alligator," he said, with automatic, absent pride. "My wife sent it to me when we were in England. Pounds don't fit in it. However . . ." He opened it and took out all the contents. There was a small pile of francs on the table in front of him. He counted them. "Four hundred francs," he said. "Eight bucks."

"Excuse me," Seeger said humbly. "I shouldn't have asked."

"Delighted," Taney said vigorously. "Absolutely delighted." He started dividing the francs into two piles. "Truth is, Seeger, most of my money goes home in allotments. And the truth is, I lost eleven hundred francs in a poker game three nights ago, and I ought to be ashamed of myself. Here . . ." he shoved one pile toward Seeger. "Two hundred francs."

Seeger looked down at the frayed, meretricious paper, which always seemed to him like stage money, anyway. "No, sir," he said, "I can't take it."

"Take it," Taney said. "That's a direct order."

Seeger slowly picked up the money, not looking at Taney. "Some time, sir," he said, "after we get out, you have to come over to my house and you and my father and my brother and I'll go on a real drunk."

"I regard that," Taney said, gravely, "as a solemn commitment."

They smiled at each other and Seeger started out.

"Have a drink for me," said Taney, "at the Café de la Paix. A small drink." He was sitting down to write his wife he loved her when Seeger went out of the tent.

Olson fell into step with Seeger and they walked silently through the mud between the tents.

"Well, *mon vieux*?" Olson said finally.

"Two hundred francs," said Seeger.

Olson groaned. "Two hundred francs! We won't be able to pinch a whore's behind on the Boulevard des Capucines for two hundred francs. That miserable, penny-loving Yankee!"

"He only had four hundred," Seeger said.

"I revise my opinion," said Olson.

They walked disconsolately and heavily back toward their tent.

Olson spoke only once before they got there. "These raincoats," he said, patting his. "Most ingenious invention of the war. Highest saturation point of any modern fabric. Collect more water per square inch, and hold it, than any material known to man. All hail the quartermaster!"

Welch was waiting at the entrance of their tent. He was standing there peering excitedly and short-sightedly out at the rain through his glasses, looking angry and tough, like a big-city hack-driver, individual and incorruptible even in the ten-million-colored uniform. Every time Seeger came upon Welch unexpectedly, he couldn't help smiling at the belligerent stance, the harsh stare through the steel-rimmed GI glasses, which had nothing at all to do with the way Welch really was. "It's a family inheritance," Welch had once explained. "My whole family stands as though we were getting ready to rap a drunk with a beer glass. Even my old lady." Welch had six brothers, all devout, according to Welch, and Seeger from time to time idly pictured them standing in a row, on Sunday mornings in church, seemingly on the verge of general violence, amid the hushed Latin and Sabbath millinery.

"How much?" Welch asked loudly.

"Don't make us laugh," Olson said, pushing past him into the tent.

"What do you think I could get from the French for my combat jacket?" Seeger said. He went into the tent and lay down on his cot.

Welch followed them in and stood between the two of them, a superior smile on his face. "Boys," he said, "on a man's errand."

"I can just see us now," Olson murmured, lying on his cot with his hands clasped behind his head, "painting Montmartre red. Please bring on the naked dancing girls. Four bucks worth."

"I am not worried," Welch announced.

"Get out of here." Olson turned over on his stomach.

"I know where we can put our hands on sixty-five bucks." Welch looked triumphantly first at Olson, then at Seeger.

Olson turned over slowly and sat up. "I'll kill you," he said, "if you're kidding."

"While you guys are wasting your time," Welch said, "fooling around with the infantry, I used my head. I went into Reems and used my head."

"Rance," Olson said automatically. He had had two years of French in college and he felt, now that the war was over, that he had to introduce his friends to some of his culture.

"I got to talking to a captain in the air force," Welch said eagerly. "A little fat old paddle-footed captain that never got higher off the ground than the second floor of Com Z headquarters, and he told me that what he would admire to do more than anything else is take home a nice shiny German Luger pistol with him to show to the boys back in Pacific Grove, California."

Silence fell on the tent and Welch and Olson looked tentatively at Seeger.

"Sixty-five bucks for a Luger, these days," Olson said, "is a very good figure."

"They've been sellin' for as low as thirty-five," said Welch hesitantly. "I'll bet," he said to Seeger, "you could sell yours now and buy another one back when you get some dough, and make a clear twenty-five on the deal."

Seeger didn't say anything. He had killed the owner of the Luger, an enormous SS major, in Coblenz, behind some paper bales in a warehouse, and the major had fired at Seeger three times with it, once knicking his helmet, before Seeger hit him in the face at twenty feet. Seeger had kept the Luger, a long, heavy, well-balanced gun, very carefully since then, lugging it with him, hiding it at the bottom of his bedroll, oiling it three times a week, avoiding all opportunities of selling it, although he had been offered as much as a hundred dollars for it and several times eighty and ninety, while the war was still on, before German weapons became a glut on the market.

"Well," said Welch, "there's no hurry. I told the captain I'd see him tonight around 8 o'clock in front of the Lion D'Or Hotel. You got five hours to make up your mind. Plenty of time."

"Me," said Olson, after a pause. "I won't say anything."

Seeger looked reflectively at his feet and the other two men avoided looking at him. Welch dug in his pocket. "I forgot," he said. "I picked up a letter for you." He handed it to Seeger.

"Thanks," Seeger said. He opened it absently, thinking about the Luger.

"Me," said Olson, "I won't say a bloody word. I'm just going to lie here and think about that nice fat air force captain."

Seeger grinned a little at him and went to the tent opening to read the letter in the light. The letter was from his father, and even from one glance at the handwriting, scrawly and hurried and spotted, so different from his father's usual steady, handsome, professorial script, he knew that something was wrong.

"Dear Norman," it read, "sometime in the future, you must forgive me for writing this letter. But I have been holding this in so long, and there is no one here I can talk to, and because of your brother's condition I must pretend to be cheerful and optimistic all the time at home, both with him and your mother, who has never been the same since Leonard was killed. You're the oldest now, and although I know we've never talked very seriously about anything before, you have been through a great deal by now, and I imagine you must have matured considerably, and you've seen so many different places and people. . . . Norman, I need help. While the war was on and you were fighting, I kept this to myself. It wouldn't have been fair to burden you with this. But now the war is over, and I no longer feel I can stand up under this alone. And you will have to face it some time when you get home, if you haven't faced it already, and perhaps we can help each other by facing it together. . . ."

"I'm redeployable," Olson was singing softly, on his cot. "It's so enjoyable, In the Pelilu mud, With the tropical crud . . ." He fell silent after his burst of song.

Seeger blinked his eyes, at the entrance of the tent, in the wan rainy light, and went on reading his father's letter, on the stiff white stationery with the University letterhead in polite engraving at the top of each page.

"I've been feeling this coming on for a long time," the letter continued, "but it wasn't until last Sunday morning that something happened to make me feel it in its full force. I don't know how much you've guessed about the reason for Jacob's discharge from the Army. It's true he was pretty badly wounded in the leg at Metz, but I've asked around, and I know that men with worse wounds were returned to duty after hospitalization. Jacob got a medical discharge, but I don't think it was for the shrapnel wound in his thigh. He is suffering now from what I suppose you call combat fatigue, and he is subject to fits of depression and hallucinations. Your mother and I thought that as time went by and the war and the army receded, he would grow better. Instead, he is growing worse. Last Sunday morning when I came down into the living room from upstairs he was crouched in his old uniform, next to the window, peering out . . ."

"What the hell," Olson was saying, "if we don't get the sixty-five bucks we can always go to the Louvre. I understand the Mona Lisa is back."

"I asked Jacob what he was doing," the letter went on. "He didn't turn around. 'I'm observing,' he said. 'V-1's and V-2's. Buzz-bombs and rockets. They're coming in by the hundreds.' I tried to reason with him and he told me to crouch and save myself from flying glass. To humor him I got down on the floor beside him and tried to tell him the war was over, that we were in Ohio, 4,000 miles away from the nearest spot where bombs had fallen, that America had never been touched. He wouldn't listen. 'These're the new rocket bombs,' he said, 'for the Jews.' "

"Did you ever hear of the Pantheon?" Olson asked loudly.

"No," said Welch.

"It's free."

"I'll go," said Welch.

Seeger shook his head a little and blinked his eyes before he went back to the letter.

"After that," his father went on, "Jacob seemed to forget about the bombs from time to time, but he kept saying that the mobs were coming up the street armed with bazookas and Browning automatic rifles. He mumbled incoherently a good deal of the time and kept walking back and forth saying, 'What's the situation? Do you know what the situation is?' And he told me he wasn't worried about himself, he was a soldier and he expected to be killed, but he was worried about Mother and myself and Leonard and you. He seemed to forget that Leonard was dead. I tried to calm him and get him back to bed before your mother came down, but he refused and wanted to set out immediately to rejoin his division. It was all terribly disjointed and at one time he took the ribbon he got for winning the Bronze star and threw it in the fireplace, then he got down on his hands and knees and picked it out of the ashes and made me pin it on him again, and he kept repeating, 'This is when they are coming for the Jews.'"

"The next war I'm in," said Olson, "they don't get me under the rank of colonel."

It had stopped raining by now and Seeger folded the unfinished letter and went outside. He walked slowly down to the end of the company street, and facing out across the empty, soaked French fields, scarred and neglected by various armies, he stopped and opened the letter again.

"I don't know what Jacob went through in the army," his father wrote, "that has done this to him. He never talks to me about the war and he refuses to go to a psychoanalyst, and from time to time he is his own bouncing, cheerful self, playing in tennis tournaments, and going around with a large group of girls. But he has devoured all the concentration camp reports, and I have found him weeping when the newspapers reported that a hundred Jews were killed in Tripoli some time ago.

"The terrible thing is, Norman, that I find myself coming to believe that it is not neurotic for a Jew to behave like this today. Perhaps Jacob is the normal one, and I, going about my business, teaching economics in a quiet classroom, pretending to understand that the world is comprehensible and orderly, am really the mad one. I ask you once more to forgive me for writing you a letter like this, so different from any letter or any conversation I've ever had with you. But it is crowding me, too. I do not see rockets and bombs, but I see other things.

"Wherever you go these days—restaurants, hotels, clubs, trains—you seem to hear talk about the Jews, mean, hateful, murderous talk. Whatever page you turn to in the newspapers you seem to find an article about

Jews being killed somewhere on the face of the globe. And there are large, influential newspapers and well-known columnists who each day are growing more and more outspoken and more popular. The day that Roosevelt died I heard a drunken man yelling outside a bar, 'Finally, they got the Jew out of the White House.' And some of the people who heard him merely laughed and nobody stopped him. And on V-E Day, in celebration, hoodlums in Los Angeles savagely beat a Jewish writer. It's difficult to know what to do, whom to fight, where to look for allies.

"Three months ago, for example, I stopped my Thursday night poker game, after playing with the same men for over ten years. John Reilly happened to say that the Jews were getting rich out of this war, and when I demanded an apology, he refused, and when I looked around at the faces of the men who had been my friends for so long, I could see they were not with me. And when I left the house no one said good night to me. I know the poison was spreading from Germany before the war and during it, but I had not realized it had come so close.

"And in my economics class, I find myself idiotically hedging in my lectures. I discover that I am loath to praise any liberal writer or any liberal act and find myself somehow annoyed and frightened to see an article of criticism of existing abuses signed by a Jewish name. And I hate to see Jewish names on important committees, and hate to read of Jews fighting for the poor, the oppressed, the cheated and hungry. Somehow, even in a country where my family has lived a hundred years, the enemy has won this subtle victory over me—he has made me disfranchise myself from honest causes by calling them foreign, Communist, using Jewish names connected with them as ammunition against them.

"And, most hateful of all, I find myself looking for Jewish names in the casualty lists and secretly being glad when I discover them there, to prove that there at least, among the dead and wounded, we belong. Three times, thanks to you and your brothers, I have found our name there, and, may God forgive me, at the expense of your blood and your brother's life, through my tears, I have felt that same twitch of satisfaction. . . .

"When I read the newspapers and see another story that Jews are still being killed in Poland, or Jews are requesting that they be given back their homes in France, or that they be allowed to enter some country where they will not be murdered, I am annoyed with them, I feel they are boring the rest of the world with their problems, they are making demands upon the rest of the world by being killed, they are disturbing everyone by being hungry and asking for the return of their property. If we could all fall through the crust of the earth and vanish in one hour, with our heroes and poets and prophets and martyrs, perhaps we would be doing the memory of the Jewish race a service. . . .

"This is how I feel today, son. I need some help. You've been to the war, you've fought and killed men, you've seen the people of other countries. Maybe you understand things that I don't understand. Maybe you see some hope somewhere. Help me. Your loving father."

Seeger folded the letter slowly, not seeing what he was doing because the tears were burning his eyes. He walked slowly and aimlessly across the dead autumn grass of the empty field, away from the camp.

He tried to wipe away his tears, because with his eyes full and dark, he kept seeing his father and brother crouched in the old-fashioned living room in Ohio and hearing his brother, dressed in the old, discarded uniform, saying, "These're the new rocket bombs. For the Jews."

He sighed, looking out over the bleak, wasted land. Now, he thought, now I have to think about it. He felt a slight, unreasonable twinge of anger at his father for presenting him with the necessity of thinking about it. The army was good about serious problems. While you were fighting, you were too busy and frightened and weary to think about anything, and at other times you were relax-

ing, putting your brain on a shelf, postponing everything
to that impossible time of clarity and beauty after the war.
Well, now, here was the impossible, clear, beautiful time,
and here was his father, demanding that he think. There
are all sorts of Jews, he thought, there are the sort whose
every waking moment is ridden by the knowledge of
Jewishness, who see signs against the Jew in every smile
on a streetcar, every whisper, who see pogroms in every
newspaper article, threats in every change of the weather,
scorn in every handshake, death behind each closed door.
He had not been like that. He was young, he was big and
healthy and easy-going and people of all kinds had
seemed to like him all his life, in the army and out. In
America, especially, what was going on in Europe had
seemed remote, unreal, unrelated to him. The chanting,
bearded old men burning in the Nazi furnaces, and the
dark-eyed women screaming prayers in Polish and Russian and German as they were pushed naked into the gas
chambers had seemed as shadowy and almost as unrelated to him as he trotted out onto the Stadium field for a
football game, as they must have been to the men named
O'Dwyer and Wickersham and Poole who played in the
line beside him.

They had seemed more related in Europe. Again and
again in the towns that had been taken back from the Germans, gaunt, gray-faced men had stopped him humbly,
looking searchingly at him, and had asked, peering at his
long, lined, grimy face, under the anonymous helmet,
"Are you a Jew?" Sometimes they asked it in English,
sometimes French, or Yiddish. He didn't know French
or Yiddish, but he learned to recognize the phrase. He
had never understood exactly why they had asked the
question, since they never demanded anything from him,
rarely even could speak to him, until, one day in Strasbourg, a little bent old man and a small, shapeless woman
had stopped him, and asked, in English, if he was Jewish.

"Yes," he said, smiling at them.

The two old people had smiled widely, like children.

"Look," the old man had said to his wife. "A young American soldier. A Jew. And so large and strong." He had touched Seeger's arm reverently with the tips of his fingers, then had touched the Garand he was carrying. "And such a beautiful rifle . . ."

And there, for a moment, although he was not particularly sensitive, Seeger got an inkling of why he had been stopped and questioned by so many before. Here, to these bent, exhausted old people, ravaged of their families, familiar with flight and death for so many years, was a symbol of continuing life. A large young man in the uniform of the liberator, blood, as they thought, of their blood, but not in hiding, not quivering in fear and helplessness, but striding secure and victorious down the street, armed and capable of inflicting terrible destruction on his enemies.

Seeger had kissed the old lady on the cheek and she had wept and the old man had scolded her for it, while shaking Seeger's hand fervently and thankfully before saying good-bye.

And, thinking back on it, it was silly to pretend that, even before his father's letter, he had been like any other American soldier going through the war. When he had stood over the huge dead SS major with the face blown in by his bullets in the warehouse in Coblenz, and taken the pistol from the dead hand, he had tasted a strange little extra flavor of triumph. How many Jews, he'd thought, has this man killed, how fitting it is that I've killed him. Neither Olson nor Welch, who were like his brothers, would have felt that in picking up the Luger, its barrel still hot from the last shots its owner had fired before dying. And he had resolved that he was going to make sure to take this gun back with him to America, and plug it and keep it on his desk at home, as a kind of vague, half-understood sign to himself that justice had once been done and he had been its instrument.

Maybe, he thought, maybe I'd better take it back with me, but not as a memento. Not plugged, but loaded.

America by now was a strange country for him. He had been away a long time and he wasn't sure what was waiting for him when he got home. If the mobs were coming down the street toward his house, he was not going to die singing and praying.

When he was taking basic training he'd heard a scrawny, clerklike-looking soldier from Boston talking at the other end of the PX bar, over the watered beer. "The boys at the office," the scratchy voice was saying, "gave me a party before I left. And they told me one thing. 'Charlie,' they said, 'hold onto your bayonet. We're going to be able to use it when you get back. On the Yids.'"

He hadn't said anything then, because he'd felt it was neither possible nor desirable to fight against every random overheard voice raised against the Jews from one end of the world to another. But again and again, at odd moments, lying on a barracks cot, or stretched out trying to sleep on the floor of a ruined French farmhouse, he had heard that voice, harsh, satisfied, heavy with hate and ignorance, saying above the beery grumble of apprentice soldiers at the bar, "Hold onto your bayonet. . . ."

And the other stories—Jews collected stories of hatred and injustice and inklings of doom like a special, lunatic kind of miser. The story of the naval officer, commander of a small vessel off the Aleutians, who, in the officers' wardroom, had complained that he hated the Jews because it was the Jews who had demanded that the Germans be beaten first and the forces in the Pacific had been starved in consequence. And when one of his junior officers, who had just come aboard, had objected and told the commander that he was a Jew, the commander had risen from the table and said, "Mister, the Constitution of the United States says I have to serve in the same navy with Jews, but it doesn't say I have to eat at the same table with them." In the fogs and the cold, swelling Arctic seas off the Aleutians, in a small boat, subject to sudden, mortal attack at any moment . . .

And the two young combat engineers in an attached

company on D Day, when they were lying off the coast right before climbing down into the landing barges. "There's France," one of them had said.

"What's it like?" the second one had asked, peering out across the miles of water toward the smoking coast.

"Like everyplace else," the first one had answered. "The Jews've made all the dough during the war."

"Shut up!" Seeger had said, helplessly thinking of the dead, destroyed, wandering, starving Jews of France. The engineers had shut up, and they'd climbed down together into the heaving boat, and gone into the beach together.

And the million other stories. Jews, even the most normal and best adjusted of them, became living treasuries of them, scraps of malice and bloodthirstiness, clever and confusing and cunningly twisted so that every act by every Jew became suspect and blameworthy and hateful. Seeger had heard the stories, and had made an almost conscious effort to forget them. Now, holding his father's letter in his hand, he remembered them all.

He stared unseeingly out in front of him. Maybe, he thought, maybe it would've been better to have been killed in the war, like Leonard. Simpler. Leonard would never have to face a crowd coming for his mother and father. Leonard would not have to listen and collect these hideous, fascinating little stories that made of every Jew a stranger in any town, on any field, on the face of the earth. He had come so close to being killed so many times, it would have been so easy, so neat and final.

Seeger shook his head. It was ridiculous to feel like that, and he was ashamed of himself for the weak moment. At the age of twenty-one, death was not an answer.

"Seeger!" It was Olson's voice. He and Welch had sloshed silently up behind Seeger, standing in the open field. "Seeger, *mon vieux,* what're you doing—grazing?"

Seeger turned slowly to them. "I wanted to read my letter," he said.

Olson looked closely at him. They had been together so long, through so many things, that flickers and hints of expression on each other's faces were recognized and acted upon. "Anything wrong?" Olson asked.

"No," said Seeger. "Nothing much."

"Norman," Welch said, his voice young and solemn. "Norman, we've been talking, Olson and me. We decided —you're pretty attached to that Luger, and maybe—if you—well . . ."

"What he's trying to say," said Olson, "is we withdraw the request. If you want to sell it, O.K. If you don't, don't do it for our sake. Honest."

Seeger looked at them, standing there, disreputable and tough and familiar. "I haven't made up my mind yet," he said.

"Anything you decide," Welch said oratorically, "is perfectly all right with us. Perfectly."

They walked aimlessly and silently across the field, away from camp. As they walked, their shoes making a wet, sliding sound in the damp, dead grass, Seeger thought of the time Olson had covered him in the little town outside Cherbourg, when Seeger had been caught going down the side of a street by four Germans with a machine gun on the second story of a house on the corner and Olson had had to stand out in the middle of the street with no cover at all for more than a minute, firing continuously, so that Seeger could get away alive. And he thought of the time outside Saint Lô when he had been wounded and had lain in a minefield for three hours and Welch and Captain Taney had come looking for him in the darkness and had found him and picked him up and run for it, all of them expecting to get blown up any second.

And he thought of all the drinks they'd had together and the long marches and the cold winter together, and all the girls they'd gone out with together, and he thought of his father and brother crouching behind the window in Ohio waiting for the rockets and the crowds armed with Browning automatic rifles.

"Say," he stopped and stood facing them. "Say, what do you guys think of the Jews?"

Welch and Olson looked at each other, and Olson glanced down at the letter in Seeger's hand.

"Jews?" Olson said finally. "What're they? Welch, you ever hear of the Jews?"

Welch looked thoughtfully at the gray sky. "No," he said. "But remember, I'm an uneducated fellow."

"Sorry, Bud," Olson said, turning to Seeger. "We can't help you. Ask us another question. Maybe we'll do better."

Seeger peered at the faces of his friends. He would have to rely upon them, later on, out of uniform, on their native streets, more than he had ever relied on them on the bullet-swept street and in the dark minefield in France. Welch and Olson stared back at him, troubled, their faces candid and tough and dependable.

"What time," Seeger asked, "did you tell that captain you'd meet him?"

"Eight o'clock," Welch said. "But we don't have to go. If you have any feeling about that gun . . ."

"We'll meet him," Seeger said. "We can use that sixty-five bucks."

"Listen," Olson said, "I know how much you like that gun and I'll feel like a heel if you sell it."

"Forget it," Seeger said, starting to walk again. "What could I use it for in America?"

Age of Reason

He had the dream only once—in December. He thought about it for a few moments the next morning, and forgot about it until one evening in April, ten minutes before his plane was scheduled to take off. Then, suddenly, it returned to him. Always, when he was about to board a plane, there was a slight tremor; an awareness of risk, however small and controlled; a slight, subconscious realization that each flight might end with death; a hidden knowledge that there was a small, lurking fatality in winds and cloud and valves and wings, and that no amount of airline skill and care and advertising could ever absolutely dispel it. It was that usual minute, buried twinge of disaster that made him remember the dream as he stood at the gate with his wife and sister, looking out at the dark field and the huge, substantial plane and the flickering lights that marked the runways.

The dream had been a simple one. In it, somehow, his sister Elizabeth had died, and he had, in a resigned and hopeless way, followed the coffin to the cemetery and watched with dry eyes as it was lowered into the ground, and then he had returned home. And somehow, in the dream, it had all happened on May 14th. The date had been absolutely clear and definite and had given the dream a real, tragic sense that it might not otherwise have had. When he woke, he tried to figure out why May 14th, an obscure day five months in the future, had been chosen so relentlessly and specifically by his dreaming mind, but it was no use. There were no birthdays in his family in May, no anniversaries, and nothing in particular had ever happened to him or anyone he knew on that day. He had laughed a little, sleepily, to himself, gently touched Alice's bare shoulder in the bed beside him, and had risen and gone to work, in the sensible, everyday atmosphere of drafting boards and blueprints, without saying a word then or later to her or anyone else about the dream.

And then—laughing at the way his five-year-old daughter had sleepily and carelessly said good-bye when he had left the apartment, standing there with the noise of engines filling the fresh April evening air, kissing his sister Elizabeth good-bye—the dream came back. Elizabeth was as rosy and sturdy as ever, a cheerful, pretty girl who looked as though she had just come triumphantly off a tennis court or from a swimming meet, and if there was any touch of doom hanging over her, it was very well hidden.

"Bring me back Cary Grant," Elizabeth said as she brushed his cheek.

"Of course," Roy said.

"I now leave you two to say a fond farewell," Elizabeth said. "Alice, give him his last-minute instructions. Tell him to behave himself."

"I've already briefed him for this mission," Alice said. "No girls. No more than three Martinis before dinner. Telephone me and report twice weekly. Get on the plane and get home the minute the job is done."

"Two weeks," Roy said. "I swear I'll be back in two weeks."

"Don't have too good a time." Alice was smiling but on the verge of tears, as she always was every time he went anyplace without her, even overnight to Washington.

"I won't," Roy said. "I promise to be miserable."

"Good enough." Alice laughed.

"No old telephone numbers secreted on your person?" Elizabeth asked.

"No." There had been a period in Roy's life, just before he married Alice, when he had been quite lively, and during the war some of his friends had come back from Europe with lurid and highly fictionized tales of wild times in Paris and London, and to the women of his family he seemed more dashing and unstable than was the fact.

"God," he said, "it'll be a relief getting away from this female board of directors for a few days."

He and Alice went up to the gate.

"Take care of yourself, darling," Alice said softly.

"Don't worry." He kissed her.

"I hate this," Alice said, holding onto him. "We're always saying good-bye. This is the last time. From now on, no matter where you go, I'm going with you."

"All right." Roy smiled down at her.

"Even if you only go to Yankee Stadium."

"Couldn't be more pleased." He held her tightly for a moment, dear and familiar and forlorn, left behind this way. Then he walked out to the plane. He turned as he started to climb into it, and waved. Alice and Elizabeth waved back, and he noticed again how much alike they looked, standing together, like two sisters in a pretty family, both of them blond and fair, trim, with little tricks of movement and holding themselves that were almost identical.

He turned and went into the plane, and a moment later the door was shut behind him and the plane started rolling toward the end of the runway.

Ten days later, over the phone between Los Angeles and New York, Roy told Alice she would have to come West. "Munson says it's going to take six months," Roy said, "and he's promised me a place to live, and you are hereby invited."

"Thanks," Alice said. "Tell Munson I would like to kick him in the teeth."

"Can't be helped, baby," Roy said. "Commerce above all. You know."

"Why couldn't he have told you before you went out? Then you could've helped me close up the apartment and we could've gone out together."

"He didn't know before I came out," Roy said patiently. "The world is very confused these days."

"I would like to kick him in the teeth."

"O.K." Roy grinned. "You come out and tell him yourself. When do you arrive? Tomorrow?"

"There's one thing you've got to learn, Roy," Alice said. "I am not a troop movement. You can't say, 'Civilian Alice Gaynor will report three thousand miles from here at 4 P.M. tomorrow,' and expect it to happen."

"O.K., you're not a troop movement. When?"

Alice chuckled. "You sound nice and anxious."

"I *am* nice and anxious."

"That's good."

"When?"

"Well"—Alice hesitated thoughtfully—"I have to get Sally out of school, I have to send some things to storage, I have to rent the apartment, I have to get plane reservations—"

"When?"

"Two weeks," Alice said, "if I can get the reservations all right. Can you wait?"

"No," Roy said.

"Neither can I." They both laughed. "Have you been very gay out there?"

Roy recognized the tentative, inquiring tone and sighed to himself. "Dull as mud," he said. "I stay in in the evenings and read. I've read six books and I'm halfway through General Marshall's report on the conduct of the war."

"There was one evening you didn't read." Alice's voice was careful and purposely light.

"All right," Roy said flatly. "Let's hear it."

"Monica came in from the Coast Tuesday and she called me. She said she saw you with a beautiful girl at a fancy restaurant."

"If there was any justice," Roy said, "they would drop Monica on Bikini Atoll."

"She had long black hair, Monica said."

"She was absolutely right," Roy said. "The girl had long black hair."

"Don't shout. I can hear perfectly well."

"What Monica neglected to say was that it was Charlie Lewis's wife—"

"She said you were alone."

"—and Charlie Lewis was twenty feet away, in the men's room."

"Are you sure?"

"No. Maybe he was in the ladies' room."

"It may be funny to you, but with your history—"

"I will match my history with any husband's," Roy said.

"I hate your sense of humor on this subject." Alice's voice began to tremble a little, and Roy relented.

"Listen, baby," he said softly. "Get out here quick. Quick as you can. Then we can stop this nonsense."

"I'm sorry." Alice's voice was soft and repentant. "It's just that we've been away from each other for so long in these last few years. I'm foolish and jittery. Who's paying for this call?"

"The company."

"That's good." Alice chuckled. "I'd hate to fight on our own money. Do you love me?"

"Get out here quick."

"Do you consider that an answer to my question?"

"Yes."

"O.K.," Alice said. "So do I. Good-bye, darling. See you soon."

"Kiss Sally for me," said Roy.

"I will. Good-bye."

Roy hung up. First he shook his head a little wearily,

remembering the argument; then he smiled, remembering the end of the conversation. He got up from his chair and went over to the calendar on the desk, to try to figure what day he could expect his wife and child.

The telegram came three days later: "RESERVATIONS ON 2 O'CLOCK FLIGHT MAY 14. WILL ARRIVE BURBANK AT 10 P.M. YOUR TIME. PLEASE SHAVE. LOVE, ALICE."

Roy grinned as he reread the telegram, then became conscious of a sensation of uneasiness that refused to be crystallized or pinned down. He walked around all that day with that undefined sense of trouble, and it wasn't until he was dozing off to sleep that night that it suddenly became clear to him. He woke and got out of bed and read the telegram again. May 14th. He kept the lamp on and lit a cigarette and sat up in the narrow bed in the impersonal hotel room and slowly allowed the thing to take control.

He had never been a superstitious man, or even a religious man, and he had always laughed at his mother, who had a fund of dreams and predictions and omens of good and evil at her command. Alice had one or two superstitious habits—like not talking about anything that she wanted to have happen, because she was sure it wouldn't happen if it were mentioned or hoped for too much—but he had always scorned them, too. During the war, when every magazine assured the world that there were no atheists in foxholes, he had never prayed, even in the most gloomy and dangerous times. He had never, in all his adult life, done anything as a result of superstition or premonition. He looked around him at his efficiently furnished, bright, twentieth-century room and felt foolish to be awake now in the heel of the night, chasing phantoms and echoing warnings and scraps of old dreams through the sensible channels of his engineer's mind.

The dream, of course, had been explicit. His sister was to die on May 14th. But dreams never were what they seemed to be, and Elizabeth and Alice looked so much alike, and they were always together and such good friends. . . . He knew enough about dreams to understand that it would be a simple transference in that shadowy, whimsical world—a wife for a sister, a sister for a wife. And now, of all the days in the year, his wife and child had picked May 14th to fly the three thousand miles over the rivers and mountains of the continent from New York to California.

He put out the light much later, with nothing decided, and tried to sleep. He stared up at the dark ceiling, listening to the occasional swift swhoosh of a car on the street outside, hurrying home through the waning night. For a man who didn't believe in Fate, he thought, who saw the world in terms of simple cause and effect; who felt that no act was inevitable, that what was going to happen tomorrow or the next second was in no place determined and was everlastingly variable; who felt that no man's death or burial place was fixed, that no event was recorded in any future book, that the human race got hints or warnings from no supernatural source—this was a ludicrous and profitless way to spend a night. For a man who walked under ladders, cheerfully broke mirrors, never had his palm read or his fortune told from cards, he felt that he was behaving idiotically, and yet he couldn't sleep.

In the morning he called New York.

"Alice," he said, "I want you to come by train."

"What's the matter?" she said.

"I'm afraid of the plane." He heard her laugh incredulously over the phone. "I'm afraid of the plane," he repeated stubbornly.

"Don't be silly," Alice said. "They haven't had an accident with that plane yet, and they won't start now."

"Even so—"

"And I'm not going to try to keep Sally amused for three days in a roomette," Alice said. "It would take me the whole summer to recover."

"Please," Roy said.

"And I couldn't get train reservations for weeks," Alice said, "and the apartment's rented and everything. What's come over you?" Her voice sounded suspicious and wary.

"Nothing," Roy said. "It's just that I'm worried about flying."

"Good God!" Alice said. "You've flown two hundred thousand miles in all sorts of contraptions."

"I know," Roy said. "That's why I'm worried."

"Are you drunk?" Alice asked.

"Alice, darling," Roy sighed. "It's eight o'clock in the morning out here."

"Well, you sound queer."

"I've been up all night, worrying."

"Well, stop worrying. I'll see you on the fourteenth. Are you sure you're all right?"

"Yes."

"This is a very strange telephone call, I must say."

"I'm sorry."

They talked for a moment more, but quite coldly, and Roy hung up feeling dissatisfied and defeated.

He called again two days later and tried once more.

"Don't ask any questions," he said. "Just do this for me, and I'll explain when you get out here. If you want to come on the plane, that's all right, but don't come on the fourteenth. Come on the fifteenth or sixteenth or seventeenth. Any other day. But not on the fourteenth."

"Roy," Alice said, "you've got me terribly worried. What's come over you? I've asked Elizabeth and she says that this doesn't sound like you at all."

"How is she?" Roy asked.

"Elizabeth is fine. She tells me to ignore you and come out as scheduled."

"Tell her to mind her own damned business." Roy had been working hard and sleeping badly and his voice was raw and nervous, and Alice reacted to it.

"I think I know what's going on," she said coldly. "Monica told me there's a big party at the Condons' on the fourteenth, and you've probably promised to take someone else, and a wife would be a big handicap—"

"Oh, God, will you stop that!" Roy shouted into the phone.

"I haven't been married to you for seven years for nothing," Alice said. "I'm not blind."

"Come out today!" Roy shouted. "Come out tomorrow! Come out the thirteenth! Only not the fourteenth!"

"You know as well as I do that if I give up my reservations, I won't get another until June. If you don't want to see me any more, tell me. You don't have to go through all this rigmarole."

"Alice, darling," Roy pleaded, "I assure you I want to see you."

"Well, then, stop this nonsense or tell me what it's all about."

"Alice, it's this way," he began, resolved to tell her, no matter how much of an idiot it made him feel, but there was a click on the wire and then three thousand miles of whispering silence. By the time he got Alice back on the phone, ten minutes later, he felt too ridiculous, felt that he could not live with himself or his wife if he at this late date exposed himself as a silly, undependable man with a brain gone soft and nervous and irresponsible after all the sane, dependable years.

"I haven't anything else to say," he told Alice when the operator finally made the connection, "except that I love you very much and I couldn't bear it if anything ever happened to you."

He heard Alice crying softly at the other end of the wire. "We have to be together soon," she said. "This is awful. And please don't call me any more, Roy, darling. You're acting so strangely, and after I talk to you, the most miserable ideas grab hold of me. Will it be all right when I get out there?"

"It'll be wonderful, darling," Roy said.

"And you'll never go away without me again? Never?"

"Never." He could close his eyes and see her crouched like a little girl over the phone in the bedroom of their quiet, pleasant home, both her hands on the instrument, her pretty, clever face screwed up with grief and longing, and it was hard to say anything more. "Good night," he said. "Be careful."

He hung up and stared wildly at the blank wall on the other side of the room, knowing he wouldn't sleep again that night.

There was an early fog on the morning of May 14th, and Roy stared at it, hot-eyed and lightheaded from lack of sleep, and went out and walked along the quiet, gray streets, with only police cars and milk-delivery carts disturbing the soft, thick dawn.

California, he thought; it's always foggy in the morning, fog is general in California before eight, and it's a different time and a different weather on the coast of the Atlantic, and her plane isn't due to leave for hours yet.

It must be the war, he thought. This would never have happened to me before the war. I thought I came out all right, but maybe I was overconfident. All the cemeteries, with the young men tucked away in the sand and spring grass, and the old ladies in black lace dresses dying on the next street in London in the air raids. A man's imagination was bound to take a morbid turn, finally. I must take hold of myself, he told himself reasonably. I'm the man who always felt sane, balanced, healthy in all situations, who always scorned mediums and table tappers, priests and psychoanalysts.

The fog was beginning to lift, and he stopped to stare at the distant smudge of mountains that stood guard over the eastern approaches of the city. Planes had to come in steeply over them and circle the city and land from the westward side. A strip of blue appeared above the mountains and widened and widened, and the fog melted away in wisps among the ugly, fat palm trees that lined the street, and soon the sun was shining on the dewy lawns, and the sky looked clear and blue from Beverly Hills to Scotland.

He went back to his hotel and lay down without even taking his shoes off. Some time later he woke up. Vaguely, in the moment before waking, there was a confusion of planes going down in puffs of smoke, like the newsreel of an air battle, and Sally's voice over it, regretfully saying, as she always did at bedtime, "Do I *really* have to go to sleep now? I'm terribly wide-awake."

He looked at the clock. It was one-forty in New York. They were at the airport now, and the big plane was waiting on the field, with the mechanics fiddling on it and the men checking the gas tanks. The hell with it, he thought. I don't care how foolish I seem.

He picked up the phone. "La Guardia Field, New York," he said.

"There will be a slight delay," the operator sang. "I will call you."

"This is very important," Roy said. "Urgent."

"There will be a slight delay," the operator said in exactly the same tones. "I will call you."

He hung up and went to the window and stared out. The sky stretched, radiant and clear, over the hills toward New York. I'll tell her the whole thing, he thought, idiotic or not. Forbid her to get on the plane. We can laugh about it later. I'll take the first plane back myself and fly back with them. That'll prove to her it has nothing to do with anything here.

He went and got out his valise and put three shirts in it, then picked up the phone again. Five minutes later he got the airport, but it took another five minutes to get through to the station manager for the airline.

"My name is Gaynor"—Roy's voice was high and hurried—"and this is a very unusual request, so please listen carefully."

"What was that name, sir?"

"Gaynor. G-a-y-n-o-r."

"Oh, yes, Gaynor. Like the dive." The distant voice laughed politely at its own joke. "What can I do for you, sir?"

"My wife and child—"

"You will have to speak louder, please."

"My wife and child!" Roy shouted. "Mrs. Alice Gaynor, on the two-o'clock flight to Los Angeles. I want you to stop them—"

"What did you say?"

"I said I wanted you to stop them. They are not to take the plane. My wife and child. Mrs. Alice Gaynor. The two-o'clock flight to Los Angeles—"

"I'm afraid that's impossible, Mr. Gaynor." The voice was puzzled but polite.

"It can't be impossible. All you have to do is announce it over the public-address system and—"

"Impossible, sir. The two-o'clock flight is just taking off at this moment. I'm terribly sorry. Is there anything else I can do for you?"

"No," Roy said flatly, and put the phone down. He sat on the edge of his bed for a moment, then got up and went to the window. He looked out at the bright sky and the green-and-yellow mountains. He remained standing there, staring at the mountains, waiting for the call from the airline.

Mixed Doubles

As Jane Collins walked out onto the court behind her husband, she felt once more the private, strong thrill of pride that had moved her again and again in the time she had known him. Jane and Stewart had been married six years, but even so, as she watched him stride before her in that curious upright, individual, half-proud, half-comic walk, like a Prussian drill sergeant on his Sunday off, Jane felt the same mixture of amusement and delight in him that had touched her so strongly when they first met. Stewart was tall and broad and his face was moody and good-humored and original, and Jane felt that even at a distance of five hundred yards and surrounded by a crowd of people, she could pick him out unerringly. Now, in well-cut white trousers and a long-sleeved Oxford shirt, he seemed elegant and a little old-fashioned among the other players, and he looked graceful and debonair as he hit the first few shots in the preliminary rallying.

Jane was sensibly dressed, in shorts and tennis shirt, and her hair was imprisoned in a bandanna, so that it wouldn't get into her eyes. She knew that the shorts made her look a little dumpy and that the handkerchief around her head gave her a rather skinned and severe appearance, and she had a slight twinge of female regret when she

looked across the net and saw Eleanor Burns soft and attractive in a prettily cut tennis dress and with a red ribbon
in her hair, but she fought it down and concentrated on
keeping her eye on the ball as Mr. Croker, Eleanor's partner, sliced it back methodically at her.

Mr. Croker, a vague, round, serious little man, was a
neighbor of the Collinses' hosts. His shorts were too tight
for him, and Jane knew, from having watched him on
previous occasions, that his face would get more serious
and more purple as the afternoon wore on, but he played
a steady, dependable game and he was useful when other
guests were too lazy or had drunk too much at lunch to
play in the afternoon.

Two large oak trees shaded part of the court, and the
balls flashed back and forth, in light and shadow, making
guitarlike chords as they hit the rackets, and on the small
terrace above the court, where the other guests were
lounging, there was the watery music of ice in glasses and
the bright flash of summer colors as people moved about.

How pleasant this was, Jane thought—to get away
from the city on a week end, to this cool, tree-shaded
spot, to slip all the stiff bonds of business and city living
and run swiftly on the springy surface of the court, feeling the country wind against her bare skin, feeling youth
in her legs, feeling, for this short Sunday hour at least, free
of desks and doors and weekday concrete.

Stewart hit a tremendous overhead smash, whipping all
the strength of his long body into it, and the ball struck the
ground at Eleanor's feet and slammed high in the air. He
grinned. "I'm ready," he said.

"You're not going to do that to me in the game, are
you?" Eleanor asked.

"I certainly am," Stewart said. "No mercy for women.
The ancient motto of the Collins family."

They tossed for service, and Stewart won. He served
and aced Eleanor with a twisting, ferocious shot that spun
off at a sharp angle.

"Jane, darling," he said, grinning, as he walked to the other side, "we're going to be sensational today."

They won the first set with no trouble. Stewart played very well. He moved around the court swiftly and easily, hitting the ball hard in loose, well-coached strokes, with an almost exaggerated grace. Again and again, the people watching applauded or called out after one of his shots, and he waved his racket, smiling at them, and said, "Oh, we're murderous today." He kept humming between shots —a tuneless, happy composition of his own—like a little boy who is completely satisfied with himself, and Jane couldn't help smiling and adoring him as he lightheartedly dominated the game and the spectators and the afternoon, brown and dashing and handsome in his white clothes, with the sun flooding around him like a spotlight on an actor in the middle of the stage.

Occasionally, when Stewart missed a shot, he would stand, betrayed and tragic, and stare up at the sky and ask with mock despair, "Collins, why don't you just go home?" And then he would turn to Jane and say, "Janie, darling, forgive me. Your husband's just no good."

And even as she smiled at him and said, "You're so right," she could sense the other women, up on the terrace, looking down at him, their eyes speculative and veiled and lit with invitation as they watched.

Jane played her usual game, steady, unheroic, getting almost everything back quite sharply, keeping the ball in play until Stewart could get his racket on it and kill it. They were a good team. Jane let Stewart poach on her territory for spectacular kills, and twice Stewart patted her approvingly on the behind after she had made difficult saves, and there were appreciative chuckles from the spectators at the small domestic vulgarity.

Stewart made the last point of the set on a slamming deep backhand that passed Eleanor at the net. Eleanor shook her head and said, "Collins, you're an impossible man," and Croker said stolidly, "Splendid. Splendid," and Stewart said, grinning, "Something I've been saving for this point, old man."

They walked off and sat down on a bench in the shade between sets, and Croker and Jane had to wipe their faces with towels and Croker's alarming purple died a little from his cheeks.

"That overhead!" Eleanor said to Stewart. "It's absolutely frightening. When I see you winding up, I'm just tempted to throw away my poor little racket and run for my life."

Jane lifted her head and glanced swiftly at Stewart to see how he was taking it. He was taking it badly, smiling a little too widely at Eleanor, being boyish and charming. "It's nothing," he said. "Something I picked up on Omaha Beach."

That, too, Jane thought bitterly. Foxhole time, too. She ducked her head into her towel to keep from saying something wifely. This is the last time, she thought, feeling the towel sticky against her sweaty forehead, the last time I am coming to any of these week-end things, always loaded with unattached or semi-attached, man-hungry, half-naked, honey-mouthed girls. She composed her face, so that when she looked up from the towel she would look like a nice, serene woman who merely was interested in the next set of tennis.

Eleanor, who had wide green eyes, was staring soberly and unambiguously over the head of her racket at Stewart, and Stewart, fascinated, as always, and a little embarrassed, was staring back. Oh, God, Jane thought, the long stare, too.

"Well," she said briskly, "I'm ready for one more set."

"What do you say," Stewart asked, "we divide up differently this time? Might make it more even. Croker and you, Jane, and the young lady and me."

"Oh," said Eleanor, "I'd be a terrible drag to you, Stewart. And besides, I'm sure your wife loves playing on your side."

"Not at all," Jane said stiffly. The young lady! How obvious could a man be?

"No," said Croker surprisingly. "Let's stay the way we are." Jane wanted to kiss the round purple face, a bleak, thankful kiss. "I think we'll do better this time. I've been sort of figuring out what to do with you, Collins."

Stewart looked at him briefly and unpleasantly, then smiled charmingly. "Anything you say, old man. I just thought . . ."

"I'm sure we'll do better," Croker said firmly. He stood up. "Come on, Eleanor."

Eleanor stood up, lithe and graceful in her short dress, which whipped around her brown legs in the summer wind. Never again, Jane thought, will I wear shorts. Dresses like that, even if they cost fifty dollars apiece, and soft false bosoms to put in them, too, and no bandanna, even if I'm blinded on each shot.

Stewart watched Eleanor follow Croker onto the court, and Jane could have brained him for the buried, measuring glint in his eye.

"Let's go," Stewart said, and under his breath, as they walked to their positions on the base line. He added, "Let's really show the old idiot this time, Jane."

"Yes, dear," Jane said, and pulled her bandanna straight and tight around her hair.

The first three games were ludicrously one-sided. Stewart stormed the net, made sizzling, malicious shots to Croker's feet, and purposely made him run, so that he panted pitifully and grew more purple than ever, and from time to time muttered to Jane, "Ridiculous old windbag," and "I thought he had me figured out," and "Don't let up, Janie, don't let up."

Jane played as usual, steady, undeviating, as predictably and sensibly as she always played. She was serving in the fourth game and was at 40-15 when Stewart dropped a shot just over the net, grinning as Croker galloped heavily in and barely got his racket on it. Croker's return wobbled over Stewart's head and landed three inches beyond the base line.

"Nice shot," she heard Stewart say. "Just in."

She looked at him in surprise. He was nodding his head emphatically at Croker.

Eleanor was at the net on the other side, looking at Stewart. "It looked out to me," she said.

"Not at all," Stewart said. "Beautiful shot. Serve them up, Janie."

Oh, Lord, Jane thought, now he's being sporting.

Jane made an error on the next point and Croker made a placement for advantage and Stewart hit into the net for the last point, and it was Croker's and Eleanor's game. Stewart came back to receive the service, not humming any more, his face irritable and dark.

Croker suddenly began to play very well, making sharp, sliding, slicing shots that again and again forced Stewart and Jane into errors. As they played, even as she swung at the ball, Jane kept remembering the shot that Stewart had called in, that had become the turning point of the set. He had not been able to resist the gallant gesture, especially when Eleanor had been standing so close, watching it all. It was just like Stewart. Jane shook her head determinedly, trying to concentrate on the game. This was no time to start dissecting her husband. They had had a lovely week end till now and Stewart had been wonderful, gay and funny and loving, and criticism could at least be reserved for weekdays, when everything else was dreary, too. But it *was* just like Stewart. It was awful how everything he did was all of a piece. His whole life was crowded with gestures. Hitting his boss that time in the boss's own office with three secretaries watching, because the boss had bawled him out. Giving up his R.O.T.C. commission and going into the Army as a private, in 1942. Giving five thousand dollars, just about the last of their savings, to Harry Mather, for Mather's business, just because they had gone to school together, when everyone knew Mather had become a hopeless drunk and none of his other friends would chip in. To an outsider, all these might seem the acts of a generous and rather noble character, but to a wife, caught in the consequences . . .

"Damn these pants," Stewart was muttering after hitting a ball into the net. "I keep tripping over them all the time."

"You ought to wear shorts, like everyone else," Jane said.

"I will. Buy me some this week," Stewart said, taking time out and rolling his cuffs up slowly and obviously. Jane had bought him three pairs of shorts a month before, but he always pretended he couldn't find them, and wore the long trousers. His legs are surprisingly skinny, Jane thought, hating herself for thinking it, and they're hairy, and his vanity won't let him. . . . She started to go for a ball, then stopped when she saw Stewart going for it.

He hit it out to the backstop. "Janie, darling," he said, "at least stay out of my way."

"Sorry," she said. Stewie, darling, she thought, Stewie, be careful. Don't lay it on. You're not really like this. I know you're not. Even for a moment, don't make it look as though you are.

Stewart ended the next rally by hitting the ball into the net. He stared unhappily at the ground. "The least they might do," he said in a low voice to Jane, "is roll the court if they invite people to play on it."

Please, Stewie, Jane begged within herself, don't do it. The alibis. The time he forgot to sign the lease for the apartment and they were put out and he blamed it on the lawyer, and the time he lost the job in Chicago and it was because he had gone to the wrong college, and the time . . . By a rigorous act of will, Jane froze her eyes on the ball, kept her mind blank as she hit it back methodically again and again.

Eleanor and Croker kept winning points. Croker had begun to chop every ball, spinning soft, deceptive shots that landed in mid-court and hardly bounced before they

fell a second time. The only way that Jane could return
them was to hit them carefully, softly, just getting them
back. But Stewart kept going in on them furiously, taking
his full, beautiful swing, sending the ball whistling into
the net or over the court into the backstop. He looked as
pretty and expert as ever as he played, but he lost point
after point.

"What a way to play tennis," he grumbled, with his
back to his opponents. "Why doesn't he play ping-pong
or jacks?"

"You can't slam those dinky little shots like that," Janie
said. "You have to get them back soft."

"You play your game," Stewart said, "and I'll play
mine."

"Sorry," Jane said. Oh, Stewart, she mourned within
her.

Stewart went after two more of Croker's soft chops,
each time whipping his backhand around in his usual,
slightly exaggerated, beautiful stroke, and each time
knocking the ball into the net.

I can't help it, Jane thought. That *is* the way he is.
Form above everything. If he were hanging over a cliff,
he'd let himself fall to the rocks below rather than risk
being ungraceful climbing to safety to save his life. He
always has to pick up the check in bars and restaurants,
no matter whom he is with or how many guests there are
at the table, always with the same lordly, laughing, slightly
derisive manner, even if we are down to our last fifty dollars. And when they had people in to dinner, there had to
be two maids to wait on table, and French wines, and
there always had to be those special bottles of brandy that
cost as much as a vacation in the country. And he became
so cold and remote when Jane argued with him about it,
reminding him they were not rich and there was no sense
in pretending they were. And his shoes. She blinked her
eyes painfully, getting a sudden vision, there in the sun
and shadow, of the long row of exquisite shoes, at seventy
dollars a pair, that he insisted upon having made to his or-

der. How ridiculous, she thought, to allow yourself to be unnerved at your husband's taste in shoes, and she loyally reminded herself how much a part of his attraction it had been in the beginning that he was always so beautifully dressed and so easy and graceful and careless of money.

The score was 4-3 in favor of Eleanor and Croker. Stewart's shots suddenly began to work again, and he and Jane took the next game with ease. Stewart's grin came back then, and he cheerfully reassured Jane, "Now we're going to take them." But after winning the first two points of the next game he had a wild streak and missed the base line by a few inches three times in a row, and they eventually lost the game.

I will make no deductions from this, Jane told herself stonily as she went up to the net for Stewart's serve. Anybody is liable to miss a few shots like that—anybody. And yet, how like Stewart! Just when it was most important to be steady and dependable. . . . The time she'd been so sick and the maid had quit, and Jane lay, broken and miserable, in bed for three weeks, with no one to take care of her except Stewart . . . He had been charming and thoughtful for the first week, fixing her meals, reading to her, sitting at her side for hours on end, cheerful and obliging, making her illness gently tolerable. And then he had suddenly grown nervous and abrupt, made vague excuses to leave her alone, and vanished for hours at a time, only to come back and hastily attend her for a few moments and vanish again, leaving her there in the rumpled bed, staring, lonely and shaken, at the ceiling as dusk faded into night and night into morning. She had been sure there was another girl then and she had resolved that when she was well and able to move around again, she would come to some decision with him, but as unpredictably as his absences had begun, they stopped. Once more he was tender and helpful, once more he sat at her side and nursed her and cheered her, and out of gratitude and love she had remained quiet and pushed her doubts deep to the back of her mind. And here they were again, in the middle of a holiday afternoon, foolishly, in this most unlikely place, during this mild, pointless game, with half a dozen people lazily watching, laughing and friendly, over their drinks.

She looked at him a few moments later, handsome and dear and familiar at her side, and he grinned back at her, and she was ashamed of herself for the thoughts that had been flooding through her brain. It was that silly girl on the other side of the net who had started it all, she thought. That practiced, obvious, almost automatic technique of flattering the male sex. That meaningless, rather pitiful flirtatiousness. It was foolish to allow it to throw her into the bitter waters of reflection. Marriage, after all, was an up-and-down affair and in many ways a fragile and devious thing, and was not to be examined too closely. Marriage was not a bank statement or a foreign policy or an X-ray photograph in a doctor's hand. You took it and lived through it, and maybe, a long time later —perhaps the day before you died—you totaled up the accounts, if you were of that turn of mind, but not before. And if you were a reasonable, sensible, mature woman, you certainly didn't do your additions and subtractions on a tennis court every time your husband hit a ball into the net. Jane smiled at herself and shook her head.

"Nice shot," she said warmly to Stewart as he swept a forehand across court, past Croker, for a point.

But it was still set point. Croker placed himself to receive Stewart's service, tense and determined and a little funny-looking, with his purple face and his serious round body a little too tight under his clothes. The spectators had fallen silent, and the wind had died, and there was a sense of stillness and expectancy as Stewart reared up and served.

Jane was at the net and she heard the sharp twang of Stewart's racket hitting the ball behind her and the rifle-like report as it hit the tape and fell away. He had just missed his first service.

Jane didn't dare look around. She could feel Stewart walking into place, in that stiff-backed, pleasant way of his, and feel him shuffling around nervously, and she couldn't look back. Please, she thought, please get this one in. Helplessly, she thought of all the times when, just at the crucial moment, he had failed. Oh, God, this is silly, she thought. I mustn't do this. The time he had old man Sawyer's account practically in his hands and he got drunk. On the sporting pages, they called it coming through in the clutch. There were some players who did and some players who didn't, and after a while you got to know which was which. If you looked at it coldly, you had to admit that until now Stewart had been one of those who didn't. The time her father died, just after her sister had run off with the vocalist in that band, and if there had been a man around, taking hold of things, her father's partner wouldn't've been able to get away with most of the estate the way he did, and the vocalist could have been frightened off. One day's strength and determination, one day of making the right move at the right time . . . But after the funeral, Stewart had pulled out and gone to Seattle on what he had said was absolutely imperative business, but that had never amounted to anything anyway, and Jane's mother and sister, and Jane, too, were still paying for that day of failure.

She could sense Stewart winding up for his service behind her back. Somewhere in her spine she felt a sense of disaster. It was going to be a double fault. She knew it. No, she thought, I mustn't. He isn't really like that. He's so intelligent and talented and good, he can go so far. She must not make this terrible judgment on her husband just because of the way he played tennis. And yet, his tennis was so much like his life. Gifted, graceful, powerful, showy, flawed, erratic . . .

Please, she thought, make this one good. Childishly, she felt, If this one is good it will be a turning point, a symbol, his whole life will be different. She hated herself for her thoughts and stared blankly at Eleanor, self-consciously alert and desirable in her pretty dress.

Why the hell did she have to come here this Sunday? Jane thought despairingly.

She heard the crack of the racket behind her. The ball whistled past her, hit the tape, rolled undecidedly on top of the net for a moment, then fell back at her feet for a double fault and the set.

"Too bad." She turned and smiled at Stewart, helplessly feeling herself beginning to wonder how she would manage to find the six weeks it would take in Reno. She shook her head, knowing that she wasn't going to Reno, but knowing, too, that the word would pass through her thoughts again and again, more and more frequently, with growing insistence, as the days went by.

She walked off the court with Stewart, holding his hand.

"The shadows," Stewart was saying. "Late in the afternoon, like this. It's impossible to see the service line."

"Yes, dear," Jane said.

The Climate of Insomnia

Cahill let himself into the silent house, softly closing the door behind him. He hung up his hat and coat, noticing the pleasant, frail smell of damp and night that came up from the cloth. Then he saw the note on the telephone table. It was scrawled in the maid's grave, childish handwriting, which always amused him a little when he saw it. "Mr. Reeves called," the message read. "He must talk to you. Very important, he says."

Cahill started to take up the phone under the mirror. Then he glanced at his watch. It was past one. Too late, he decided; it will have to wait till morning. He looked at himself in the dim glass, noting with satisfaction that his face was still thin and rather young-looking and that his eyes, despite the three drinks after the meeting that night, were not bloodshot. With dissatisfaction, he noted also that the gray was gaining over the black at his temples and that the lines under his eyes were now permanent. He sighed with agreeable melancholy, thinking gently: Older, older . . .

He put out the light and started upstairs. He was a large, bulky man, but he moved gracefully up the carpeted steps of his home. He touched the smooth wood of the banister, smelling the mixed but orderly aromas of living that the house breathed into the still darkness—the lemony fragrance of furniture polish, the autumnal dust of chrysanthemums from the living room, the hint of his wife's perfume, lingering here after the day's comings and goings.

He walked past the adjoining doors behind which slept his son and his daughter. He thought of the dark-haired, seventeen-year-old girl lying neatly in the quilted bed, the almost womanly mouth relaxed back into childishness by sleep. He brushed the door with his fingertips sentimentally. As he passed his son's door, he could hear a low, dreamy mumble, then, more clearly, Charlie's voice calling, "Intercept! Intercept!" Then the voice stopped. Cahill grinned, reflecting on what vigorous, simple dreams of green fields and sunny afternoons visited the sleep of his fifteen-year-old son. Cahill, the miser, he thought, quietly going past the closed doors, counting his treasures at midnight.

He went into the bathroom and undressed there, so as not to wake his wife. After he had put on his pajamas and slippers, he stood for a moment in front of the medicine chest, debating whether or not to take the sedative for his stomach that Dr. Manners had prescribed for him on Tuesday. He patted his stomach thoughtfully. It bulged a little, as it had been doing for seven or eight years now, but it felt relaxed and healthy. The hell with it, he thought. I am going to break the tyranny of the Pill.

Unmedicined, he put out the bathroom light and padded into the bedroom. He sat carefully on the edge of his bed and silently took off his slippers, moving with domestic caution, watching his wife, in the next bed. She did not stir. A little moonlight filtered in through the curtained windows and softly outlined the head against the pillows. She slept steadily, not moving even when Cahill inadvertently knocked against the base of the lamp on the bed table, making a resonant metallic noise. She looked young, pretty, defenseless in the obscure light, although Cahill noticed, with a grimace, that she had her hair up in curlers, leaving only a small bang loose in front as a sop to marital attractions. A woman must be awfully certain of her husband, he thought, to appear in bed night after night in those grim ringlets. He grinned to himself as he got under the covers, amused at his strong feelings on the subject.

As the warmth of the blankets slowly filled in around him, he stretched, enjoying the softness of the bed, his muscles luxuriously delivering him over to the long weariness of the day. The curtains, folded in moonlight, rustled gently at the windows. A fragile, tenuous sense of peace settled drowsily upon him. His son and his daughter slept youthfully and securely beyond the bedroom wall. His first class the next morning was not until ten o'clock. His wife confidently clamped her hair in ludicrous curls, knowing nothing could disturb her marriage. At the meeting, he had spoken quite well, and Professor Edwards, who was the head of the department, had come over afterward and approved of it. In the next morning's second class, Philosophy 12, there were three of the brightest young people in the college—two boys and a girl, and the girl was rather pretty, too—and they had all made it plain that they admired him enormously, and were constantly quoting him in the classes of other instructors. Cahill moved softly under the covers as the pleasant, half-formed images of contentment drifted across his brain. Tomorrow, he thought, will be clear and warmer—that's what the paper says. I'll wear my new brown tweed suit.

Just before he dozed off, he thought of the message from Joe Reeves. Important, he thought a little irritably, important—now, what could that be? He twitched a little, uneasily, nearly coming back to wakefulness. Then, with the steady breathing of his wife sounding from the next bed, he dropped off to sleep.

The siren must have been wailing for some time before Cahill woke, because it entered harshly into his dream, and somehow he was back in London, in the cold billet, and the planes were overhead and the guns were going off, and he had the old feeling that neighbors were dying by chance in burning buildings on the street outside his window. He could feel himself moaning softly and shivering under the blankets and hoping he would be alive in the morning, and then he awoke.

He gazed blindly at the dark ceiling, feeling the cold, unreasonable sweat come out on his body. What is it? he thought. What is it? Then he realized that he was at home, in his own bed, and that the war was over. The noise of the siren howled down the quiet street outside— a police car going to investigate a burglary or pick up a drunk—echoing among the untouched homes, behind their undamaged lawns. He shook his head, irritated with himself for his nervousness. He looked across at his wife. She slept, unperturbed, her breath coming evenly, her arms primly down at her sides, her captured hair untossed on the pillow, happily beyond the reach of sirens and the memory of sirens.

He felt tremblingly awake. Every sound now reached him clearly and with individual significance: the wind troubling the curtains in a starched rhythm; the insubstantial creak of the stairs reacting to the obscure strain that years put upon old houses; the distant crashing of a truck's gears past a faraway street corner, attacking all insomniacs within a radius of a mile; the even intake and exhalation of his wife's breath, too mild to be called a snore but now as annoying as a suddenly loud clock, holding the hours of the night too strictly to account, reminding the would-be sleeper that every moment of wakefulness now would be answered by weariness tomorrow.

Cahill looked at the low radium gleam of the clock on the bed table. Four-thirty. He fell back onto his pillow heavily. Too late to take a sleeping pill. If he took a pill now, he'd be doped all day; he wouldn't have time to sleep it off. The ubiquitous problem of modern civilization, he thought: Is it too late for a pill? Too early? Which way will it be worse tomorrow? All over the country, sleepy, nervous hands reaching out for the clock, troubled heads calculating, It will wear off in six hours, but I have to get up in four. Sleep, he thought, the first great natural resource to be exhausted by modern man. The erosion of the nerves, not to be halted by any reclamation project, private or public.

He lay rigid in his bed, conscious now of various dull, unpleasant sensations in his body. His eyelids felt harsh and granular and seemed to scrape his eyeballs when he blinked. He was too warm, but a damp breeze from the window felt cold and uncomfortable on his forehead. The muscles of his right leg felt cramped, and he had a curious sensation that the tendon running up from his ankle had grown too short during the night. His stomach, just under the diaphragm, was moving in little spasms. He put his hand on the spot and felt the sick, erratic fluttering. He could taste the whiskey he had drunk, high and sour in his throat. That damned siren, he thought. I was feeling so well . . .

Then Cahill remembered the message. It must be something really pressing, he thought, for Joe Reeves to call like that. Cahill couldn't recall another occasion, in all the time he'd known Joe, when Joe had left that sort of a message for him. Early in his college career, Joe had decided to be urbane, debonair, off-hand, and his manner of treating all matters light-handedly and without urgency had become, if anything, more pronounced with the years. And there was nothing off-handed about leaving a disturbing note like that waiting for a man to pick up at one o'clock in the morning. After all, he saw Joe almost every day, at lunch. You'd think a man could wait until noon the next day. Unless it was a matter of the most drastic importance . . .

Cahill twisted restlessly in his bed, trying to keep his eyes closed, sullenly inviting sleep. I will think about this tomorrow, he thought. I will think about this tomorrow. But the restful emptiness of mind he sought evaded him. Unpleasantly, he remembered that Joe had good reason to call him. Subconsciously, he realized, he had been waiting for just such a message, and dreading it. For the twentieth time, he wondered if Joe had heard what he, Cahill, had said about him at the Faculty Club two weeks before. He had felt guilty about it ever since, and ashamed of himself. Even giving himself the excuse that he had drunk a little too much had not helped. In a discussion about teaching techniques, the subject of Joe's popularity with his classes had come up, and Cahill had said cruelly, "Joe Reeves charms his classes into believing they're learning a great deal about economics when what they're really learning is how charming Joe Reeves can be." It was a stupid thing to say, even though it was partly true, and Lloyd and Evarts, who had been listening to him, had chuckled maliciously. Reeves had seemed rather cool for the last two weeks, and Cahill was almost certain that the remark had got back to him, as was almost inevitable in the narrow companionship of a college town. It was too bad. He and Joe Reeves had been close friends for over twenty years, and even though the relationship by now had more the form than the substance of the earlier friendship (how really remain friendly with any man after you are married?), it was silly to risk it for a light and mischievous judgment over a glass of whiskey. And it didn't even represent what Cahill really felt about Reeves. True, there was a superficiality about Reeves, especially in recent years, that came with his easy success with everyone—university presidents, faculty wives, students—but buried beneath that were the shrewdness, the good sense, the honorable instincts that had attracted Cahill to him in the first place. Jealousy, Cahill thought, ashamed of himself. How can a grown man give himself to it so easily? Probably, Cahill thought, Reeves had heard about the remark the very next morning and had mulled it over for the last two weeks, growing angrier and angrier, until this evening, when he had decided to have a showdown with Cahill about it. And Cahill couldn't deny having said it, or disguise in any way the envy and criticism that had called it forth, and that would be the end of the friendship. Joe, for all his easy assurance, was terribly touchy, vain, unforgiving. Cahill pondered on what it would be like not to be friendly with Joe. They had gone through college together, traveled through Europe together, lent each other money, books, opinions, neckties, celebrated together, mourned, exulted together. Even now, they and their wives had dinner together once or twice a week and made free of each other's homes in a carefully preserved informality that was pleasant, if not quite honest, and that kept alive for them a kind of gentle memory of their exciting younger days. And now, for a phrase, for a drop of wanton acid, to lose it all.

Cahill stared bitterly at the ceiling. The tongue, he thought, grows looser and more destructive with the years. Give a talkative man enough listeners and he will bring down stone with his indiscretions.

The curtains scraped in their humble starch at the windows, rasping across his consciousness. Of course, Cahill thought, it is possible that Joe did not hear what I said about him. The message could be about a dozen other things. What things? Joe was so intimately connected with his life, with the people and events of his past, with the problems and promises of the present, that the message might be concerned with his wife, his children, his job, his health, his finances, anything.

Edith moved a little in the next bed, sighing—a forlorn, sleep-bound, homeless, unremembered intake of breath—then settled back into that steady almost snore. Cahill looked over at her shadowed face. She slept, resting, secure, masked, giving no information, volunteering no help. Suddenly, he disliked and mistrusted her. Just to be so calmly and happily unconscious at a moment like this, when her husband lay awake, remorseful and torn by doubt, was a kind of willful absence, a tacit infidelity, a form of uncaring callousness.

Cahill considered his wife coldly. Her face looked surprisingly young. Twenty-eight, you might say—thirty.

Frivolity, he thought, has preserved her youth. Age needed some assistance from thought and feeling to carve lines into a face, and in Edith's case age had had to work unaided. Still, she looked pretty, attractive, despite the net and curlers. Why was she so finickingly careful about the way she looked? Not for his sake, that was sure. Another man? How could anyone ever possibly know? Lectures in other towns took him away from home quite often. And then there were the whole long days that were hers to spend unquestioned. Maybe Joe had something to say on this subject—something that couldn't wait.

Unwillingly, Cahill remembered the evening, the week before, at the Crowells', when he'd gone out onto the darkened porch and come upon Joe and Edith sitting close to each other, both of them speaking in low, urgent whispers. They'd seemed embarrassed when they saw Cahill, and Edith had looked startled. And Joe's rather heavy standard joke about being caught in the act had not served to clear the air. Cahill had been troubled for a moment; then he had dismissed it from his mind. There could be a hundred reasons, all innocent, for Joe and Edith to be talking secretly together. They'd always been friendly, right from the beginning. They kissed each time they met, Cahill suddenly recalled. Why was that? He, Cahill, never kissed Joe's wife, except ceremonially, on New Year's Eve and birthdays. The whole modern world, Cahill thought with distaste, kisses too damned much. Sly, without innocence, full of subtle invitation and hidden implication, these public embraces of the married. And, considered coldly, Joe was ripe for experiment. He and his wife didn't get along at all well. She bored Joe; that was plain enough. He was impatient with her in discussions, and she often gave the impression that she had been crying before guests arrived. And she was one of those women who are always going off on long visits to their families, in the Midwest. No woman who had a happy married life remained that attached to her mother and father. And in those bachelorlike periods

God knew what Joe did with himself. Also, Cahill remembered, Joe had not been spectacularly celibate in his youth, and in his speech, at least, gave no indication that he had reformed. Another thing: Edith, Cahill remembered, always laughed at Joe's jokes. Damaging, Cahill thought, very damaging. She laughed markedly seldom at his. Well, the truth was he wasn't terribly witty, and a woman might be expected to catch on in eighteen years of marriage. He mourned briefly over the fact that he was not witty, and mourned even more bitterly because now, at the age of forty, he realized it. When he was younger, he had had a higher opinion of himself. Edith had laughed at his jokes then, and so had other people, but now he knew that it was not wit so much as the good humor and vitality of youth that had created an air of cheerfulness about him. That was gone, there was no doubt about that, and it would be unseemly and embarrassing to pretend it wasn't. I must turn, as gracefully as possible, he thought, into a grave old man. Let people like Joe Reeves, who had the talent, say the bright things. He thought of Reeves, with his arched, actor's eyebrows and his dry, knowing delivery, at the center of things at parties, surrounded by eagerly listening, easily laughing people. Of course, Cahill thought bleakly, that's bound to be attractive to women. Also, Reeves wasn't fat. He had never exercised in all his life, but he was still as thin and straight and young-looking as ever. God has a vicious habit, Cahill thought, of putting all the gifts in one basket. Weighing the matter objectively, a woman would have to be crazy to prefer Cahill to Joe Reeves. Cahill thought of all the stories he'd heard, through the years, of good friends who had switched wives. And of the man he had met during the war who had arrived back from Europe to find his brother and his wife waiting for him on the dock with the brave, honorable, up-to-date news that they were in love with each other and wanted to marry, but not without his permission. What permission would he be able to give Joe

Reeves and his sleeping wife, and what permission had they already given themselves?

Hating Edith, Cahill twitched under the rumpled covers and groaned softly. I should have taken the pill when I woke up, regardless of the time, he thought.

It might not be Edith, Cahill thought, violently keeping his eyes shut; it might be about the Mitchell girl. There was no doubt about it, he'd been a fool about that, and trouble waited there inevitably. Dora Mitchell had been in one of his classes the year before and had decided that she was in love with him. She was nineteen years old, with a dark, unstable look to her and a kind of solemn, uncertain beauty that Cahill thought most attractive. They had met several times out of class, by accident. (At least, Cahill had thought it was by accident until Dora had told him that she waited for him outside his classroom and on the steps of the library building.) And then, more times than he wished to remember, Cahill had met her in quiet bars and had taken her on drives to the country and to a small inn for tea, fifteen miles out of town. He had been flattered by her devotion, and some obscure, middle-aged hunger in him had fed on her youth and her ingenuous high estimate of him. He had known enough, of course, never to touch her. In fact, he had never even kissed her. But who, seeing them together in a clandestine corner of the Red Wheel Inn—the animated, unaccustomedly high-spirited man and the tall, adoring girl— would ever believe that? And he knew they'd been observed several times. And, besides that, Dora had once or twice wept and rather hysterically declared she could not go on this way and had even suggested, with the melodrama born of a hundred movies full of Other Women, that she have a heart-to-heart talk with Edith.

Cahill shuddered in his bed. It was all too possible that Dora had gone to Reeves, whom she knew, and unburdened herself to him, sobbing and overflowing with grandiose, youthful passion. Perhaps she had been to see Reeves that very night, and that's why Reeves had been so anxious to have Cahill call him. Tenderness, Cahill thought, the blind, many-edged weapon for the cutting down of fools. Bitterly, he made himself imagine what it would be like the day his own daughter, Elizabeth, herself only two years younger than Dora, found out (from a malicious sorority sister, a newspaper report, from a process server for divorce proceedings, from Dora herself over ice-cream sodas after a basketball game). Grotesque, he thought, for a few hours of gentle conversation, for an illusory, ephemeral buttressing of the vanity, for the titillating suggestion of sin without the sin itself, to risk so much! Maybe, he thought despairingly, I should go to a psychoanalyst; the urge for self-destruction has overcome me.

That, of course, was out of the question. He couldn't afford it. He could be as mad as Peter the Great, or as any lunatic screaming in a padded cell, and he couldn't pay the first bill of the rawest young practitioner, just past his initial reading of Freud and Jung. Absolutely sane or raving like an ape in a tree, he would still have to conduct classes in Philosophy 22, Philosophy 12, Philosophy 53A, for Students in Pre-Educational Courses. Money. He thought about money and groaned again. Still three payments on the car. Elizabeth's tuition, due in two weeks. Butter, how many cents a pound? Roast beef once a week, eighty cents a pound, and Charles, his son, and Margaret, the maid, between them devoured four whole ribs each time. Insurance, he calculated in the darkness, in a well-remembered, dreadful nighttime litany, taxes, clothes, dentist, doctor, gifts to his wife's large family, amusement. Perhaps, he thought, Reeves had called him to tell him about promotion. God knew he was up for it, and Old Man Edwards was almost due to retire, and that would leave some room near the top. Reeves was very friendly with the president. Dinner there once a month. First names and private confidences. Reeves had been in to see the president that afternoon. Cahill knew because Lloyd, in his own department, who had all the gossip of

the university at his fingertips, had told him so. Perhaps
Reeves had been given the good word and wanted to
pass it on. Cahill played luxuriously with the idea of promotion. Twelve, fifteen hundred more a year. No more
Philosophy 53A, the dullest course in the curriculum.
No eight-o'clock classes. Then the glow passed. Probably, he thought, it's the other way around. The president had never been any more than polite to him, and it
was to be remembered that he had been passed over
twice on the promotion lists, for Kennedy and O'Rourke,
younger men than he. It wouldn't be too surprising, all
things considered, if they had decided to get rid of him.
He was far from being the most popular instructor on the
campus. To be absolutely honest, he wouldn't blame them
for firing him. Ever since he'd come back from the war,
the job had bored him. Not that there was anything else
that he particularly wanted to do. Just sit, perhaps, and
stare into an open fire. Drink more whiskey than was
good for him. Not pretend to anyone that he knew anything much, or not pretend he thought it was valuable
that anyone learn anything much. Dangerous doctrine for
professors, assistant professors, instructors, tutors. Probably others had caught on. Come to think of it, the last
time he had seen the president at a faculty meeting, the
president had been . . . frosty. That was the word—
frosty. Purge by frost. Execution, university style. The polite death among the library shelves. He could almost hear
Joe Reeves' troubled voice on the phone, warning him,
trying to break it to him gently, trying to cheer him up
with lies about other jobs, in other colleges.

Cahill lay in bed thinking about what it would be like
not to have a job. Rent, taxes, roast beef, tuition, clothes.
The advantage of marrying a rich wife. Nothing, finally,
was crucial. There was always the net of fat relatives to
fall back on, like a high-wire artist who slipped in the
circus. Edith's father had worked for the Pennsylvania
Railroad and had retired on a pension of a hundred and

thirty-five dollars a month. Not much of a net there. Cahill thought of the rich wives he might have married. Rowena . . . Rowena what? Twenty years ago, in Chicago. Shipping. Father in Lake steamers. How could a man be expected to marry a girl named Rowena? Also, she had weighed a hundred and seventy pounds. No exaggeration. Maybe a hundred and eighty. Amorous as the gilded fly, too. Who wanted a wife like that, Lake steamers or no Lake steamers, especially at that weight? Anyway, that had been his one chance of marrying into wealth. Some people were lucky, of course. They met pretty girls, very nice, whose fathers controlled the Chase National Bank or owned mining empires in Central America. Still, if he had married Rowena—Rowena Grumman, that was it; good God, what a name—he wouldn't be trembling like this tonight. Seven hundred dollars in the bank, debts three fifty-five, and that was that. One month and then relief. For this relief, very little thanks. He supposed that nine-tenths of the people in the country walked, as he did, on this thin edge of disaster all their lives, smiling, dissembling, not sleeping some nights, hoping their nerve would hold out as they saw the edge crumbling, crumbling. And then the people in China, scouring sidewalks for lost grains of rice, running before the armies with two pans and a blanket on their backs, dying politely, with Oriental good manners, of starvation. Maybe Reeves ought to call them up, too. Perhaps he had an important message for the Chinese as well. Still, all the philosophical identification in the world would not help if the frost set in. Somehow, he thought regretfully, I should have arranged things better. Somewhere, I missed a chance, was too lazy, too stupid, too complacent.

Of course, Reeves might be calling him about something entirely different. Maybe Elizabeth. Reeves had a nephew, name of Richard, and he and Elizabeth had been seeing a good deal of each other recently. Fact was, last Saturday night Cahill had surprised them kissing at

the door. Quite a shock. Item: What do you do when you
see your seventeen-year-old daughter kissing the nephew
of your best friend? Bringing up a daughter was a little
like sitting over one of those dud bombs that had been
dropped into cellars during the war. A year might go by,
two years. Nothing might happen. Or, the world was full
of women who had gone bad, and at one time they had
all been seventeen and some father's dewy darling. Ministers' daughters, admirals' daughters, daughters of the
leaders of society. How could any father know what obscure, shameful invitations of the flesh his daughter was
accepting and succumbing to among the college pennants
and dimity and framed photographs in the next room?
And Elizabeth was no help. She had always been a secretive, self-willed child, going her own way, disdainful
of help or advice, not lying, exactly, but never telling any
more of the truth than she was forced to. He tried to think
of her as someone else's daughter, in order to get an ob-
jective impression of her. Handsomely developed, pre-
maturely womanly, he would have to say, with a promising, challenging look in her eye, a hidden, guarded sen-
suality, very much like her mother's. Oh, God, he thought
torturedly, I hope the message isn't about her!

Or Reeves might want to talk to him about Charlie.
Cahill considered the question of Charlie. In addition to
eating an enormous amount of expensive roast beef when
he got the chance, Charlie did very badly in his studies
(was it possible that he was fundamentally stupid?) and
got into trouble regularly with all authorities. A smooth-
tongued truant, a brawler in schoolyards, a mischievous
vandal in locker rooms, Charlie had been the occasion,
again and again, for long visits of apology on the part of
Cahill to parents of broken-nosed children, angry and insulted teachers, even, once, to the police station, when
Charlie had broken into the country-club tennis shop and
stolen a dozen cans of balls and two lengths of chrome
twist. At what moment did the high-spirited schoolboy
turn into the juvenile delinquent? Cahill thought of Char-

lie's sly, blond, unruly face. Consider your son objectively. What did you see? The insolence of the radio-and-comic-book age. The violence and irresponsibility of the double- and triple-featured generation of movie gangsters and movie sensualists. The restless superficiality of the book haters, who slid into whiskey, divorce courts, bankruptcy, worse, as the years wore on. Cahill had a vision of himself at the age of seventy, supporting his son, paying various blonde women alimony for him, bailing him out of magistrates' courts, and trying to hush up charges of drunken driving and cop-fighting. Tomorrow, he thought gloomily, I am going to have a serious talk with that young man. Though who knew what good it might do? John Dillinger's father probably had several talks with his son on the farm back in Indiana, and old Mr. Capone no doubt had the parish priest in to talk sternly to his dark-eyed boy in the crowded home in Brooklyn.

Cahill hoped that Reeves was not going to talk to him about Charlie when they finally met the next day.

The bed now seemed intolerably warm, and Cahill could feel the sweat collecting in the crease of his chest. He threw back the covers. They made a loud, electric crackle and static electricity from the friction jumped in strange blue flashes around him. Edith stirred a little at the noise but did not wake. Cahill glared gloomily at her, listening to her breathe. If she had been home, as she had said she was going to be, that evening, it would have been she who had talked to Reeves. He'd have given her some inkling of what it was he wanted to talk to Cahill about and he'd have been spared this agonizing night of conjecture. Tomorrow, Cahill thought, I'm going to damn well ask her a question or two, too. No, he thought, I'll be sly. If I seem to be quizzing her, she'll get suspicious or angry and sulk for days, and there'll be hell to pay around the house, and I'll have to give in to her on everything from now to Easter Sunday. I'll be nonchalant, elaborately offhand—pretend to be reading the paper, mix it up with questions about the kids, surprise her into revelations, if there are any. Then he was ashamed of himself for plotting this way against his wife, sleeping so trustfully and innocently in the next bed. He had an impulse to go over to her and hold her in his arms. He even sat up, tentatively. Then he thought better of it. Edith was terribly grouchy when he woke her in the middle of the night, and could be depended on to make him suffer for it the next day. He stared at her, resenting her. The business of the two beds, now. Until the war, they'd slept in one big old bed, as married people should. You felt really married, two people defending themselves as a unit against the world, if each night you retired into the warm fortress of the marital bed. Two beds brought with them the inevitable warning of division, oneness, loneliness, rejection. And when he'd come back from the war, Edith had said she couldn't sleep that way any more, she'd got too used to sleeping alone. And, like a fool, he'd consented. The two beds, with the extra mattresses and blankets, had cost nearly three hundred dollars, too. All his terminal-leave pay. Your bonus for fighting the war was that your wife made you sleep alone. Beds fit for heroes to sleep in—singularly.

It was silly to worry about that any more. It was a battle he'd lost, definitely, a long time ago. Each night to its own insomnia. Tonight, he thought—by now a little lightheaded and oratorical, even in his thoughts—we take up the problem of the message of Joseph Reeves.

The thing was to systematize it, attack the problem scientifically. Like *Time* magazine: Business, Politics, National Affairs, Science, Religion, Sex. Everything in its neat, crisp department. Two minutes with each one and you're ready with enough facts and opinions to carry you until the next publication date.

National Affairs. In the twentieth century, Reeves had said at lunch three days before, National Affairs had become a euphemism for butchery. Butchery accomplished, butchery in progress, butchery contemplated. Slaughter in three tenses, with a corresponding rise in the budget.

In the last few months, Reeves had become more and more obsessed with the idea of war. At the same lunch, they'd had a gloomy conversation about the possibility that it would break out soon. Reeves, so optimistic about other things, sombrely dug around in newspapers and magazines to find new and disturbing items about the imminence of conflict and the dreadful new tools that might be employed. Cahill had even tried to avoid Reeves recently, because it was a subject he preferred not to reflect on. And his friend's dark flood of statistics about the range of atomic missiles and the mortal potential of biologic agents was not calculated to improve the delicate lunchtime appetite. Also, Reeves had made an unpleasant survey of the various and all too frequent occasions in history on which whole nations and, in fact, whole civilizations had committed suicide, deducing from that that it was entirely possible, and, indeed, probable, that in the next few years just such a widespread immolation would take place. To preserve his sanity, Cahill thought, resentfully trying to crowd Reeves' apocalyptic arguments out of his mind, a man must keep himself from speculating on these matters. Impotent and haunted, frozen in the slow, massive tide of events beyond his control, the night waker could only hope to ignore the question, or at least think about it in daylight, when the nerves were steadier. War, he thought angrily and helplessly, war. He remembered the cemeteries of Normandy and the sound shells made going over his head. At this moment, in a dozen places on the crust of the earth, machine guns were flicking and men were joyfully and devotedly putting other men to death and inviting the Americans, the Russians, the Berbers, the Malayans, the Yugoslavs, the Finns, and the Bulgars to join them.

Read a newspaper, listen to a news broadcast, wake for a quarter hour in your own bed some time before dawn, and death came familiarly to hand. When he'd come home in 1945, he'd thought all that was behind him. My limit, he always said—not seriously, but meaning it, too—is one war. But other people, of more influence, seemed to have other limits. It was one thing, at the age of thirty-three, bravely to don the uniform and sail off to a relatively old-fashioned war, in which comprehensible weapons like machine guns and bombs were being used. It was quite another, seven years later, a sedentary forty, to contemplate exposing yourself to the atom and the microbe, feeling, too, all the while, that your well-run home, enclosing your wife and children, might at any moment dissolve in radioactive dust or become the harbor for the germs of plague. He looked over at his wife, comfortably at rest. How, he wondered, does anyone sleep this year?

The dim light of dawn was washing through the curtains now. God, Cahill thought, his hot eyes resentfully taking it in, I am going to be a wreck today. Masochistically, he continued with his list. Politics. There we have a subject, he reflected, to keep a man's eyes open a night or two. According to Lloyd again, after Reeves had visited the president's office that afternoon, he had been called into a secret session of the committee of state senators who were down from the capital investigating Communist influence on the campus. Lloyd, who had been active in several questionable organizations for years, and who didn't trust Reeves, had been none too happy about that. "A company man," Lloyd had said resentfully, in Cahill's presence. "He'd sell his best friend for a smile from the stockholders." Lloyd had peered meaningfully at Cahill when he said it, too, and Cahill was sure that the phrase "his best friend" had not been a random choice of words. Cahill thought of various things that Reeves might have told the committee and twitched uneasily. Back in the years before the war, when Communism was an almost respectable doctrine, Cahill had been on various committees with people he was sure belonged to the Party, and had let his name be used again and again on a flood of well-meaning petitions and statements that, if not promulgated by the Communists, certainly had their endorsement. Once, he and Reeves had even gone to a kind of polite, open Party meeting, at which several people he knew had made amorphous speeches about Communism's being twentieth-century Americanism, and stuff like that. He had even been invited to join, he remembered, although he couldn't remember who had actually come up to him and spoken the fateful words. He hadn't joined, and he'd never gone to another meeting, but what if the committee, armed with informers' information, demanded of him whether he had ever attended a meeting and if he had ever been asked to join. What would he do? Perjure himself, and say he had never gone, or tell the truth, and leave himself open to the next question. Was Professor Kane there? Did Mr. Ryan, instructor in chemistry, make a speech about the working of the Communist Party? Will you kindly look over this list of names and check off the ones you can swear were present? What do you do in a situation like that? Professor Kane had been there and had made a speech, but Cahill knew that he had quietly resigned from the Party at the time of the Pact and had had no more to do with it. Still, who knew what Kane had told the committee? Kane was a friend of his, and needed the job. And if Cahill told the truth, Kane would be out of his job, disgraced, in a month. And poor Ryan. He'd been suspended on suspicion already, and his wife was sick, and he'd had to pay a lawyer to defend him. And, Communist or no, he'd always seemed to Cahill to be a very decent, shy, undangerous man. Cahill had given Ryan fifty dollars toward his defense, secretly, in cash. It was hard to understand just why. He was opposed to Ryan's politics, but he liked Ryan and felt sorry for him, and fifty dollars was not much, one way or another. Cahill had told Reeves about the fifty dollars and had even asked Reeves to help, too. Reeves, coldly, saying Ryan had it coming to him, had refused. What if Reeves had been trapped into saying something about the fifty dollars to the committee? What could Cahill tell them when he was questioned? How would he act? Would he be brave, considered, honorable? Just what was honorable in a situation like this? Was there honor in perjury? Or did honor lie in destroying your friends? Or destroying yourself? Did he actually believe that Ryan, for example, was an innocent, idealistic fellow, or did he believe that Ryan, the soft-voiced, scholarly, shyly smiling family man Ryan, was a potential traitor, a patient murderer, a dangerous conspirator against all the values that he, Cahill, held dear? I am too weary, Cahill thought pettishly, to decide this this morning. What if they asked about the meeting? What day was it? What year? Who invited you? The mists of memory shifted thickly around the fact. Whatever you answered was bound to be wrong. And if you said honestly, "I don't remember," how would that look on the record and in the newspapers? Like evasion, guilt, worthy only of disbelief and disdain.

So much for the crisp, neat two minutes of Politics. It was simpler in a magazine, where another issue was coming out in seven days, with another capsule of highly polished, anonymous, streamlined facts. A new man, Cahill thought, should be published every week, under a different title, anonymously. Each issue built around a different fact. The honorable man. The perjured man. The sensual man. The devout man. The economic man. Fifty-two times a year, something new and interesting in each copy. No irreconcilable facts to be found in any single volume. For Christmas, we plan to give you the friendly man, to be followed shortly by the betraying man, all in fine, unlimited editions. And, as a dividend to our subscribers, bound in blood, stitched with nerve ends, and illustrated by the leading artists of the age, with copious notes, the doubtful man, on which our editors have been working continuously for three hundred years at great personal expense.

There was a soft, sighing sound at the window, and Cahill saw that the wind had grown stronger and that it had begun to snow. A thin shower of snow sifted in through the open window, making a pale pattern on the floor. Fair and warmer, Cahill thought angrily, that's what the forecasters said. The liars of science, portentously surrounded by inaccurate instruments, confidently deluding you with false visions of the future. Like Dr. Manners, armed with stethoscope and X ray, patting him heartily on the back last Tuesday, telling him of course he occasionally must expect to feel a twinge here, a pain there; he was not as young as he used to be. How many men died on Sunday who had been told during the week by their doctors that they were not as young as they used to be? The breezy assumption on the part of the medical profession that agony was the ordinary condition of life. Manners, he thought resentfully, would be considerably less breezy with himself if it were his chest that trembled to the tone of pain, secret and until now distant, but there, warning, definite. Experimentally, Cahill lifted his left arm and stretched it. Again, as always in the last few months, there was the small answering pressure, dull, lurking, across his chest, across his heart. "A slight irregularity," Manners had said. "Just nerves. Nothing to worry about." Nothing for Manners to worry about, perhaps. And the constriction across the stomach; that, too, according to Manners, was nerves. Nerves, the modern equivalent for Fate, the substitute for the medieval Devil, which attacked mankind in the form of obscure, and often mortal, ills. Nerves, the perfect formula for the lazy diagnostician. Or—and Cahill could feel his breath catching in his throat at the thought—perhaps Manners, out of kindness, was hiding the true information from him. A hearty clap on the back, an innocuous prescription for sugar water and belladonna, and, after the door had closed, a thoughtful, sorrowful shrug, and the fateful entry in the case history of Philip Cahill "Prognosis negative."

Cahill put the palm of his hand under his pajama jacket, on the warm skin of his abdomen, as though by the touch of flesh on flesh he might discover the dreadful secret that lay there. Within him, under his hand, he could feel a faint, erratic quivering. Not good, he thought, not good at all. His mind touched regretfully on the edge of the word he was afraid to say. The papers were so damned full of it, the posters on the buses, even the radio. And if it occurred in the stomach, it was fatal at least eighty per cent of the time, and you almost never found out about it before it was too late. Maybe that was what Reeves had called about. Maybe Manners had gone to Reeves and explained to him and asked what Reeves thought should be done. The services that friends had to do for each other. You start out as gay children, playing tennis with each other, racing each other across the lakes of summer, roaring jubilantly together on your first drunks, and twenty years later, all that far in the past, you have to go in and announce to your friend that his death is at hand.

Ridiculous, Cahill thought. I'm not going to lie here any longer. He got out of bed and stood up. His legs felt weary and uncertain, and there was the tense, stretched sensation in his stomach as he put on his robe and slippers. He looked over at Edith. She still slept, the rhythm of her breathing unchanged. Walking slowly, his slippers shuffling across the rug, he went silently out of the bedroom. He descended the stairs, holding the banister, shivering a little in the night-frozen house. In the hall below, he went over to the telephone, on the table under the mirror. He hesitated, staring at the phone. The clock in the living room said ten minutes to seven. He picked up the phone and dialed Joe Reeves' number. While he listened to the long succession of buzzes in the receiver, he stared at himself in the mirror. His face was haggard, his eyes thick and glazed and encircled completely by muddy blue shadows. His rumpled hair looked slack and lustreless, his face exhausted and—hunted. He looked for a moment, then turned his back on the mirror.

Finally, there was the sound of someone picking up the receiver at the other end. Whoever it was fumbled a long time with the instrument, and Cahill said impatiently, "Hello! Hello!" Then he heard a sleepy, dark voice mumbling irritatedly, "Mr. Reeves' residence. Who that calling?"

"Hello," Cahill said eagerly. "Violet?"

"Yes. This Violet. Who calling?"

"Violet," Cahill said, making his voice even and clear, because he remembered with what suspicion Violet regarded the telephone, "this is Mr. Cahill."

"Who?"

"Cahill. Mr. Cahill."

"It's an awful early hour of the mawnin', Mr. Cahill," Violet said aggrievedly.

"I know," Cahill said, "but Mr. Reeves has a message for me. He especially asked me to call him as soon as I could. Is he up yet?"

"I dunno, Mr. Cahill," said Violet. He could hear her yawn enormously at the other end of the wire. "He's not here."

"What's that?"

"He's gone. Went last night. He and Mis' Reeves. They gone for the weekend. I'm the only livin' soul in the house. And"—her voice took on a tone of impatient complaint—"I'm freezin' here in my nightshirt in this drafty old hall."

Cahill could sense that Violet was on the verge of hurling the receiver down on the hook—an amusing trick of hers, with which she concluded telephone conversations in mid-message. It was not amusing now. "Violet," he said urgently, "don't hang up. Where did they go?"

"Don't ask me," Violet said. "They didn't tell me. You know Mr. Reeves. He was sittin' around the house last night, real restless, like he is, and all of a sudden he jumped up and said to Mis' Reeves, 'Let's get into the car and get away from here for a couple of days.' They just packed one little bag. Mis' Reeves was wearing slacks and she didn't even bother to change 'em. They just gone for a ride, I guess. They'll be back by Monday, never you worry."

Slowly, Cahill put the receiver down. He looked up and

saw that Elizabeth was standing at the foot of the stairs, in an almost transparent nightgown, her bathrobe carelessly open and hanging loose from her shoulders. Her dark hair was down, flowing thickly around her throat. Her face was creamy with sleep and her eyes were half closed in an amused, almost condescending smile. "Daddy," she said, "who on earth are you calling at this fantastic hour? One of your other girls?"

Cahill stared dully at her. Through the frail rayon of her nightdress, he could see, very plainly, the swell of her breasts, rising generously from the exposed, rich skin of her bare bosom. "None of your business," he said harshly. "Now go upstairs. And when you come down again, make sure you're decently covered! This is your home. It is not a burlesque house! Is that clear?"

He could see the incredulous, hurt grimace gripping her features, and then the blush, rising from her bosom, flaming on her cheeks. "Yes," she said faintly. "Yes, Daddy." She turned, hugging her robe around her ashamedly. Cahill watched her walk slowly and painfully up the stairs. He wanted to say something, call her back, but by now he knew there was nothing to say and that the child would not come back.

He went into the living room and sank into a chair, feeling cold. Wildly, he contemplated the thought of living until Monday.

The Green Nude

As a young man, Sergei Baranov, although he preferred painting large still lifes of red apples, green pears and very orange oranges, joined the Red Army and did a mild amount of damage in several engagements against the Whites around Kiev. He was a sturdy, good-humored, dreamy youth who did not like to refuse anyone anything, and since all his friends were joining the Revolution he went along and served faithfully and cheerfully, eating the soldier's black bread, sleeping on the soldier's straw, pulling the trigger of his ancient rifle when the people around him ordered him to do so, advancing bravely when everyone else was advancing and running in fear of his life when that seemed like the necessary thing to do. When the Revolution was over, he retired from the military, equipped with a modest decoration for an action at which he was not present, and took up quarters in Moscow and began once more to paint red apples, green pears, and very orange oranges. All his friends were enthusiastically convinced that the Revolution was an excellent thing, and Sergei, never one to strike out on his own, amiably and decorously concurred. The truth was that he was only really interested in his highly colored fruits and vegetables and when, in his studio or in the café which he frequented, discussions would start about Lenin and Trotsky or the new economic program, he would laugh his hearty and agreeable laugh and say, bashfully, "Eh, who knows? It is for the philosophers." Besides, being a decorated hero of the Revolution and an artist to boot, he was treated well, and was assigned an excellent studio with a skylight and permitted heavy laborer's rations. His paintings, too, were warmly approved by everyone, since he had the trick of making all his garden products seem marvelously edible. They sold without delay and his work was to be seen in the homes and offices of many quite-important officials of the new regime, warm and appetizing globs of color on the otherwise bleak and functional walls.

When, in 1923, he met and conquered an ample and beautiful young lady from Soviet Armenia, his painting took a new turn. He began to paint nudes. Since his technique remained the same, despite the change in subject matter, his success increased in leaps and bounds. As edible as ever, his paintings now combined the most satisfactory features of the orchard and the harem, and examples of his work, rosy, healthy, and very round, were much sought after by even more important officials of the regime.

He undoubtedly would have continued thus to this day, happily producing a succession of canvases of hearty, lightly clad, appetizing girls, alternating with piled heaps of oversized purple grapes and bananas, going from success to success, honor to honor, if he had not met, at a literary party, the woman who was finally to become his wife.

Anna Kronsky was one of those sharp-featured and overpoweringly energetic women that the liberation of women from the nursery and kitchen has turned loose on the male world. Angular, voracious, and clever, with a tongue like an iron clapper in a new bell, racked by indigestion and a deep contempt for the male sex, she was the sort of woman who in this country would run a department store or report wars for the Luce publications. As one of her friends said of her, in attempting to put his finger on the exact difference between Anna and her more gentle contemporaries, "Anna does not make up her face when she goes out in the morning—she hones it."

In Moscow, at the time Sergei met her, she had gravitated inexorably into the education system. With twenty-three day nurseries for the children of working parents under her supervision, and a staff of over five hundred cowed men and women, she had already made her mark on the new population of the growing state. The children under her care were known as the cleanest and most precocious in the Soviet Union, and it was not until 1938 that a routine survey of neurotic diseases disclosed the fact that the graduates of Anna Kronsky's immaculate creches led all other population groups of the nation by three to one in absolute nervous breakdowns.

In a necessarily incomplete study, prepared by a thoughtful Artillery Colonel during a slow month on the Southern front in 1944, the estimate was made that the ministrations of Anna Kronsky to the rising generation had cost the Red Army more manpower than a full armored brigade of the Nazi 9th Army. However, the study was accepted with a grain of salt by the Colonel's superiors, since his OGPU dossier revealed that he had been the lover of Miss Kronsky between the dates of August third and August seventh, 1922, and had sent into headquarters a fervent request for transfer to Archangel on August eighth of the same year.

It was this lady, who, flanked by a heroic poet and an aging test-pilot, set her eyes on the sturdy Baranov as he came through the door, and, in one moment of iron speculation, made the decision that was to transform the painter's life. Her carborundum eyes glittering, she crossed the room, introduced herself to her prey, ignored the beautiful girl from Soviet Armenia who had come with Baranov, and started the necessary process which resulted three months later in marriage. Just what it was that made Baranov so immediately attractive to her, none of her friends could decide. Perhaps she saw, in the painter's simple docility and good-humored health, evidence of a fine digestion and an uncomplicated nervous system, excellent attributes for the husband of a busy lady executive who came home each night jangled and worried with the day's thousand cares. Whatever the reasons, Anna left no escape possible for Sergei. He had a tearful scene with his beloved Soviet Armenian, painted one last, pink, fruity nude, and helped carry the poor girl's meager belongings to the new room Anna had managed to find for her in a slum section three-quarters of an hour away from the center of town. Then Anna moved in, bringing with her a new bedspread, three packing cases of pamphlets and reports, and a large gooseneck lamp.

The marriage seemed from the beginning to be a thoroughly happy one, and there was only one noticeable change in Baranov, outside of a subtle, but growing tendency toward silence in company. He no longer painted nudes. Not one painting, not one sketch, not even a wash from the waist up, of the ripe, unclad female form, came from his studio. Confined once more entirely to the vegetable world, he seemed to have mastered a new understanding of the problems of the apple, the orange, and the pear. As edible as ever, a new dust seemed to be powdered over his work, a haunting and melancholy fragrance, as though the fruit he chose to paint came now from autumnal boughs, the last sweet bounty of the closing year, the final, nostalgic yield of trees and vines through whose dying leaves and frozen branches the cruel winds of winter were already moaning.

This new development in Baranov's work was greeted with respectful praise by critics and public alike and examples of the new phase were hung in many museums and public places. Success did not change him, however. More silent than ever, he painted steadily, experimenting with beets and pumpkins in ever darker reds and yellows, going everywhere with his sallow and brilliant wife, listening with model attention night after night as she monopolized conversations in literary, artistic, political, educational,

and industrial circles. Once, it is true, at the request of his
wife, he went to one of her nurseries and started a painting of a group of children he saw there. He painted for
about an hour, then put his brush down, tore the canvas in
half and had it burned in the stove, and went into the
men's room, where he was reported sobbing uncontrol-
lably. This story was not believed by anyone, as it was re-
tailed by a young teacher who had crossed swords with
Anna Kronsky and who was removed later at her instiga-
tion as unreliable. Whatever the truth of the matter was,
Baranov returned to his studio and went back to his beets
and pumpkins.

It was about this time that he took to painting at night,
using the gooseneck lamp that Anna had brought with her
as part of her dowry. They had their own apartment by
now, as a result of their double importance, more than a
mile away from the studio, and the sturdy though now
slightly bent figure of the painter, trudging through the
snow late at night was a common sight on the almost deserted streets between his home and his studio. He became
very secretive, locking his door at all times, and when
friends asked him about his current work, he would merely
smile vaguely and politely and change the subject. Anna,
of course, never asked him about his work, as she was a
very busy woman, and it was not until the opening of his
one-man show, an affair attended by many of the intellec-
tual élite of the government and the arts, that she saw for
the first time the painting that had engaged her husband for
the past many months.

It was a nude. But it was like no nude that Baranov had
painted before. There was no touch of pink anywhere on
the enormous and frightening canvas. The prevailing color
was green, that green that lurks in the sky before cyclones
and hurricanes, sallow, lurid, oppressive to the eye. The figure itself, of a slack-breasted and lank-haired woman with
a wrinkled abdomen and stringy but somehow violent
loins, was also done in mottled green, and the staring and
demonic eyes under the dry brow were another shade of

the dominant hue. The mouth, the most fearful feature of the work, was done in dead black and somehow gave the startling impression of howling speech, as though the painter had caught his model in a full flood of maniac oratory. The mouth seemed to fill the canvas, indeed the entire room, with a tumbling, morbid, glittering torrent of horrid rhetoric, and it was to be noticed that the viewers attempted, uneasily, to avoid, as much as possible, looking at that particular section of the work. The background, so different from Baranov's usual arrangement of carefully painted, richly figured materials, was spume and wreckage, jagged stony ruins of temples and tenements against a green and charcoal sky. The only recognizable link with Baranov's past work was a cherry tree in the right foreground. But the tree was stunted and uprooted; a green fungus ate at the branches; a thick and snakelike vine wound murderously around the suffering trunk, and minutely painted green worms munched among the unripe fruit. The entire effect was of madness, genius, energy, disaster, sorrow, and despair.

When Anna Kronsky Baranov entered the room, people were standing in muted groups, staring with horrid fascination at the new painting. "Great," she heard Suvarnin, the critic for *The Sickle,* mutter. And, "Incredible," whispered Levinoff, the painter, as she passed him.

Baranov himself was standing in a corner, shyly and excitedly accepting the awed congratulations of friends. Anna stared incredulously at the painting, then again at her husband, who, with his rosy complexion and pleasantly smiling, obedient face, looked not one whit different from the man she had known all these years. She started to go over to congratulate him, although the painting seemed very unlifelike to her, but she was intercepted by two men who ran a tractor factory in Rostov, and she became so interested in lecturing to them about tractor manufacture that she forgot to mention anything about the painting to Baranov until much later in the evening.

From time to time, various of the guests stole sidelong

and speculative glances at Anna, especially when she happened to be standing in front of her husband's masterpiece. Although Anna was conscious of their regard and also conscious of something vaguely disturbing in their eyes, she dismissed the feeling, since she was well-used by now to glances of varying intensity from her subordinates in the halls and offices of the nurseries under her command. The real reason for the hurried, measuring appraisals of the people in the gallery she never discovered and no one in the Soviet Union had the courage to apprise her of it. The wild and nightmare face that topped the terrible body of the green nude bore a family resemblance to Anna Kronsky that no amount of stylization on the part of the artist could erase. Sisters, twin souls, the painted and the living woman existed in a hideous relationship that escaped the notice of none. The only other person in Moscow who did not know that the artist had painted his wife's portrait was the man who went home obediently each night with her. Ignorant and happy in his new glory, Sergei Baranov took his wife to the ballet that night to celebrate and later ordered three bottles of champagne at a café, most of which was drunk by the two tractor men from Rostov.

The week following the opening of the show marked the highpoint of Sergei Baranov's early life. Feted, pointed out wherever he went, especially when accompanied by his wife, saluted in the press, urged to create murals to cover acres of walls, he swam in a bright stream of praise. The critic Suvarnin, who had barely acknowledged his greeting before this, even deigned to come to Baranov's studio to interview him, and, breaking all precedent, appeared sober.

"Tell me," said Suvarnin, squinting at Baranov through his pale, cold eyes, those eyes which had riddled holes in so many canvases before this, "tell me how a man who has only painted fruit before this comes to do such a painting."

"Well," said Baranov, who had recaptured some of his early loquacity and expansiveness in the past week,

"Well, it happened something like this. As you know, if you have seen any of my painting recently, my work has become more and more melancholy."

Suvarnin nodded thoughtfully, agreeing.

"The palette became more and more subdued. Brown, dark brown, entered increasingly into the canvases. The fruit . . . well, the truth is, the fruit began to be withered, frostbitten, sad. I would come here to my studio and I would sit down and cry. For an hour. Two hours at a time. All by myself. I began to dream every night. Dreams of death, dreams of trains going out of stations, dreams of boats leaving me on the dock, in the rain, dreams of being buried alive and being sniffed at by dark brown foxes and other small animals . . ." Baranov spoke with lively animation, as a perfectly healthy man might describe symptoms of a dreadful disease which he has suffered and proudly conquered. "The worst dream, and one that I had over and over again, was that I was in a small room and it was crowded with women, only women. All the women could talk, but I couldn't. I tried. I moved my lips. My tongue quivered between my teeth. The conversation around me filled the air deafeningly like locomotive whistles and French horns. And I could not make a sound. You have no idea how terrible this simple thing can be. It was like being committed each night to a new kind of awful prison. I began to fear going to bed. I would come and stare at the blank canvas on my easel, at the arrangement of potatoes and eggplants on which I intended to work, and I could not move my fingers to the brushes. An artist, as you know, must create out of his emotions. How could I transfer how I felt into the image of an eggplant, into potatoes? I felt I was lost. I felt I would never be able to paint again. I contemplated suicide."

Suvarnin nodded. He even thought of making notes, something he hadn't done for twenty years, since he was of the firm opinion that accuracy in reporting was the foe of creative criticism. He put his hand into his pocket for a pencil, but discovered he had neglected to bring one along with him. He took his hand out of his pocket and gave up the thought of taking notes.

"Suicide," Baranov repeated, flushed with joy at having the redoubtable Suvarnin pay such close attention to his confession. "I moaned. I shrieked." Baranov knew that he had done no such thing, and had, in fact, merely gloomed silently in front of the easel, but he felt that these active expressions of passion would sit well with the critic, as indeed they did. "I cried out. I despaired." Suvarnin moved restively, glancing instinctively at the vodka bottle on the table, and licking the corner of his mouth, and Baranov hurried on, feeling anxiously that he had perhaps gone a little far with his synonyms. "I slashed out blindly at the canvas. I did not guide my hand. I did not search for colors. I did not look at the potatoes or the eggplant. My terrors painted through me. I was the instrument of my dreams. I hardly looked to see what I was doing. I painted all night long, one night after another. I did not know what I was doing . . ." By now Baranov had forgotten that he was trying to make an impression. By now he was letting the simple truth pour out. "All I knew was, that as the painting grew, a great weight was being lifted from me. My subconscious was being delivered from its prison. When I slept, I no longer dreamed of being struck dumb or being nosed by dark brown foxes. Now my dreams were of vineyards in the springtime and large-breasted young women I wished to approach on the streets. Finally, when I was finished, and I sat back and looked at the green nude and the ruins, I was as surprised by what I had done as if I had come into my studio and found that another man, a complete stranger, had used my easel while I was away on holiday. And I was grateful to him, whoever he was. And I was grateful to the green lady on the canvas. Between them," Baranov said simply, "they had delivered me from Hell."

Suvarnin stood up and silently shook the painter's hand.

"Out of anguish," he said finally, "comes the great art. Out of the depths of despair only can we reach to the skies. Look at Dostoyevsky."

Baranov nodded, although a little uneasily, as he had tried to read *The Brothers Karamazov* three times and had never got past page 165. But Suvarnin did not press the point. "Read my article on Saturday," he said modestly. "I think you will be pleased."

"Thank you," Baranov said humbly, resolving to call Anna immediately Suvarnin left to impart to her the heady news. "I am in your debt."

"Nonsense," said Suvarnin, with the concision and gift for a phrase that had made his reputation secure in a dozen cities. "Art is in your debt. And now," he asked, "what is the next painting going to be?"

Baranov smiled happily. "Cherries," he said. "Six kilos of red cherries in a wicker basket. They are being delivered here at two o'clock from the market."

"Good," said Suvarnin. They shook hands once more and the critic departed, with only one tentative glance at the vodka bottle.

Baranov sat down, waiting dreamily for the arrival of the cherries, thinking, as he sat there, Perhaps it is time that I started a scrapbook for my reviews.

On Saturday, Baranov opened the magazine with trembling fingers. There, on the page with Suvarnin's photograph, was a streaming black title, "FILTH IN THE GALLERIES." Baranov blinked. Then he began to read. "Last week," Suvarnin had written, "the Counter-Revolution struck one of its most audacious blows at Russian Art. From the bestial brushes of one, Sergei Baranov, who has until now concealed his heretical infamies under bushels of rotten fruit, and who now feels that he can come out boldly and shamelessly in his true colors, we have received a nauseating sample of decadent, bourgeois 'art.'"

Baranov sat down, trying to get air into his aching lungs. Then he forced himself to read on. "In this gangrenous excrescence," Suvarnin continued, using what Baranov, even in his extremity, recognized as a pet phrase, "the dying world of Capitalism, allied with the Trotskyist bandits, has served notice on the Soviet Union that its minions and agents have wormed their way into the heart of the fatherland's cultural life. By what treachery and corruption the notorious Baranov managed to get his monstrosity hung on a gallery wall, we shall leave to the public prosecutor to discover. But while waiting for the reports on the investigation that will surely take place, we of the art world must join ranks to defend ourselves. We must not permit the insidious Baranov and others of his ilk, slavishly devoted to the fads and aberrations of their plutocratic masters, to desecrate our walls with these samples of dada-istic despair, reactionary cubism, retrogressive abstractionism, surrealistic archaism, aristocratic individualism, religiostic mysticism, materialistic Fordism."

Baranov put the magazine down carefully. He did not have to read further. He had read it often enough before so that he could have recited the rest of the piece without glancing once more at the page. He sat on his stool, his world in ruins, staring unhappily at the six kilos of bright red cherries, arranged prettily in their wicker basket.

There was a knock on the door. Before he could say, "Come in," the door opened and Suvarnin came in. The critic went directly to the table and poured himself five fingers of vodka and drained it. Then he turned to Baranov. "I see," he said, gesturing toward the still-open magazine, "that you've read the piece."

"Yes," said Baranov hoarsely.

"Here," said Suvarnin, taking some manuscript pages out of his pocket. "You might be interested in reading what I wrote originally."

Baranov numbly took the sheets and stared at them. Suvarnin poured himself another drink while Baranov read through swimming eyes, ". . . a great new unfolding of talent . . . a courageous grappling with the problems of doubt and disillusionment which are the beginning of understanding . . . a blazing display of technical ability . . . a pioneering plunge into the depths of the modern psyche in paint . . ."

Baranov pushed the pages aside. "What . . . what happened?" he asked dimly.

"The Committee," Suvarnin said. "They saw your painting. Then they saw my reivew. They asked me to make certain changes," he said delicately. "That Klopoyev, the president of the Committee, the one who has made eighty-four portrait heads of Stalin, he was especially anxious."

"What's going to happen to me now?"

Suvarnin shrugged. "Nothing good," he said. "As a friend, I advise you . . . leave the country." He went over and picked up the manuscript sheets of his first review. He tore them into small pieces, made a little pile of them on the floor and put a match to them. He watched until the flame had burnt itself out, then carefully scattered the ashes with his foot. He finished the vodka, drinking this time directly from the bottle, and went out.

Baranov did not dream that night. He was up all night listening to his wife.

She spoke vigorously from eight in the evening until eight the next morning, a full-length address in which every relevant topic was stated and developed with a balance and fullness which Edmund Burke, in another country and a more leisurely century, would have wholeheartedly admired. She had been notified that afternoon that their apartment was being taken over by a cellist with a cousin on the Central Committee and she had been removed from her position as head of the nursery system at five P.M. and relegated to the post of assistant dietician at a ward for backward and criminally inclined children in a penal camp some thirty kilometers outside Moscow. With these facts as a springboard and with her audience of one wanly rooted against the bedpillows, she ran through her eloquent twelve hours of recrimination without noticeably pausing for breath and without repeating herself.

"Ruined," she said clearly, with no sign of hoarseness,

as the eight o'clock factory whistles sounded outside, "we are completely ruined. And for what? For an idiotic, senseless daub that no one can make head or tail of! A man wants to be a painter. All right! It is childish—but all right, I do not complain. A man wants to paint apples. Silly? All right. But apples can be understood. Apples do not have political implications. Apples do not turn into bombshells. But this . . . this naked witch . . . Why? Why have you done this to me? Why?"

Dumbly, Baranov leaned against the pillows, staring at his wife.

"Come," Anna called. "Come, you must have something to say. You can't sit without speaking forever. Say something. Say one word."

"Anna," Baranov said brokenly, "Anna . . . please . . ." He hesitated. He wanted to say, "Anna, I love you," but he thought better of it.

"Well," Anna demanded. "Well?"

"Anna," Baranov said, "let us have hope. Maybe it will all blow over."

Anna glared at him coldly. "Nothing," she said, "nothing blows over in Moscow."

Then she got dressed and went out to the penal camp to report to her new job in the kitchen there.

Anna's prediction proved only too well-founded. Attacks which made Suvarnin's article seem like an unrestrained paean of praise by comparison, were loosed on him in newspapers and magazines all over the Soviet Union. *The New Masses,* in New York City, which had never before mentioned his name, printed, opposite a full page pen and ink drawing of Stalin by Klopoyev, a heated diatribe which called him, among other things, a "traitor to the working class of the world, a lecher after Western fleshpots, a Park Avenue sensationalist, a man who would be at home drawing cartoons for *The New Yorker*." In a follow-up article, a writer who later joined the Catholic Church and went to work for Metro-Goldwyn-Mayer preparing scenarios for a dog star, used the Baranov case to point out that Michelangelo had been the first proponent of Socialist-realism. In Moscow, a painters' congress, led by the fiery Klopoyev, dropped Baranov from the Painters' Union by the customary vote of 578 to nothing. On one morning, between the hours of ten and twelve, every painting of Baranov's disappeared from every wall in Russia on which they had been hanging. Baranov's studio, which he had held for ten years, was taken from him and given to a man who drew signs for the Moscow subway. Two large plainclothesmen appeared and followed Baranov day and night for three months. His mail was always late and always opened. Anna Kronsky discovered a dictaphone under the sink in the kitchen in which she now worked. Old friends crossed over to the other side of the street when they spotted Baranov in the distance and he no longer found it possible to get tickets for the ballet or the theater. A woman he had never seen before claimed that he was the father of her illegitimate child and when the case came to trial he lost and was ordered to pay 90 rubles a week for her support and only barely avoided being sent to a work-camp.

Sensing which way the wind was blowing, Baranov put an old camel's brush and the gooseneck lamp into a bag, and haggard and thin, with Anna at his side, fled the country.

Six months later, in the summer of 1929, Baranov and Anna were established in Berlin. The climate of the German capital at that time was most propitious for artists, and Baranov, who had set to work industriously painting oranges, lemons, and apples, in his early edible style, enjoyed an immediate success. "We will be very happy here," Anna prophesied, correctly. "You will paint only fruits and vegetables. You will use dark colors very sparingly. You will avoid nudes and political implications. You will keep your mouth shut and permit me to do all the talking."

Baranov was only too happy to obey these simple and salutary injunctions. Aside from a certain vagueness of outline, a kind of subtle mist, which seemed to arise from the artist's subconscious hesitancy to come out too definitely on any subject, even the exact location of a lemon on a tablecloth, his work compared very favorably with the first canvases he had done when he returned from the Revolution. He prospered. His cheeks filled out and grew rosy again and he developed a little paunch. He took a small chalet for the summer in Bavaria and rented a superb studio near the Tiergarten. He learned to sit in rathskellers and drink Munich beer and say, with a hearty laugh, when politics was discussed, as it often was in those days, "Eh, who knows? That is for the philosophers."

When Suvarnin, who had slid from official suspicion to official ostracism in Moscow, as a result of his first, unpublished tribute to Baranov, appeared in Berlin, looking somewhat the worse for wear, Baranov generously took him in and let the critic live in the spare room under the studio, even managing a warm, reminiscent chuckle when Suvarnin told him that the green nude had the most conspicuous place in a new museum for decadent art in Leningrad.

Anna found herself a position as a physical-training instructress in one of the new organizations for young women that were springing up at the time and soon became noted for the vigor of her programs. She turned out battalions of iron-thewed females with enormous hips who could march eighteen hours a day through plowed country and who could, bare-handed, disarm strong men equipped with rifles and bayonets. When Hitler came to power, she was called into the government and given command of the entire women's training program for Prussia and Saxony. Much later, the Bureau of Statistics for the Women's Motherhood-and-National-Honor-Front put out a report disclosing that the graduates of Anna's classes led all other Germans in incidence of miscarriage and death in childbirth seven to one, but by that time, of course, the Baranovs had left the country.

Between 1933 and 1937, the life the Baranovs led was very much as it had been in the good days in Moscow. Baranov painted steadily, and his ripe fruit was hung on many famous walls, including, it was said, the Fuehrer's private gas-proof bomb shelter under the Chancellery, where it considerably brightened the otherwise rather austere atmosphere. Much in demand socially because of Anna's prominence and Baranov's good humor, the couple attended a constant round of parties, at which Anna, as usual, monopolized the conversation, holding forth at great length and with her famous clarity and sharpness on such matters as military tactics, steel production, diplomacy and the upbringing of children.

It was during this period, friends later recalled, that Baranov seemed to grow more and more silent. At parties, he would stand near Anna, listening attentively, munching on grapes and almonds, answering questions with absent-minded monosyllables. He began to fall off in weight, too, and his eyes had the look about them of a man who slept poorly and had bad dreams. He began to paint at night, locking his door, pulling down the blinds, his studio lit by the functional glare of the gooseneck lamp.

It came as a complete surprise, both to Anna and the Baranovs' friends when the green nude was discovered. Suvarnin, who had seen both the original and the Berlin canvas, has said that, if possible, the second was even better than the first, although the main figure was, in conception at least, almost identical in the two paintings. "The anguish," said Suvarnin, who at that time was employed by the government as a roving critic of official architecture, a post, he sensibly figured, in which errors of judgment could not be as spectacular and dangerous as those that might be made in the field of easel painting, "the anguish by now in the painting seemed intolerable. It was heroic, gigantic, god-size. Baranov had plunged to the sub-cellers of despair. [Perhaps it was because I knew of Baranov's nightmares, particularly the one in which he could not say a word in a roomful of conversing women, that I got so strong an impression that this was all humanity, locked in dumbness, protesting, wordlessly and hopelessly, against the tragic predicament of life.] I liked especially the nice new touch of the dwarf hermaphrodite nude, done in pink, being nosed in the left foreground by a brace of small dark brown animals."

It is doubtful that Baranov was rash enough to contemplate showing the painting publicly. [Whatever necessity drove him to re-creating his masterpiece was adequately served by its completion and his memories of the damage he had suffered in Moscow must have been too fresh to allow him to court disaster in Berlin by unveiling his work.] But the matter was taken out of his hands, by the Gestapo, who, in their routine weekly search of the homes and offices of all people who read foreign newspapers (a habit to which Baranov was foolishly addicted) came upon the green nude on the very day Baranov had finished it. The two detectives were simple fellows, but they were well-enough imbued with National Socialist culture to sense detection and heresy here. Arranging for reinforcements and throwing a cordon around the building, they called the chief of the bureau which dealt in these matters. One hour later, Baranov was under arrest and Anna had been removed from her post and sent to work as an assistant dietician in a home for unwed mothers near the Polish border. As was the case in Moscow, no one, not even a fire-eating Colonel in an SS Armored division with whom Anna had quite an intimate relationship, ever dared point out to Anna that her husband had not gone out of his home for his model.

Baranov was questioned by the Gestapo for one month. The questioning, more or less routine, during the course of which Baranov lost three teeth and was twice condemned to death, was aimed largely at getting Baranov to deliver over his lists of accomplices and fellow-conspirators and to confess to certain acts of sabotage in nearby airplane factories which had been committed in the past several months. While he was in the hands of the Gestapo, Baranov's painting was put on public view in a large exhibition arranged by the Propaganda Ministry to acquaint the population with the newest trends in decadent and unGerman art. The exhibition was enormously successful and was attended by a hundred thousand more people than had ever witnessed a showing of paintings in Berlin until that time.

On the day that Baranov was released from jail, considerably stooped and doomed to eat soft foods for some months to come, the leading critic of the Berlin *Tageblatt* came out with the official judgment on the painting. Baranov bought a paper and read, "This is Judaeo-Anarchism at its most insolent peak. Egged on by Rome (there was a new addition in the background of the ruins of a village church), with the connivance of Wall Street and Hollywood, under orders from Moscow, this barbaric worm of a Baranov, né Goldfarb, has insinuated himself into the heartland of German culture in an attempt to bring discredit on our German health and our German institutions of justice. It is a pacifistic attack on our Army, Navy and Air Force, a vile Oriental slander of our glorious German women, a celebration of the lecherous so-called psychology of the Viennese ghetto, a noxious fume from the Paris sewers of the French degenerates, a sly agrument from the British Foreign office for their bloodthirsty Imperialism. With our usual reticent dignity, we Germans of the German art world, we monitors of the proud and holy German soul, must band together and demand, in respectful, firm, reserved tones that this gangrenous excrescence on our national life be expunged. Heil Hitler!"

That night, in bed with Anna, who had luckily managed to get a three-day leave to welcome her husband home, listening to what was now a standard twelve-hour lecture on his wife's part, Baranov looked back with something like fondness on the comparatively delicate phrasing of the *Tageblatt* critic.

The next morning he saw Suvarnin. Suvarnin noted that despite the physical ravages of the past month, his friend seemed to have regained some secure inner peace, some great lessening of the weight of an impalpable but soul-destroying burden. Also, despite the night of oratory he had just passed through and the thirty days of police handling, he seemed rested, as if he had been sleeping well recently.

"You shouldn't have done it," Suvarnin said with mild reproach.

"I know," said Baranov. "But I couldn't help it. It just came out."

"Do you want some advice?'

"Yes."

"Leave the country," Suvarnin said. "Fast."

But Anna, who liked Germany and was convinced that she could win her way up the ladder once more, refused. And it was inconceivable to Baranov that he go without her. But in the next three months, he was twice beaten up severely on the street by SA gangs and a man who lived three blocks away who resembled him slightly was kicked to death by five young men by mistake; all his paintings were collected and officially burned; he was accused by his janitor of homosexuality and was given a suspended sentence after a trial of four days; he was arrested and questioned for twenty-four hours when he was caught carrying a camera past the Chancellery on the way to a pawnshop and the camera was confiscated. All this would not have shaken Anna in her determination to remain in Germany, but when proceedings were put under way to have Baranov sterilized as a threat to the German bloodstream, she crossed the border with him into Switzerland in the middle of a snowstorm.

It took the Baranovs more than a year to get to America,

but as Sergei walked down 57th Street in New York City, staring at the windows of the art galleries, in which the most extreme styles of painting, from lurid surrealism to sugary naturalism were peacefully on display, he felt that all his trials and troubles had been worthwhile because they had eventually brought him to this harbor. Gratefully and emotionally he made application within the first week for citizenship for Anna and himself. As further demonstration of his new-born allegiance he even took to watching the Giants play at the Polo Grounds, although it never became quite clear to him what, exactly, the players were doing around second base, and he patriotically developed a taste for Manhattan cocktails, which he rightly assumed to be the native drink.

The next few years were the happiest of the Baranovs' lives. Critics and patrons alike found that the soft-voiced Russian brought a mysterious European flavor, melancholy and classic, to homely American tomatoes and cucumbers, and his shows almost invariably sold out at good prices. A large wine company used Baranov grapes on all their labels and advertising and a large Baranov still life of a basket of oranges was bought by a California packing company and blown up into twenty-four sheets and plastered on billboards from one end of the country to the other. Baranov bought a small house in Jersey, not far from New York, and when Suvarnin turned up, having left Germany with a price on his head because he had been overheard, in his cups, saying that the German Army could not reach Moscow in three weeks, Baranov gladly invited the critic to live with them.

Heady with his new sense of freedom, Baranov even went so far as to paint a nude, very pink and firm-fleshed, from memory. But Anna, who by this time was attached to a nationally circulated news magazine as an authority on Communism and Fascism, was very firm in her handling of the situation. She ripped the painting to shreds with a breadknife and dismissed the robust, apple-cheeked

Czech girl who did their cooking, although the girl went to the rather extreme length of having a reputable physician testify to her virginity in an attempt to retain her position.

Anna's success in America, where men have long been conditioned to listen to women, and where her particular brand of crisp, loquacious efficiency was regarded with stunned fascination by her male colleagues, was even more dazzling than any she had enjoyed in Europe. By the end of the war the magazine for which she worked had put her in charge of the departments of Political Interpretation, Medicine for Women, Fashion, Books, and, of course, Child Care. She even got a job for Suvarnin on the magazine, reviewing motion pictures, a job he held until the autumn of '47, when he lost his eyesight.

Anna became a well-known figure in Washington, testifying at great length as a friendly witness before several important committees, discoursing on such varied subjects as the sending of subversive literature through the mails and the effect of sex education in the public school systems of several Northern states. She even had the exhilarating experience of having her girdle pinched in an elevator by a senior Senator from the West. As was inevitable, she was invited to countless dinners, receptions, congresses, and parties, and to all of them Baranov faithfully escorted her. In the beginning, living in the free atmosphere of literary and artistic America, Baranov had seemed to shed the taciturnity that had set in during the last part of his years in Moscow. He laughed frequently, he sang old Red Army songs without much urging, he insisted on mixing Manhattans at the homes of his friends, he spoke up on all subjects with disarming and agreeable gusto. But after a while he began to sink back into his old silences. Munching peanuts, occasionally muttering a monosyllable, he would stand by Anna's side at parties, watching her closely, listening with strange concentration as she spoke out, clearly and fully, on the destiny of the Republican Party, trends in the theater, and the intricacies of the American Constitution. It was at this time, too, that Baranov began to have trouble sleeping. His weight fell off and he began to work at night.

Half-blind as he was, Suvarnin saw what was happening. Excitedly, he waited for the great day. In advance, he composed once more the stirring tribute to his friend's genius that he had first written so long ago in Moscow. Suvarnin was one of those writers who hates to see any word of his go unpublished and the fact that nearly twenty years had passed since he had been forced to jettison his appreciation only made him more eager to get it finally into print. Also, it was a great relief to write about painting again, after the long months of Betty Grable and Van Johnson.

On the morning that, Anna being in the city and the house quiet, Baranov came to him and said, "I would like you to come into my studio," Suvarnin found himself trembling. Stumbling a little, he hurried out of the house and followed Baranov across the driveway to the barn which had been converted into a studio. He peered through his darkening eyes for a long time at the enormous canvas. "This," he said humbly, "this is the great one. Here," he took out some manuscript papers from his pocket, "here, read what I have to say about it."

When he had finished reading his friend's eulogy, Baranov wiped a tear from his eye. Then he went over to Suvarnin and kissed him. There was no question this time about hiding the masterpiece. Baranov rolled it up carefully, put it in a case, and with Suvarnin at his side, drove in with it to his dealer. However, by silent agreement, he and Suvarnin tactfully refrained from telling Anna anything about the matter.

Two months later Sergei Baranov was the new hero of the world of art. His dealer had to put up velvet ropes to contain the crowds who came to see the green nude. Suvarnin's tribute now seemed pale and insubstantial in the torrent of adjectives poured out by the other critics. Picasso was mentioned in the same sentence as Baranov countless times and several writers brought up the name of El Greco. Bonwit Teller had six green nudes in their windows, wearing lizard shoes and draped with mink. A Baranov *Grapes and Local Cheese*, which the painter had sold in 1940 for two hundred dollars brought 5600 dollars at an auction. The Museum of Modern Art sent a man around to arrange about a retrospective show. The World Good Will Association, whose letterhead boasted the names of many dozen legislators and leaders of industry, requested it as the leading item in a show of American art which they proposed to send, at government expense, to fourteen European countries. Even Anna, to whom, as usual, no one dared mention the interesting resemblance of painter's wife and painter's model, seemed pleased, and for a whole evening allowed Baranov to speak without interrupting once.

At the opening of the show of American art, which was being revealed in New York preliminary to its trip overseas, Baranov was the center of attention. Photographers took his picture in all poses, toying with a Manhattan, munching on a smoked salmon canapé, talking to the wife of an Ambassador, looking up gravely at his masterpiece, surrounded by admirers. It was the crowning moment of his life and if he had been struck dead that midnight he would have expired happily. In fact, later on, looking back at that evening, from the vantage point of the events that followed, Baranov often bitterly wished that he *had* died that night.

For, one week later, on the floor of Congress, an economy-minded representative, enraged at what he called the irresponsible money-squandering proclivities of the Administration, which had put up good American dollars to send this sinister travesty on America to our late allies, demanded a thorough investigation of the entire enterprise. The lawmaker went on to describe the main exhibit, a green nude by a Russian foreigner, as sickening twaddle, Communist-inspired, an insult to American womanhood, a blow to White Supremacy, atheistic, psychological, un-

American, subversive, Red-Fascistic, not the sort of thing he would like his fourteen-year-old daughter to see either alone or accompanied by her mother, decadent, likely to inspire scorn for the Republic of the United States in foreign breasts, calculated aid to Stalin in the cold war between America and the Soviet Union, a slap in the face to the heroes of the Berlin air lift, injurious to trade, an offense to our neighbors to the South, artistic gangsterism, a natural result of our letting down our immigration barriers, proof of the necessity of Federal censorship of the press, the radio, and the movies, and a calamitous consequence of the Wagner Labor Relations Act.

Other developments followed quickly. A conservative, mellow-voiced radio commentator, broadcasting from Washington, announced that he had warned the country over and over again that New Deal paternalism would finally spawn just such monstrosities and hinted darkly that the man responsible for the painting had entered the United States illegally, being put ashore from a submarine by night with a woman he alleged to be his wife.

Several newspaper chains took up the matter in both their editorial and news columns, sending their least civil employees down to the Baranov farm to question the culprit and reporting that a samovar stood in a place of honor in the Baranov living room and that the outside of the studio was painted red. One editor demanded to know why no cover from the *Saturday Evening Post* was included in the collection of paintings. Leaders of the American Legion filed a formal protest against sending the paintings in question over to the lands where our boys had fought so bravely so shortly before and pointing out that Baranov was not a veteran.

The House Committee on Un-American Activities served a subpoena on both Baranovs and put a tap on their telephone wires, hiring a man who knew Russian to monitor it. At the hearing, it was brought out that Baranov in 1917, 1918, and 1919, had served in the Red Army and the Bureau of Immigration was publicly denounced for allowing such doubtful human material into the country. Ministers of all three religions circulated a petition calling upon the government to halt the shipment of the paintings to Europe, a place which all knew was badly shaken in the department of religious faith as it was. A well-known jurist was quoted as saying he was tired of modern art experts and that he could paint a better picture than the green nude with a bucket of barn paint and a paperhanger's brush. A psychiatrist, quoted in a national magazine, said that the painting in question had obviously been done by a man who felt rejected by his mother and who had unstable and violent tendencies which were bound to grow worse with the years. The FBI threw in a squad of investigators who conducted interviews with seventy-five friends of the Baranovs and discovered that the couple had subscriptions to the Book-of-the-Month Club, *House and Garden,* and the *Daily News,* and that they often spoke Russian in front of their servants.

A cross was burned on the Baranov lawn on a rainy evening, but even so, wind-blown sparks ignited a privy on a neighbor's property and reduced it to the ground. Irate, the neighbor fired a shotgun at the Baranovs' Siamese cat, nicking it twice in the rear.

The local Chamber of Commerce petitioned the Baranovs to move away, as they were giving the town a bad name, just at a time when they were trying to attract a plumbing factory to set up business there.

A Communist civil-liberties group held a mass meeting to raise funds for Baranov, who denounced them. They, in turn, denounced the Baranovs and demanded that they be deported to Russia.

The Treasury Department, attracted by the commotion, went over Baranov's last five income-tax returns and disallowed several items and sent in a bill for an additional eight hundred and twenty dollars. The Baranovs' citizenship papers were carefully scanned and it was revealed that Mrs. Baranov had lied about her age.

At a radio forum on the subject "What Should We Do with the Green Nude" Baranov's name was hissed by the audience every time it was mentioned and the next day the postmaster in a small Massachusetts town announced that a mural of cranberry pickers and fishermen that Baranov had painted for the postoffice in the days of the WPA, would be torn down.

Anna Baranov, due to the unwelcome publicity given her, was deprived by her editor first of the Department of Political Interpretation, then of Medicine for Women, then of Books and Fashion, and finally, of Child Care, after which she was allowed to resign.

Baranov moved through all this in a dull haze, dreading more than anything else the long hours of mounting rhetoric which were loosed on him by his wife between midnight and eight each morning. Occasionally, huddled for disguise into the turned-up collar of his overcoat, he would go to the gallery where the disputed painting still hung, and would stare mournfully and puzzledly at it. When, one day, the director of the gallery took him aside, and told him, not unkindly, that in response to certain pressures, the authorities had decided to disband the show and not send it to Europe after all, he wept.

That night, he was sitting alone, slumped in a wooden chair in the middle of his cold studio. The blinds were drawn because of the habit the small boys of the neighborhood had developed of hurling rocks through the windows at any moving shadows they saw within. In Baranov's hand he held a small world atlas, opened to a map of the Caribbean and Central America, but he did not look at it.

The door opened and Suvarnin came in. He sat down without a word.

Finally, Baranov spoke, without looking at his friend. "I was at the gallery today," he said, his voice low and troubled. "I looked at the painting for a long time. Maybe it's my imagination," he said, "but I thought I noticed something."

"Yes?"

"Suddenly," Baranov said, "the painting reminded me of someone. I thought and thought who it could be. Just now I remembered. Suvarnin," he twisted anxiously in his chair to face the critic, "Suvarnin, have you ever noticed that there was any resemblance there to my wife, Anna?"

Suvarnin said nothing for a while. He closed his movie-destroyed eyes thoughtfully and rubbed his nose. "No," he said, finally. "Not the slightest."

Baranov smiled wanly. "Oh, what a relief," he said. "It would be a terrible shock to her." He spread the book on his knees and stared down at the small red and blue countries of the warm middle Atlantic. "Suvarnin," he said, "have you ever been to the Caribbean?"

"No," said Suvarnin.

"What sort of fruit," Baranov asked, peering at the map, "do you think a man could find to paint in Costa Rica?"

Suvarnin sighed and stood up. "I will go pack my things," he said heavily, and went out, leaving Baranov alone in the cold studio, staring at his brightly colored, repetitious map.

Tip on a Dead Jockey

Lloyd Barber was lying on his bed reading *France-Soir* when the phone rang. It was only two o'clock in the afternoon, but it was raining for the fifth consecutive day and he had no place to go anyway. He was reading about the relative standing of the teams in the Rugby leagues. He never went to Rugby games and he had no interest in the relative standings of Lille and Pau and Bordeaux, but he had finished everything else in the paper. It was cold in the small, dark room, because there was no heat provided between ten in the morning and six in the evening, and he lay on the lumpy double bed, his shoes off, covered with his overcoat.

He picked up the phone, and the man at the desk downstairs said, "There is a lady waiting for you here, M. Barber."

Barber squinted at himself in the mirror above the bureau across from the bed. He wished he was better-looking. "Did she give her name?" he asked.

"No, Monsieur. Should I demand it?"

"Never mind," Barber said. "I'll be right down."

He hung up the phone and put on his shoes. He always put the left one on first, for luck. He buttoned his collar

288

and pulled his tie into place, noticing that it was frayed at the knot. He got into his jacket and patted his pockets to see if he had cigarettes. He had no cigarettes. He shrugged, and left the light on vindictively, because the manager was being unpleasant about the bill, and went downstairs.

Maureen Richardson was sitting in the little room off the lobby, in one of those age-colored plush chairs that fourth-rate Parisian hotels furnish their clientele to discourage excessive conviviality on the ground floor. None of the lamps was lit, and a dark, dead, greenish light filtered in through the dusty curtains from the rainy street outside. Maureen had been a young, pretty girl with bright, credulous blue eyes when Barber first met her, during the war, just before she married Jimmy Richardson. But she had had two children since then and Richardson hadn't done so well, and now she was wearing a worn cloth coat that was soaked, and her complexion had gone, and in the greenish lobby light she seemed bone-colored and her eyes were pale.

"Hello, Beauty," Barber said. Richardson always called her that, and while it had amused his friends in the squadron, he had loyally stuck to it, and finally everyone had picked it up.

Maureen turned around quickly, almost as though he had frightened her. "Lloyd," she said, "I'm so glad I found you in."

They shook hands, and Barber asked if she wanted to go someplace for a coffee.

"I'd rather not," Maureen said. "I left the kids with a friend for lunch and I promised I'd collect them at two-thirty and I don't have much time."

"Sure," Barber said. "How's Jimmy?"

"Oh, Lloyd . . ." Maureen pulled at her fingers, and Barber noticed that they were reddened and the nails were uneven. "Have you seen him?"

"What?" Barber peered through the gloom at her, puzzled. "What do you mean?"

"Have you seen him?" Maureen persisted. Her voice was thin and frightened.

"Not for a month or so," Barber said. "Why?" He asked it, but he almost knew why.

"He's gone, Lloyd," Maureen said. "He's been gone thirty-two days. I don't know what I'm going to do."

"Where did he go?" Barber asked.

"I don't know." Maureen took out a pack of cigarettes and lit one. She was too distracted to offer the pack to Barber. "He didn't tell me." She smoked the cigarette avidly but absently. "I'm so worried. I thought maybe he'd said something to you—or that you'd bumped into him."

"No," Barber said carefully. "He didn't say anything."

"It's the queerest thing. We've been married over ten years and he never did anything like this before," Maureen said, trying to control her voice. "He just came to me one night and he said he'd got leave of absence from his job for a month and that he'd be back inside of thirty days and he'd tell me all about it when he got back, and he begged me not to ask any questions."

"And you didn't ask any questions?"

"He was acting so strangely," Maureen said. "I'd never seen him like that before. All hopped up. Excited. You might even say happy, except that he kept going in all night to look at the kids. And he's never given me anything to worry about in the—the girl department," Maureen said primly. "Not like some of the other boys we know. And if there was one thing about Jimmy, it was that you could trust him. So I helped him pack."

"What did he take?"

"Just one Valpak," Maureen said. "With light clothes. As though he was going off on a summer vacation. He even took a tennis racket."

"A tennis racket," Barber nodded, as though it were the most natural thing in the world for husbands to take tennis rackets along when disappearing. "Did you hear from him at all?"

"No," Maureen said. "He told me he wouldn't write. Did you ever hear of anything like that?" Even in her anguish, she permitted herself a tone of wifely grievance. "I knew we shouldn't have come to Europe. It's different for you. You're not married and you were always kind of wild anyway, not like Jimmy—"

"Did you call his office?" Barber asked, interrupting. He didn't want to hear how wild people thought he was, or how unmarried.

"I had a friend call," Maureen said. "It would look too fishy—his wife calling to ask where he was."

"What did they say?"

"They said that they had expected him two days ago but he hadn't come in yet."

Barber took one of Maureen's cigarettes and lit it. It was the first one in four hours and it tasted wonderful. He had a little selfish twinge of gratitude that Maureen had come to his hotel.

"Lloyd, do you know anything?" Maureen asked, worn and shabby in her damp, thin coat in the foggy green light.

Barber hesitated. "No," he said. "But I'll put in a couple of calls and I'll telephone you tomorrow."

They both stood up. Maureen pulled on gloves over her reddened hands. The gloves were worn and greenish black. Looking at them, Barber suddenly remembered how neat and shining Maureen had been when they first met, in Louisiana, so many years before, and how healthy and well-dressed he and Jimmy and the others had been in their lieutenants' uniforms with the new wings on their breasts.

"Listen, Beauty," Barber said. "How are you fixed for dough?"

"I didn't come over for that," Maureen said firmly.

Barber took out his wallet and peered judiciously into it. It wasn't necessary. He knew exactly what was there. He took out a five-thousand-franc note. "Here," he said, handing it to her. "Try this on for size."

Maureen made a motion as though to give it back to him. "I really don't think I should . . ." she began.

"Sh-h-h, Beauty," Barber said. "There isn't an American girl in Paris who couldn't use five *mille* on a day like this."

Maureen sighed and put the bill in her pocketbook. "I feel terrible about taking your money, Lloyd."

Barber kissed her forehead. "In memory of the wild blue yonder," he said, pocketing the wallet, with its remaining fifteen thousand francs, which, as far as he knew, would have to last him for the rest of his life. "Jimmy'll give it back to me."

"Do you think he's all right?" Maureen asked, standing close to him.

"Of course," Lloyd said lightly and falsely. "There's nothing to worry about. I'll call you tomorrow. He'll probably be there, answering the phone, getting sore at me for sucking around his wife when he's out of town."

"I bet." Maureen smiled miserably. She went through the cavelike murk of the lobby, out into the rainy street, on her way to pick up the two children, who had been sent out to lunch at the home of a friend.

Barber went to his room and picked up the phone and waited for the old man downstairs to plug in. There were two suitcases standing open on the floor, with shirts piled in them, because there wasn't enough drawer space in the tiny bureau supplied by the hotel. On top of the bureau there were: a bill, marked overdue, from a tailor; a letter from his ex-wife, in New York, saying she had found an Army pistol of his in the bottom of a trunk and asking him what he wanted her to do with it, because she was afraid of the Sullivan Law; a letter from his mother, telling him to stop being a damn fool and come home and get a regular job; a letter from a woman in whom he was not interested, inviting him to come and stay with her in her villa near Eze, where it was beautiful and warm, she said, and where she needed a man around the house; a letter from a boy who had flown as his waist-gunner during the war and who insisted that Barber had saved his life when he was hit in the stomach over Palermo, and who, surprisingly, had written a book since then. Now he sent long, rather literary letters at least once a month to Barber. He was an odd, intense boy, who had been an excitable gunner, and he was constantly examining himself to find out whether he and the people he loved, among whom he rather embarrassingly included Barber, mostly because of the eight minutes over Palermo, were living up to their promise. "Our generation is in danger," the boy had typed in the letter on the bureau, "the danger of diminution. We have had our adventures too early. Our love has turned to affection, our hate to distaste, our despair to melancholy, our passion to preference. We have settled for the life of obedient dwarfs in a small but fatal sideshow."

The letter had depressed Barber and he hadn't answered it. You got enough of that sort of thing from the French. He wished the ex-waist-gunner would stop writing him, or at least write on different subjects. Barber hadn't answered his ex-wife, either, because he had come to Europe to try to forget her. He hadn't answered his mother, because he was afraid she was right. And he hadn't gone down to Eze, because no matter how broke he was, he wasn't selling that particular commodity yet.

Stuck into the mirror above the bureau was a photograph of himself and Jimmy Richardson, taken on the beach at Deauville the summer before. The Richardsons had taken a cottage there, and Barber had spent a couple of weekends with them. Jimmy Richardson was another one who had attached himself to Barber during the war. Somehow, Barber was always being presented with the devotion of people whose devotion he didn't want. "People hang on to you," a girl who was angry at him once told him, "because you're an automatic hypocrite. As soon as somebody comes into the room, you become gay and confident."

Jimmy and he had been in bathing trunks when the picture was snapped, and Barber was tall and blessed with a blond, California kind of good looks next to Jimmy, who seemed like a fat, incompetent infant, standing there with the sunny sea behind him.

Barber peered at the photograph. Jimmy didn't look like the sort of man who would ever be missing from any-where for thirty-two days. As for himself, Barber thought wryly, he looked automatically gay and confident.

He leaned over and took the picture down and threw it into a drawer. Then, holding the phone loosely, he stared around him with distaste. In the glare of the un-shaded lamp, the dark woodwork looked gloomy and ter-mite-ridden, and the bed, with its mottled velours spread, the color of spoiled pears, looked as though it had been wallowed on by countless hundreds of obscenely shaped men and women who had rented the room for an hour at a time. For a second, he was piercingly homesick for all the rooms of all the Hotel Statlers he had slept in and all the roomettes on trains between New York and Chicago, and St. Louis and Los Angeles.

There was a whistling, static-like sound in the phone, and he shook himself and gave the number of the George V. When he got the George V, he asked for M. Smith, M. Bert Smith. After a while, the girl said M. Smith was no longer at the hotel. Barber asked hurriedly, before the girl could cut him off, whether M. Smith was expected to return shortly or if he had left a forwarding address. No, the girl said after a long wait, he was not expected to re-turn and there was no forwarding address.

Barber hung up. He was not surprised about Bert Smith. He was a man who wandered mysteriously from hotel to hotel, and he might have used a half-dozen names besides Smith since Barber had spoken to him last.

With a conscious effort, Barber tried not to think about Jimmy Richardson or his wife, who was called, as a friendly squadron joke, Beauty, or about Jimmy Rich-ardson's two small sons.

Scowling, Barber went over to the window. The winter rain of Paris was seeping down into the narrow street, blurring it with the unproductive malice of city rain, chipping colorlessly at the buildings opposite, making it impossible to imagine what they had looked like when they were new. A workman was unloading cases of wine from a truck, looking persecuted by the weather, the Paris sound of clinking bottles muted and made hollow and mournful by the flow of gray water from the skies and from window ledges and signs and rolled awnings. It was not a day for a husband to be missing, for a friend to be missing. It was not a day to be alone or to have only fifteen thousand francs in your pocket or to be in a narrow hotel room where the heat was off from ten in the morning till six at night. It was not a day to be without a job or cigarettes or lunch. It was not a day on which to examine yourself and realize that no matter how many excuses you gave yourself, you were going to wind up knowing that, finally, you were responsible.

Barber shook himself again. There was no sense in just staying in the room all day. If he was going to do any good, he would have to find Bert Smith. He looked at his watch. It was nearly two-thirty. He tried to remember all the places he had ever seen Bert Smith at two-thirty in the afternoon. The fancy restaurant near the Rond-Point, where the movie people and the French newspaper owners and the rich tourists ate; the bistro on the Boulevard Latour-Maubourg, on the Left Bank; the restaurants at Auteuil and Longchamp and St. Cloud. Barber looked at the newspaper. They were running at Auteuil today.

If he was not at the races and if he was still in Paris, Bert Smith was likely to be in one art gallery or another in the middle of the afternoon. Bert Smith was an art lover, or at least he bought pictures, shrewdly and knowingly. Since Smith lived in hotel rooms, which were unlikely places for a collection, it was probable that he bought paintings on speculation or as an agent or, when they were important ones that the government did not wish to have leave the country, to be smuggled out of France.

Barber had also seen Smith late in the afternoons in the steam room at Claridge's, a small, round man with surprisingly well-shaped legs, sitting in the vapor, wrapped in a sheet, growing pinker and pinker, smiling luxuriously in the steam, sweating off the fat that he had accumulated in many years of eating in the best restaurants in Europe.

He had also seen Smith several times around six o'clock in the evening in the barbershop at the George V getting shaved, and after that in the bar upstairs, and in the bar at the Relais Plaza and the English bar downstairs at the Plaza-Athénée. And late at night he had seen him at various night clubs—L'Eléphant Blanc, Carroll's, La Rose Rouge . . .

Barber thought unhappily of the last fifteen thousand francs in his wallet. It was going to be a long, wet, hard, expensive day. He put on his hat and coat and went out. It was still raining, and he hailed a taxi and gave the driver the address of the restaurant near the Rond-Point.

It had started about two months before, in the stand at Auteuil just before the sixth race. The day was misty and there weren't many spectators, and Barber had not been doing very well, but he had got a tip on the sixth race, on an eight-to-one shot. He put five thousand down on the nose and climbed high up in the stand to get a good view of the race.

There was only one other spectator near him in the stand, a small, round man wearing an expensive-looking velours hat, and carrying a pair of binoculars and a rolled umbrella, like an Englishman. He smiled at Barber and nodded. As Barber smiled back politely, he realized that he had seen the man many times before, or his brother, or a half-dozen other men who looked like him, in restaurants and in bars and on the street, usually with tall girls who might have been lower-class mannequins or upper-class tarts.

The man with the umbrella moved over to him along the damp concrete row of seats. He had little, dapper feet and a bright necktie, and he had a well-cared-for, international kind of face, with large, pretty dark eyes, fringed by thick black lashes. He had what Barber had come to call an import-export face. It was a face that was at the same time bland, cynical, self-assured, sensual, hopeless, and daring, and its owner might be Turkish or Hungarian or Greek or he might have been born in Basra. It was a face you might see in Paris or Rome or Brussels or Tangier, always in the best places, always doing business. It was a face, you felt somehow, that was occasionally of interest to the police.

"Good afternoon," the man said, in English, tipping his hat. "Are you having a lucky day?" He had an accent, but it was difficult to place it. It was as though as a child he had gone to school everywhere and had had ten nurses of ten different nationalities.

"Not bad," Barber said carefully.

"Which do you like in this one?" The man pointed with his umbrella at the track, where the horses were gingerly going up to the distant starting line on the muddied grass.

"Number Three," Barber said.

"Number Three." The man shrugged, as though he pitied Barber but was restrained by his good breeding from saying so. "How is the movie business these days?" the man asked.

"The movie business went home a month ago," Barber said, slightly surprised that the man knew anything about it. An American company had been making a picture about the war, and Barber had had four lucky, well-paid months as a technical expert, buckling leading men into parachutes and explaining the difference between a P-47 and a B-25 to the director.

"And the blond star?" the man asked, taking his glasses away from his eyes. "With the exquisite behind?"

"Also home."

The man moved his eyebrows and shook his head gently, indicating his regret that his new acquaintance and the city of Paris were now deprived of the exquisite behind. "Well," he said, "at least it leaves you free in the afternoon to come to the races." He peered out across the track through the glasses. "There they go."

No. 3 led all the way until the stretch. In the stretch, he was passed rapidly by four other horses.

"Every race in this country," Barber said as the horses crossed the finish line, "is a hundred metres too long." He took out his tickets and tore them once and dropped them on the wet concrete.

He watched with surprise as the man with the umbrella took out some tickets and tore them up, too. They were on No. 3, and Barber could see that they were big ones. The man with the umbrella dropped the tickets with a resigned, half-amused expression on his face, as though all his life he had been used to tearing up things that had suddenly become of no value.

"Are you staying for the last race?" the man with the umbrella asked as they started to descend through the empty stands.

"I don't think so," Barber said. "This day has been glorious enough already."

"Why don't you stay?" the man said. "I may have something."

Barber thought for a moment, listening to their footsteps on the concrete.

"I have a car," the man said. "I could give you a lift into town, Mr. Barber."

"Oh," Barber said, surprised, "you know my name."

"Of course," the man said, smiling. "Why don't you wait for me at the bar? I have to go and cash some tickets."

"I thought you lost," Barber said suspiciously.

"On Number Three," the man said. From another pocket he took out some more tickets and waved them gently. "But there is always the insurance. One must always think of the insurance," he said. "Will I see you at the bar?"

"O.K.," Barber said, not because he hoped for anything in the way of information on the next race from the man with the umbrella but because of the ride home. "I'll be there. Oh—by the way, what's your name?"

"Smith," the man said. "Bert Smith."

Barber went to the bar and ordered a coffee, then changed it to a brandy, because coffee wasn't enough after a race like that. He stood there, hunched over the bar, reflecting sourly that he was one of the category of people who never think of the insurance. Smith, he thought, Bert Smith. More insurance. On how many other names, Barber wondered, had the man lost before he picked that one?

Smith came to the bar softly, on his dapper feet, smiling, and laid a hand lightly on Barber's arm. "Mr. Barber," he said, "there is a rumor for the seventh race. Number Six."

"I never win on Number Six," Barber said.

"It is a lovely little rumor," Smith said. "At present, a twenty-two-to-one rumor."

Barber looked at the man doubtfully. He wondered briefly what there was in it for Smith. "What the hell," he said, moving toward the seller's window. "What have I got to lose?"

He put five thousand francs on No. 6 and superstitiously remained at the bar during the race, drinking brandy. No. 6 won, all out, by half a length, and, although the odds had dropped somewhat, paid eighteen to one.

Barber walked through the damp twilight, across the discarded newspapers and the scarred grass, with its farmlike smell, patting his inside pocket with the ninety thousand francs in a comforting bulge there, pleased with the little man trotting beside him.

Bert Smith had a Citroën, and he drove swiftly and well and objectionably, cutting in on other cars and swinging wide into the outside lane to gain advantage at lights.

"Do you bet often on the races, Mr. Barber?" he was saying as they passed a traffic policeman, forlorn in his white cape on the gleaming street.

"Too often," Barber said, enjoying the warmth of the car and the effects of the last brandy and the bulge in his pocket.

"You like to gamble?"

"Who doesn't?"

"There are many who do not like to gamble," Smith said, nearly scraping a truck. "I pity them."

"Pity them?" Barber looked over at Smith, a little surprised at the word. "Why?"

"Because," Smith said softly, smiling, "in this age there comes a time when everyone finds that he is forced to gamble—and not only for money, and not only at the seller's window. And when that time comes, and you are not in the habit, and it does not amuse you, you are most likely to lose."

They rode in silence for a while. From time to time, Barber peered across at the soft, self-assured face above the wheel, lit by the dashboard glow. I would like to get a look at his passport, Barber thought—at all the passports he's carried for the last twenty years.

"For example," Smith said, "during the war . . ."

"Yes?"

"When you were in your plane," Smith said, "on a mission. Weren't there times when you had to decide suddenly to try something, to depend on your luck for one split second, and if you hesitated, if you balked at the act of gambling—ssssszt!" Smith took one hand from the wheel and made a gliding, falling motion, with his thumb down. He smiled across at Barber. "I suppose you are one of the young men who were nearly killed a dozen times," he said.

"I suppose so," Barber said.

"I prefer that in Americans," Smith said. "It makes them more like Europeans."

"How did you know I was in the war?" Barber said. For the first time, he began to wonder if it was only a coincidence that Smith had been near him in the stand before the sixth race.

Smith chuckled. "You have been in Paris how long?" he said. "A year and a half?"

"Sixteen months," Barber said, wondering how the man knew *that*.

"Nothing very mysterious about it," Smith said. "People talk at bars, at dinner parties. One girl tells another girl. Paris is a small city. Where shall I drop you?"

Barber looked out the window to see where they were. "Not far from here," he said. "My hotel is just off the Avenue Victor Hugo. You can't get in there with a car."

"Oh, yes," Smith said, as though he knew about all hotels. "If it doesn't seem too inquisitive," he said, "do you intend to stay long in Europe?"

"It depends."

"On what?"

"On luck." Barber grinned.

"Did you have a good job in America?" Smith asked, keeping his eyes on the traffic ahead of him.

"In thirty years, working ten hours a day, I would have been the third biggest man in the company," Barber said.

Smith smiled. "Calamitous," he said. "Have you found more interesting things to do here?"

"Occasionally," Barber said, beginning to be conscious that he was being quizzed.

"After a war it is difficult to remain interested," Smith said. "While it is on, a war is absolutely boring. But then when it is over, you discover peace is even more boring. It is the worst result of wars. Do you still fly?"

"Once in a while."

Smith nodded. "Do you maintain your license?"

"Yes."

"Yes, that's wise," Smith said.

He pulled the car sharply in to the curb and stopped, and Barber got out.

"Here you are," Smith said. He put out his hand, smiling, and Barber shook it. Smith's hand was softly fleshed, but there was a feeling of stone beneath it.

"Thanks for everything," Barber said.

"Thank you, Mr. Barber, for your company," Smith said. He held Barber's hand for a moment, looking across the seat at him. "This has been very pleasant," he said. "I hope we can see each other again soon. Maybe we are lucky for each other."

"Sure," Barber said, grinning. "I'm always at home to people who can pick eighteen-to-one shots."

Smith smiled, relinquishing Barber's hand. "Maybe one of these days we'll have something even better than an eighteen-to-one shot," he said.

He waved a little and Barber closed the car door. Smith spurted out into the traffic, nearly causing two *quatre chevaux* to pile up behind him.

It had taken two weeks for Smith to declare himself. From the beginning, Barber had known that something was coming, but he had waited patiently, curious and amused, lunching with Smith in the fine restaurants Smith patronized, going to galleries with him and listening to Smith on the subject of the Impressionists, going out to the race tracks with him and winning more often than not on the information Smith picked up from tight-lipped men around the paddocks. Barber pretended to enjoy the little, clever man more than he actually did, and Smith, on his part, Barber knew, was pretending to like *him* more than he actually did. It was a kind of veiled and cynical wooing, in which neither party had yet committed himself. Only, unlike more ordinary wooings, Barber for the first two weeks was not sure in just which direction his desirability, as far as Smith was concerned, might lie.

Then, late one night, after a large dinner and a desultory tour of the night clubs, during which Smith had seemed unusually silent and abstracted, they were standing in front of Smith's hotel and he made his move. It was a cold night, and the street was deserted except for a prostitute with a dog, who looked at them without hope as she passed them on the way to the Champs-Elysées.

"Are you going to be in your hotel tomorrow morning, Lloyd?" Smith asked.

"Yes," Barber said. "Why?"

"Why?" Smith repeated absently, staring after the chilled-looking girl and her poodle walking despairingly down the empty, dark street. "Why?" He chuckled irrelevantly. "I have something I would like to show you," he said.

"I'll be in all morning," Barber said.

"Tell me, my friend," Smith said, touching Barber's sleeve lightly with his gloved hand. "Do you have any idea why I have been calling you so often for the last two weeks, and buying you so many good meals and so much good whiskey?"

"Because I am charming and interesting and full of fun," Barber said, grinning. "And because you want something from me."

Smith chuckled, louder this time, and caressed Barber's sleeve. "You are not absolutely stupid, my friend, are you?"

"Not absolutely," said Barber.

"Tell me, my friend," Smith said, almost in a whisper. "How would you like to make twenty-five thousand dollars?"

"What?" Barber asked, certain that he had not heard correctly.

"Sh-h-h," Smith said. He smiled, suddenly gay. "Think about it. I'll see you in the morning. Thank you for walking me home." He dropped Barber's arm and started into the hotel.

"Smith!" Barber called.

"Sh-h-h." Smith put his finger playfully to his mouth. "Sleep well. See you in the morning."

Barber watched him go through the glass revolving doors into the huge, brightly lit, empty lobby of the hotel.

Barber took a step toward the doors to follow him in, then stopped and shrugged and put his collar up, and walked slowly in the direction of his own hotel. I've waited this long, he thought, I can wait till morning.

Barber was still in bed the next morning when the door opened and Smith came in. The room was dark, with the curtains drawn, and Barber was lying there, half asleep, thinking drowsily, Twenty-five thousand, twenty-five thousand. He opened his eyes when he heard the door open. There was a short, bulky silhouette framed in the doorway against the pallid light of the corridor.

"Who's that?" Barber asked, without sitting up.

"Lloyd. I'm sorry," Smith said. "Go back to sleep. I'll see you later."

Barber sat up abruptly. "Smith," he said. "Come in."

"I don't want to disturb—"

"Come in, come in." Barber got out of bed and, bare-footed, went over to the window and threw back the curtains. He looked out at the street. "By God, what do you know?" he said, shivering and closing the window. "The sun is shining. Shut the door."

Smith closed the door. He was wearing a loose gray tweed overcoat, very British, and a soft Italian felt hat, and he was carrying a large manila envelope. He looked newly bathed and shaved, and wide awake.

Barber, blinking in the sudden sunshine, put on a robe and a pair of moccasins and lit a cigarette. "Excuse me," he said. "I want to wash." He went behind the screen that separated the washbasin and the *bidet* from the rest of the room. As he washed, scrubbing his face and soaking his hair with cold water, he heard Smith go over to the window. Smith was humming, in a soft, true, melodious tenor voice, a passage from an opera that Barber knew he had heard but could not remember. Aside from everything else, Barber thought, combing his hair roughly, I bet the bastard knows fifty operas.

Feeling fresher and less at a disadvantage with his teeth

washed and his hair combed, Barber stepped out from
behind the screen.

"Paris," Smith said, at the window, looking out. "What
a satisfactory city. What a farce." He turned around, smiling. "Ah," he said, "how lucky you are. You can afford to
put water on your head." He touched his thin, well-
brushed hair sadly. "Every time I wash my hair, it falls
like the leaves. How old did you say you are?"

"Thirty," Barber said, knowing that Smith remembered
it.

"What an age." Smith sighed. "The wonderful moment
of balance. Old enough to know what you want, still
young enough to be ready for anything." He came back
and sat down and propped the manila envelope on the
floor next to the chair. "Anything." He looked up at Barber, almost coquettishly. "You recall our conversation, I
trust," he said.

"I recall a man said something about twenty-five thousand dollars," Barber said.

"Ah—you do remember," Smith said gaily. "Well?"

"Well what?"

"Well, do you want to make it?"

"I'm listening," Barber said.

Smith rubbed his soft hands together gently in front of
his face, his fingers rigid, making a slight, dry, sliding
sound. "A little proposition has come up," he said. "An
interesting little proposition."

"What do I have to do for my twenty-five thousand
dollars?" Barber asked.

"What do you have to do for your twenty-five thousand dollars?" Smith repeated softly. "You have to do a
little flying. You have flown for considerably less, from
time to time, haven't you?" He chuckled.

"I sure have," Barber said. "What else do I have to do?"

"Nothing else," Smith said, sounding surprised. "Just
fly. Are you still interested?"

"Go on," said Barber.

"A friend of mine has just bought a brand-new single-engine plane. A Beechcraft, single engine. A perfect, pleasant, comfortable, one-hundred-per-cent dependable aircraft," Smith said, describing the perfect little plane with pleasure in its newness and its dependability. "He himself does not fly, of course. He needs a private pilot, who will be on tap at all times."

"For how long?" Barber asked, watching Smith closely.

"For thirty days. Not more." Smith smiled up at him. "The pay is not bad, is it?"

"I can't tell yet," Barber said. "Go on. Where does he want to fly to?"

"He happens to be an Egyptian," Smith said, a little deprecatingly, as though being an Egyptian were a slight private misfortune, which one did not mention except among friends, and then in lowered tones. "He is a wealthy Egyptian who likes to travel. Especially back and forth to France. To the South of France. He is in love with the South of France. He goes there at every opportunity."

"Yes?"

"He would like to make two round trips from Egypt to the vicinity of Cannes within the next month," Smith said, peering steadily at Barber, "in his private new plane. Then, on the third trip, he will find that he is in a hurry and he will take the commercial plane and his pilot will follow two days later, alone."

"Alone?" Barber asked, trying to keep all the facts straight.

"Alone, that is," Smith said, "except for a small box."

"Ah," Barber said, grinning. "Finally the small box."

"Finally." Smith smiled up at him delightedly. "It has already been calculated. The small box will weigh two hundred and fifty pounds. A comfortable margin of safety for this particular aircraft for each leg of the journey."

"And what will there be in the small two-hundred-and-fifty-pound box?" Barber asked, cool and relieved now that he saw what was being offered to him.

"Is it absolutely necessary to know?"

"What do I tell the customs people when they ask me what's in the box?" Barber said. " 'Go ask Bert Smith'?"

"You have nothing to do with customs people," Smith said. "I assure you. When you take off from the airport in Cairo, the box is not on board. And when you land at the airport at Cannes, the box is not on board. Isn't that enough?"

Barber took a last pull at his cigarette and doused it. He peered thoughtfully at Smith, sitting easily on the straight-backed chair in the rumpled room, looking too neat and too well-dressed for such a place at such an hour. Drugs, Barber thought, and he can stuff them . . .

"No, Bertie boy," Barber said roughly. "It is not enough. Come on. Tell."

Smith sighed. "Are you interested up to now?"

"I am interested up to now," Barber said.

"All right," Smith said regretfully. "This is how it will be done. You will have established a pattern. You will have been in and out of the Cairo airport several times. Your papers always impeccable. They will know you. You will have become a part of the legitimate routine of the field. Then, on the trip when you will be taking off alone, everything will be perfectly legitimate. You will have only a small bag with you of your personal effects. Your flight plan will show that your destination is Cannes and that you will come down at Malta and Rome for re-fueling only. You will take off from Cairo. You will go off course by only a few miles. Some distance from the coast, you will be over the desert. You will come down on an old R.A.F. landing strip that hasn't been used since 1943. There will be several men there. . . . Are you listening?"

"I'm listening." Barber had walked to the window and was standing there, looking out at the sunny street below, his back to Smith.

"They will put the box on board. The whole thing will not take more than ten minutes," Smith said. "At Malta, nobody will ask you anything, because you will be in

transit and you will not leave the plane and you will stay
only long enough to refuel. The same thing at Rome.
You will arrive over the south coast of France in the evening, before the moon is up. Once more," Smith said,
speaking as though he was savoring his words, "you will
be just a little off course. You will fly low over the hills between Cannes and Grasse. At a certain point, you will see
an arrangement of lights. You will throttle down, open
the door, and push the box out, from a height of a hundred feet. Then you will close the door and turn toward
the sea and land at the Cannes airport. Your papers will
be perfectly in order. There will have been no devia-
tions from your flight plan. You will have nothing to declare. You will walk away from the airplane once and for
all, and we will pay you the twenty-five thousand dollars
I have spoken of. Isn't it lovely?"

"Lovely," Barber said. "It's just a delicious little old
plan, Bertie boy." He turned away from the window.
"Now tell me what will be in the box."

Smith chuckled delightedly, as though what he was going to say was too funny to keep to himself. "Money," he
said. "Just money."

"How much money?"

"Two hundred and fifty pounds of money," Smith said,
his eyes crinkled with amusement. "Two hundred and
fifty pounds of tightly packed English notes in a nice,
strong, lightweight metal box. Five-pound notes."

At that moment, it occurred to Barber that he was
speaking to a lunatic. But Smith was sitting there, matter-
of-fact and healthy, obviously a man who had never for
a minute in all his life had a single doubt about his sanity.

"When would I get paid?" Barber asked.

"When the box was delivered," Smith said.

"Bertie boy . . ." Barber shook his head reprovingly.

Smith chuckled. "I have warned myself that you were
not stupid," he said. "All right. We will deposit twelve
thousand five hundred dollars in your name in a Swiss
bank before you start for the first time to Egypt."

"You trust me for that?"

Fleetingly the smile left Smith's face. "We'll trust you for that," he said. Then the smile reappeared. "And immediately after the delivery is made, we will deposit the rest. A lovely deal. Hard currency. No income tax. You will be a rich man. Semi-rich." He chuckled at his joke. "Just for a little plane ride. Just to help an Egyptian who is fond of the South of France and who is naturally a little disturbed by the insecurity of his own country."

"When will I meet this Egyptian?" Barber asked.

"When you go to the airfield to take off for your first flight," Smith said. "He'll be there. Don't you worry. He'll be there. Do you hesitate?" he asked anxiously.

"I'm thinking," Barber said.

"It's not as though you were involved in your own country," Smith said piously. "I wouldn't ask a man to do that, a man who had fought for his country in the war. It isn't even as though it had anything to do with the English, for whom it is possible you have a certain affection. But the Egyptians . . ." He shrugged and bent over and picked up the manila envelope and opened it. "I have all the maps here," he said, "if you would like to study them. The route is all marked out, but, of course, it would be finally in your hands, since it would be you who was doing the flying."

Barber took the thick packet of maps. He opened one at random. All it showed was the sea approaches to Malta and the location of the landing strips there. Barber thought of twenty-five thousand dollars and the map shook a little in his hands.

"It is ridiculously easy," Smith said, watching Barber intently. "Foolproof."

Barber put the map down. "If it's so easy, what are you paying twenty-five thousand bucks for?" he said.

Smith laughed. "I admit," he said, "there may be certain little risks. It is improbable, but one never knows. We pay you for the improbability, if you want to put it that way." He shrugged. "After all, after a whole war you must be somewhat hardened to risks."

"When do you have to know?" Barber asked.

"Tonight," Smith said. "If you say no, naturally we have to make other plans. And my Egyptian friend is impatient."

"Who is we?" Barber asked.

"Naturally," Smith said, "I have certain colleagues."

"Who are they?"

Smith made a small regretful gesture. "I am terribly sorry," he said, "but I cannot tell you."

"I'll call you tonight," said Barber.

"Good." Smith stood up and buttoned his coat and carefully put the soft Italian felt hat on his head, at a conservative angle. He played gently and appreciatively with the brim. "This afternoon, I will be at the track. Maybe you would like to join me there."

"Where're they running today?"

"Auteuil," Smith said. "Jumping today."

"Have you heard anything?"

"Perhaps," Smith said. "There is a mare who is doing the jumps for the first time. I have spoken to the jockey and I have been told the mare has responded in training, but I'll hear more at three o'clock."

"I'll be there."

"Good," Smith said enthusiastically. "Although it is against my interests, of course, to make you too rich in advance." He chuckled. "However, for the sake of friendship . . . Should I leave the maps?"

"Yes," said Barber.

"Until three o'clock," Smith said as Barber opened the door. They shook hands, and Smith went out into the corridor, a rich, tweedy, perfumed figure in the impoverished light of the pallid hotel lamps.

Barber locked the door behind him and picked up the packet of maps and spread them on the bed, over the rumpled sheets and blankets. He hadn't looked at aerial maps for a long time. Northern Egypt. The Mediterra-

nean. The island of Malta. Sicily and the Italian coast.
The Gulf of Genoa. The Alpes-Maritimes. He stared at
the maps. The Mediterranean looked very wide. He didn't
like to fly over open water in a single-engined plane. In
fact, he didn't like to fly. Since the war, he had flown as
little as possible. He hadn't made any explanations to
himself, but when he had had to travel, he had gone by
car or train or boat whenever he could.

Twenty-five thousand dollars, he thought.

He folded the maps neatly and put them back into
the envelope. At this point, the maps weren't going to
help.

He lay down on the bed again, propped against the pillows, with his hands clasped behind his head. Open water, he thought. Five times. Even that wouldn't be too
bad. But what about the Egyptians? He had been in Cairo
briefly during the war. He remembered that at night the
policemen walked in pairs, carrying carbines. He didn't
like places where the policemen carried carbines. And
Egyptian prisons . . .

He moved uneasily on the bed.

Who knew how many people were in on a scheme like
this? And it would only take one to cook you. One dissatisfied servant or accomplice, one greedy or timid partner . . . He closed his eyes and almost saw the fat,
dark uniformed men with their carbines walking up to
the shiny, new little plane.

Or suppose you blew a tire or crumpled a wheel on the
landing strip? Who knew what the strip was like, aban-
doned in the desert since 1943?

Twenty-five thousand dollars.

Or you would think you were making it. The box
would be on the seat beside you and the coast of Egypt
would be falling off behind you and the sea stretching
blue below and ahead and the engine running like a watch
—and then the first sign of the patrol. The shimmering
dot growing into . . . What did the Egyptian Air Force
fly? Spitfires, left over from the war, he supposed. Com-

ing up swiftly, going twice as fast as you, signaling you to turn around . . . He lit a cigarette. Two hundred and fifty pounds. Say the box alone—it would have to be really solid—weighed a hundred and fifty pounds. How much did a five-pound note weigh? Would there be a thousand to a pound? Five thousand multiplied by a hundred, with the pound at two-eighty. Close to a million and a half dollars.

His mouth felt dry, and he got up and drank two glasses of water. Then he made himself sit down on the chair, keeping his hands still. If there was an accident, if for any reason you failed to come through with it . . . If the money was lost, but you were saved. Smith didn't look like a murderer, although who knew what murderers looked like these days? And who knew what other people he was involved with? My colleagues, as Smith called them, who would then be your colleagues. The wealthy Egyptian, the several men at the old R.A.F. landing strip in the desert, the people who were to set out the lights in the certain arrangement in the hills behind Cannes— How many others, sliding across frontiers, going secretly and illegally from one country to another with guns and gold in their suitcases, the survivors of war, prison, denunciation— How many others whom you didn't know, whom you would see briefly in the glare of the African sun, as a running figure on a dark French hillside, whom you couldn't judge or assess and on whom your life depended, who were risking prison, deportation, police bullets for their share of a box full of money . . .

He jumped up and put on his clothes and went out, locking the door. He didn't want to sit in the cold, disordered room, staring at the maps.

He walked around the city aimlessly for the rest of the morning, looking blindly into shopwindows and thinking of the things he would buy if he had money. Turning away from a window, he saw a policeman watching him incuriously. Barber looked speculatively at the policeman, who was small, with a mean face and a thin mustache. Looking at the policeman, Barber remembered some of the stories about what they did to suspects when they questioned them in the back rooms of the local prefectures. An American passport wouldn't do much good if they picked you up with five hundred thousand English pounds under your arm.

This is the first time in my life, Barber thought curiously, walking slowly on the crowded street, that I have contemplated moving over to the other side of the law. He was surprised that he was considering it so calmly. He wondered why that was. Perhaps the movies and the newspapers, he thought. You get so familiar with crime it becomes humanized and accessible. You don't think about it, but then, suddenly, when it enters your life, you realize that subconsciously you have been accepting the idea of crime as an almost normal accompaniment of everyday life. Policemen must know that, he thought, all at once seeing things from the other side. They must look at all the shut, ordinary faces going past them and they must know how close to theft, murder, and defaulting everyone is, and it must drive them crazy. They must want to arrest everybody.

While Barber was watching the horses move in their stiff-legged, trembling walk around the paddock before the sixth race, he felt a light tap on his shoulder.

"Bertie boy," he said, without turning around.

"I'm sorry I'm late," Smith said, coming up to the paddock rail beside Barber. "Were you afraid I wouldn't come?"

"What's the word from the jock?" Barber asked.

Smith looked around him suspiciously. Then he smiled. "The jockey is confident," Smith said. "He is betting himself."

"Which one is it?"

"Number Five."

Barber looked at No. 5. It was a light-boned chestnut mare with a delicate, gentle head. Her tail and mane were braided, and she walked alertly but not too nervously, well-mannered and with a glistening coat. Her jockey was a man of about forty, with a long, scooped French nose. He was an ugly man, and when he opened his mouth, you saw that most of his front teeth were missing. He wore a maroon cap, with his ears tucked in, and a white silk shirt dotted with maroon stars.

Barber, looking at him, thought, It's too bad such ugly men get to ride such beautiful animals.

"O.K., Bertie boy," he said. "Lead me to the window."

Barber bet ten thousand francs on the nose. The odds were a comfortable seven to one. Smith bet twenty-five thousand francs. They walked side by side to the stands and climbed up together as the horses came out on the track. The crowd was small and there were only a few other spectators that high up.

"Well, Lloyd?" Smith said. "Did you look at the maps?"

"I looked at the maps," Barber said

"What did you think?"

"They're very nice maps."

Smith looked at him sharply. Then he decided to chuckle. "You want to make me fish, eh?" he said. "You know what I mean. Did you decide?"

"I . . ." Barber began, staring down at the cantering horses. He took a deep breath. "I'll tell you after the race," he said.

"Lloyd!" The voice came from below, to the right, and Barber turned in that direction. Toiling up the steps was Jimmy Richardson. He had always been rather round and baby-plump, and Parisian food had done nothing to slim him down, and he was panting, his coat flapping open, disclosing a checkered vest, as he hurried toward Barber.

"How are you?" he said breathlessly as he reached their level. He clapped Barber on the back. "I saw you up here and I thought maybe you had something for this race. I can't figure this one and they've been murdering me all day. I'm lousy on the jumps."

"Hello, Jimmy," Barber said. "Mr. Richardson. Mr. Smith."

"Pleased to meet you," Richardson said. "How do you spell it?" He laughed loudly at his joke. "Say, really, Lloyd, do you know anything? Maureen'll murder me if I go home and tell her I went into the hole for the afternoon."

Barber looked across at Smith, who was watching Richardson benignly. "Well," he said, "Bertie boy, here, thinks he heard something."

"Bertie boy," Richardson said, "please . . ."

Smith smiled thinly. "Number Five looks very good," he said. "But you'd better hurry. They're going to start in a minute."

"Number Five," Richardson said. "Roger. I'll be right back." He went galloping down the steps, his coat flying behind him.

"He's a trusting soul, isn't he?" Smith said.

"He was an only child," Barber said, "and he never got over it."

Smith smiled politely. "Where do you know him from?"

"He was in my squadron."

"In your squadron." Smith nodded, looking after Richardson's hurrying, diminishing figure on the way to the seller's window. "Pilot?"

"Uh-huh."

"Good?"

Barber shrugged. "Better ones got killed and worse ones won every medal in the collection."

"What is he doing in Paris?"

"He works for a drug company," Barber said.

The bell rang and the horses raced toward the first jump.

"Your friend was too late, I'm afraid," Smith said, putting his binoculars to his eyes.

"Yep," Barber said, watching the bunched horses.

No. 5 fell on the fourth jump. She went over with two other horses, and suddenly she was down and rolling. The pack passed around her. The fourth jump was far off down the track, and it was hard to see what, exactly, was happening until, a moment later, the mare struggled to her feet and cantered after the pack, her reins broken and trailing. Then Barber saw that the jockey was lying there motionless, crumpled up clumsily on his face, with his head turned in under his shoulder.

"We've lost our money," Smith said calmly. He took his binoculars from his eyes and pulled out his tickets and tore them and dropped them.

"May I have those, please?" Barber reached over for the binoculars. Smith lifted the strap over his head, and Barber trained the glasses on the distant jump where the jockey was lying. Two men were running out to him and turning him over.

Barber adjusted the binoculars, and the figures of the two men working on the motionless figure in the maroon-starred shirt came out of the blur into focus. Even in the glasses, there was something terribly urgent and despairing in the movements of the distant men. They picked the jockey up between them and started running clumsily off with him.

"Damn it!" It was Richardson, who had climbed up beside them again. "The window closed just as I—"

"Do not complain, Mr. Richardson," Smith said. "We fell at the fourth jump."

Richardson grinned. "That's the first bit of luck I had all day."

Down below, in front of the stands, the riderless mare was swerving and trotting off down the track to avoid a groom who was trying to grab the torn reins.

Barber kept the glasses on the two men who were carrying the jockey. Suddenly, they put him down on the grass, and one of the men bent down and put his ear against the white silk racing shirt. After a while, he stood up. Then the two men started to carry the jockey again, only now they walked slowly, as though there was no sense in hurrying.

Barber gave the glasses back to Smith. "I'm going home," he said. "I've had enough of the sport for one day."

Smith glanced at him sharply. He put the glasses to his eyes and stared at the men carrying the jockey. Then he put the glasses into their case and hung the case by its strap over his shoulder. "They kill at least one a year," he said in a low voice. "It is to be expected in a sport like this. I'll take you home."

"Say," Richardson said. "Is that fellow dead?"

"He was getting too old," Smith said. "He kept at it too long."

"Holy man!" Richardson said, staring down the track. "And I was sore because I came too late to bet on him. That was some tip." He made a babyish grimace. "A tip on a dead jock."

Barber started down toward the exit.

"I'll come with you," Richardson said. "This isn't my lucky day."

The three men went down under the stands without speaking. People were standing in little groups, and there was a queer rising, hissing sound of whispering all over the place, now that the news was spreading.

When they reached the car, Barber got into the back, allowing Richardson to sit next to Smith, on the front seat. He wanted to be at least that much alone for the time being.

Smith drove slowly and in silence. Even Richardson spoke only once. "What a way to get it," he said as they drove between the bare, high trees. "In a lousy, three-hundred-thousand-franc claiming race."

Barber sat in the corner, his eyes half closed, not looking out. He kept remembering the second time the two men had picked up the jockey. Smith's selection for the afternoon, Barber thought. He closed his eyes altogether and saw the maps spread out on the bed in his room. The Mediterranean. The wide reaches of open water. He remembered the smell of burning. The worst smell. The smell of your dreams during the war. The smell of hot metal, smoldering rubber. Smith's tip.

"Here we are," Smith was saying.

Barber opened his eyes. They were stopped at the corner of the dead-end street down which was the entrance to his hotel. He got out.

"Wait a minute, Bertie boy," Barber said. "I have something I want to give you."

Smith looked at him inquiringly. "Can't it wait, Lloyd?" he asked.

"No. I'll just be a minute." Barber went into his hotel and up to his room. The maps were folded in a pile on the bureau, except for one, which was lying open beside the others. The approaches to Malta. He folded it quickly and put all the maps into the manila envelope and went back to the car. Smith was standing beside the car, smoking, nervously holding on to his hat, because a wind had come up and dead leaves were skittering along the pavement.

"Here you are, Bertie boy," Barber said, holding out the envelope.

Smith didn't take it. "You're sure you know what you're doing?" he said.

"I'm sure."

Smith still didn't take the maps. "I'm in no hurry," he said softly. "Why don't you hold on to them another day?"

"Thanks, no."

Smith looked at him silently for a moment. The fluorescent street lamps had just gone on, hard white-blue light, and Smith's smooth face looked powdery in the shadows under his expensive hat, and his pretty eyes were dark and flat under the curled lashes.

"Just because a jockey falls at a jump—" Smith began.

"Take them," Barber said, "or I'll throw them in the gutter."

Smith shrugged. He put out his hand and took the envelope. "You'll never have a chance like this again," he said, running his finger caressingly over the envelope edge.

"Good night, Jimmy." Barber leaned over the car and

spoke to Richardson, who was sitting there watching them, puzzled. "Give my love to Maureen."

"Say, Lloyd," Richardson said, starting to get out. "I thought maybe we could have a couple of drinks. Maureen doesn't expect me home for another hour yet and I thought maybe we could cut up some old touches and—"

"Sorry," Barber said, because he wanted, more than anything else, to be alone. "I have a date. Some other time."

Smith turned and looked thoughtfully at Richardson. "He always has a date, your friend," Smith said. "He's a very popular boy. I feel like a drink myself, Mr. Richardson. I would be honored if you'd join me."

"Well," Richardson said uncertainly, "I live way down near the Hôtel de Ville and—"

"It's on my way," Smith said, smiling warmly.

Richardson settled back in his seat, and Smith started to get into the car. He stopped and looked up at Barber. "I made a mistake about you, didn't I, Lloyd?" he said contemptuously.

"Yes," Barber said. "I'm getting too old. I don't want to keep at it too long."

Smith chuckled and got into the car. They didn't shake hands. He slammed the door, and Barber watched him pull sharply away from the curb, making a taxi-driver behind him jam on his brakes to avoid hitting him.

Barber watched the big black car weave swiftly down the street, under the hard white-blue lights. Then he went back to the hotel and up to his room and lay down, because an afternoon at the races always exhausted him.

An hour later, he got up. He splashed cold water on his face to wake himself, but even so he felt listless and empty. He wasn't hungry and he wasn't thirsty and he kept thinking about the dead jockey in his soiled silks. There was no one he wanted to see. He put on his coat and went out, hating the room as he closed the door behind him.

He walked slowly toward the Etoile. It was a raw

night and a fog was moving in from the river, and the streets were almost empty, because everybody was inside eating dinner. He didn't look at any of the lighted windows, because he wasn't going to buy anything for a long time. He passed several movie houses, neon in the drifting fog. In the movies, he thought, the hero would have been on his way to Africa by now. He would nearly be caught several times in Egypt, and he would fight his way out of a trap on the desert, killing several dark men just in time on the airstrip. And he would develop engine trouble over the Mediterranean and just pull out, with the water lapping at the wing tips, and he would undoubtedly crash, without doing too much damage to himself, probably just a photogenic cut on the forehead, and would drag the box out just in time. And he would turn out to be a Treasury agent or a member of British Intelligence and he would never doubt his luck and his nerve would never fail him and he would not end the picture with only a few thousand francs in his pocket. Or, if it was an artistic picture, there would be a heavy ground mist over the hills and the plane would drone on and on, desperate and lost, and then, finally, with the fuel tanks empty, the hero would crash in flames. Battered and staggering as he was, he would try to get the box out, but he wouldn't be able to move it, and finally the flames would drive him back and he would stand against a tree, laughing crazily, his face blackened with smoke, watching the plane and the money burn, to show the vanity of human aspiration and greed.

Barber grinned bleakly, rehearsing the scenarios in front of the giant posters outside the theatres. The movies do it better, he thought. They have their adventures happen to adventurers. He turned off the Champs-Elysées, walking slowly and aimlessly, trying to decide whether to eat now or have a drink first. Almost automatically, he walked toward the Plaza-Athénée. In the two weeks that he had been wooed by Smith, they had met in the English bar of the Plaza-Athénée almost every evening.

He went into the hotel and downstairs to the English

bar. As he came into the room, he saw, in the corner, Smith and Jimmy Richardson.

Barber smiled. Bertie boy, he thought, are you whatever wasting your time. He stood at the bar and ordered a whiskey.

". . . fifty missions," he heard Richardson say. Richardson had a loud, empty voice that carried anywhere. "Africa, Sicily, Italy, Yugo—"

Then Smith saw him. He nodded coolly, with no hint of invitation. Richard swiveled in his chair then, too. He smiled uncomfortably at Barber, getting red in the face, like a man who has been caught by a friend with his friend's girl.

Barber waved to them. For a moment, he wondered if he ought to go over and sit down and try to get Richardson out of there. He watched the two men, trying to figure out what they thought of each other. Or, more accurately, what Smith thought of Richardson. You didn't have to speculate about Jimmy. If you bought Jimmy a drink, he was your friend for life. For all that he had been through— war and marriage and being a father and living in a foreign country—it had still never occurred to Jimmy that people might not like him or might try to do him harm. When you were enjoying Jimmy, you called it trustfulness. When he was boring you, you called it stupidity.

Barber watched Smith's face carefully. By now, he knew Smith well enough to be able to tell a great deal of what was going on behind the pretty eyes and the pale, powdered face. Right now, Barber could tell that Smith was bored and that he wanted to get away from Jimmy Richardson.

Barber turned back to his drink, smiling to himself. It took Bertie boy just about an hour, he thought, an hour of looking at that good-natured empty face, an hour of listening to that booming, vacant voice, to decide that this was no man to fly a small box of five-pound notes from Cairo to Cannes.

Barber finished his drink quickly and went out of the

bar before Smith and Richardson got up from the table. He had nothing to do for the evening, but he didn't want to get stuck with Jimmy and Maureen Richardson for dinner.

And now it was almost two months later and nobody had heard from Jimmy Richardson for thirty-two days.

In the whole afternoon of searching, Barber had not come upon any trace of Bert Smith. He had not been at the restaurants or the track or the art galleries, the barbershop, the steam bath, the bars. And no one had seen him for weeks.

It was nearly eight o'clock when Barber arrived at the English bar of the Plaza-Athénée. He was wet from walking in the day's rain, and tired, and his shoes were soggy and he felt a cold coming on. He looked around the room, but it was almost empty. Indulging himself, thinking unhappily of all the taxi fares he had paid that day, he ordered a whiskey.

Barber sipped his whiskey in the quiet room, thinking circularly, I should have said something. But what could I have said? And Jimmy wouldn't have listened. But I should have said something. *The omens are bad, Jimmy, go on home. . . . I saw a plane crashing at the fourth jump, I saw a corpse being carried across dead grass by Egyptians, Jimmy, I saw silks and maps stained by blood.*

I had to be so damned superior, Barber thought bitterly. I had to be so damned sure that Jimmy Richardson was too stupid to be offered that much money. I had to be so damned sure that Bert Smith was too clever to hire him.

He hadn't said any of the things he should have said, and it had all wound up with a frantic, husbandless, penniless girl pleading for help that could only be too late now. Penniless. Jimmy Richardson had been too stupid even to get any of the money in advance.

He remembered what Jimmy and Maureen had looked like, smiling and embarrassed and youthfully important, standing next to Colonel Sumners, the Group Commander, at their wedding in Shreveport. He remembered Jimmy's plane just off his wing over Sicily; he remembered Jimmy's face when he landed at Foggia with an engine on fire; he remembered Jimmy's voice singing drunkenly in a bar in Naples; he remembered Jimmy the day after he arrived in Paris, saying, "Kid, this is the town for me, I got Europe in my blood."

He finished his drink and paid and went upstairs slowly. He went into a phone booth and called his hotel to see if there were any messages for him.

"Mme. Richardson has been calling you all day," the old man at the switchboard said. "Ever since four o'clock. She wanted you to call her back."

"All right," Barber said. "Thank you." He started to hang up.

"Wait a minute, wait a minute," the old man said irritably. "She called an hour ago to say she was going out. She said that if you came in before nine o'clock, she would like you to join her at the bar of the Hotel Bellman."

"Thanks, Henri," Barber said. "If she happens to call again, tell her I'm on my way." He went out of the hotel. The Bellman was nearby, and he walked toward it slowly, even though it was still raining. He was in no hurry to see Maureen Richardson.

When he reached the Bellman, he hesitated before going in, feeling too tired for this, wishing Maureen could be put off at least until the next day. He sighed, and pushed the door open.

The bar was a small one, but it was crowded with large, well-dressed men who were taking their time over drinks before going out to dinner. Then he saw Maureen. She was sitting in a corner, half turned away from the room, her shabby, thin coat thrown back over her chair. She was sitting alone and there was a bottle of champagne in a bucket in a stand beside her.

Barber went over to her, irritated by the sight of the

champagne. Is that what she's doing with my five thousand francs, he thought, annoyed. Women are going crazy, too, these days.

He leaned over and kissed the top of her head. She jumped nervously, then smiled when she saw who it was. "Oh, Lloyd," she said, in a funny kind of whisper. She jumped up and kissed him, holding him hard against her. There was a big smell of champagne on her breath and he wondered if she was drunk. 'Lloyd, Lloyd . . .'' she said. She pushed him away a little, holding on to both his hands. Her eyes were smeary with tears and her mouth kept trembling.

"I came as soon as I got your message," Lloyd said, trying to sound practical, afraid Maureen was going to break down in front of all the people in the bar. She kept standing there, her mouth working, her hands gripping his avidly. He looked down, embarrassed, at her hands. They were still reddened and the nails were still uneven, but there was an enormous ring glittering, white and blue, on her finger. It hadn't been there when she came to his hotel, and he knew he had never seen her with a ring like that before. He looked up, almost frightened, thinking, What the hell has she started? What has she got herself into?

Then he saw Jimmy. Jimmy was making his way among the tables toward him. He was smiling broadly and he had lost some weight and he was dark brown and he looked as though he had just come from a month's vacation on a southern beach.

"Hi, kid," Jimmy said, his voice booming across the tables, across the barroom murmur of conversation. "I was just calling you again."

"He came home," Maureen said. "He came home at four o'clock this afternoon, Lloyd." She sank suddenly into her chair. Whatever else had happened that afternoon, it was plain that she had had access to a bottle. She sat in her chair, still holding on to one of Barber's hands, looking up, with a shimmering, half-dazed expression on her face, at her husband.

Jimmy clapped Barber on the back and shook hands fiercely. "Lloyd," he said. "Good old Lloyd. *Garçon!*" he shouted, his voice reverberating through the whole room. "Another glass. Take your coat off. Sit down. Sit down."

Lloyd took his coat off and sat down slowly.

"Welcome home," he said quietly. He blew his nose. The cold had arrived.

"First," Jimmy said, "I have something for you." Ceremoniously he dug his hand into his pocket and brought out a roll of ten-thousand-franc notes. The roll was three inches thick. He took off one of the notes. "Maureen told me," he said seriously. "You were a damn good friend, Lloyd. Have you got change of ten?"

"I don't think so," Barber said. "No."

"Garçon," Jimmy said to the waiter, who was putting down a third glass, "get me two fives for this, please." When he spoke French, Jimmy had an accent that made even Americans wince.

Jimmy filled the three glasses carefully. He lifted his glass and clinked it first against Barber's and then against Maureen's. Maureen kept looking at him as though she had just seen him for the first time and never hoped to see anything as wonderful again in her whole life.

"To crime," Jimmy said. He winked. He made a complicated face when he winked, like a baby who has trouble with a movement of such subtlety and has to use the whole side of its face and its forehead to effect it.

Maureen giggled.

They drank. It was very good champagne.

"You're having dinner with us," Jimmy said. "Just the three of us. The victory dinner. Just Beauty and me and you, because if it hadn't been for you . . ." Suddenly solemn, he put his hand on Barber's shoulder.

"Yes," said Barber. His feet were icy and his trousers hung soddenly around his wet socks and he had to blow his nose again.

"Did Beauty show you her ring?" Jimmy asked.

"Yes," Barber said.

"She's only had it since six o'clock," Jimmy said.

Maureen held her hand up and stared at her ring. She giggled again.

"I know a place," Jimmy said, "where you can get pheasant and the best bottle of wine in Paris and . . ."

The waiter came back and gave Jimmy the two five-thousand-franc notes. Dimly, Barber wondered how much they weighed.

"If ever you're in a hole," Jimmy said, giving him one of the notes, "you know where to come, don't you?"

"Yes," Barber said. He put the note in his pocket.

He started to sneeze then, and ten minutes later he said he was sorry but he didn't think he could last the evening with a cold like that. Both Jimmy and Maureen tried to get him to stay, but he could tell that they were going to be happier without him.

He finished a second glass of champagne, and said he'd keep in touch, and went out of the bar, feeling his toes squish in his wet shoes. He was hungry and he was very fond of pheasant and actually the cold wasn't so bad, even if his nose kept running all the time. But he knew he couldn't bear to sit between Maureen and Jimmy Richardson all night and watch the way they kept looking at each other.

He walked back to his hotel, because he was through with taxis, and went up and sat on the edge of his bed in his room, in the dark, without taking his coat off. I better get out of here, he thought, rubbing the wet off the end of his nose with the back of his hand. This continent is not for me.

In the French Style

Beddoes got in from Egypt in the middle of the morning. He went to his hotel and shook hands with the concierge and told him that the trip had been fine but that Egyptians were impossible. From the concierge he found out that the city was crowded, as usual, and that the price of the room had gone up once more, as usual.

"The tourist season now lasts twelve months a year," the concierge said, giving Beddoes his key. "Nobody stays home any more. It is exhausting."

Beddoes went upstairs and told the porter to put his typewriter in the closet, because he didn't want to see it for a while. He opened the window and looked out with pleasure at the Seine flowing past. Then he took a bath and put on fresh clothes and gave Christina's number over the telephone to the woman at the switchboard. The woman at the switchboard had an insulting habit of repeating numbers in English, and Beddoes noticed, with a smile, that that had not changed. There was the familiar hysteria on the wires as the woman on the switchboard got Christina's number. The telephone in Christina's hotel was down the hall from her room, and Beddoes had to spell the name slowly—Mlle. "T" for Théodore, "A" for André, "T" for Théodore, "E" for Edouard—before the man on the other end understood and went away to tell Christina an American gentleman demanded her on the telephone.

Beddoes heard Christina's footsteps coming down the hall toward the telephone and he thought he could tell from the sound that she was wearing high heels.

"Hello," Christina said. There was a sudden crackle on the wire as Christina spoke, but even so Beddoes could recognize the breathless, excited tone of her voice. Christina answered the phone as though she expected each call to be an invitation to a party.

"Hi, Chris," Beddoes said.

"Who's this?"

"The voice of Egypt," said Beddoes.

"Walter!" Christina said happily. "When did you get in?"

"This minute," Beddoes said, lying by an hour to please her. "Are you wearing high heels?"

"What?"

"You're wearing high heels, aren't you?"

"Wait a minute while I look," Christina said. Then, after a pause, "Did you turn psychic in Cairo?"

Beddoes chuckled. "Semi-Oriental fakery," he said. "I brought back a supply. Where're we going for lunch?"

"Walter!" Christina said. "I'm in despair."

"You have a date."

"Yes. When are you going to learn to cable?"

"That's O.K.," Beddoes said carelessly. He made a point of never sounding disappointed. He had a feeling that if he asked Christina to break the date she would, but he also made a point of never pleading for anything. "We'll make it later."

"How about a drink this afternoon?"

"We can start with that," Beddoes said. "Five?"

"Make it five-thirty," Christina said.

"Where're you going to be?" Beddoes asked, minutely annoyed at the postponement.

"Near the Etoile," Christina said.

"Alexandre's?"

"Fine," Christina said. "Will you be on time for once?"

"Be more polite," Beddoes said, "the first day the man comes to town."

"A tout à l'heure," Christina said.

"What did you say, Ma'am?"

"All the kids are speaking French this year." Christina laughed. "Isn't it nice to have you back in town."

There was a click as she hung up. Beddoes put the phone down slowly and went over to the window. He stared at the river, thinking that this was the first time in a long while that Christina hadn't come over immediately when he arrived in Paris. The river appeared cold and the trees were bare and the sky looked as though it had been gray for months. But with all that, the city looked promising. Even the sunless, snowless winter weather couldn't prevent Paris from looking promising.

He had lunch with a man from the A.P. who had just come back from America. The man from the A.P. said that things were in unholy shape in America and that even if you ate in drugstores it cost at least a dollar and a half for lunch and Beddoes ought to be damned glad he wasn't there.

Beddoes got to the café a little late, but Christina hadn't arrived. He sat on the glass-enclosed terrace, next to the huge window, feeling it cold from the winter afternoon against his sleeve. The terrace was crowded with women drinking tea and men reading the evening newspapers. Outside, under the trees, a little parade was forming, the veterans of some World War I unit, huddling, middle-aged, and chilled in their overcoats, with their flags and decorations, preparing to walk behind an Army band up to the Arch and put a wreath on the tomb in memory of comrades who had fallen in battles that no one any longer remembered. The French, Beddoes thought sourly, because Christina was late and the afternoon had failed its promise, are always finding occasions to block traffic. They have an endless supply of dead to celebrate.

He ordered a beer, because he had drunk too much at lunch. He had also eaten too much, in the first wave of gluttony after Egyptian food. His stomach felt uncomfortable, and he was suddenly very tired from all the miles he had traveled in the past twenty-four hours. After the age of thirty-five, he thought, in evening melancholy, no matter how swift the plane, how calm the air, how soft the cushion, the bones record the miles inexorably. He had turned thirty-five three months before and he had begun to reflect uneasily upon age. He stared at his face in mirrors, noticing wrinkles under his eyes and gray in his beard when he shaved. He remembered hearing that aging ballplayers shaved two and three times a day to keep managers and sportswriters from seeing the telltale flecks in beard stubble. Maybe, he thought, career men in the foreign service ought to do the same thing. Seventy minus thirty-five leaves thirty-five, he thought. It was an equation that came ominously to mind, especially late in the afternoon, more and more often after the midway anniversary. He stared out through the cold glass at the shuffling veterans, ranked shabbily behind their flags, their breath, mingled with cigarette smoke, rising in little clouds above their heads. He wished they'd start marching and get away from there. "Veteran" was a word that suddenly fell on his ear with an unpleasant sound.

He also wished that Christina would arrive. It wasn't like her to be late. She was one of those rare girls who always got to places exactly on the appointed hour. Irrelevantly, he remembered that she also dressed with great speed and took only a minute or two to comb her hair. She had blond hair, cut in the short Parisian manner, which left the back of her neck bare. Beddoes thought about the back of Christina's neck and felt better.

They would give themselves a gay evening, he thought. One should not permit himself to feel tired or old in Paris. If the feeling ever gets chronic, he told himself, I'll move away for good.

He thought about the evening ahead of him. They'd

wander around to a couple of bars, avoiding their friends and not drinking too much, and go to a *bistro* in the markets where there were thick steaks and a heavy red wine, and after that maybe they'd go to the night club where there was a queer, original puppet show and three young men who sang funny songs that, unlike so many night-club songs, really did turn out to be funny. When you came out into the street after their act you were charmed and amused and you had the sense that this was the way a man should feel in Paris at two o'clock in the morning.

The night before he left for Cairo, he had taken Christina there. The prospect of going back on this first night home gave him an unexplained but pleasant feeling of satisfactory design. Christina had looked very pretty, the prettiest girl in the room full of handsome women, he'd thought, and he had even danced, for the first time in months. The music was supplied by a pianist and a man who got quivering, rich sounds from an electric guitar, and they played those popular French songs that always made you feel how sweet was love in the city, how full of sorrow and tempered regret.

The music had made Christina a little moony, he remembered, which was strange for her, and she had held his hand during the show, and kissed him when the lights went out between numbers. Her eyes had filled with tears for a moment and she had said, "What am I going to do without you for two months?" when he spoke of his departure the next morning. He had felt, a little warily, because he was affected, too, that it was lucky he was leaving, if she was moving into that phase. That was the pre-yearning-for-marriage phase, and you had to be on guard against it, especially late at night, in Paris, in darkened rooms where pianists and electric guitars played songs about dead leaves and dead loves and lovers who were separated by wars.

Beddoes had been married once, and he felt, for the time being, that that was enough. Wives had a tendency to produce children, and sulk and take to drink or other

men when their husbands were called away to the other
side of the earth for three or four months at a time on jobs.

He had been a little surprised at Christina. Yearning
was not in her line. He had known her, although until recently not very well, almost from the time she arrived from
the States four years before. She did some modeling for
photographers and was pretty enough to have done very
well at it, except that, as she said, she felt too silly making
the fashionable languorous, sexy grimaces that were demanded of her. She knew how to type and take dictation
and she found odd jobs with American businessmen who
had work for a month or two at a time in Paris. She had
picked up French immediately, and drove a car, and from
time to time she got curious little jobs as a companion for
old American ladies who wanted to tour through the châ-
teau country or into Switzerland. She never seemed to
need any sleep (even now she was only about twenty-six)
and she would stay up all night with anybody and she went
to all the parties and had had, to Beddoes' knowledge, affairs with two friends of his—a free-lance photographer
and an Air Transport Command pilot who had been killed
in a crash outside Frankfurt. You could telephone her at
any hour of the day or night without making her angry
and you could introduce her into any group and be pleased
with the way she behaved. She always knew which *bistro*
was having a rage at the moment and who was singing at
which night club and which new painter was worth seeing
and who was in town and who was going to arrive next
week and which little hotels outside Paris were pleasant
for lunch or a weekend. She obviously didn't have much
money, but she dressed charmingly, French enough to
amuse her French friends and not so French that she made
Americans feel she was trying to pretend she was European. All in all, while she was not a girl of whom your
grandmother was likely to approve, she was, as Beddoes
had once told her, an ornament to the wandering and
troubled years of the second half of the twentieth century.

The veterans started to move off, the banners flapping a little in the dusk as the small parade turned past the TWA office and up the Champs-Elysées. Beddoes watched them, thinking vaguely of other parades, other banners. Then he saw Christina striding diagonally across the street, swift and sure of herself in the traffic. She could live in Europe the rest of her life, Beddoes thought, smiling as he watched her, and all she'd have to do would be to walk ten steps and everybody would know she had been born on the other side of the ocean.

He stood when she opened the door into the terrace. She was hatless, and Beddoes noticed that her hair was much darker than he remembered and she was wearing it longer. He kissed her on both cheeks as she came up to the table. "Welcome," he said. "In the French style."

She hugged him momentarily. "Well, now," she said, "here's the man again."

She sat down, opening her coat, and smiled across the table at him. Her cheeks were flushed from the cold and her eyes were shining and she looked glitteringly young.

"The spirit of Paris," Beddoes said, touching her hand on the table. "American division. What'll it be to drink?"

"Tea, please. I'm so glad to see you."

"Tea?" Beddoes made a face. "Anything wrong?"

"No." Christina shook her head. "I just want tea."

"That's a hell of a drink to welcome a traveler home on," Beddoes said.

"With lemon, please," Christina said.

Beddoes shrugged, and ordered one tea from the waiter.

"How was Egypt?" Christina asked.

"Was I in Egypt?" Beddoes stared at Christina, enjoying her face.

"That's what it said in the papers."

"Oh, yes," Beddoes said. "A new world struggling to be born," he said, his voice deep and expert. "Too late for feudalism, too early for democracy . . ."

Christina made a face. "Lovely phrases for the State Department archives," she said. "I mean over a drink how is Egypt."

"Sunny and sad," Beddoes said. "After two weeks in Cairo you feel sorry for everybody. How is Paris?"

"Too late for democracy," Christina said, "too early for feudalism."

Beddoes grinned and leaned across the little table and kissed her gently. "I mean over a kiss," he said, "how is Paris?"

"The same," Christina said. She hesitated. "Almost the same."

"Who's around?"

"The group," Christina said carelessly. "The usual happy exiles. Charles, Boris, Anne, Teddy . . ."

Teddy was the free-lance photographer. "You see much of him?" Beddoes asked, very lightly.

"Uh?" Christina smiled, just a little, at him.

"Merely checking." Beddoes grinned.

"No, I haven't," Christina said. "His Greek's in town."

"Still the Greek?"

"Still the Greek," Christina said.

The waiter came and placed the tea in front of her. She poured it into the cup and squeezed the lemon. She had long, competent fingers, and Beddoes noticed that she no longer used bright nail polish.

"Your hair," he said. "What happened?"

Christina touched her hair absently. "Oh," she said. "You noticed?"

"Where're the blondes of yesteryear?"

"I decided to go natural." Christina stirred her tea. "See what that was like for a change. Like it?"

"I haven't decided yet. It's longer, too."

"Uh-huh. For the winter. The back of my neck was cold. People say it makes me look younger."

"They're absolutely right," Beddoes said. "You now look exactly eleven."

Christina smiled and lifted her cup to him. "To those who return," she said.

"I don't accept toasts in tea," Beddoes said.

"You're a finicky, liquor-loving man," Christina said, and placidly sipped at her tea.

"Now," Beddoes said, "the evening. I thought we might skip our dear friends and go to that place in the markets for dinner, because I'm dying for a steak, and after that—" He stopped. "What's the matter? Can't we have dinner together?"

"It's not that, exactly." Christina kept her head down and stirred her tea slowly. "I have a date—"

"Cancel him," Beddoes said promptly. "Cancel the swine."

"I can't really." Christina looked soberly up at him. "He's coming to meet me here any minute now."

"Oh." Beddoes nodded. "That makes it different, doesn't it?"

"Yes."

"Can't we shake him?"

"No," Christina said. "We can't shake him."

"The man doesn't live who can't be shaken," said Beddoes. "Old friend, you say, who just arrived from the horrors of the desert, just escaped dysentery and religious wars by the skin of his teeth, needs soothing, you say, and tender attention for his shattered nerves, et cetera."

Christina was smiling, but shaking her head. "Sorry," she said. "It can't be done."

"Want me to do it?" Beddoes said. "Man to man. See here, old fellow, we're all grown-up, civilized human beings— That sort of thing?"

"No," Christina said.

"Why not?" Beddoes asked, conscious that he was breaking a long-standing and until now jealously adhered-to rule about not pleading for anything. "Why can't we?"

"Because I don't want to," Christina said.

"Oh," said Beddoes. "The wind is in that direction."

"Variably," Christina said softly, "in that direction. We could all have dinner together. The three of us. He's a very nice man. You'd like him."

"I never like any man the first night I'm in Paris," Beddoes said.

They sat in silence for a moment while Beddoes remembered all the times that Christina had said over the phone, "O.K., it's sinful, but I'll brush him. Meet you at eight." It was hard to believe, sitting across from her, noticing that there was no obvious change in the way she looked at him, in the way she touched his hand, that she wouldn't say it in the next minute or so.

"Two months is a long time, isn't it?" Beddoes said. "In Paris?"

"No," Christina said. "It's not a long time. In Paris or anywhere else."

"Hello, Christina." It was a tall, rather heavy-set young man, smiling and blond, who was standing, holding a hat, next to the table. "I found the place all right." He leaned over and kissed her forehead.

Beddoes stood up.

"Jack," Christina said, "this is Walter Beddoes. John Haislip. Dr. Haislip."

The two men shook hands.

"He's a surgeon," Christina said as Haislip gave his hat and coat to the attendant and sat down beside her. "He nearly had his picture in *Life* last year for something he did with kidneys. In thirty years he's going to be enormously famous."

Haislip chuckled. He was a big, placid, self-confident-looking man, with the air of an athlete, who was probably older than he looked. And just with one glance Beddoes could tell how the man felt about Christina. Haislip wasn't hiding anything in that department.

"What'll you drink, Doctor?" Beddoes asked.

"Lemonade, please."

"*Un citron pressé,*" Beddoes said to the waiter. He

peered curiously at Christina, but she was keeping her face straight.

"Jack doesn't drink," Christina said. "He says it isn't fair for people who make a living out of cutting other people up."

"When I retire," Haislip said cheerfully, "I'm going to soak it up and let my hands shake like leaves in the wind." He turned to Beddoes. You could tell that it took a conscious wrench for him to stop looking at Christina. "Did you have a good time in Egypt?" he asked.

"Oh," Beddoes said, surprised. "You know about my being in Egypt?"

"Christina's told me all about you," Haislip said.

"I swore a solemn oath that I was going to forget Egypt for a month once I got here," Beddoes said.

Haislip chuckled. He had a low, unforced laugh and his face was friendly and unself-conscious. "I know how you feel," he said. "The same way I feel about the hospital sometimes."

"Where is the hospital?" Beddoes asked.

"Seattle," Christina said quickly.

"How long have you been here?" Beddoes saw Christina glance at him obliquely as he spoke.

"Three weeks," said Haislip. He turned back toward Christina, as though he could find comfort in no other position. "The changes that can take place in three weeks. My Lord!" He patted Christina's arm and chuckled again. "One more week and back to the hospital."

"You here for fun or for business?" Beddoes asked, falling helplessly into the pattern of conversation of all Americans who meet each other abroad for the first time.

"A little of both," Haislip said. "There was a conference of surgeons I was asked to attend, and I moseyed around a few hospitals on the side."

"What do you think of French medicine now you've had a chance to see some of it?" Beddoes asked, the investigator within operating automatically.

"Well"—Haislip managed to look away from Christina

for a moment—"they function differently from us over here. Intuitively. They don't have the equipment we have, or the money for research, and they have to make up for it with insight and intuition." He grinned. "If you're feeling poorly, Mr. Beddoes," he said, "don't hesitate to put yourself in their hands. You'll do just about as well here as anyplace else."

"I feel all right," Beddoes said, then felt that it had been an idiotic thing to say. The conversation was beginning to make him uncomfortable, not because of anything that had been said but because of the way the man kept looking, so openly and confessingly and completely, at Christina. There was a little pause and Beddoes had the feeling that unless he jumped in, they would sit in silence forever. "Do any sightseeing?" he asked lamely.

"Not as much as I'd like," Haislip said. "Just around Paris. I'd've loved to go down south this time of the year. That place Christina keeps talking about. St. Paul de Vence. I guess that's about as different from Seattle as a man could wish for and still get running water and Christian nourishment. You've been there, haven't you, Mr. Beddoes?"

"Yes," Beddoes said.

"Christina told me," said Haislip. "Oh, thank you," he said to the waiter who put the lemonade down in front of him.

Beddoes stared at Christina. They had spent a week together there early in the autumn. He wondered what, exactly, she had told the Doctor.

"We'll make it the next trip," Haislip said.

"Oh," said Beddoes, noting the "we" and wondering whom it included. "You planning to come over again soon?"

"In three years." Haislip carefully extracted the ice from his lemonade and put it on the saucer. "I figure I can get away for six weeks in the summer every three years. People don't get so sick in the summertime." He stood up.

"Pardon me," he said, "but I have to make a couple of telephone calls."

"Downstairs and to the right," Christina said. "The woman'll put the calls through for you. She speaks English."

Haislip laughed. "Christina doesn't trust my French," he said. "She says it's the only recognizable Puget Sound accent that has ever been imposed upon the language." He started away from the table, then stopped. "I sincerely hope you'll be able to join us for dinner, Mr. Beddoes."

"Well," Beddoes said, "I made a tentative promise I'd meet some people. But I'll see what I can do."

"Good." Haislip touched Christina's shoulder lightly, as though for some obscure reassurance, and walked away between the tables.

Beddoes watched him, thinking unpleasantly, Well, one thing, I'm better-looking, anyway. Then he turned to Christina. She was stirring the tea leaves at the bottom of her cup absently with her spoon. "That's why the hair is long and natural," Beddoes said. "Isn't it?"

"That's why." Christina kept stirring the tea leaves.

"And the nail polish."

"And the nail polish."

"And the tea."

"And the tea."

"What did you tell him about St. Paul de Vence?"

"Everything."

"Look up from that damned cup."

Slowly Christina put down the spoon and raised her head. Her eyes were glistening, but not enough to make anything of it, and her mouth was set, as with an effort.

"What do you mean by everything?" Beddoes demanded.

"Everything."

"Why?"

"Because I don't have to hide anything from him."

"How long have you known him?"

"You heard," Christina said. "Three weeks. A friend of mine in New York asked him to look me up."

"What are you going to do with him?"

Christina looked directly into his eyes. "I'm going to marry him next week and I'm going back to Seattle with him."

"And you'll come back here three years from now for six weeks in the summertime, because people don't get so sick in the summertime," Beddoes said.

"Exactly."

"And that's O.K.?"

"Yes."

"You said that too defiantly," Beddoes said.

"Don't be clever with me," Christina said harshly. "I'm through with all that."

"Waiter!" Beddoes called. "Bring me a whiskey, please." He said it in English, because for the moment he had forgotten where he was. "And you," he said to Christina. "For the love of God, have a drink."

"Another tea," Christina said.

"Yes, Madame," said the waiter, and went off.

"Will you answer some questions?" Beddoes asked.

"Yes."

"Do I rate straight answers?"

"Yes."

Beddoes took a deep breath and looked through the window. A man in a raincoat was walking past, reading a newspaper and shaking his head.

"All right," Beddoes said. "What's so great about him?"

"What can I be expected to say to that?" Christina asked. "He's a gentle, good, useful man. And now what do you know?"

"What else?"

"And he loves me." She said it in a low voice. In all the time they'd been together, Beddoes hadn't heard her use the word before. "He loves me," Christina repeated flatly.

"I saw," said Beddoes. "Immoderately."

"Immoderately," Christina said.

"Now let me ask another question," Beddoes said. "Would you like to get up from this table and go off with me tonight?"

Christina pushed her cup away, turning it thoughtfully. "Yes," she said.

"But you won't," said Beddoes.

"No."

"Why not?"

"Let's talk about something else," said Christina. "Where're you going on your next trip? Kenya? Bonn? Tokyo?"

"Why not?"

"Because I'm tired of people like you," Christina said clearly. "I'm tired of correspondents and pilots and promising junior statesmen. I'm tired of all the brilliant young men who are constantly going someplace to report a revolution or negotiate a treaty or die in a war. I'm tired of airports and I'm tired of seeing people off. I'm tired of not being allowed to cry until the plane gets off the ground. I'm tired of being so damned prompt. I'm tired of answering the telephone. I'm tired of all the spoiled, hung-over international darlings. I'm tired of sitting down to dinner with people I used to love and being polite to their Greeks. I'm tired of being handed around the group. I'm tired of being more in love with people than they are with me. That answer your question?"

"More or less," Beddoes said. He was surprised that no one at any of the other tables seemed to be paying any special attention to them.

"When you left for Egypt," Christina went on, her voice level, "I decided. I leaned against that wire fence watching them refueling all those monstrous planes, with the lights on, and I dried the tears and I decided. The next time, it was going to be someone who would be shattered when *I* took off."

"And you found him."

"I found him," Christina said flatly. "And I'm not going to shatter him."

Beddoes put out his hands and took hers. They lay limp in his grasp. "Chris . . ." he said. She was looking out the window. She sat there, outlined against the shining dusk beyond the plate glass, scrubbed and youthful and implacable, making him remember, confusedly, the first time he had met her, and all the best girls he had ever known, and what she had looked like next to him in the early-morning autumnal sunlight that streamed, only three months before, into the hotel room in the south, which overlooked the brown minor Alps and the distant sea. Holding her hands, with the familiar touch of the girlish fingers against his, he felt that if he could get her to turn her head everything would be different.

"Chris . . ." he whispered.

But she didn't turn her head. "Write me in Seattle," she said, staring out the window, which was streaked with moisture and in which the lights from within the café and the lights from the restaurant across the street were reflected and magnified and distorted.

Beddoes let her hands go. She didn't bother to move them. They lay before her, with their pale nail polish glistening dully, on the stained wood table. Beddoes stood up. "I'd better go." It was difficult to talk, and his voice sounded strange to him inside his head, and he thought, God, I'm getting senile, I'm tempted to cry in restaurants. "I don't want to wait for the check," he said. "Tell your friend I'm sorry I couldn't join you for dinner and that I apologize for leaving him with the check."

"That's all right," Christina said evenly. "He'll be happy to pay."

Beddoes leaned over and kissed her, first on one cheek, then on the other. "Good-bye," he said, thinking he was smiling. "In the French style."

He got his coat quickly and went out. He went past the TWA office to the great boulevard and turned the corner, where the veterans had marched a half hour before. He walked blindly toward the Arch, where the laurel leaves of the wreath were already glistening in the evening mist before the tomb and the flame.

He knew that it was a bad night to be alone and that he ought to go in somewhere and telephone and ask someone to have dinner with him. He passed two or three places with telephones, and although he hesitated before each one, he didn't go in. Because there was no one in the whole city he wanted to see that night.

Voyage Out, Voyage Home

Constance sat impatiently in the little chair in the first-class cabin, taking occasional sips of the champagne that Mark had sent. Mark had been called out of town and hadn't been able to come, but he'd sent champagne. She didn't like champagne, but she didn't know what else to do with it, so she drank it. Her father stood in front of the porthole, drinking, too. From his expression, Constance could guess that he didn't like champagne either. Or perhaps he didn't like this particular vintage. Or he didn't like it because Mark had sent it. Or maybe it wasn't the champagne at all but just that he was embarrassed.

Constance knew that she was looking sullen, and she tried to change the set of her face, because she also knew that she looked younger, childish, sixteen, seventeen, when she was sullen. She was sure that everything she did with her face at that moment made her look more sullen than ever, and she wished the horn would blow and her father would get off the ship.

"You'll probably drink a lot of this," her father said. "In France."

"I don't expect to stay in France long," she said. "I'm going to look for someplace quiet." Her voice sounded to

344

her as though it were coming out of the nursery, wailing and spiteful and spoiled. She tried to smile at her father. The last few weeks in the apartment, while the argument had been going on and the hostility had been so close to the surface, had been painful to her, and now, in the last ten minutes before the ship pulled away, she wanted to recapture an earlier, easier relationship as far as she could. So she smiled, but she had the impression that the smile was crafty and cold and coquettish. Her father turned around and looked vaguely out the porthole at the covered wharf. It was rainy and there was a cold wind blowing and the men on the dock waiting to throw off the lines looked miserable.

"It's going to be a choppy night," her father said. "Have you got the Dramamine?"

The hostility returned, because he asked about the Dramamine. At a moment like that. "I won't need Dramamine," Constance said shortly. She took a long drink of the champagne. The label on the bottle was impeccable, like all Mark's gifts, but the wine was sourish and acidy.

Her father turned back toward her. He smiled at her, and she thought, bitterly, This is the last time he's going to get away with patronizing me. He stood there, a robust, confident, healthy, youngish-seeming man, looking privately amused, and Constance thought, How would you like it if I just got out of here and walked off this precious boat—how would you ever like it?

"I envy you," her father said. "If someone had only sent me to Europe when I was twenty . . ."

Twenty, twenty, Constance thought. He's always harping on twenty. "Please, Father, let's cut that out," she said. "I'm here and I'm going and it's all settled, but let's spare ourselves the envy."

"Every time I happen to remind you that you're twenty," her father said mildly, "you react as though I'd insulted you."

He smiled, pleased with himself that he was so damned perceptive, that he understood her so well, that he was not one of those fathers whose children slide irrevocably away from them into mysterious, modern depths.

"Let's not discuss it," Constance said, pitching her voice low. When she remembered, she always made a point of pitching her voice low. It sometimes made her sound forty years old on the telephone, or like a man.

"Have a great time," her father said. "Go to all the bright places. And if you decide you want to stay on, just let me know. Maybe I'll be able to come over and join you for a few weeks—"

"Three months from now," Constance said crisply, "to this day, I'll be coming up the harbor."

"Whatever you say, my dear."

When he said "my dear," Constance knew he was humoring her. She couldn't bear being humored there in the ugly little cabin, with the weather bad outside, and the ship ready to leave, and the sounds of people saying good-bye, laughing loudly, in the next room. If she had been on better terms with her father, she would have cried.

The horn blew for visitors to go ashore, and her father came and kissed her, holding her for an extra second, and she tried to be polite. But when he said, very seriously, "You'll see—three months from now you'll thank me for this," she pushed him back, furious with him for his obnoxious assurance, and mournful at the same time that they, who had been so close to each other, were no longer friends.

"Good-bye," she said, her voice choked and not pitched low. "The whistle's blowing. Good-bye."

He picked up his hat, patted her shoulder, hesitated a moment at the door, looking thoughtful but not disturbed, and went out into the corridor and disappeared among the other visitors who were streaming up toward the gangplank and the shore.

When she was sure her father was off, Constance went up to the boat deck and stood there, alone in the sharp, blowy rain, watching the tugs pull the ship into the stream. As the ship went slowly downriver into the harbor and then headed into open water, she shivered in the wintry air, and, approving of herself a little for the grandeur of the sentiment, thought, I am approaching a continent to which I have no connection.

Constance braced herself against the crossbar of the lift as she approached the mid-point of the hill. She made sure that her skis were firmly in the ruts as she came up onto the flat section of packed snow where there was a short line of skiers who had come down only halfway and were waiting to pick up empty hooks and go back to the top. She always felt a little uncertain here, because if you were alone on one side of the T bar, the first person in the line would swing into place alongside you and there would be an extra, sudden pull as the new weight caught that could throw you off balance. She saw that there was a man waiting for the place next to her, and she concentrated on keeping erect gracefully as he settled into place beside her. He did it smoothly, and they skidded easily past the waiting line. She was conscious that he was looking across at her, but she was too occupied for the moment with the terrain in front of her to turn her head.

"Oh, I know you," the man said as they started safely up the hill again, leaning against the pull of the bar, their skis bumping a little in the ruts. "You're the grave young American."

Constance looked at him for the first time. "And you," she said, because everybody talked to everybody else on the hills, "you're the gay young Englishman."

"Half right," he said. He smiled. His face was a skier's brown, with an almost girlish flush of blood along the cheekbones. "At least, one-third right." She knew his name was Pritchard, because she had heard people talking to him in the hotel. She remembered hearing one of the ski teachers say about him, "He is too reckless. He thinks he is better than he actually is. He does not have the technique for so much speed." She glanced across at him and decided he *did* look reckless. He had a long nose—the kind that doesn't photograph well but that looks all right just the same, especially in a long, thin face. Twenty-five, Constance thought, twenty-six. No more. He was leaning easily against the bar, not holding on with his hands. He took off his gloves and fished a package of cigarettes out of his pockets and offered them to Constance. "Players," he said. "I hope you won't hate me."

"No, thank you," Constance said. She was sure that if she tried to light a cigarette she would fall off the lift.

He lit his cigarette, bending over a little and squinting over his cupped hands as the smoke twisted up past his eyes. He had long, thin hands, and ordinarily you had the feeling that people with hands like that were nervous and easily upset. He was tall and slender, and his ski pants were very downhill, Constance noted, and he wore a red sweater and a checked scarf. He had the air of a dandy, but a dandy who was amused at himself. He moved easily on his skis, and you could tell he was one of the people who weren't afraid of falling.

"I never see you in the bar," he said, tossing the match into the snow and putting on his gloves.

"I don't drink," she said, not quite telling the truth.

"They have Coca-Cola," he said. "Switzerland, the forty-ninth state."

"I don't like Coca-Cola."

"Used to be one of the leading British colonies," he said, grinning. "Switzerland. But we lost it, along with India. Before the war, in this town, the English covered the hills like the edelweiss. If you wanted to find a Swiss between January 1st and March 13th, you had to hunt with dogs."

"Were you here before the war?" Constance asked, surprised.

"With my mother. She broke a leg a year."

"Is she here now?"

"No," he said. "She's dead."

I must be careful, Constance thought, avoiding looking

at the man beside her, not to ask people in Europe about their relatives. So many of them turn out to be dead.

"It used to be very gay," he said, "the hotels swarming, and dances every night, and everybody dressing for dinner, and singing 'God Save the King' on New Year's. Did you know it was going to be this quiet?"

"Yes," Constance said. "I asked the man at the travel bureau in Paris."

"Oh. What did he say?"

"He said everybody was a serious skier here and went to bed by ten o'clock."

The Englishman glanced at her momentarily. "You're not a serious skier, are you?"

"No. I've only been two or three times before."

"You're not one of the delicate ones, are you?"

"Delicate?" Constance looked at him, puzzled. "What do you mean?"

"You know," he said, "the advertisements. Schools for delicate children. Swiss for t.b."

Constance laughed. "Do I look as though I have t.b.?"

He regarded her gravely, and she felt plump and un-austere and a little too bosomy in her tight clothes. "No," he said. "But you never can tell. Did you ever read *The Magic Mountain*?"

"Yes," she said, feeling proud that she could show she was not completely uncultured, although American and very young, and remembering that she had skipped the philosophic discussions and cried over the death of the cousin. "I read it. Why?"

"The sanitarium it was written about isn't far from here," Pritchard said. "I'll show it to you someday when the snow's bad. Do you think this place is sad?"

"No," she said, surprised. "Why?"

"Some people do. The mixture. The pretty mountains and the healthy types walloping down the hills, risking their necks and feeling marvelous, and the people with the bad lungs hanging on, watching them and wondering if they're ever going to leave here alive."

"I guess I didn't think about it," Constance admitted honestly.

"It was worse right after the war," he said. "There was a boom here right after the war. All the people who hadn't eaten enough or had been living underground or in prison and who had been frightened so long—"

"Where're they now?"

Pritchard shrugged. "Dead, discharged, or destitute," he said. "Is it true that people refuse to die in America?"

"Yes," she said. "It would be an admission of failure."

He smiled and patted her gloved hand, which was clutching tightly onto the middle bar. "You mustn't be angry that we're jealous," he said. "It's the only way we can show our gratitude." Gently, he loosened her fingers from the wood. "And you mustn't be so tight when you ski. Not even with your fingers. You mustn't even frown until you go in for tea. The drill is—loose, desperate, and supremely confident."

"Is that how you are?"

"Mostly desperate," he said.

"What are you doing on this little beginners' slope, then?" Constance asked. "Why didn't you take the *téléphérique* up to the top?"

"I twisted my ankle yesterday," Pritchard said. "Overrated myself. The February disease. Out of control and into a gully, with a great deal of style. So today I can only do slow, majestic turns. But tomorrow we attack that one once more—" He gestured up toward the peak, half closed in by fog, with the sun a wet, pale ball above it, making it look forbidding and dangerous. "Come along?" He looked at her inquiringly.

"I haven't been up there yet," Constance said, regarding the mountain respectfully. "I'm afraid it's a little too much for me so far."

"You must always do things that are a little too much for you," he said. "On skis. Otherwise, where's the fun?"

They were silent for several moments, moving slowly up the hill, feeling the wind cut across their faces, noticing the quiet and the queer, fogged mountain light. Twenty yards ahead of them, on the preceding bar, a girl in a yellow parka moved evenly upward like a bright, patient doll.

"Paris?" Pritchard said.

"What's that?" He jumps around entirely too much, Constance thought, feeling heavy.

"You said you came from Paris. Are you one of those nice people who come here to give us your government's money?"

"No," said Constance. "I just came over on a—well, on a vacation. I live in New York, really. And French food makes me break out."

He looked at her critically. "You look completely unbroken out now," he said. "You look like the girls who advertise soap and beer in American magazines." Then he added hastily, "If that's considered insulting in your country, I take it back."

"And the men in Paris," she said.

"Oh. Are there men in Paris?"

"Even in the museums. They follow you. With homburg hats. Looking at you as though they're weighing you by the pound, In front of religious pictures and everything."

"Girl I knew, English girl," Pritchard said, "was followed from Prestwick, Scotland, to the tip of Cornwall by an American gunner in 1944. Three months. No religious pictures, though, as far as I know."

"You know what I mean. It's an impolite atmosphere," she said primly, knowing he was making fun of her in that straight-faced English way but not knowing whether to be offended or not.

"Were you brought up in a convent?"

"No."

"It's amazing how many American girls sound as though they were brought up in a convent. Then it turns out they drink gin and roar in bars. What do you do at night?"

"Where? At home?"

"No. I know what people do at night in America. They look at television," he said. "I mean here."

"I—I wash my hair," she said defensively, feeling foolish. "And I write letters."

"How long are you staying up here?"

"Six weeks."

"Six weeks." He nodded, and swung his poles to his outside hand, because they were nearing the top. "Six weeks of shining hair and correspondence."

"I made a promise," she said, thinking, I might as well let him know now, just in case he's getting any ideas. "I promised someone I'd write him a letter a day while I was gone."

Pritchard nodded soberly, as though sympathizing with her. "Americans," he said as they came to the top and slid out from the T bar onto the flat place. "Americans baffle me."

Then he waved his poles at her and went straight down the hill, his red sweater a swift, diminishing gay speck against the blue-shadowed snow.

The sun slipped between the peaks, like a gold coin in a gigantic slot, and the light got flat and dangerous, making it almost impossible to see the bumps. Constance made her last descent, falling twice and feeling superstitious, because it was always when you said, "Well, this is the last one," that you got hurt.

Running out and coming to a stop on the packed snow between two farmhouses at the outskirts of the town, she kicked off her skis with a sense of accomplishment and relief. Her toes and fingers were frozen, but she was warm everywhere else and her cheeks were bright red and she breathed the thin, cold air with a mountain sense of tasting something delicious. She felt vigorous and friendly, and smiled at the other skiers clattering to a stop around her. She was brushing the snow of the last two falls off her clothes, so that she would look like a good skier as she walked through the town, when Pritchard came down over the last ridge and flicked to a stop beside her.

"I see you," he said, bending to unlock his bindings, "but I won't tell a soul."

Constance gave a final, self-conscious pat to the icy crystals on her parka. "I only fell four times all afternoon," she said.

"Up there, tomorrow"—he made a gesture of his head toward the mountain—"you'll crash all day."

"I didn't say I was going up there." Constance buckled her skis together and started to swing them up to her shoulder. Pritchard reached over and took them from her. "I can carry my own skis," she said.

"Don't be sturdy. American girls are always being sturdy about inessential points." He made a big V out of the two pairs of skis on his shoulders, and they started walking, their boots crunching on the stained, hard snow of the road. The lights came on in the town, pale in the fading light. The postman passed them, pulling his sled with his big dog yoked beside him. Six children in snowsuits on a linked whip of sleds came sliding down out of a steep side street and overturned in front of them in a fountain of laughter. A big brown horse with his belly clipped to keep the ice from forming there slowly pulled three huge logs toward the station. Old men in pale-blue parkas passed them and said *"Grüezi,"* and a maid from one of the houses up the hill shot out on a little sled, holding a milk can between her knees as she rocketed around the turns. They were playing a French waltz over at the skating rink, and the music mingled with the laughter of the children and the bells on the horse's bridle and the distant, old-fashioned clanging of the gong at the railroad station, announcing a train's departure.

"Departure," the station bell said, insistent among the other sounds.

There was a booming noise far off in the hills, and Constance looked up, puzzled. "What's that?" she asked.

"Mortars," said Pritchard. "It snowed last night, and the patrols have been out all day firing at the overhangs. For the avalanches."

There was another shot, low and echoing, and they stopped and listened. "Like old times," Pritchard said as they started walking again. "Like the good old war."

"Oh," said Constance, feeling delicate, because she had never heard guns before. "The war. Were you in it?"

"A little." He grinned. "I had a little war."

"Doing what?"

"Night fighter," he said, shifting the yoke of skis a little on his shoulders. "I flew an ugly black plane across an ugly black sky. That's the wonderful thing about the Swiss —the only thing they shoot is snow."

"Night fighter," Constance said vaguely. She had been only twelve years old when the war ended, and it was all jumbled and remote in her memory. It was like hearing about the graduating class two generations before you in school. People were always referring to names and dates and events that they expected you to recognize, but which you could never quite get straight. "Night fighter. What was that?"

"We flew interceptor missions over France," Pritchard said. "We'd fly on the deck to avoid the radar and flak, and hang around airfields making the Hun miserable, waiting for planes to come in slow, with their wheels down."

"Oh, I remember now," Constance said firmly. "You're the ones who ate carrots. For night vision."

Pritchard laughed. "For publication we ate carrots," he said. "Actually, we used radar. We'd locate them on the screen and fire when we saw the exhaust flares. Give me a radar screen over a carrot any day."

"Did you shoot down many planes?" Constance asked, wondering if she sounded morbid.

"*Grüezi,*" Pritchard said to the owner of a *pension* who was standing in front of his door looking up at the sky to see if it was going to snow that night. "Twenty centimetres by morning. Powder."

"You think?" the man said, looking doubtfully at the evening sky.

"I guarantee," Pritchard said.

"You're very polite," the man said, smiling. "You must come to Switzerland more often." He went into his *pension*, closing the door behind him.

"A couple," Pritchard said carelessly. "We shot down a couple. Should I tell you how brave I was?"

"You look so young," Constance said.

"I'm thirty," said Pritchard. "How old do you have to be to shoot down a plane? Especially poor, lumbering transports, running out of gas, full of clerks and rear-echelon types, wiping their glasses and being sorry the airplane was ever invented."

In the hills, there was the flat sound of the mortars again. Constance wished they'd stop. "You don't look thirty," she said to Pritchard.

"I've led a simple and salutary life. Here," he said. They were in front of one of the smaller hotels, and he put the skis in the rack and jammed the poles into the snow beside them. "Let's go in here and get a simple and salutary cup of tea."

"Well," said Constance, "I really—"

"Make the letter two pages shorter tonight, and more intense." He took her elbow gently, barely touching it, as he guided her toward the door. "And polish your hair some other night."

They went into the bar and sat down at a heavy, carefully carved wood table. There were no other skiers in the bar—just some village men sitting under the chamois antlers on the wall, quietly playing cards on felt cloths and drinking coffee out of small stemmed glasses.

"I told you," Pritchard said, taking off his scarf. "This country is being overrun by the Swiss."

The waitress came over, and Pritchard ordered, in German.

"What did you ask for?" Constance asked, because she could tell it wasn't only tea.

"Tea and lemon and black rum," said Pritchard.

"Do you think I ought to have rum?" she asked doubtfully.

"Everybody in the whole world should have rum," he said. "It will keep you from committing suicide in the twilight."

"You speak German, don't you?"

"I speak all the dead languages of Europe," he said. "German, French, Italian, and English. I was carefully educated for a world of interchangeable currency." He sat back, rubbing the knuckles of one hand against the palm of the other, to warm them. His head was leaning against the wood-paneled wall and he was smiling at her and she couldn't tell whether she was uncomfortable or not. "Let me hear you say 'Hi-ho, Silver.' "

"What?" she asked, puzzled.

"Isn't that what people say in America? I want to perfect my accent for the next invasion," he said.

"They stopped that," she said, thinking, My, he's a jumpy boy, I wonder what happened to him to make him that way. "They don't say it any more. It's out of date."

"All the best things go out of date so quickly in your country," he said regretfully. "Observe the Swiss." He gestured with his head toward where the men were playing. "That game has been going on since 1910," he said. "Living among the Swiss is so placid. It's like living alongside a lake. Many people can't stand it, of course. You remember that joke about the Swiss in that film about Vienna?"

"No," Constance said. "What film?" This is the first time, she thought, I've ever called a movie a film. I must be careful.

"One of the characters says, 'The Swiss haven't had a war in a hundred and fifty years and what have they produced? The cuckoo clock.' I don't know." Pritchard shrugged. "Maybe it's better to live in a country that invents the cuckoo clock than one that invents radar. Time is nothing serious to a cuckoo clock. A little toy that makes a silly, artificial sound every half hour. For people who invent radar, time is ominous, because it's the difference between the altitude of a plane and the location of the battery that's going to bring it down. It's an invention for people who are suspicious and are thinking of ambush. Here's your tea. As you see, I'm making a serious effort to amuse you, because I've been watching you for five days and you give the impression of a girl who cries herself to sleep several times a week."

"How much of this stuff do I put in?" Constance asked, confused by the flood of talk, holding up the glass of rum, and carefully making sure not to look at Pritchard.

"Half," he said. "You have to have something in reserve for the second cup."

"It smells good," Constance said, sniffing the fragrance that rose from the cup after she had measured out half the glass of rum and squeezed the lemon into it.

"Perhaps"—Pritchard prepared his own cup—"perhaps I'd better talk only on impersonal subjects."

"Perhaps that would be better," Constance said.

"The chap who receives all those letters," Pritchard said. "Why isn't he here?"

Constance hesitated for a moment. "He works," she said.

"Oh. That vice." He sipped his tea, then put down his cup and rubbed his nose with his handkerchief. "Hot tea does that to you, too?"

"Yes."

"Are you going to marry him?"

"You said impersonal."

"So. The marriage is arranged."

"I didn't say that."

"No. But you would have said no if it wasn't."

Constance chuckled. "All right," she said. "Arranged. Anyway, approximately arranged."

"When?"

"When the three months're up," she said, without thinking.

"Is that a law in New York?" Pritchard asked. "That you have to wait three months? Or is it a private family taboo?"

Constance hesitated. Suddenly, she felt that she hadn't really talked to anyone in a long time. She had ordered meals and asked directions in railroad stations and said good morning to the people in shops, but everything else had been loneliness and silence, no less painful because she had imposed it on herself. Why not, she thought, self-ishly and gratefully. Why not talk about it, for once?

"It's my father," she said, twisting her cup. "It's his idea. He's against it. He said wait three months and see. He thinks I'll forget Mark in three months in Europe."

"America," Pritchard said. "The only place left where people can afford to act in an old-fashioned manner. What's the matter with Mark? Is he a fright?"

"He's beautiful," Constance said. "Melancholy and beautiful."

Pritchard nodded, as though noting all this down. "No money, though," he said.

"Enough," said Constance. "At least, he has a good job."

"What's the matter with him, then?"

"My father thinks he's too old for me," Constance said. "He's forty."

"A grave complaint," Pritchard said. "Is that why he's melancholy?"

Constance smiled. "No. He was born that way. He's a thoughtful man."

"Do you only like forty-year-old men?" Pritchard asked.

"I only like Mark," said Constance. "Although it's true I never got along with the young men I knew. They—they're cruel. They make me feel shy—and angry with myself. When I go out with one of them, I come home feeling crooked."

"Crooked?" Pritchard looked puzzled.

"Yes. I feel I haven't behaved like me. I've behaved

the way I think the other girls they've gone out with have behaved. Coquettish, cynical, amorous. Is this too complicated?"

"No."

"I hate the opinions other people have of me," Constance said, almost forgetting the young man at the table with her, and talking bitterly, and for herself. "I hate being used just for celebrations, when people come into town from college or from the Army. Somebody for parties, somebody to maul on the way home in the taxi. And my father's opinion of me." She was getting it out for the first time. "I used to think we were good friends, that he thought I was a responsible, grown-up human being. Then when I told him I wanted to marry Mark, I found out it was all a fraud. What he really thinks of me is that I'm a child. And a child is a form of idiot. My mother left him when I was ten and we've been very close since then, but we weren't as close as I thought we were. He was just playing a game with me. Flattering me. When the first real issue came up, the whole thing collapsed. He wouldn't let me have my own opinion of me at all. That's why I finally said all right to the three months. To prove it to him once and for all." She looked suddenly, distrustfully, at Pritchard, to see whether he was smiling. "Are you being amused at me?"

"Of course not," he said. "I'm thinking of all the people I've known who've had different opinions of me than I've had of myself. What a frightening idea." He looked at her speculatively, but it was hard for her to tell how serious he was. "And what's your opinion of yourself?"

"It's not completely formed yet," she said slowly. "I know what I want it to be. I want to be responsible and I don't want to be a child and I don't want to be cruel— and I want to move in a good direction." She shrugged, embarrassed now. "That's pretty lame, isn't it?"

"Lame," Pritchard said, "but admirable."

"Oh, I'm not admirable yet," she said. "Maybe in ten years. I haven't sorted myself out completely yet." She laughed nervously. "Isn't it nice," she said, "you're going away in a few days and I'll never see you again, so I can talk like this to you."

"Yes," he said. "Very nice."

"I haven't talked to anyone for so long. Maybe it's the rum."

Pritchard smiled. "Ready for your second cup?"

"Yes, thank you." She watched him pour the tea and was surprised to notice that his hand shook. Perhaps, she thought, he's one of those young men who came out of the war drinking a bottle of whisky a day.

"So," he said. "Tomorrow we go up to the top of the mountain."

She was grateful to him for realizing that she didn't want to talk about herself any more and switching the conversation without saying anything about it.

"How will you do it—with your ankle?" she asked.

"I'll get the doctor to put a shot of Novocain in it," he said. "And for a few hours my ankle will feel immortal."

"All right," she said, watching him pour his own tea, watching his hand shake. "In the morning?"

"I don't ski in the morning," he said. He added the rum to his tea and sniffed it appreciatively.

"What do you do in the morning?"

"I recover, and write poetry."

"Oh." She looked at him doubtfully. "Should I know your name?"

"No," he said. "I always tear it up the next morning."

She laughed, a little uncertainly, because the only other people she had ever known who wrote poetry had been fifteen-year-old boys in prep school. "My," she said, "you're a queer man."

"Queer?" He raised his eyebrows. "Doesn't that mean something a little obscene in America? Boys with boys, I mean."

"Only sometimes," Constance said, embarrassed. "Not now. What sort of poetry do you write?"

"Lyric, elegiac, and athletic," he said. "In praise of

youth, death, and anarchy. Very good for tearing. Shall we have dinner together tonight?"

"Why?" she asked, unsettled by the way he jumped from one subject to another.

"That's a question that no European woman would ever ask," he said.

"I told the hotel that I was going to have dinner up in my room."

"I have great influence at the hotel," he said. "I think I may be able to prevent them from taking the tray up."

"Besides," Constance said, "what about the lady you've been having dinner with all week—the French lady?"

"Good." He smiled. "You've been watching me, too."

"There're only fifteen tables in the whole dining room," Constance said uncomfortably. "You can't help . . ." The French lady was at least thirty, with a short, fluffed haircut and a senselessly narrow waist. She wore black slacks and sweaters and very tight, shiny belts, and she and Pritchard always seemed to be laughing a great deal together over private jokes in the corner in which they sat every night. Whenever Constance was in the room with the French lady, she felt young and clumsy.

"The French lady is a good friend," Pritchard said, "but Anglo-Saxons are not *nuancé* enough for her, she says. The French are patriots down to the last bedsheet. Besides, her husband is arriving tomorrow."

"I think I'd really rather stick to my plan," Constance said formally. She stood up. "Are we ready to go?"

He looked at her quietly for a moment. "You're beautiful," he said. "Sometimes it's impossible to keep from saying that."

"Please," she said. "Please, I do have to go now."

"Of course," he said. He stood up and left some money on the table. "Whatever you say."

They walked the hundred yards to their hotel in silence. It was completely dark now, and very cold, and their breath crystallized in little clouds before their mouths as they walked.

"I'll put your skis away," he said, at the door of the hotel.

"Thank you," she said in a low voice.

"Good night. And write a nice letter," he said.

"I'll try," she said. She turned and went into the hotel.

In her room, she took off her boots but didn't bother changing her clothes. She lay down on her bed, without putting on the lights, and stared at the dark ceiling, thinking, Nobody ever told me the English were like that.

"Dearest," she wrote. "Forgive me for not writing, but the weather has been glorious and for a little while I've just devoted myself to making turns and handling deep snow. . . . There's a young man here, an Englishman," she wrote conscientiously, "who's been very nice, who has been good enough to act as an instructor, and even if I say it myself, I'm really getting pretty good. He was in the R.A.F. and his father went down with the Hood and his mother was killed in a bombing—"

She stopped. No, she thought, it sounds tricky. As though I'm hiding something, and putting in the poor, dead, patriotic family as artful window dressing. She crumpled the letter and threw it in the wastebasket. She took out another sheet of paper. "Dearest," she wrote.

There was a knock on the door, and she called *"Ja."*

The door opened and Pritchard came in. She looked up in surprise. In all the three weeks, he'd never come to her room. She stood up, embarrassed. She was in her stocking feet, and the room was littered with the debris of the afternoon's skiing—boots standing near the window, sweaters thrown over a chair, gloves drying on the radiator, and her parka hanging near the bathroom door, with a little trickle of melting snow running down from the collar. The radio was on, and an American band was playing "Bali Ha'i" from an Armed Forces station in Germany.

Pritchard, standing in front of the open door, smiled

at her. "Ah," he said, "some corner of a foreign room that is forever Vassar."

Constance turned the radio off. "I'm sorry," she said, waving vaguely and conscious that her hair was not combed. "Everything's such a mess."

Pritchard went over to the bureau and peered at Mark's picture, which was standing there in a leather frame. "The receiver of letters?" he asked.

"The receiver of letters." There was an open box of Kleenex on the bureau, and an eyelash curler, and a half-eaten bar of chocolate, and Constance felt guilty to be presenting Mark so frivolously.

"He's very handsome." Pritchard squinted at the photograph.

"Yes," Constance said. She found her moccasins and put them on, and felt a little less embarrassed.

"He looks serious." Pritchard moved the Kleenex to get a better view.

"He *is* serious," said Constance. In all the three weeks that she had been skiing with Pritchard, she had said hardly anything about Mark. They had talked about almost everything else, but somehow, by a tacit agreement, they had avoided Mark. They had skied together every afternoon and had talked a great deal about the necessity of leaning forward at all times, and about falling relaxed, and about Pritchard's time in public school in England, and about his father, and about the London theatre and American novelists, and they had talked gravely about what it was like to be twenty and what it was like to be thirty, and they had talked about Christmastime in New York and what football weekends were like at Princeton, and they had even had a rather sharp discussion on the nature of courage when Constance lost her nerve in the middle of a steep trail late one afternoon, with the sun going down and the mountain deserted. But they had never talked about Mark.

Pritchard turned away from the picture. "You didn't

have to shoe yourself for me," he said, indicating her moccasins. "One of the nicest things about skiing is taking those damned heavy boots off and walking around on a warm floor in wool socks."

"I'm engaged in a constant struggle not to be sloppy," Constance said.

They stood there, facing each other in silence for a moment. "Oh," Constance said. "Sit down."

"Thank you," Pritchard said formally. He seated himself in the one easy chair. "I just came by for a minute. To say good-bye."

"Good-bye," Constance repeated stupidly. "Where're you going?"

"Home. Or at least to England. I thought I'd like to leave you my address," Pritchard said.

"Of course."

He reached over and picked up a piece of paper and her pen and wrote for a moment. "It's just a hotel," he said. "Until I find a place of my own." He put the paper down on the desk but kept the pen in his hand, playing with it. "Give you somebody else to write to," he said. "The English receiver of letters."

"Yes," she said.

"You can tell me what the snow's like," he said, "and how many times you came down the mountain in one day and who got drunk at the bar the night before."

"Isn't this sudden?" Constance asked. Somehow, after the first few days, it had never occurred to her that Pritchard might leave. He had been there when she arrived and he seemed to belong there so thoroughly, to be so much a part of the furniture of the place, that it was hard to conceive of being there without him.

"Not so sudden," Pritchard said. He stood up. "I wanted to say good-bye in private," he said. She wondered if he was going to kiss her. In all the three weeks, he hadn't as much as held her hand, and the only times he had touched her had been when he was helping her up after a particularly bad fall. But he made no move. He

stood there, smiling curiously, playing with the pen, unusually untalkative, as though waiting for her to say something. "Well," he said, "will I see you later?"

"Yes," she said.

"We'll have a farewell dinner. They have veal on the
menu, but I'll see if we can't get something better, in
honor of the occasion." He put the pen down carefully
on the desk. "Until later," he said, and went out, closing
the door behind him.

Constance stared at the closed door. Everybody goes
away, she thought. Unreasonably, she felt angry. She
knew it was foolish, like a child protesting the end of a
birthday party, but she couldn't help feeling that way.
She looked around the room. It seemed cluttered and un-
tidy to her, like the room of a silly and careless school-
girl. She shook her head impatiently and began to put
things in place. She put the boots out in the hall and hung
the parka in the closet and carried the box of Kleenex
into the bathroom and gave the half bar of chocolate to
the chambermaid. She straightened the coverlet of the
bed and cleaned the ashtray and, on a sudden impulse,
dropped the eyelash curler into the wastebasket. It's too
piddling, she thought, to worry about curling your eyelashes.

Pritchard ordered a bottle of Burgundy with dinner,
because Swiss wine, he said, was too thin to say farewell
on. They didn't talk much during dinner. It was as
though he had already departed a little. Once or twice,
Constance almost started to tell him how grateful she was
for his patience with her on the hills, but somehow it
never came out, and the dinner became more and more
uncomfortable for both of them. Pritchard ordered brandy
with the coffee, and she drank it, although it gave
her heartburn. The three-piece band began to play for
the evening's dancing while they were drinking their
brandy, and then it was too noisy to talk.

"Do you want to dance?" he asked.

"No," she said.

"Good," he said. "I despise dancing."

"Let's get out of here," Constance said. "Let's take a walk."

They went to their rooms to get some warm clothes, and Pritchard was waiting for her outside the hotel door when she came down in her snow boots and the beaver coat her father had given her the year before. Pritchard was leaning against a pillar on the front porch and she stared at him for a moment before he turned around, and she was surprised to see how tired and suddenly old he seemed when he was unaware that he was being watched.

They walked down the main street, with the sounds of the band diminishing behind them. It was a clear night, and the stars shone above the mountains, electrically blue. At the top of the highest hill, at the end of the *téléphérique,* a single light glittered from the hut there, where you could warm yourself before the descent, and buy spiced hot wine and biscuits.

They walked down to the bottom of the street and crossed over onto the path alongside the dark skating rink. The ice reflected the stars dimly and there was the noise of water from the brook that ran along one side of the rink and scarcely ever froze.

They stopped at a small, snow-covered bridge, and Pritchard lit a cigarette. The lights of the town were distant now and the trees stood around them in black silence. Pritchard put his head back, with the smoke escaping slowly from between his lips, and gestured up toward the light on top of the mountain.

"What a life," he said. "Those two people up there. Night after winter night alone on top of the hills, waiting for the world to arrive each morning." He took another puff of the cigarette. "They're not married, you know," he said. "Only the Swiss would think of putting two people who weren't married on top of a hill like that. He's an old man and she's a religious fanatic and they hate each other, but neither of them will give the other the satisfaction of taking another job." He chuckled as they both looked at the bright pinpoint above them. "Last year there was a blizzard and the *téléphérique* didn't run for a week and the power lines were down and they had to stay up there for six days and nights, breaking up chairs for firewood, living off chocolate and tins of soup, and not talking to each other." He stared reflectively at the faraway high light. "It will do as a symbol this year for this pretty continent," he said softly.

Suddenly Constance knew what she had to say. "Alan" —she moved squarely in front of him—"I don't want you to go."

Pritchard flicked at his cigarette. "Six days and six nights," he said. "For their hardness of heart."

"I don't want you to go."

"I've been here for a long time," he said. "I've had the best of the snow."

"I want you to marry me," Constance said.

Pritchard looked at her. She could see he was trying to smile. "That's the wonderful thing about being twenty years old," he said. "You can say things like that."

"I said I want you to marry me."

He tossed away his cigarette. It glowed on the snow. He took a step toward her and kissed her. She could taste the fumed grape of the brandy faint on his lips. He held her for a moment, then stepped back and buttoned her coat, like a nurse being careful with a little girl. "The things that can happen to a man," he said. He shook his head slowly.

"Alan," Constance said.

"I take it all back," Pritchard said. "You're not at all like the girls who advertise soap and beer."

"Please," she said. "Don't make it hard."

"What do you know about me?" He knocked the snow off the bridge railing and leaned against it, brushing the snow off his hands with a dry sound. "Haven't you ever been warned about the young men you're liable to meet in Europe?"

"Don't confuse me," she said. "Please."

"What about the chap in the leather frame?"

Constance took a deep breath. She could feel the cold tingling in her lungs. "I don't know," she said. "He's not here."

Pritchard chuckled, but it sounded sad. "Lost," he said. "Lost by an ocean."

"It's not only the ocean," she said.

They walked in silence again, listening to the sound of their boots on the frozen path. The moon was coming up between the peaks and reflecting milkily off the snow.

"You ought to know one bit of information," Pritchard said in a low voice, looking down at the long shadow the moon cast on the path ahead of him. "I've been married."

"Oh," Constance said. She was very careful to walk in the footprints of the others who had tamped the path down before her.

"Not gravely married," Pritchard said, looking up. "We were divorced two years ago. Does that make a difference to you?"

"Your business," Constance said.

"I must visit America someday," Pritchard said, chuckling. "They are breeding a new type."

"What else?" Constance asked.

"The next thing is unattractive," Pritchard said. "I don't have a pound. I haven't worked since the war. I've been living off what was left of my mother's jewelry. There wasn't much and I sold the last brooch in Zurich last week. That's why I have to go back, even if there were no other reasons. You can see," he said, grinning painfully, "you've picked the prize of the litter."

"What else?" Constance asked.

"Do you still want to hear more?"

"Yes."

"I would never live in America," Pritchard said. "I'm a weary, poverty-stricken, grounded old R.A.F. type, and I'm committed to another place. Come on." He took her elbow brusquely, as though he didn't want to talk any more. "It's late. We'd better get to the hotel."

Constance hung back. "You're not telling me everything," she said.

"Isn't that enough?"

"No."

"All right," he said. "I couldn't go with you to America if I wanted to."

"Why not?"

"Because they wouldn't let me in."

"Why not?" Constance asked, puzzled.

"Because I am host to the worm," Pritchard said.

"What're you talking about?"

"Swiss for delicate," he said harshly. "They kicked D. H. Lawrence out of New Mexico and made him die along the Riviera for it. You can't blame them. They have enough diseases of their own. Now let's go back to the hotel."

"But you seem so healthy. You ski—"

"Everybody dies here in the best of health," Pritchard said. "It goes up and down with me. I almost get cured, then the next year"—he shrugged and chuckled soundlessly—"the next year I get almost uncured. The doctors hold their heads when they see me going up in the lift. Go home," he said. "I'm not for you. I'm oppressed. And you're not oppressed. It is the final miscegenation. Now shall we go back to the hotel?"

Constance nodded. They walked slowly. The town on the hill ahead of them was almost completely dark now, but they could hear the music of the dance band, thin and distant in the clear night air.

"I don't care," Constance said as they came to the first buildings. "I don't care about anything."

"When I was twenty—" Pritchard said. "When I was twenty I once said the same thing."

"First, we'll be practical," Constance said. "You'll need money to stay here. I'll give it to you tomorrow."

"I can't take your money."

"It's not mine," Constance said. "It's my father's."

"England is forever in your debt," Pritchard said. He was trying to smile. "Be careful of me."

"What do you mean?"

"I am beginning to feel as though I can be consoled."

"What's wrong with that?"

"It can prove to be mortal," Pritchard whispered, taking her clumsily and bulkily in his arms, "for those of us who are inconsolable."

When they woke in the morning, they were solemn at first, and disconnectedly discussed the weather, which was revealed through the not quite closed curtains to be gray and uncertain. But then Pritchard asked, "How do you feel?" and Constance, taking her time and wrinkling her eyebrows in a deep attempt to be accurate, said, "I feel *enormously* grown up." Pritchard couldn't help roaring with laughter, and all solemnity was gone. They lay there comfortably discussing themselves, going over their future like misers, and Constance was worried, although not too seriously, about scandalizing the hotel people, and Pritchard said that there was nothing to worry about—nothing that foreigners could do could scandalize the Swiss—and Constance felt more comfortable than ever at being in such a civilized country.

They made plans about the wedding, and Pritchard said they'd go to the French part of Switzerland to get married, because he didn't want to get married in German, and Constance said she was sorry she hadn't thought of it herself.

Then they decided to get dressed, because you could not spend the rest of your life in bed, and Constance had a sorrowful, stinging moment when she saw how thin he was, and thought, conspiratorially, Eggs, milk, butter, rest. They went out of the room together, bravely determined to brazen it out, but there was no one in the corridor or on the stairway to see them, so they had the double pleasure of being candid and being unobserved at the same time, which Constance regarded as an omen of good luck. They discovered that it was almost time for lunch, so they had some kirsch first, and then orange juice and bacon and eggs and wonderful, dark coffee in the scrubbed, wood-paneled dining room, and in the middle of it tears came into Constance's eyes and Pritchard asked why she was crying and she said, "I'm thinking of all the breakfasts we're going to eat together." Pritchard's eyes got a little wet then, too, as he stared across the table at her, and she said, "You must cry often, please."

"Why?" he asked.

"Because it's so un-English," she said, and they both laughed.

After breakfast, Pritchard said he was going up the hill to make a few runs and asked if she wanted to go with him, but she said she felt too melodious that day to ski, and he grinned at the "melodious."

She said she was going to write some letters, and he grew thoughtful. "If I were a gentleman, I'd write your father immediately and explain everything," he said.

"Don't you dare," she said, meaning it, because she knew her father would be over on the next plane if he got a letter like that.

"Don't worry," he said. "I'm not that much of a gentleman."

She watched him stride off between the snowbanks with his red sweater and his skis, looking boyish and jaunty, and then went to her room and wrote a letter to Mark, saying that she had thought it over and that she was sorry but she had decided it was a mistake. She wrote the letter calmly, without feeling anything, cozy in her warm room. She didn't mention Pritchard, because that was none of Mark's business.

Then she wrote a letter to her father and told him that she had broken off with Mark. She didn't mention Pritchard in the letter to her father, either, because she didn't want him over on the next plane, and she didn't say anything about coming home. All that could wait.

She sealed the letters, then lay down dreamily to nap, and slept without dreaming for more than an hour. She dressed for the snow and went to the post office to mail the letters and walked down to the skating rink to watch the children on the ice, and on her way back to the hotel she stopped at the ski shop and bought Pritchard a light-weight yellow sweater, because soon the sun would be very hot all day and the clothes of winter would all be too warm.

She was in the bar, waiting unhurriedly for Pritchard, when she heard that he was dead.

Nobody had come to tell her, because there was no particular reason for anybody to come to tell her.

There was an instructor with whom Pritchard had sometimes skied talking in the bar to some Americans, and he was saying, "He was out of control and he miscalculated and he went into a tree and he was dead in five minutes. He was a jolly fine fellow"—the ski teacher had learned his English from his British pupils before the war —"but he went too fast. He did not have the technique to handle the speed."

The ski teacher did not sound as though it were routine to die on skis, but he did not sound surprised. He himself had had many of his bones broken, as had all his friends, crashing into trees and stone walls and from falls in the summertime, when he was a guide for climbers, and he sounded as though it were inevitable, and even just, that from time to time people paid up to the mountain for faults of technique.

Constance stayed for the funeral, walking behind the black-draped sled to the churchyard and the hole in the snow and the unexpected dark color of the earth after the complete white of the winter. No one came from England, because there was no one to come, although the ex-wife telegraphed flowers. A good many of the villagers came, but merely as friends, and some of the other skiers, who had known Pritchard casually, and as far as anyone could tell, Constance was just one of them.

At the grave, the ski teacher, with the professional habit of repetition common to teachers, said, "He did not have the technique for that much speed."

Constance didn't know what to do with the yellow sweater, and she finally gave it to the chambermaid for her husband.

Eight days later, Constance was in New York. Her father was waiting for her on the pier and she waved to him and he waved back, and she could tell, even at that distance, how glad he was to see her again. They kissed when she walked off the gangplank, and he hugged her, very hard, then held her off at arm's length and stared at her delightedly, and said, "God, you look absolutely wonderful! See," he said, and she wished he hadn't said it, but she realized he couldn't help himself. "See—wasn't I right? Didn't I know what I was talking about?"

"Yes, Father," she said, thinking, How could I ever have been angry with him? He's not stupid or mean or selfish or uncomprehending—he is merely alone.

Holding her hand the way he used to do while they took walks together when she was a little girl, he led her into the customs shed, to wait for her trunk to come off the ship.

The Sunny Banks of the River Lethe

Hugh Forester always remembered everything. He remembered the dates of the Battle of New Cold Harbor (May 31-June 12, 1864); he remembered the name of his teacher in the first grade (Webel; red-haired; weight, one-forty-five; no eyelashes); he remembered the record number of strikeouts in one game in the National League (Dizzy Dean, St. Louis Cards, July 30, 1933, seventeen men, against the Cubs); he remembered the fifth line of "To a Skylark" (Shelley: "In profuse strains of unpremeditated art"); he remembered the address of the first girl he ever kissed (Prudence Collingwood, 248 East South Temple Street, Salt Lake City, Utah; March 14, 1918); he remembered the dates of the three partitions of Poland and the destruction of the Temple (1772, 1793, 1795, and 70 A.D.); he remembered the number of ships taken by Nelson at the Battle of Trafalgar (twenty), and the profession of the hero of Frank Norris's novel *McTeague* (dentist); he remembered the name of the man who won the Pulitzer Prize for history in 1925 (Frederic L. Paxson), the name of the Derby winner at Epsom in 1923 (Papyrus), and the number he drew in the draft in 1940 (4726); he remembered the figures for his blood pressure (a hundred and sixty-five over ninety;

too high), his blood type (O), and his vision (forty over twenty for the right eye and thirty over twenty for the left); he remembered what his boss told him when he was fired from his first job ("I'm getting a machine to do the job"), and what his wife said when he proposed to her ("I want to live in New York"); he remembered the correct name of Lenin (Vladimir Ilyich Ulyanov), and what caused the death of Louis XIV (gangrene of the leg). He also remembered the species of birds, the mean depths of the navigable rivers of America; the names, given and assumed, of all the Popes, including the ones at Avignon; the batting averages of Harry Heilmann and Heinie Groh; the dates of the total eclipses of the sun since the reign of Charlemagne; the speed of sound; the location of the tomb of D. H. Lawrence; all of the *Rubáiyát* of Omar Khayyámm; the population of the lost settlement of Roanoke; the rate of fire of the Browning automatic rifle; the campaigns of Caesar in Gaul and Britain; the name of the shepherdess in *As You Like It* and the amount of money he had in the Chemical Bank & Trust on the morning of December 7, 1941 ($2,367.58).

Then he forgot his twenty-fourth wedding anniversary (January 25th). His wife, Narcisse, looked at him strangely over breakfast that morning, but he was reading the previous night's newspaper and thinking, They will never get it straight in Washington, and he didn't pay much attention. There was a letter from their son, who was at the University of Alabama, but he put it in his pocket without opening it. It was addressed only to him, so he knew it was a request for money. When Morton wrote his dutiful, familial notes they were addressed to both his parents. Morton was at Alabama because his marks had not been high enough to get him into Yale, Dartmouth, Williams, Antioch, the College of the City of New York, or the University of Colorado.

Narcisse asked if Hugh wanted fish for dinner and he said yes, and Narcisse said that fish was criminally expensive, too, and he said yes, and she asked if anything was the matter and he said no and kissed her and walked out of the apartment to the 242nd Street subway station and stood all the way down to the office, reading the morning newspaper. Narcisse's parents had lived in France for some time and that was where the name came from; by now he was used to it. As he read his newspaper in the crowded car he wished, mildly, that most of the people whom people wrote about in the newspapers would vanish.

Hugh was the first one in the office, and he went to his cubbyhole and sat at his desk, leaving the door open, enjoying the empty desks and the sound of silence. He remembered that Narcisse's nose had twitched at the breakfast table and that she had seemed about to cry. He wondered briefly why, but knew that he would be told in good time, and dismissed it. Narcisse cried between five and eight times a month.

The company for which he worked was putting out a one-volume encyclopedia, absolutely complete, on Indian paper, with seven hundred and fifty illustrations. There was some talk of its being called the Giant Pocket Encyclopedia, but no final decision had as yet been reached. Hugh was working on the "S"s. Today he had Soap, Sodium, Sophocles, and Sorrento before him. He remembered that Maxim Gorki had lived in Sorrento, and that of the hundred and twenty-three plays that Sophocles wrote, only seven had been discovered. Hugh was not actually unhappy at his work except when Mr. Gorsline appeared. Mr. Gorsline was the owner and editor-in-chief of the house, and believed in standing behind the backs of his employees, silently watching them at their labors. Whenever Mr. Gorsline came into the room, Hugh had the curious feeling that blood was running slowly over his groin.

Mr. Gorsline was gray-haired, wore tweed suits, had the face and figure of a picador, and had started with calendars. The house still put out a great variety of calendars—pornographic, religious and occasional. Hugh was very useful on calendars because he remembered things like the death of Oliver Cromwell (September 3, 1658) and the date on which Marconi sent the first wireless message across the Atlantic (December 12, 1901) and the date of the first steamboat run from New York to Albany (August 17, 1807).

Mr. Gorsline appreciated Hugh's peculiar talents and was relentlessly paternal about his welfare. Mr. Gorsline was a believer in homeopathic medicines and the health-giving properties of raw vegetables, particularly eggplant. He was also opposed to glasses, having thrown his away in 1944 after reading a book about a series of exercises for the muscles of the eyes. He had persuaded Hugh to discard his glasses for a period of seven months in 1948, during which time Hugh had suffered from continual headaches, for which Mr. Gorsline had prescribed minute doses of a medicine from a homeopathic pharmacy which made Hugh feel as though he had been hit in the skull with bird shot. Now whenever Mr. Gorsline stood behind Hugh, he stared at Hugh's glasses with the stubborn, Irredentist expression of an Italian general surveying Trieste. Hugh's health, while not actively bad, was shabby. He had frequent, moist colds, and his eyes had a tendency to become bloodshot after lunch. There was no hiding these lapses or the fact that in cold weather he had to make several trips an hour to the men's room. At such times, Mr. Gorsline would break his customary silence to outline diets designed to improve the tone of the nasal passages, the eyes and the kidneys.

During the morning, Mr. Gorsline came into Hugh's room twice. The first time, he stood behind Hugh's chair without saying a word for five minutes, then said, "Still on sodium?" and left. The next time, he stood silently for eight minutes, then said, "Forester, you're putting on weight. White bread," and left. Each time, Hugh had the familiar feeling in the groin.

Just before lunch, Hugh's daughter came into his office. She kissed him and said, "Many happy returns of the day, Daddy," and gave him a small oblong package with a bow of colored ribbon on top of it. Clare was twenty-two and had been married four years but she refused to stop saying "Daddy." Hugh opened the package, feeling confused. There was a gold-topped fountain pen in it. It was the fourth fountain pen Clare had given him in the last six years, two on birthdays and the third on Christmas. She had not inherited her father's memory.

"What's this for?" Hugh asked.

"Daddy!" Clare said. "You're kidding."

Hugh stared at the pen. He knew it wasn't his birthday (June 12th). And it certainly wasn't Christmas (December 25th).

"It can't be," Clare said incredulously. "You didn't *forget!*"

Hugh remembered Narcisse's face at breakfast, and the twitching of her nose. "Oh, my," he said.

"You better load yourself with flowers before you set foot in the house tonight," Clare said. She peered anxiously at her father. "Daddy, are you all right?" she asked.

"Of course I'm all right," Hugh said, annoyed. "Everybody forgets an anniversary once in a while."

"Not you, Daddy."

"Me, too. I'm human, too," he said, but he felt shaken. He unscrewed the top of the pen and wrote TWENTY-FOUR YEARS, in capitals, on a pad, keeping his head down. He now owned eight fountain pens. "It's just what I needed, Clare," he said, and put it in his pocket. "Thank you very much."

"You haven't forgotten that you promised to take me to lunch, have you?" Clare had phoned the day before to make the appointment for lunch, because, she told Hugh, she had some serious problems to discuss.

"Of course not," Hugh said briskly. He put on his overcoat, and they went out together. Hugh ordered sole, then changed to a lamb chop, because he remembered that

Narcisse had said at breakfast they were to have fish for dinner. Clare ordered roast chicken and Waldorf salad, and a bottle of wine, because, she said, the afternoons became less sad after a bottle of wine. Hugh didn't understand why a pretty twenty-two-year-old girl needed wine to keep her from being sad in the afternoons, but he didn't interfere.

While Clare was going over the wine card, Hugh took Morton's letter out of his pocket and read it. Morton was asking for two hundred and fifty dollars. It seemed that he had borrowed a fraternity brother's Plymouth and gone into a ditch with it after a dance and the repairs had come to a hundred and twenty-five dollars. There had been a girl with him, too, and her nose had been broken and the doctor had charged a hundred dollars for the nose and Morton had promised to pay. Then, there was ten dollars for two books in a course on ethics and fifteen dollars just, as Morton phrased it, to make it a round number. Hugh put the letter back in his pocket without saying anything about it to Clare. At least, Hugh thought, it wasn't as bad as last year, when it looked as though Morton was going to be kicked out of school for cheating on a calculus examination.

As Clare ate her chicken and drank her wine, she told her father what was troubling her. Mostly, it was Freddie, her husband. She was undecided, she said as she ate away steadily at her chicken, whether to leave him or have a baby. She was sure Freddie was seeing another woman, on East Seventy-eighth Street, in the afternoons, and before she took a step in either direction she wanted Hugh to confront Freddie man to man and get a statement of intentions from him. Freddie wouldn't talk to her. Whenever she brought the subject up, he left the house and went to a hotel for the night. If it was to be a divorce, she would need at least a thousand dollars from Hugh for the six weeks in Reno, because Freddie had already told her he wouldn't advance a cent for any damn thing like that. Besides, Freddie was having a little financial trouble at

the moment. He had overdrawn against his account at
the automobile agency for which he worked, and they
had clamped down on him two weeks ago. If they had
the baby, the doctor Clare wanted would cost eight hundred dollars, and there would be at least another five hundred for the hospital and nurses, and she knew she could
depend on Daddy for that.

She drank her wine and talked on as Hugh ate silently.
Freddie, she said, was also five months behind in his dues
and greens fees at the golf club, and they were going to
post his name if he didn't pay by Sunday, and that was
really urgent, because of the disgrace, and Freddie had
behaved like an absolute savage around the house ever
since he received the letter from the club secretary.

"I told him," Clare said, with tears in her eyes and eating steadily, "I told him I would gladly go out and work,
but he said he'd be damned if he'd let people say he
couldn't support his own wife, and, of course, you have to
respect a feeling like that. And he told me he wouldn't
come to you for another cent, either, and you can't help
admiring him for that, can you?"

"No," Hugh said, remembering that his son-in-law had
borrowed from him, over a period of four years, three
thousand eight hundred and fifty dollars and had not paid
back a cent. "No, you can't. Did he know you were going
to come and talk to me today?"

"Vaguely," Clare said, and poured herself another glass
of wine. As she carefully harvested the last bits of apple
and walnut from her salad, Clare said she didn't really
like to burden him with her problems but he was the only
one in the whole world whose judgment she really trusted.
He was so solid and sensible and smart, she said, and she
didn't know any more whether she really loved Freddie
or not and she was so confused and she hated to see Freddie so unhappy all the time about money and she wanted
to know whether Hugh honestly felt she was ready for
motherhood at the age of twenty-two. By the time they
finished their coffee, Hugh had promised to talk to Fred-

die very soon about the woman on Seventy-eighth Street and to underwrite either the trip to Reno or the obstetrician, as the case might be, and he had made a half promise about the back dues and the greens fees.

On the way to the office, Hugh bought an alligator handbag for Narcisse for sixty dollars and worried sharply, for a moment, about inflation as he wrote out the check and handed it to the salesgirl.

It was a little difficult to work after lunch, because he kept thinking about Clare and what she had been like as a little girl (measles at four, mumps the year after, braces from eleven to fifteen, acne between fourteen and seventeen). He worked very slowly on Sorrento. Mr. Gorsline came in twice during the afternoon. The first time he said, "Still on Sorrento?" and the second time he said, "Who the hell cares if that Communist Russian wrote a book there?"

In addition to the usual sensation in the groin, Hugh noticed a quickening of his breath, which was almost a gasp, when Mr. Gorsline stood behind him during the afternoon.

After work, he went into the little bar on Lexington Avenue where he met Jean three times a week. She was sitting there, finishing her first whisky, and he sat down beside her and squeezed her hand in greeting. They had been in love for eleven years now, but he had kissed her only once (V-E Day), because she had been a classmate of Narcisse's at Bryn Mawr and they had decided early in the game to be honorable. She was a tall, majestic woman who, because she had led a troubled life, still looked comparatively young. They sat sadly and secretly in sad little bars late in the afternoon and talked in low, nostalgic tones about how different everything could have been. In the beginning, their conversation had been more animated, and for a half hour at a time Hugh had recovered some of the optimism and confidence that he had had as a young man who had taken all the honors at college, before it had become apparent that a retentive memory and talent and intelligence and luck were not all the same thing.

"I think, very soon," Jean said while he was sipping his drink, "we'll have to give this up. It isn't going anywhere, really, is it, and I just don't feel right about it. I feel guilty. Don't you?"

Until then, it hadn't occurred to Hugh that he had done anything to feel guilty about, with the possible exception of the kiss on V-E Day. But now that Jean had said it, he realized that he probably would feel guilty from now on, every time he entered the bar and saw her sitting there.

"Yes," he said sadly. "I suppose you're right."

"I'm going away for the summer," Jean said. "In June. When I come back I'm not going to see you any more."

Hugh nodded miserably. The summer was still five months away, but behind him he had a sense of something slipping, with a rustling noise, like a curtain coming down.

He had to stand in the subway all the way home, and the car was so crowded that he couldn't turn the pages of his newspaper. He read and reread the front page, thinking, I certainly am glad I wasn't elected President.

It was hot in the train, and he felt fat and uncomfortable jammed among the travelers, and he had a new, uneasy feeling that his flesh was overburdening him. Then, just before he came to Two hundred and forty-second Street, he realized that he had left the alligator bag on his desk in the office. He felt a little tickle of terror in his throat and knees. It was not so much that, empty-handed, he faced an evening of domestic sighs, half-spoken reproaches, and almost certain tears. It was not even so much the fact that he mistrusted the cleaning woman who did his office every night and who had once (November 3, 1950), he was sure, taken a dollar and thirty cents' worth of airmail stamps from the upper right-hand drawer. But, standing there in the now uncrowded car, he had to face the fact that twice in one day he had forgotten something. He couldn't remember when anything like that had ever happened to him before. He touched his head with his fingertips, as though there might be some obscure explanation to be found that way. He decided to give up drinking. He drank only five or six whiskies a week, but the induction of partial amnesia by alcohol was a well-established medical principle, and perhaps his level of tolerance was abnormally low.

The evening passed as he had expected. He bought some roses at the station for Narcisse, but he couldn't tell her about the alligator bag left on his desk, because he figured, correctly, that that would only compound the morning's offense. He even suggested that they return to the city for an anniversary dinner, but Narcisse had had the whole day alone to augment her self-pity and brood upon her martyrdom, and she insisted on eating the fish, which had cost ninety-three cents a pound. By ten-thirty she was crying.

Hugh slept badly and got to the office early the next morning, but even the sight of the alligator bag, left squarely in the middle of the desk by the cleaning woman, did not raise his spirits. During the day he forgot the names of three of Sophocles' plays (*Oedipus at Colonus, Trachiniae,* and *Philoctetes*) and the telephone number of his dentist.

It started that way. Hugh began to make more and more frequent trips to the reference library on the thirteenth floor, dreading the trip through the office, because of the way his fellow-workers commenced to look at him, curious and puzzled, as he traversed the room again and again in the course of an hour. One day he forgot the titles of the works of Sardou, the area of Santo Domingo, the symptoms of silicosis, the definition of syndrome, and the occasion of the mortification of Saint Simeon Stylites.

Hoping it would pass, he said nothing about it to any-one—not even to Jean, in the little bar on Lexington Avenue.

Mr. Gorsline took to standing for longer and longer periods behind Hugh's desk, and Hugh sat there, pretending to be working, pretending he didn't look haggard, his jowls hanging from his cheekbones like gallows ropes, his brain feeling like a piece of frozen meat that was being nibbled by a wolf. Once, Mr. Gorsline muttered something about hormones, and once, at four-thirty, he told Hugh to take the afternoon off. Hugh had worked for Mr. Gorsline for eighteen years and this was the first time Mr. Gorsline had told him to take an afternoon off. When Mr. Gorsline left his office, Hugh sat at his desk, staring blindly into terrifying depths.

One morning, some days after the anniversary, Hugh forgot the name of his morning newspaper. He stood in front of the news dealer, staring down at the ranked *Times* and *Tribunes* and *News* and *Mirrors,* and they all looked the same to him. He knew that for the past twenty-five years he had been buying the same paper each morning, but now there was no clue for him in their makeup or in their headlines as to which one it was. He bent down and peered more closely at the papers. The President, a headline announced, was to speak that night. As Hugh straightened up, he realized he no longer remembered the President's name or whether he was a Republican or a Democrat. For a moment, he experienced what could be described only as an exquisite pang of pleasure. But he knew it was deceptive, like the ecstasy described by T. E. Lawrence on the occasion when he was nearly beaten to death by the Turks.

He bought a copy of *Holiday,* and stared numbly at the colored photographs of distant cities all the way down to the office. That morning, he forgot the date on which John L. Sullivan won the heavyweight championship of the world, and the name of the inventor of the submarine. He also had to go to the reference library because he wasn't sure whether Santander was in Chile or Spain.

He was sitting at his desk that afternoon, staring at his hands, because for an hour he had had the feeling that mice were running between his fingers, when his son-in-law came into the office.

"Hi, Hughie, old boy," his son-in-law said. From the very first night his son-in-law had appeared at the house, he had been unfalteringly breezy with Hugh.

Hugh stood up and said "Hello——" and stopped. He stared at his son-in-law. He knew it was his son-in-law. He knew it was Clare's husband. But he couldn't remember the man's name. For the second time that day he experienced the trilling wave of pleasure that he had felt at the newsstand when he realized he had forgotten the name and political affiliations of the President of the United States. Only this time it seemed to last. It lasted while he shook hands with his son-in-law and all during the trip down in the elevator with him, and it lasted in the bar next door while he bought his son-in-law three Martinis.

"Hughie, old boy," his son-in-law said during the third Martini, "let's get down to cases. Clare said you had a problem you wanted to talk to me about. Spit it out, old boy, and let's get it over with. What have you got on your mind?"

Hugh looked hard at the man across the table. He searched his brain conscientiously, but he couldn't think of a single problem that might possibly involve them. "No," Hugh said slowly. "I have nothing in particular on my mind."

His son-in-law kept looking at Hugh belligerently while Hugh was paying for the drinks, but Hugh merely hummed under his breath, smiling slightly at the waitress. Outside, where they stood for a moment, his son-in-law cleared his throat once and said, "Now, look here, old boy, if it's about——" but Hugh shook his hand warmly and walked briskly away, feeling deft and limber.

But back in his office, looking down at his cluttered desk, his sense of well-being left him. He had moved on to the "T"s by now, and as he looked at the scraps of paper and the jumble of books on his desk, he realized that he had forgotten a considerable number of facts about Tacitus and was completely lost on the subject of Taine. There was a sheet of notepaper on his desk with the date and the beginning of a salutation: "Dear . . ."

He stared at the paper and tried to remember who it was he had been writing to. It was five minutes before it came to him; the letter was to have been to his son, and he had meant, finally, to enclose the check for the two hundred and fifty dollars, as requested. He felt in his inside pocket for his checkbook. It wasn't there. He looked carefully through all the drawers of his desk, but the checkbook wasn't there, either. Shaking a little, because this was the first time in his life that he had misplaced a checkbook, he decided to call up his bank and ask them to mail him a new book. He picked up the phone. Then he stared at it blankly. He had forgotten the telephone number of the bank. He put the phone down and opened the classified telephone directory to "B." Then he stopped. He swallowed dryly. He had forgotten the name of his bank. He looked at the page of banks. All the names seemed vaguely familiar to him, but no one name seemed to have any special meaning for him. He closed the book and stood up and went over to the window. He looked out. There were two pigeons sitting on the sill, looking cold, and across the street a bald man was standing at a window in the building opposite, smoking a cigarette and staring down as though he were contemplating suicide.

Hugh went back to his desk and sat down. Perhaps it was an omen, he thought, the thing about the checkbook. Perhaps it was a sign that he ought to take a sterner line with his son. Let him pay for his own mistakes for once. He picked up his pen, resolved to write this to Alabama. "Dear . . ." he read. He looked for a long time at the word. Then he carefully closed his pen and put it back in his pocket. He no longer remembered his son's name.

He put on his coat and went out, although it was only three-twenty-five. He walked all the way up to the Museum, striding lightly, feeling better and better with each block. By the time he reached the Museum, he felt like a man who has just been told that he has won a hundred-dollar bet on a fourteen-to-one shot. In the Museum, he went and looked at the Egyptians. He had meant to look at the Egyptians for years, but he had always been too busy.

When he got through with the Egyptians, he felt wonderful. He continued feeling wonderful all the way home in the subway. He no longer made any attempt to buy the newspapers. They didn't make any sense to him. He didn't recognize any of the people whose names appeared in the columns. It was like reading the Karachi *Sind Observer* or the Sonora *El Mundo.* Not having a paper in his hands made the long ride much more agreeable. He spent his time in the subway looking at the people around him. The people in the subway seemed much more interesting, much more pleasant, now that he no longer read in the newspapers what they were doing to each other.

Of course, once he opened his front door, his euphoria left him. Narcisse had taken to looking at him very closely in the evenings, and he had to be very careful with his conversation. He didn't want Narcisse to discover what was happening to him. He didn't want her to worry, or try to cure him. He sat all evening listening to the phonograph, but he forgot to change the record. It was an automatic machine and it played the last record of the second Saint-Saëns piano concerto seven times before Narcisse came in from the kitchen and said, "I'm going out of my mind," and turned it off.

He went to bed early. He heard Narcisse crying in the next bed. It was the third time that month. There were between two and five more times to go. He remembered that.

The next afternoon, he was working on Talleyrand. He was bent over his desk, working slowly but not too badly, when he became conscious that there was someone standing behind him. He swung in his chair. A gray-haired man in a tweed suit was standing there, staring down at him.

"Yes?" Hugh said curtly. "Are you looking for someone?"

The man, surprisingly, turned red, then went out of the room, slamming the door behind him. Hugh shrugged incuriously and turned back to Talleyrand.

The elevator was crowded when he left for the day, and the hall downstairs was thronged with clerks and secretaries hurrying out of the building. Near the entrance, a very pretty girl was standing, and she smiled and waved at Hugh over the heads of the homeward-bound office workers. Hugh stopped for an instant, flattered, and was tempted to smile back. But he had a date with Jean, and anyway he was too old for anything like that. He set his face and hurried out in the stream of people. He thought he heard a kind of wail, which sounded curiously like "Daddy," but he knew that was impossible, and didn't turn around.

He went to Lexington Avenue, enjoying the shining winter evening, and started north. He passed two bars and was approaching a third when he slowed down. He retraced his steps, peering at the bar fronts. They all had chromium on them, and neon lights, and they all looked the same. There was another bar across the street. He went and looked at the bar across the street, but it was just like the others. He went into it, anyway, but Jean wasn't there. He ordered a whisky, standing at the bar, and asked the bartender, "Have you seen a lady alone in here in the last half hour?"

The bartender looked up at the ceiling, thinking. "What's she look like?" he asked.

"She—" Hugh stopped. He sipped his drink. "Never mind," he said to the bartender. He laid a dollar bill on the counter and went out.

Walking over to the subway station he felt better than he had felt since he won the hundred-yard dash at the age of eleven at the annual field day of the Brigham Young Public School in Salt Lake City on June 9, 1915.

The feeling lasted, of course, only until Narcisse put the soup on the table. Her eyes were puffed, and she had obviously been crying that afternoon, which was curious, because Narcisse never cried when she was alone. Eating his dinner, conscious of Narcisse watching him closely across the table, Hugh began to feel the mice between his fingers again. After dinner, Narcisse said, "You can't fool me. There's another woman." She also said, "I never thought this would happen to me."

By the time Hugh went to bed, he felt like a passenger on a badly loaded freighter in a winter storm off Cape Hatteras.

He awoke early, conscious that it was a sunny day outside. He lay in bed, feeling warm and healthy. There was a noise from the next bed, and he looked across the little space. There was a woman in the next bed. She was middle-aged and was wearing curlers and she was snoring and Hugh was certain he had never seen her before in his life. He got out of bed silently, dressed quickly, and went out into the sunny day.

Without thinking about it, he walked to the subway station. He watched the people hurrying toward the trains and he knew that he probably should join them. He had the feeling that somewhere in the city to the south, in some tall building on a narrow street, his arrival was expected. But he knew that no matter how hard he tried he would never be able to find the building. Buildings these days, it occurred to him suddenly, were too much like other buildings.

He walked briskly away from the subway station in the direction of the river. The river was shining in the sun and there was ice along the banks. A boy of about twelve, in a plaid mackinaw and a wool hat, was sitting on a bench and regarding the river. There were some schoolbooks, tied with a leather strap, on the frozen ground at his feet.

Hugh sat down next to the boy. "Good morning," he said pleasantly.

"Good morning," said the boy.

"What're you doing?" Hugh asked.

"I'm counting the boats," the boy said. "Yesterday I counted thirty-two boats. Not counting ferries. I don't count ferries."

Hugh nodded. He put his hands in his pockets and looked down over the river. By five o'clock that afternoon he and the boy had counted forty-three boats, not including ferries. He couldn't remember having had a nicer day.

Then We Were Three

Munnie Brooks was awakened by the sound of two shots outside the window. He opened his eyes and looked at the ceiling. By the quality of the light, even through the drawn curtains, he could tell that it was sunny outside. He turned his head. In the other bed Bert was still asleep. He slept quietly, the blankets neat, in control of his dreams. Munnie got out of his bed and, barefooted, in his pajamas, went over to the window and parted the curtains.

The last mists of morning were curling up from the fields, and far off and below, the sea was smooth in the October sunlight. In the distance, along the curve of the coast, the Pyrenees banked back in green ridges toward a soft sky. From behind a haystack more than a hundred yards away, beyond the edge of the hotel terrace, a hunter and his dog appeared, walking slowly, the hunter reloading. Watching him, Munnie remembered, with mild, gluttonous pleasure, that he had had partridge, newly killed and plump with the summer's feeding, for dinner the night before.

The hunter was an old man, dressed in fisherman's blue and wearing fisherman's rubber boots. He moved solidly and carefully behind his dog, through the cut stubble. When I am an old man, thought Munnie, who was

391

twenty-two, I hope I look and feel like that on an October morning.

He opened the curtains wider and looked at his watch. It was after ten o'clock. They had been up late the night before, all three of them, at the casino in Biarritz. Earlier in the summer, when they had been on the Côte d'Azur, a paratroop lieutenant on leave had showed them a foolproof system for beating the roulette table, and whenever they could, they frequented casinos. The system took a lot of capital and they had never made more than 8000 francs in one night among them on it, and sometimes it meant sitting up till three o'clock in the morning following the wheel, but they hadn't lost yet, either, since they met the lieutenant. It had made their trip unexpectedly luxurious, especially when they got to places where there was a casino. The system ignored the numbers and concentrated on the red and the black and involved a rather complicated rhythm of doubling. The night before they had won only 4500 francs and it had taken them until two o'clock, but still, waking late, with the weather clear and an old man hunting birds outside your window, the thousand-franc notes on the dresser added a fillip of luck and complacency to the morning.

Standing there, feeling the sun warm on his bare feet and smelling the salt and hearing the distant calm mutter of the surf, remembering the partridge and the gambling and everything else about the summer that had just passed, Munnie knew he didn't want to start home that morning as they had planned. Staring down at the hunter following his dog slowly across the brown field on the edge of the sea, Munnie knew that when he was older he would look back upon the summer and think, Ah, it was wonderful when I was young. This double ability to enjoy a moment with the immediacy of youth and the reflective melancholy of age had made Bert say to him, half seriously, half as a joke, "I envy you, Munnie. You have a rare gift—the gift of instantaneous nostalgia. You get twice your investment out of everything."

The gift had its drawbacks. It made moving away from places he liked difficult for Munnie and packed all endings and farewells with emotion, because the old man who traveled within him was always saying, in his autumnal whisper, It will never be like that again.

But putting an end to this long summer, which had stretched into October, was going to be more painful than any other finish or departure that Munnie had known. These were the last days of the last real holiday of his life, Munnie felt. The trip to Europe had been a gift from his parents upon his graduation from college and now when he went back, there they would all be on the dock, the kind, welcoming, demanding faces, expecting him to get to work, asking him what he intended to do, offering him jobs and advice, settling him lovingly and implacably into the rut of being a grownup and responsible and tethered adult. From now on all holidays would be provisional, hurried interludes of gulped summertime between work and work. The last days of your youth, said the old man within. The boat docks in seven days.

Munnie turned and looked at his sleeping friend. Bert slept tranquilly, extended and composed under his blankets, his sunburned long thin nose geometrically straight in the air. This would change, too, Munnie thought. After the boat docked they would never be as close again. Never as close as on the rocks over the sea in Sicily or climbing through the sunny ruins at Paestum or chasing the two English girls through the Roman nightclubs. Never as close as the rainy afternoon in Florence when they talked, together, for the first time, to Martha. Never as close as on the long, winding journey, the three of them packed into the small open car, up the Ligurian coast toward the border, stopping whenever they felt like it for white wine or a swim at the little beach pavilions with all the small, brightly colored pennants whipping out in the hot Mediterranean afternoon. Never as close as the conspiratorial moment over the beers with the paratrooper in the bar of the casino at Juan-les-Pins, learning about the unbeatable system. Never as close as in the lavender, hilarious dawns, driving back to their hotel gloating over their winnings, with Martha dozing between them. Never as close as on the blazing afternoon at Barcelona, sitting high up on the sunny side, sweating and cheering and shading their eyes as the matador walked around the ring holding up the two bull's ears, with the flowers and the wineskins sailing down around him. Never as close at Salamanca and Madrid and on the road through the straw-colored, hot, bare country up to France, drinking sweet, raw Spanish brandy and trying to remember how the music went that the gypsies danced to in the caves. Never so close, again, finally, as here in this small whitewashed Basque hotel room, with Bert still asleep, and Munnie standing at the window watching the old man disappear with his dog and his shotgun, and upstairs in the room above them, Martha, sleeping, as she always did, curled like a child, until they came in, as they always did, together, as though they didn't trust themselves or each other to do it alone, to wake her and tell her what they planned to do for the day.

Munnie threw the curtains wide open and let the sun stream in. If there's one boat that I have a right to miss in my life, he thought, it's the one that's sailing from Le Havre the day after tomorrow.

Munnie went over to Bert's bed, stepping carefully over the clothes that were crumpled on the floor. He poked Bert's bare shoulder with his finger. "Master," he said, "rise and shine." The rule was that whoever lost in tennis between them had to call the other Master for twenty-four hours. Bert had won the day before 6-3, 2-6, 7-5.

"It's after ten." Munnie poked him again.

Bert opened both eyes and stared coldly at the ceiling. "Do I have a hangover?" he asked.

"We only had one bottle of wine amongst us for dinner," said Munnie, "and two beers after."

"I do not have a hangover," Bert said, as if the news depressed him. "But it's raining outside."

"It's a bright, hot sunny morning," Munnie said.

"Everybody always told me it rained all the time on the Basque coast," said Bert, lying still, complaining.

"Everybody is a liar," Munnie said. "Get the hell out of bed."

Bert swung his legs slowly over the side of the bed and sat there, thin, bony and bare from the waist up, in his pajama pants that were too short for him and from which his big feet dangled loosely. "Do you know why American women live longer than American men, Fat Man?" he asked, squinting at Munnie in the sunlight.

"No."

"Because they sleep in the morning. My ambition," Bert said, lying back on the bed again, but with his legs still over the side, "is to live as long as the American Woman."

Munnie lit a cigarette and tossed one to Bert, who managed to light it without lifting his head from the blanket. "I had an idea," Munnie said, "while you were wasting the precious hours of your childhood sleeping."

"Put it in the suggestion box." Bert yawned and closed his eyes. "The management will give a buffalo-hide saddle to every employee who presents us with an idea that is put into practice by the . . ."

"Listen," Munnie said eagerly. "I think we ought to miss that damned boat."

Bert smoked in silence for a moment, narrowing his eyes and pointing his nose at the ceiling. "Some people," he said, "are born boat-missers and train-missers and plane-missers. My mother, for example. She once saved herself from getting killed by ordering a second dessert at lunch. The plane left just as she got to the field and came down in flames thirty-five minutes later. Not a single survivor. It was ice cream, with crushed fresh strawberries . . ."

"Come on, Bert." Sometimes Munnie got very impatient with Bert's habit of going off on tangents while he was making up his mind. "I know all about your mother."

"In the springtime," Bert said, "she goes mad for strawberries. Tell me, Munnie, have you ever missed anything in your life?"

"No," Munnie said.

"Do you think it's wise," Bert asked, "at this late stage, to fiddle with the patterns of a lifetime?"

Munnie went into the bathroom and filled a glass with water. When he came back into the bedroom, Bert was still lying on the bed, his legs dangling over the side, smoking. Munnie stood over him, then slowly tipped the glass over Bert's bare brown chest. The water splashed a little and ran in thin trickles over Bert's ribs onto the sheets.

"Ah," Bert said, still smoking. "Refreshing."

They both laughed and Bert sat up.

"All right, Fat Man," Bert said. "I didn't know you were serious."

"My idea," said Munnie, "is to stay here until the weather changes. It's too sunny to go home."

"What'll we do about the tickets?"

"We'll send a telegram to the boat people and tell them we'll take passage later. They've got a waiting list a mile long. They'll be delighted."

Bert nodded judiciously. "What about Martha?" he asked. "Maybe she has to get to Paris today."

"Martha doesn't have to go anyplace. Anytime," Munnie said. "You know that."

Bert nodded again. "The luckiest girl in the world," he said.

Outside the window there was the sound of the shotgun again. Bert turned his head, listening. There was a second report. "My," Bert said, running his tongue over his teeth, "that was wonderful partridge last night." He stood up, looking, in his flapping pajama pants like a boy who would be a good prospect for the college crew if he could be induced to eat heavily for a year. He had been chubby until he went into the Army, but by the time he got out in May, he was long and stringy and his ribs showed. When she wanted to make fun of him, Martha told him he looked like an English poet in his bathing trunks. He went to the window and Munnie crossed over and stood beside him, looking out over the mountains and the sea and the sunlight.

"You're right," Bert said. "Only an idiot would dream of starting home on a day like this. Let's go tell Martha the party's still on."

They dressed quickly, in espadrilles and cotton trousers and tennis shirts and went upstairs together and into Martha's room, without knocking. The wind was making one of the shutters rap against the window, but Martha was still asleep, curled around herself, only the top of her head showing above the blanket, the hair dark and tangled and short. The pillow was on the floor.

Munnie and Bert stood in silence for a moment, looking down at the curled, blanketed figure and the dark head, each of them convinced that the other did not know what he was thinking.

"Awake," Bert said softly. "Awake to glory." He went over to the bed and touched the top of Martha's head. Watching him, Munnie could feel the tips of his own fingers twitching electrically.

"Please," Martha said, her eyes still closed. "It's the middle of the night."

"It's nearly noon," Munnie said, lying by nearly two hours, "and we have to tell you something."

"Tell it to me," said Martha, "and get out of here."

"The Fat Man here," said Bert, standing at her head, "has come up with an idea. He wants us to stay here until it begins to rain. How do you feel about it?"

"Of course," Martha said.

Bert and Munnie smiled at each other, because they felt they understood her so well. "Martha," said Bert, "you're the only perfect girl alive."

Then they went out of the room to give her a chance to get dressed.

They had met Martha Holm in Florence. They seemed to have the same ideas about which museums and which churches to go to and they kept bumping into her and she was alone and obviously American and as Bert said, they didn't come prettier, and finally they started talking to each other. Maybe it was because they had first seen her in the Uffizi Gallery among the Botticellis that gave Munnie the idea, but he thought, privately, that, aside from the fact that her hair was short and dark and irregularly cut, she looked like the Primavera, tall, slender, and girl-ish, with a long narrow nose and deep, brooding, danger-ous eyes. He felt extravagant and embarrassed to be thinking things like this about a twenty-one-year-old American girl who wore slacks and had gone for a year to Smith, but he couldn't help himself. He never told Martha about it and, of course, he never said a word on the sub-ject to Bert.

Martha knew a lot of people in and around Florence (later on, it turned out that she knew a lot of people in and around everyplace) and she got them invited to a tea in Fiesole at a villa where there was a swimming pool and to a party at which Munnie found himself dancing with a Contessa. Martha had been in Europe for nearly two years and she was wonderful at telling you what places to go to and what places were traps, and she spoke Italian and French, and she was ready when you told her to be ready, and she didn't scream for pity when she had to walk a few blocks on her own two feet, and she laughed at Bert's and Munnie's jokes and made some of her own, and she didn't giggle, weep or sulk, which put her several notches above every other girl Munnie had ever known. After they had been together for three days in Florence and were due to start for Portofino and France, it seemed unbearable just to leave her behind. As far as Munnie and Bert could tell, she had no plans of her own. "I tell my mother," Martha explained, "that I'm taking courses at the Sorbonne, and it's almost true, at least in the win-tertime."

Martha's mother lived in Philadelphia, after three divorces, and every once in awhile, Martha said, she sent back a photograph, so that when she finally did arrive back home, there wouldn't be an embarrassing moment on the dock when her mother wouldn't recognize her.

So Munnie and Bert talked it over very seriously and sat at a café table with Martha in the Piazza del Signoria and ordered coffee and put it up to her.

"What we've decided," Bert said, with Munnie sitting beside him, silently agreeing, "is that the Brooks-Carboy unguided tour of Europe could use you, as interpreter, hotel-finder, and chief taster of foreign foods. Aside from supplying a welcome feminine touch. Are you interested?"

"Yes," Martha said.

"We'd like to know if we could mesh schedules, more or less," Munnie said.

Martha smiled. "I'm on a schedule of drift," she said. "Didn't you know?"

"Does that mean," Munnie asked, because he liked to have everything absolutely clear, "that you want to come along?"

"It means that I want to come along very much," said Martha, "and I was hoping you'd ask me." She looked at each of them for exactly the same number of seconds, cheerful, grateful, ready for anything.

"Now," said Bert, "Munnie and I have talked it over and we're going to lay it on the line. Something like this has to be planned out in advance or there comes a dark and hideous night of disaster. We've thought up a good, workable set of rules and if you agree, off we go tomorrow. If not—no harm done—and we hope you spend a pleasant summer."

"Get to it, Bert," Munnie said, impatiently. "Don't recite the preamble to the Constitution."

"Rule Number One," Bert said, with Martha sitting still, nodding, gravely listening, "rule number one is basic. No entanglements. Munnie and I're old friends and we've planned this summer for years and we've been hav-

ing a wonderful time and we don't want to wind up fighting duels with each other or anything like that. Now, I
know women . . ." He paused, daring either of them to
smile. They didn't smile.

"He wouldn't have said that," Munnie explained, "before the Army."

"What do you know about women?" Martha asked, being serious.

"What I know is that women're always busy choosing,"
Bert went on. "They come into a room and if there're
five men present, their minds get to work like a business
machine, punching holes. First Choice, Second Choice,
Acceptable, Perhaps, Impossible."

"Oh, my." Martha began to laugh. She covered her
mouth with her hand apologetically and tried to straighten
her face. "Forgive me. Munnie . . . do you believe
this?"

"I don't know," he said embarrassedly. "I haven't had
Bert's advantages. I wasn't in the Army."

"I'll even tell you how you'd choose," Bert said, "between Munnie and me, so you won't have to wonder or
waste your time."

"Tell me," Martha said. "Do tell me."

"In the beginning," said Bert, "the tendency is to
choose me. I'll go into the reasons some other time. Then,
after awhile, the switch sets in, and Munnie gets the final
decision."

"Poor Bert," Martha said, chuckling. "How awful for
you! Only winning the opening game of the season all the
time. Why are you telling me all this?"

"Because you've got to promise not to choose anybody," Bert said. "And if you *do* choose, you have to go
to the grave with your secret."

"To the grave," Martha repeated, trying to be solemn.

"Until the boat sails," Bert said, "we treat each other
like brothers and sister, and that's all. *D'accord?*"

"*D'accord,*" Martha said.

"Good." Bert and Munnie nodded at each other, pleased with how reasonable everybody was.

"Rule Number Two," Bert said, "if after awhile we get to feel you're a nuisance—we say farewell and you leave. No tears. No recriminations. No scenes. Just a friendly shake of the hand and off to the nearest railroad station. *D'accord?*"

"*D'accord* two times," Martha said.

"Rule Number Three—everybody pays exactly one-third of the expenses."

"Of course," said Martha.

"Rule Number Four," Bert went on, like the director of a company explaining a plan of operations to his board, "everybody is free to go wherever he or she wants to, and with anyone else whoever, and no questions asked. We are not an inseparable unit, because inseparable units are boring. O.K.?"

"A free, loose confederation of sovereign states," Martha said. "I got it. Whomever."

They all shook hands on it, surrounded by the looming oversized statues, and started out together early the next morning, after figuring out a way to squeeze Martha into the car and strap her baggage onto the back, and it all couldn't have worked out better. There hadn't been a single argument all summer, although they had discussed, among other things, sex, religion, politics, marriage, the choice of careers, the position of women in modern society, the theatre in New York and Paris, and the proper size of bathing costumes for young girls on the beaches of Italy, France and Spain. And when Bert had taken up with a plump little blonde American girl in St. Tropez for a week or so, it hadn't seemed to disturb Martha for a minute, even when the girl moved into the hotel they were staying at and frankly installed herself in the room next to Munnie's and Bert's.

The truth was, nothing seemed to disturb Martha very much. She greeted the events of each day with a strange

and almost dreamlike placidity. She seemed to make no
decisions herself and whatever decisions the others made,
regardless of how they turned out, she accepted with exactly the same good-natured, smiling, rather vague approval. Linked in Munnie's mind with this pleasant will-
lessness was Martha's extraordinary talent for sleeping.
If nobody went in to awaken her in the morning, she
would sleep on till noon, till two o'clock in the afternoon,
even if she had gone to bed early the evening before. It
wasn't anything physical, either, because she didn't need
the sleep and never suggested, herself, that it was time to
go to bed, no matter how late they stayed up at night or
at what hour she had arisen in the morning. She never
wrote any letters and rarely received any, since she hardly
ever remembered to leave a forwarding address when
they moved. When she needed money she would wire
the bank in Paris that handled her allowance, and when it
came she spent it carelessly. She took almost no interest
in clothes and the reason she cut her hair short the way
she did, she told Bert and Munnie, was that she didn't
want to be bothered having to comb it all the time.

When the three of them talked about what they would
like to do with their lives, she was vaguer than ever. "I
don't know," she said, shrugging, smiling, seeming to be
mildly and indulgently puzzled about herself. "I suppose
I'll just hang around. Wait and see. For the moment, I'm
on a policy of float. I don't see anybody else our age doing anything so damned attractive. I'm waiting for a revelation to send me in a permanent direction. I'm in no hurry
to commit myself, no hurry at all . . ."

In a curious way, Martha's lack of direction made her
much more interesting to Munnie than all the other girls
he had ever known, the positive but limited girls who
knew they wanted to be married and have babies and
join a country club, the girls who wanted to go on the
stage and be famous, the girls who wanted to become
editors or deans of women's colleges. Martha hadn't settled for anything yet, Munnie felt, because nothing good

enough had come up. And there was always the chance, he believed, that when she finally did commit herself it would be for something huge, original and glorious.

The only way that the plans hadn't worked out as outlined in Florence had been that, except for the week of the plump blonde in St. Tropez, they had been an inseparable unit, but that was only because all three of them enjoyed being with one another better than being with anyone else. It wouldn't have worked if Martha had been a different kind of girl, if she had been a coquette or greedy or foolish, and it wouldn't have worked if Munnie and Bert hadn't been such good friends and hadn't trusted each other so completely, and finally, it wouldn't have worked if they had all been a little older. But it *had* worked, at least up until the first week of October, and with luck, it would continue to work, until they kissed Martha good-bye and got on the boat train, and started for home.

They lay on the deserted beach until nearly two o'clock and then took a swim. They had a race, because the water was cold, and it was the best way to keep warm. The race was a short one, only about fifty yards, and Munnie was completely out of breath by the time he finished, trying to keep up with Martha. Martha won easily and was floating serenely on her back when Munnie came up to her, blowing heavily and fighting to get air in his lungs.

"It would be a different story," Munnie said, grinning, but a little ashamed, "if I didn't have asthma."

"Don't be gloomy about it," Martha said, kicking her legs gently. "Women're more naturally buoyant."

They both stood up and watched Bert plowing doggedly up toward them.

"Bert," Martha said, as he reached them and stopped, "you're the only man I know who looks like an old lady driving an electric automobile when he swims."

"My talents," said Bert, with dignity, "run in another direction."

They went in then, shouting and pink from the cold water and waving their arms. They dressed on the beach, under the big towel, one after another, for modesty's sake. Martha wore slacks that came down only to the middle of her calf and a fisherman's jersey, striped blue and white. Watching her arrange her clothes with light, careless movements, Munnie felt that never in his life would he see again anything so gay and obscurely touching as Martha Holm, dressed in a sailor's striped shirt, on a sunny beach, shaking the sea water out of her short, dark hair.

They decided to have a picnic rather than to go to a restaurant for lunch and they got into the little two-seater MG that Munnie's brother had left for him, when he had had his summer in Europe the year before. With Martha sitting on the cushioned brake in the middle they went into town and bought a cold chicken and a long loaf of bread and a piece of Gruyère cheese. They borrowed a basket from the fruit dealer from whom they bought a huge bunch of blue grapes and picked up two bottles of pink wine and got back into the car and drove all around the harbor to the old fort, which had been besieged and which had fallen at other times but which was used now in the summertime as a school to teach young people how to sail. They parked the car and walked out along the broad, bleached top of the sea wall, carrying the basket and the wine and the big, slightly damp towel, to serve as a tablecloth.

From the wall they could see the wide stretch of the oval harbor, empty now except for a dory with a home-made sail heading toward the point of Sainte Barbe, and the deserted beach and the white and red buildings of Saint Jean de Luz. The boatyard near the fort was crammed with small blue Snipe-class boats, lashed down and on blocks for the winter, and from somewhere in the distance came the faint sound of hammering, lonely and out-of-season, where a single workman was putting new planks into the bow of a small fishing vessel. Out at sea, almost lost against the gray-blue wash of the horizon, the boats of the tuna fleet bobbed in the swell. The tide was out and the waves rolled in, white and spumy, but not ominous, over the slanting uncovered rocks on which the sea wall was built. Close to the wall, on the bay side, the ruined, circular bastions of the old wall, which the sea had broken in another century, loomed out of the quiet water, irregular, crumbling, useless, looking somehow Roman and reminding Munnie of aqueducts that had brought mountain water to cities that had long since vanished and dungeons in which the last prisoners had died five hundred years before.

They didn't go all the way out to the end of the wall, which was separated from the middle section of the breakwater by a wide channel through which the shipping entered and left the harbor. Even on the calmest day, Munnie felt something wild and dangerous out there on the flat point of stone, where the full force of the unbroken ocean probed, however quietly, at the guarded waters of the bay and the land beyond. Munnie suffered a little from vertigo and when he looked down the sheer sides of the wall into the shifting green depths and the fringe of foam he had a helpless picture of himself caught there below, or plunging down to fight against the tides and the rocks and the waves coming and going and crossing each other with upcurling tips of spray. He didn't say anything about it, of course, but he was grateful when Martha said, "This is good enough," before they had gone very far, and he carefully helped weight the towel down as a tablecloth squarely in the middle of the wall.

There was a little wind, capricious and sporadically chilly, but Bert took off his shirt, to maintain his tan. Munnie, who had a soft, rather full growth of fuzzy reddish hair on his chest, and who was embarrassed by it, said that the wind was too cold for undressing. Bert glanced at him ironically, because he knew how Munnie felt about his chest, but he didn't say anything.

As Martha cut up the chicken and arranged the cheese and bread and grapes on pieces of paper in the center of the towel, where they could all get at them neatly, Bert cocked his head, listening to the distant, slow, rhythmic hammering from the boatyard. "Whenever I hear that noise in a place like this," he said, "it reminds me of the end of *The Cherry Orchard*. Everything melancholy and closed up and ready to die and the autumn setting in . . ."

"Whenever I hear it," Martha said, arranging the grapes, "I think, 'Divorce, divorce.' "

"That's the difference," said Bert, "between Russia and America." He walked over to the edge of the wall and stood there, his toes dangerously over the brink, staring out at the horizon, a tall, spare, loose-limbed figure, reciting, his arms ritually upraised, "Break, break, break, On thy cold gray stones, Oh, sea, And I would that my heart could utter, The thoughts that arise in me . . ."

"Lunch is on," Martha said, sitting cross-legged and pushing her sleeves above the elbows, her bare arms, under the bunched jersey, brown and surprisingly full and solid for such a slender girl. She took a piece of chicken and bit into it and said, "It's the only kind of picnic that makes picnics worth while. And no ants."

Munnie drank some of the wine from the bottle, because they had neglected to bring glasses, and broke a piece of bread off the long loaf and took some of the dark meat. Bert sat on the other side of Martha, folding his long legs down in slow motion. He reached for a piece of chicken, and said, as he munched at it, "Do you think a bright, sober young American would make a fortune setting up a factory in France to manufacture paper plates and paper cups?"

"It would spoil all the ineffable medieval charm," Martha said.

"Oh, that old, lowdown, ineffable, medieval, greasy-paper charm," Bert said. "Trust a woman to notice things like that, eh, Munnie?" He lifted his eyebrow in an exaggerated, theatrical leer. "God, isn't it lucky we walked into that gallery in Florence and found Martha? Otherwise, you know what our summer would've been like?

We'd have been delivered over to all the female riffraff of Europe—all those Italian movie starlets, bursting out of their shirtwaists, all those skinny French models, all those hungry-eyed, golden-brown American divorcees, smelling from Arpège. God, Munnie, doesn't it make you feel as though Something was watching over you that day in the museum? Tell me the truth, Fat Man, doesn't it make you feel supernaturally serene?"

"Where did you ever learn to talk like that?" Martha asked, sitting cross-legged, placidly lifting the wine bottle to her lips.

"My grandfather was a Baptist preacher in Memphis, Tennessee," Bert said, "and he taught me to fear the Lord, read the Bible, relish corn, and speak in balanced sentences." He stood up and waved the drumstick of the chicken at the Atlantic Ocean. "Repent, ye sinners, because ye have swum in the warm waters, and ogled the virgins . . ." He made a bow in Martha's direction. "And ye have played at the tables and ye have neglected to send postcards home. Repent, because ye have found pleasure and ye have missed the boat."

"Do you want some cheese?" Martha asked.

"With mustard." Bert sat down again. He peered thoughtfully at Munnie. "What do you think, Munnie?" he asked. "Are we really as happy as we feel or do we only *think* we're this happy? The philosopher's everlasting cud—illusion or reality. Is this wall stone?" he demanded oratorically. "Is this ocean blue, this water wet? Is this girl beautiful? Is this money we have in our pockets or is it really coupons for prizes that were given away in Duluth in 1922 by a tobacco company that went bankrupt the first Thursday after the crash? Is this the good wine of France we're drinking or is it vinegar spiked with blood and seawater? Rosé de Béarn," he said, reading the label on the bottle. "It seems real, doesn't it, but *is* it? Are we three over-privileged, white-toothed, splendid young American princes, visiting our greatest colony, or are we, without knowing it, pitiful refugees, in flight, with our backs to the sea? . . . Have you read a newspaper this morning, do you know the answer? Are we friends and brothers, or will we betray each other by sunset? Search the lady for daggers."

"Holy man," Martha said, "the self-starter got loose."

Munnie smiled dreamily, in appreciation of Bert's performance. He himself was literal and direct and always said exactly what he meant and no more. But he was entertained by Bert's flights of rhetoric and appreciated Bert much the way a man with no talent, but a love for music, appreciates a friend who is a skillful pianist and who generously performs at just the right moments, without being asked. It went all the way back to the time when they were both sixteen and in school together and Bert used to make scandalous improvisations in blank verse about the assumed sexual habits of the middle-aged and slightly bald lady who taught them chemistry. It got Bert into trouble from time to time because he was recklessly brave and once he started he let himself be carried away and say outrageous things, no matter who was listening. Just this summer, they had had to fight four young Germans in a *brasserie* in Nice and run from the police because of one of his performances. Bert had struck up a conversation with the young men and asked them where they came from and they had said, after a little hesitation, that they were Swiss. "What part of Switzerland?" Bert had asked blandly. "Düsseldorf? Hamburg?"

The Germans, who were large, solid men, had looked uncomfortable and turned away from him toward the beers that were standing on the bar in front of them, but Bert wouldn't leave it alone. "The part of Switzerland I find most charming," Bert said loudly, "is Belsen. So rural, so cosy, so full of memories. What I always have said is that Switzerland would have won the war if it hadn't been stabbed in the back by the watchmakers. And a good thing, too."

"Cut it out," Munnie had whispered, and Martha had

shaken her head warningly too, and pulled at Bert's arm. "There're four of them. They'll murder us."

But Bert had gone right on. "I'm proud to tell you gentlemen," he had said, smiling broadly, "that I have always been a believer in a Greater Switzerland and there are plenty of good, red-blooded Americans who go right along with me." The Germans were muttering among themselves by now and Munnie took off his watch and slipped it into his pocket because he didn't want it broken when the fight began.

"Shut up, Bert," Martha said. "They're going to hit you with a beermug."

"Now, boys," Bert went on, lifting his glass, "I'd like you to join me in a toast to the greatest little old Swiss of them all, that kindly, sweet old lovable fellow, Adolf Hitler, and after that we'll all join in singing Switzerland Über Alles. I'm sure you know the words . . ."

Munnie had edged around by now and when the first German swung, he grabbed the man's arm and clubbed him twice with his right hand. The Germans were slow, but strong, and very angry, and by the time Munnie dragged Bert to the door, he had a bloody nose and Bert's coat collar was half torn off and all the waiters were screaming for the police.

The three of them ran through the back streets of Nice, hearing confused shouting dying down behind them. Bert was chuckling as he ran, and shaking his right hand, which was numb from a German skull, and he kept saying to Munnie, "What part of Switzerland you from, Bud? Leipzig? Nuremberg?"

A half hour later, when they were sitting safely in a bar along the Promenade des Anglais, it had begun to seem funny to Martha and Munnie, too, and for the rest of the summer, whenever any one of them did something that seemed objectionable or foolish, the others would ask, incredulously, "What part of Switzerland are *you* from?"

Now Bert was sitting, waving the wine bottle gently,

beaming out at the bay. "I think I am going to start a new kind of travel service. Out-of-season tours to slightly run-down resorts. I'll write a brochure, entitled 'Know bliss! Be Unfashionable! Get Away from Your Fellow Man on Your Next Vacation!' Do you think your father would be inclined to put up the dough to get us started, Munnie?"

Bert had an unshakable belief that Munnie's father was enormously wealthy and avid for unusual business opportunities, which Bert was happy to find for him. The opportunities had included the planting of an avocado grove near Grasse, and the building of a 4000-foot téléphérique for skiing in a village of twenty-two houses in the Spanish Pyrenees. All of Bert's projects, aside from involving great outlays of capital on the part of Munnie's father, also included the necessity of Bert's remaining permanently in Europe as manager.

"Munnie," Bert said, "don't you think we ought to send your father a cable?"

"No," said Munnie.

"The chance of a lifetime," Bert said. "What does he want to hold onto all that money for? The inheritance people'll just take it from him in the hideous end. Well, I'll find something. That's not the only way to turn a dollar." He peered speculatively at Martha, who was eating the grapes by now. "Martha," he said, "do you know that you represent a source of vast potential income?"

"I'm going to donate my body to science," Martha said, "at the age of eighty-five."

"The essential thing," said Bert, "is not to marry an American."

"Report that man to a committee," Martha said.

"America is not the place for a pretty woman," Bert went on. "The houses're getting too small, the help too expensive, a beauty suddenly finds herself in a cosy little nest in Scarsdale surrounded by television sets and labor-saving devices and invitations to join the Parent-Teachers Association. A beautiful woman does better in a country which is decaying a little, and rather uneconomically run

—like France. You could marry a nice forty-five-year-old man with a clean mustache and large, rolling feudal estates on the banks of the Loire. Wonderful shooting in the autumn and good, light wines grown on the property and dozens of servants taking off their caps and bowing when the station wagon went by. Your husband would adore you and invite all your friends down to keep you happy and he'd leave you alone a good deal of the time when he went up to Paris to attend to his affairs and have his doctor probe his liver."

"Where do you fit into this picture?" Martha asked.

"He'd be one of the friends invited to keep you happy," Munnie said. He wasn't enjoying the conversation. Even though Bert was joking, Munnie knew that actually Bert would approve if Martha *did* go out and marry an old man with a lot of money. Just the other day, when they had been talking about the careers that might lie ahead of them, Bert had said, "The important thing is to recognize your gift and then use it. And the best way to use it is to keep you from the insufferable boredom of work. Now your gift—" he had grinned at Martha "—your gift is beauty. That's easy. You use it on a man and the sky's the limit. My gift is a double one, but in the long run less hopeful. I have charm . . ." He grinned more widely, making fun of himself, "and I don't give a damn. Still, if I'm clever enough and don't rise to the wrong bait, I may go a long way on it. As for Munnie . . ." He shook his head doubtfully. "His gift is virtue. Poor sod. What can he do with that?"

Now, sitting on the corner of the towel, picking the grapes appreciatively off their stems, one by one, Bert was shaking his head. "No," he said, "I won't be one of the invited friends. I'm a permanent fixture. I'm the overseer of the estates, the curious American with no ambition who likes to live in France on the banks of the pretty river. I walk around in an old tweed jacket smelling a little from horses and new wine barrels, loved by one and all, making wry comments on the state of the world, playing

backgammon in front of the fire with the mistress of the
house when her husband is away, and going up the stairs
later, with the last glass of Armagnac in my hand, to en-
tertain her in my wry, American way in the ancestral
bed . . ."

"Ah," Martha said, "how idyllic!"

"Every age," Bert said gravely, "to its own particular
idyll. This is this year, among the wars."

Munnie felt very uncomfortable and when he looked
over at Martha he felt even more uncomfortable, because
she was laughing. They had laughed together at a lot of
things since Florence, and they had covered all the subjects, but Munnie didn't want to hear Martha laughing
now at this.

He stood up. "I think I'm going down the wall a way,"
he said, "and take a siesta. Wake me when you want to
go."

He walked about thirty yards, carrying a sweater to use
as a pillow, and as he stretched out on the smooth sun-
warmed stone, he heard Martha and Bert laughing together, the laughter private and small in the wide, bright
emptiness.

Closing his eyes against the glare of the sun, listening
to the distant laughter, Munnie realized that he was in
pain. The pain was not localized and it had a curious,
evasive quality. Just when Munnie felt, *There, I've got it,
it's in my throat,* it slipped away, not to disappear, but to
put vague, sharp, almost detectable fingers somewhere
else. Then, lying there, with the curtain of heat on his
eyelids, Munnie understood that what he was feeling was
not pain, but sorrow.

The sorrow was deep and complex, and was composed
of many elements—a sense of deprivation, a shadow of
impending departure, a nostalgia for memories that were
moving irrevocably away from innocence, a confusion of
emotion more profound than anything he had ever experienced before in his life. Engulfed and shaken as he

was, Munnie also knew that if, telepathically affected, Martha would stop laughing with Bert and get up and walk the thirty yards along the wall to where he lay, and if she were to sit down beside him and touch his hand, all would instantaneously be well.

But she didn't move, and he heard her laugh more loudly at something that Bert had said and which Munnie couldn't hear.

Suddenly, Munnie knew what he was going to do. As soon as he was on the boat, and all bargains were over, all rules no longer in effect, he was going to write Martha and ask her to marry him. Clumsily, he began to compose the letter in his mind. *This will come as a surprise to you, I suppose, because all summer long I never said a word, but I didn't realize for a long time what had been happening to me, and besides there was the arrangement you and Bert and I made in Florence to keep everything on a purely friendly basis, which I am happy we did. But now I'm on the boat and I feel free to tell you how I feel about you. I love you and I want to marry you. I don't know how you feel about me, but maybe the arrangement kept you from saying anything, just the way it did me. Anyway, I hope so. I am going to get a job and get settled just as soon as I get home, and then you could come back and meet my family and all that . . ."*

The letter stopped writing itself inside his head. He thought of his mother sitting down having tea with Martha, saying, "You say your mother lives in Philadelphia? And your father . . . oh . . . Do try one of these cakes. And you say you met Munnie in Florence and then just you and he and Bert went all around Europe for the rest of the summer all together . . . Lemon, cream?"

Munnie shook his head. He'd handle his mother when the time came. He went back to writing the imaginary letter.

You said once that you didn't know what you wanted to do with yourself, that you were waiting for some kind

*of revelation to send you in a permanent direction. Maybe
you'll laugh at me for offering myself as a revelation, but
maybe you'll feel that marrying me will . . .*

Munnie shook his head disgustedly. God, even if she
was crazy in love with him, he thought, a sentence like
that would queer it forever.

I don't know about you and other men, he went on
jumpily in his head. *You never seemed interested in anybody else while you were with us and you never mentioned anybody else in any particular way and as far as I
could tell you never showed any preference between
Bert and me . . .*

Munnie opened his eyes and turned his head to look at
Bert and Martha. They were sitting close together, almost
head to head, facing each other, talking in low, serious
voices.

He remembered Bert's description of what he called
his gift. I have charm and I don't give a damn. Well, Munnie thought, with satisfaction, even if she overlooked the
egotism, that can't have attracted her so much. And besides, there was that open and avowed blonde in St. Tropez. If Bert had planned to do anything with Martha, or
if Martha, as Bert had predicted, was interested in making
a choice, that certainly would have put an end to it,
wouldn't it? Bert, Munnie decided, could be the amusing,
bachelor friend of the family. The best kind.

Munnie dozed a little, a succession of warm and delicious images pouring through his mind. Martha coming
off the airplane at Idlewild, because after getting his letter
the boat was too slow, and walking away from the runway
into his arms. Martha and he waking late on a Sunday
morning in their own apartment and deciding to doze for
another hour and then go out to breakfast. Martha coming into a party on his arm and a slight, approving, envi-
ous, subtle hush sweeping the room for a moment, because she was so beautiful. Martha . . .

Someone was shouting. Far off, someone was shouting.

Munnie opened his eyes and blinked, thinking, puzzled. Now, why did anyone shout in my dream?

The cry came again and Munnie stood up and looked out at the bay. In the water, at least three hundred yards away, was a small boat. It was the dory they had seen before. It had capsized and it was low in the water and there were two figures clinging to it. As he watched, he heard the cry again, wordless, desperate. A hand and arm flashed in the sunlight, waving.

Munnie turned and looked over at Bert and Martha. They were stretched out, their heads together on the towel, their bodies making a wide V, sleeping.

"Bert!" Munnie called. "Martha! Get up!"

Bert stirred, then sat up, rubbing his eyes. The shout came again, wailing, from the bay.

"Out there," Munnie said, pointing. Bert swung around, still sitting, and looked at the capsized boat and the two almost-submerged figures clinging to it, a man and a woman. "Good God," Bert said. "What do they think they're doing there?" He nudged Martha. "Wake up," he said, "and watch the shipwreck."

The boat lay almost motionless in the water, only shifting a little as the two figures moved, changing their positions. As Munnie watched, he saw the man push off from the boat and start to swim toward the beach. The man swam slowly and every thirty seconds he stopped and shouted and waved. After each stop he slid under, then reappeared, splashing and frantic.

"Oh, my," Bert said. "He's leaving her out there!"

Bert was standing by now, with Martha at his side, peering across the bay. The man had a good three hundred yards to go before he could touch down on the beach and with his screaming and waving and going under twice a minute, it didn't look as though he was going to make it. The woman who had been left hanging onto the boat shouted from time to time, too, and her voice sounded shrill and angry as it floated across the glittering quiet water.

Finally, Munnie could make out what the swimmer was shouting. *"Au secours! Je noye, je noye!"* Munnie felt a little flicker of annoyance with him. It seemed melodramatic and overdone to be shouting "I'm drowning," especially in such a powerful voice, on a peaceful afternoon in the calm, sunny bay. He went over to the edge of the wall, joining Bert and Martha.

"He seems to be doing all right," Bert said. "He's got a nice, strong stroke there."

"He's going to have to do a little explaining later," Martha said, "leaving his girl friend out there like that."

As they watched, the man went under again. He seemed to stay under a long time and Munnie began to fell his mouth get very dry, watching the spot where the man had disappeared. Then the man surfaced again, this time with his shoulders and arms bare, white and glistening against the deep blue water. He had taken off his shirt underwater and a moment later the shirt came up and floated away, billowing soddenly. The man shouted again. By now it was plain that he was calling directly to the three of them, standing on the wall. The man started swimming again, thrashing heavily.

Munnie scanned the beach and the wharf on which the Snipes were put up on blocks for the winter. There wasn't a boat of any kind he could use, or even a length of rope. He listened for the sound of the hammer they had heard when they had first come onto the wall. Then he realized it had stopped a long time ago, while they were still eating. Far across, on the other side of the bay, there was no movement in front of the houses that faced the water and there were no swimmers or fishermen or children playing anywhere in sight. The entire world of stone, sand and sea that afternoon seemed to be given over to the three of them standing on the wall, and the woman clinging to the bottom of the capsized boat calling shrilly and angrily to the half-naked man struggling in the water and moving slowly and painfully away from her.

Why couldn't this have happened in August? Mun-

nie thought irritably. He looked down at the water rip-
pling in gentle regular swells against the base of the wall.
It wasn't very deep now, with the tide out, four or five
feet at the most, and huge chunks of rock and concrete
broke the surface irregularly. If you jumped it was a drop
of at least fifteen feet and there would be no avoiding the
rocks.

Munnie looked, almost embarrassedly, across at
Martha and Bert. Martha was squinting and there were
lines on her forehead. She was biting her thumbnail absently like a little girl puzzling over a problem in school.
Bert seemed critical and mildly interested, as though he
were watching the performance of an acrobat in a third-
rate circus.

"The damn fool," Bert said mildly. "If he couldn't
handle a boat any better than that you'd think he'd have
had the sense to stick close to the shore."

"Frenchmen," Martha said. "They think they can do
anything." She went back to chewing on her nail.

The man called again, aiming it at them.

"What're we going to do?" Munnie asked.

"Bawl the stupid bastard out," Bert said, "when he
comes ashore, for being such a lousy sailor."

Munnie peered at the swimmer. He was going more
slowly now and he seemed to be settling deeper in the
water after each stroke. "I don't think he's going to make
it," Munnie said.

"Well," said Bert, "that'll be too bad."

Martha said nothing.

Munnie swallowed dryly. Later on, he thought, I won't
be able to bear remembering today, standing here, watching a man drown.

Then another picture flicked before his eyes. It was
sharp and clear and there was nothing missing. It was of
Bert and Martha and himself standing in front of a French
policeman, seated at a desk, with his cap on, scratching
away with a leaking fountain pen in a little black book.

"So," the policeman was saying, "you wish to report a drowning?"

"Yes."

"So—you saw this gentleman, some distance from the shore, waving at you, and then he disappeared?"

"Yes."

"And the lady?"

"The last we saw of her she was still holding onto the boat, floating out to sea."

"Ah. And—uh—what steps did you take, personally?"

"We . . . we came here and reported it."

"Oh, yes. Of course." More scratching in the book. A hand reaching out. "Your passports, please." A quick riffling through the pages and one short, coldly smiling glance as the policeman tossed them on the desk. "Ah, Americans, all of you . . ."

The man out in the water went under again for a second.

Munnie tried to swallow again. This time he couldn't manage it.

"I'm going to go get him," he said. But for a moment he didn't move, as though, somehow, just saying it would fix everything, put the man on dry land, right the boat, stop the screams.

"It's two hundred and fifty yards at least from the beach," Bert said, very calmly. "And then two hundred and fifty yards back, or a little less, with a crazy Frenchman holding onto your neck."

Munnie listened gratefully. "Yes," he said. "At least."

"You never swam five hundred yards in your life," Bert said, sounding friendly and reasonable.

The man screamed again and now his voice was hoarse and terrified.

Munnie started walking swiftly along the wall, back to where there was a narrow flight of steps leading down to the little beach in front of the fort. He didn't run because he didn't want to be out of breath when he went into the water.

"Munnie!" he heard Bert call behind him. "Don't be a damn fool!"

Even as he started down the steep flight of steps, slippery with moss, Munnie noticed that Martha hadn't said anything. When he got down to the beach he trotted across it, at the water line, to get to the point nearest the man. He stopped, breathing heavily, and waved at the swimmer, encouraging him. Now, down at water level, it looked a good deal more than two hundred and fifty yards. He kicked off his shoes and tore off his shirt. The wind felt cold on his skin. He took off his pants, tossing them to one side on the sand, and stood there in his shorts. He hesitated. They were old shorts and they had torn at the crotch and he had mended them, clumsily, himself. He had a sudden picture of his body washed ashore and people noticing the shabby mending job and smiling a little. He unbuttoned the shorts, his fingers fumbling thickly at the buttons and let the shorts drop to the sand. As he walked deliberately into the water, he thought, She's never seen me naked, I wonder what she thinks.

He scraped his toes on a rock and the pain made the tears come into his eyes. He kept walking until the water was up to his chest, then pushed off and began to swim. The water was cold and his skin felt tight and frozen almost at once. He tried not to swim too fast, so that he would have some strength left when he reached the drowning man. Whenever he looked up to see how far he'd gone it seemed to him that he had hardly moved at all, and it was hard to keep going in a straight line. Somehow he always seemed to be veering to his left, in the direction of the wall, and he had to keep correcting himself all the time. Once, he looked up at the wall, searching for Bert and Martha. He couldn't see them and he had a moment of panic. What the hell have they done? he thought. They've left. He turned over on his back, losing precious seconds, and saw them on the beach, standing at the water's edge, watching him. Of course, he thought.

He turned over and kept on swimming methodically

toward the Frenchman. Whenever he picked his head out of the water, the Frenchman seemed to be screaming, and just as far away as ever. He decided not to look again for awhile. It was too discouraging.

Then his arms began to feel tired. It can't be, he thought. I haven't even gone fifty yards yet. Still, the muscles between his shoulders and his elbows seemed to be contracted, twisting his bones, and there was a deep ache of weariness in the back of his arms. His right hand began to cramp a little, too, and he let it flutter loosely through the water, which slowed him down, but he didn't know what else to do about it. The cramp reminded him that he had eaten not very long before and had a lot of wine and grapes and cheese. As he swam, with the water a green blur in his eyes and the slow, steady push of it going past his ears, he remembered his mother, in all the summers of his boyhood, on the shores of the lake in New Hampshire, saying, "No swimming for at least two hours after meals." Sitting on a little wooden chair, under a striped umbrella, watching the children play on the narrow, pebbly beach.

The back of his neck and the base of his skull started to ache now, and his thoughts wavered across his consciousness, disconnected and slippery. He had never liked swimming much, he remembered. He just went in to cool off and play around. Swimming had always seemed like a boring sport. The same old thing, over and over again, lift one arm, lift the other arm, kick, lift one arm, lift the other arm, kick, never really get anyplace. And he had never learned to keep the water out of his ears and sometimes he'd feel deaf for hours and the water wouldn't come out until he'd gone to bed and slept on one side for a long time.

His arms began to feel numb and he rolled more and more, in an effort to get his shoulders into the job, and he seemed to be swimming lower in the water than he ever had before. There's no sense in wasting time, he thought, making himself worry about something else besides his arms, I might as well figure out what to do once I get there. Laboriously, he tried to phrase what he would say to the man in French when he approached him. *Monsieur, J'y suis. Doucement. Doucement.* He would stay off from the man and try to calm him down before grabbing him. Dimly, he remembered having seen a demonstration of life-saving at a pool when he was fourteen years old. He hadn't paid much attention, because the boy behind him had surreptitiously kept flicking at him with a wet towel. But there was something about letting yourself sink if the drowning man put his arms around your neck, then twisting and putting your hand under his chin and pushing back. He hadn't believed it when he was fourteen years old and he didn't believe it now. It was one of those things that looked good in practice, on dry land. Then there were all the stories about hitting people on the chin and knocking them out. More dry land. He had never knocked anybody out in his whole life. His mother hated fighting. *Monsieur, soyez tranquille. Roulez sur votre dos, s'il vous plaît.* Then he'd go in and grab him by the hair and start towing him, sidestroke. If the man understood him. He had an awful lot of trouble getting Frenchmen to understand his accent, especially here in the Basque country. Martha had no trouble at all. They all said what a charming accent she had. Well, why not, after all that time at the Sorbonne? She should have come with him as an interpreter, if for nothing else. *Tournez sur votre dos.* That was better.

He swam heavily and slowly, his eyes beginning to smart from the salt water. When he lifted his head there were white and silver spots before his eyes and everything seemed to be blurred and he couldn't really see anything much. He kept on swimming. After fifty strokes he decided he'd stop and tread water and look around. The idea of treading water now seemed like the greatest pleasure ever vouchsafed the human race.

He started to count the strokes. Fourteen, fifteen, sixteen . . . Lord, he thought, what if he's bald? He tried to remember what the man's head had looked like, far out, splashing away from the overturned boat. There had been a funny pale gleam. Bald, Munnie decided desperately. Nothing is going to go right.

He started counting strokes all over again. By the time he got to thirty-five he knew he would have to stop for awhile. He made himself do five more, then stopped and rolled over on his back, gasping and blowing water and looking up at the sky. He got his breath back and turned again and trod water, searching for the Frenchman.

He blinked his eyes and rubbed them with the back of his hand, sinking up to his mouth as he did so. The Frenchman wasn't there. Oh, God, he thought, he went down.

Then he heard the chugging and twisted in the water. A fishing boat was bearing away from the spot where Munnie had last seen the Frenchman, and was going toward the overturned dory. Munnie trod water, watching while the tuna boat stopped, and two fishermen reached down and pulled the woman on board. The tuna boat, Munnie realized, must have been coming up from the south, concealed by the little headland on which the fort was built, and must have coasted along the seaward side of the wall and entered the channel while he was swimming blindly out from the beach.

The men on the tuna boat threw a line onto the dory, then swung around and headed for Munnie. He waited for it, fighting his lungs. The tuna boat, painted blue, and slow and old, approached him, looking big and safe as it drew nearer. Munnie saw grinning, tanned wide faces, capped by blue berets in the bow, and he waved, with great effort, as the tuna boat slowed down and came to a stop next to him.

"Ça va?" a fisherman shouted, grinning down at him. A cigarette, burned almost to the end, hung plastered to his lips.

Munnie managed to smile. "Ça va bien," he called. "Très bien."

The man who had been rescued came to the rail, still naked to the waist, and peered curiously down at Munnie. Munnie saw that he had plenty of hair. The Frenchman didn't say anything. He was a fat young man with a hurt and dignified expression on his face. At his side appeared a woman. She had been heavily made up and the seawater had done a great deal of damage to the rouge and mascara. She stared furiously down at Munnie, then turned to the Frenchman. She grabbed him by both ears and shook him. *"Crapaud!"* she said loudly. *"Espèce de cochon."*

The Frenchman closed his eyes and allowed his head to be shaken, keeping his face sad and dignified. The fisherman grinned more broadly.

"Alors," one of the fishermen said, throwing a line out toward Munnie, *"allons-y."*

Munnie looked longingly at the line. Then he remembered that he was naked. He shook his head. One thing that was not going to happen to him that afternoon was to be fished out of the sea naked in front of that woman pulling her friend's ears and calling him a pig and a toad. "I'm O.K.," Munnie said, up to the brown, tough, amused faces, used to all sorts of comical, salty accidents and escapes. *"Je suis O.K.* I want to swim. I mean—*Je voudrais bien nager."*

"O.K., O.K.," the fishermen said, laughing, as though what he had said was enormously witty. They pulled in the line and waved and the tuna boat swung around and started in toward the harbor, towing the dory. As it went, over the sound of the engine, Munnie could still hear the sound of the woman screaming.

Well, Munnie thought, watching the boat sail off, at least they understood me.

Then he turned and looked at the beach. It looked miles away and Munnie was surprised that he had swum that far. He had never swum that far before in his life. On the beach, at the water line, with the tower of the fort behind them, Bert and Martha were standing, small, sharp figures, throwing long shadows now in the declining sun.

Taking a deep breath, Munnie started to swim in.

He had to turn over and float every ten yards or so and for awhile it seemed to him that he wasn't moving at all, only going through the motions of swimming, but finally, putting his feet down, he touched bottom. It was still fairly deep, up to his chin, and he pulled his feet up and stubbornly kept on swimming. And as a gesture, which he didn't try to understand, even as he did it, he swam all the way in, making himself spurt and do a proper crawl, until the water was so shallow that his finger tips scraped the sand.

Then he stood up. He wavered a little, but he stood up and, making himself smile, walked slowly, naked, with the water streaming off him, toward where Bert and Martha stood next to the little pile of his clothes on the beach.

"Well," Bert said as Munnie came up to them, "what part of Switzerland are *you* from, Bud?"

As he bent over and picked up the towel and began to dry himself, shivering under the rough cloth, Munnie heard Martha laugh.

He rubbed himself dry. He took a long time, shivering badly, too weary and not interested enough to try to cover his nakedness. They drove back to the hotel in silence and when Munnie said that he thought he'd lie down and try to rest for awhile, they both agreed that it was probably the best thing to do.

He slept uneasily, his ears half deaf and stopped with water and the blood pounding in them like a distant, fitful sea. When Bert came in and said it was time for dinner, Munnie told him he wasn't hungry and that he wanted to rest. "We're going to the Casino after dinner," Bert said, "Should we stop by and pick you up?"

"No," Munnie said. "I don't feel lucky tonight."

There was a little silence in the darkened room. Then Bert said, "Good night. Sleep well, Fat Man," and went out.

Alone, Munnie lay staring at the shadowed ceiling,

thinking. *I'm not fat. Why does he call me that? He only started it in the middle of the summer.* Then he slept again and only awakened when he heard the car drive up outside the hotel and the steps going softly up the stairs, past his door, to the floor above. He heard a door open and close gently upstairs and he made himself shut his eyes and try to sleep.

When he awoke the pillow was wet, where the water had run out of his ears, and he felt better. When he sat up the blood stopped pounding inside his head, too. He turned on the lamp and looked at Bert's bed. It was empty. He looked at his watch. It was four-thirty.

He got out of bed and lit a cigarette and went to the window and opened it. The moon was just going down and the sea was milky and was making an even, grumbling sound, like an old man complaining about the life that lay behind him.

For a moment, he wondered where he would have been at this hour if the tuna boat hadn't come in around the breakwater. Then he doused his cigarette and began to pack. It didn't take long, because they had been traveling light all summer.

When he finished he made sure that the extra key for the car was on his ring. Then he wrote a short note for Bert, telling him that he'd decided to take off for Paris. He hoped to get to Paris in time to catch the boat. He hoped this wouldn't inconvenience Bert too much and he knew that Bert would understand. He didn't mention Martha.

He carried his bag out to the car through the dark hotel and threw the bag into the empty space next to the driver's seat. He put on a raincoat and a pair of gloves and started the car and drove carefully out the driveway, without looking back to see whether the sound of the engine had awakened anyone or whether anyone had come to a window to watch him leave.

There was mist in the low places on the road, and he drove slowly, feeling it wet against his face. With the sighing regular noise of the windshield wipers and the steady, damp light of the headlights on the road ahead of him almost hypnotizing him, he drove mechanically, not thinking of anything at all.

It was only far past Bayonne, when the dawn had broken and he had cut off the lights and the road stretched gray and glistening through the dark pine aisles of Les Landes, that he allowed himself to remember the day and night that had just passed. And then all he could think was, It's my fault. I let the summer go on one day too long.

The Best of the World's Best Books

COMPLETE LIST OF TITLES IN

THE MODERN LIBRARY

For convenience in ordering use number at right of title

MISCELLANEOUS

MODERN LIBRARY GIANTS

A series of full-sized library editions of books that formerly were available only in cumbersome and expensive sets.

THE MODERN LIBRARY GIANTS REPRESENT A
SELECTION OF THE WORLD'S GREATEST BOOKS

These volumes contain from 600 to 1,400 pages each

G1. TOLSTOY, LEO. War and Peace.
G2. BOSWELL, JAMES. Life of Samuel Johnson.
G3. HUGO, VICTOR. Les Miserables.
G4. THE COMPLETE POEMS OF KEATS AND SHELLEY.
G5. PLUTARCH'S LIVES (The Dryden Translation).
G6. ⎫
G7. ⎬ GIBBON, EDWARD. The Decline and Fall of the Roman
G8. ⎭   Empire (Complete in three volumes).
G9. GREAT VOICES OF THE REFORMATION.
G10. TWELVE FAMOUS RESTORATION PLAYS (1660-1820)
       (Congreve, Wycherley, Gay, Goldsmith, Sheridan, etc.)
G11. JAMES, HENRY. The Short Stories of
G12. THE MOST POPULAR NOVELS OF SIR WALTER
       SCOTT (Quentin Durward, Ivanhoe and Kenilworth).
G13. CARLYLE, THOMAS. The French Revolution.
G14. BULFINCH'S MYTHOLOGY (Illustrated).
G15. CERVANTES. Don Quixote (Illustrated).
G16. THE EUROPEAN PHILOSOPHERS FROM DESCARTES TO
       NIETZSCHE.
G17. THE POEMS AND PLAYS OF ROBERT BROWNING.
G18. ELEVEN PLAYS OF HENRIK IBSEN.
G19. THE COMPLETE WORKS OF HOMER.
G20. THE LIFE AND WRITINGS OF ABRAHAM LINCOLN.
G21. SIXTEEN FAMOUS AMERICAN PLAYS.
G22. THIRTY FAMOUS ONE-ACT PLAYS.
G23. TOLSTOY, LEO. Anna Karenina.
G24. LAMB, CHARLES. The Complete Works and Letters of
G25. THE COMPLETE PLAYS OF GILBERT AND SULLIVAN.
G26. MARX, KARL. Capital.
G27. DARWIN, CHARLES. Origin of Species & The Descent of Man.
G28. THE COMPLETE WORKS OF LEWIS CARROLL.
G29. PRESCOTT, WILLIAM H. The Conquest of Mexico and
       The Conquest of Peru.
G30. MYERS, GUSTAVUS. History of the Great American
       Fortunes.
G31. FAMOUS SCIENCE-FICTION STORIES: ADVENTURES IN
       TIME AND SPACE
G32. SMITH, ADAM. The Wealth of Nations.
G33. COLLINS, WILKIE. The Moonstone and The Woman in White.
G34. NIETZSCHE, FRIEDRICH. The Philosophy of Nietzsche.
G35. BURY, J. B. A History of Greece.
G36. DOSTOYEVSKY, FYODOR. The Brothers Karamazov.
G37. THE COMPLETE NOVELS AND SELECTED TALES OF
       NATHANIEL HAWTHORNE.